image comics presents

THE WALKING DEAD

™

ROBERT KIRKMAN
CREATOR, WRITER

CHARLIE ADLARD
PENCILER

STEFANO GAUDIANO
INKER

CLIFF RATHBURN
GRAY TONES

RUS WOOTON
LETTERER

CHARLIE ADLARD
&
DAVE STEWART
COVER

SEAN MACKIEWICZ
EDITOR

SKYBOUND™
For SKYBOUND ENTERTAINMENT

Robert Kirkman - CEO
Sean Mackiewicz - Editorial Director
Shawn Kirkham - Director of Business Development
Brian Huntington - Online Editorial Director
June Alian - Publicity Director
Helen Leigh - Assistant Editor
Rachel Skidmore - Office Manager
Lizzy Iverson - Administrative Assistant
Dan Petersen - Operations Manager
Nick Palmer - Operations Coordinator

International inquiries: foreign@skybound.com
Licensing inquiries: contact@skybound.com
WWW.SKYBOUND.COM

IMAGE COMICS, INC.
Robert Kirkman – Chief Operating Officer
Erik Larsen – Chief Financial Officer
Todd McFarlane – President
Marc Silvestri – Chief Executive Officer
Jim Valentino – Vice-President

Eric Stephenson – Publisher
Ron Richards – Director of Business Development
Jennifer de Guzman – Director of Trade Book Sales
Kat Salazar – Director of PR & Marketing
Jeremy Sullivan – Director of Digital Sales
Emilio Bautista – Sales Assistant
Branwyn Bigglestone – Senior Accounts Manager
Emily Miller – Accounts Manager
Jessica Ambriz – Administrative Assistant
Tyler Shainline – Events Coordinator
David Brothers – Content Manager
Jonathan Chan – Production Manager
Drew Gill – Art Director
Meredith Wallace – Print Manager
Monica Garcia – Senior Production Artist
Jenna Savage – Production Artist
Addison Duke – Production Artist
Tricia Ramos – Production Assistant
IMAGECOMICS.COM

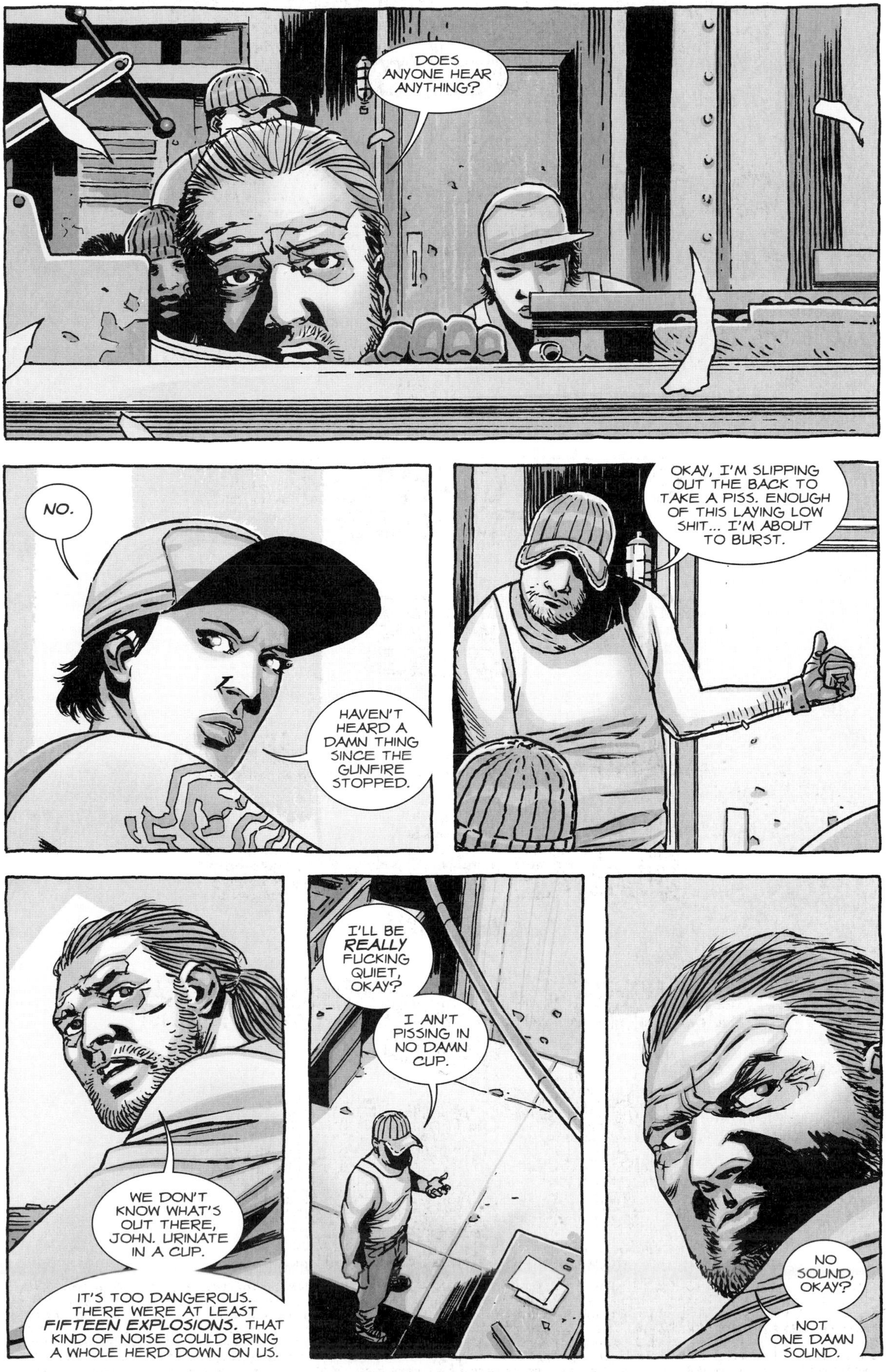
DOES ANYONE HEAR ANYTHING?
NO.
HAVEN'T HEARD A DAMN THING SINCE THE GUNFIRE STOPPED.
OKAY, I'M SLIPPING OUT THE BACK TO TAKE A PISS. ENOUGH OF THIS LAYING LOW SHIT... I'M ABOUT TO BURST.
WE DON'T KNOW WHAT'S OUT THERE, JOHN. URINATE IN A CUP.
IT'S TOO DANGEROUS. THERE WERE AT LEAST FIFTEEN EXPLOSIONS. THAT KIND OF NOISE COULD BRING A WHOLE HERD DOWN ON US.
I'LL BE REALLY FUCKING QUIET, OKAY?
I AIN'T PISSING IN NO DAMN CUP.
NO SOUND, OKAY?
NOT ONE DAMN SOUND.

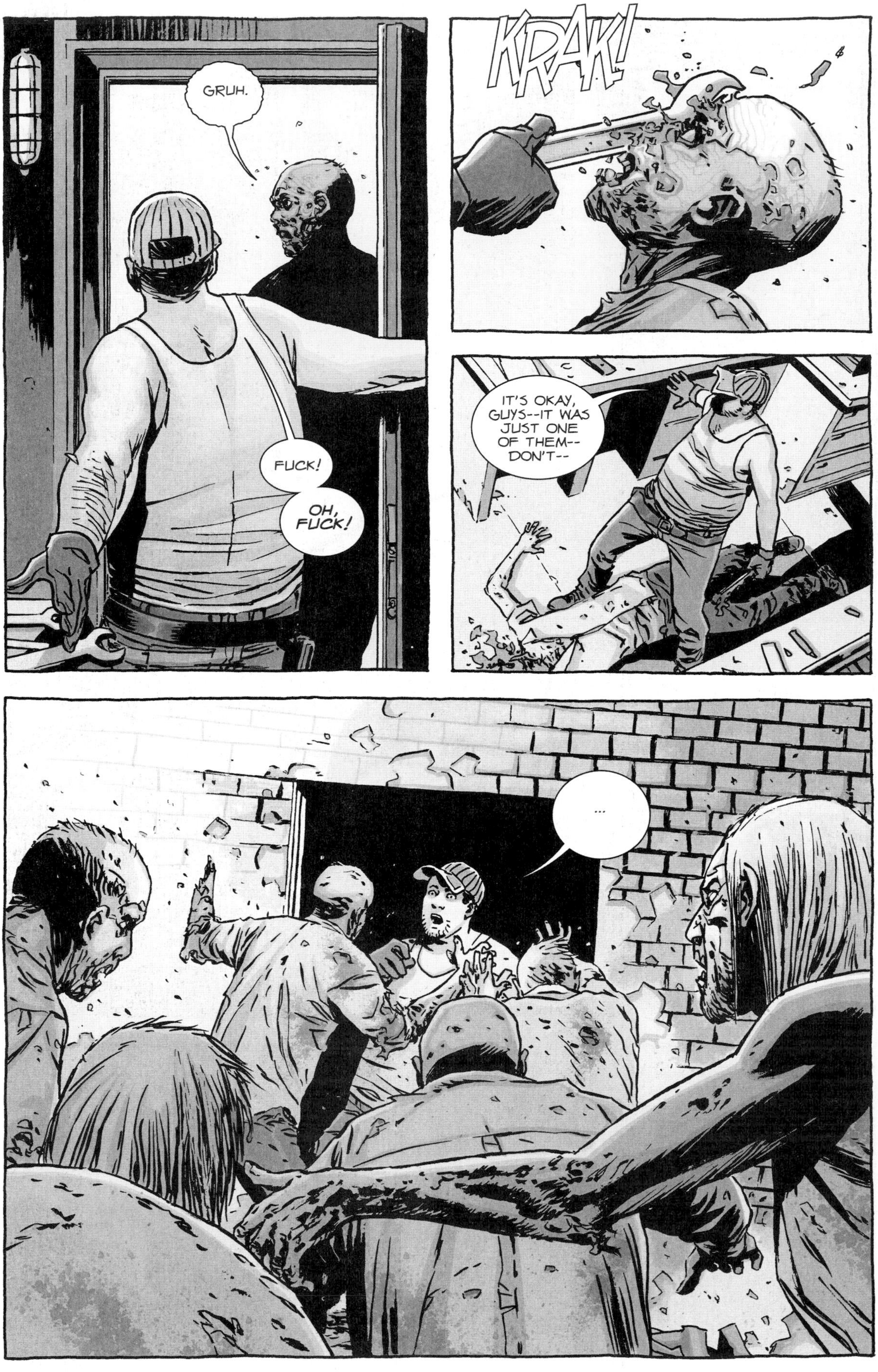
GRUH.
FUCK!
OH, FUCK!
KRAK!
IT'S OKAY, GUYS--IT WAS JUST ONE OF THEM-- DON'T--
...

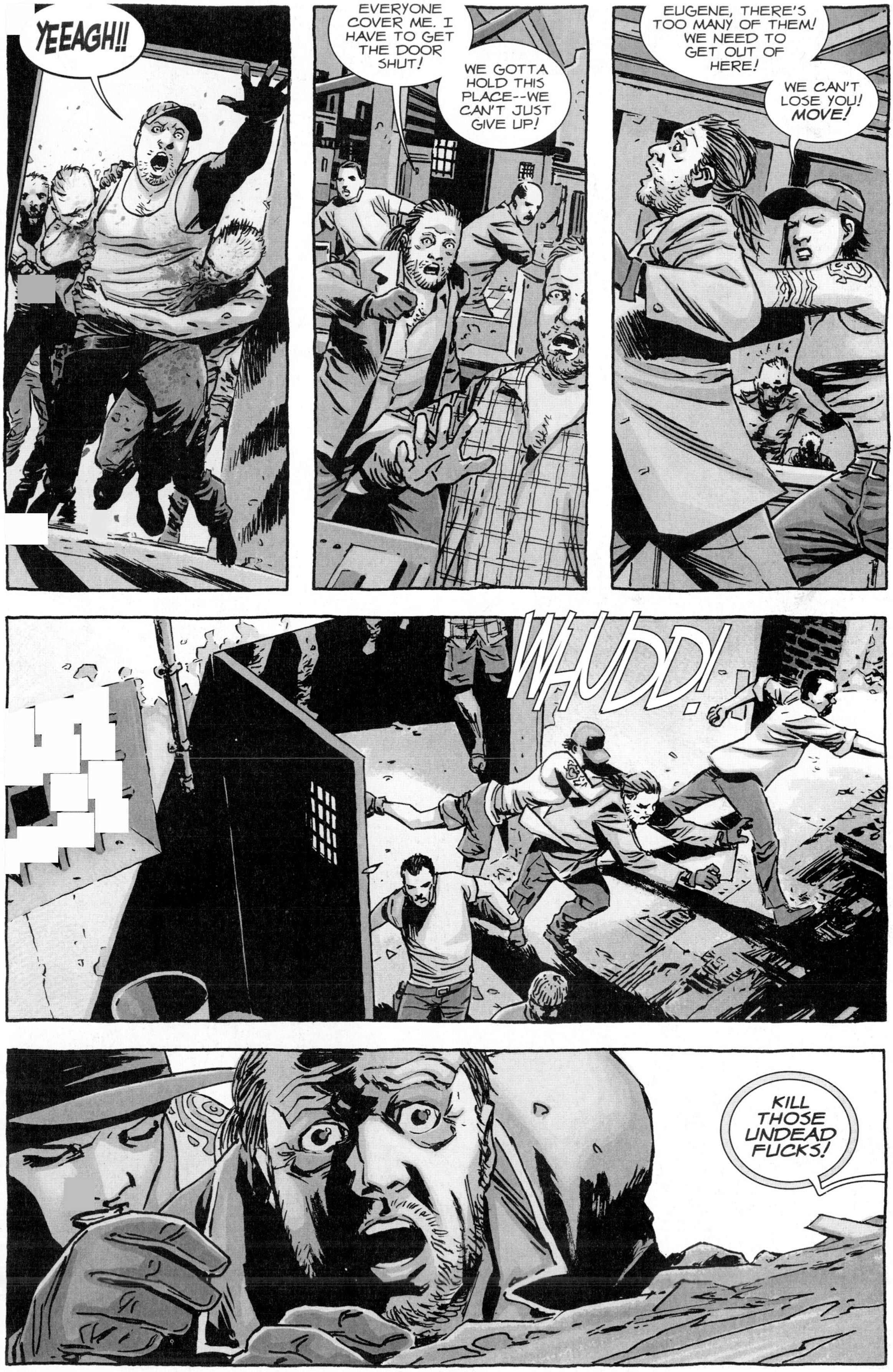
YEEAGH!!
EVERYONE COVER ME. I HAVE TO GET THE DOOR SHUT!
WE GOTTA HOLD THIS PLACE--WE CAN'T JUST GIVE UP!
EUGENE, THERE'S TOO MANY OF THEM! WE NEED TO GET OUT OF HERE!
WE CAN'T LOSE YOU! MOVE!
WHUDD!
KILL THOSE UNDEAD FUCKS!

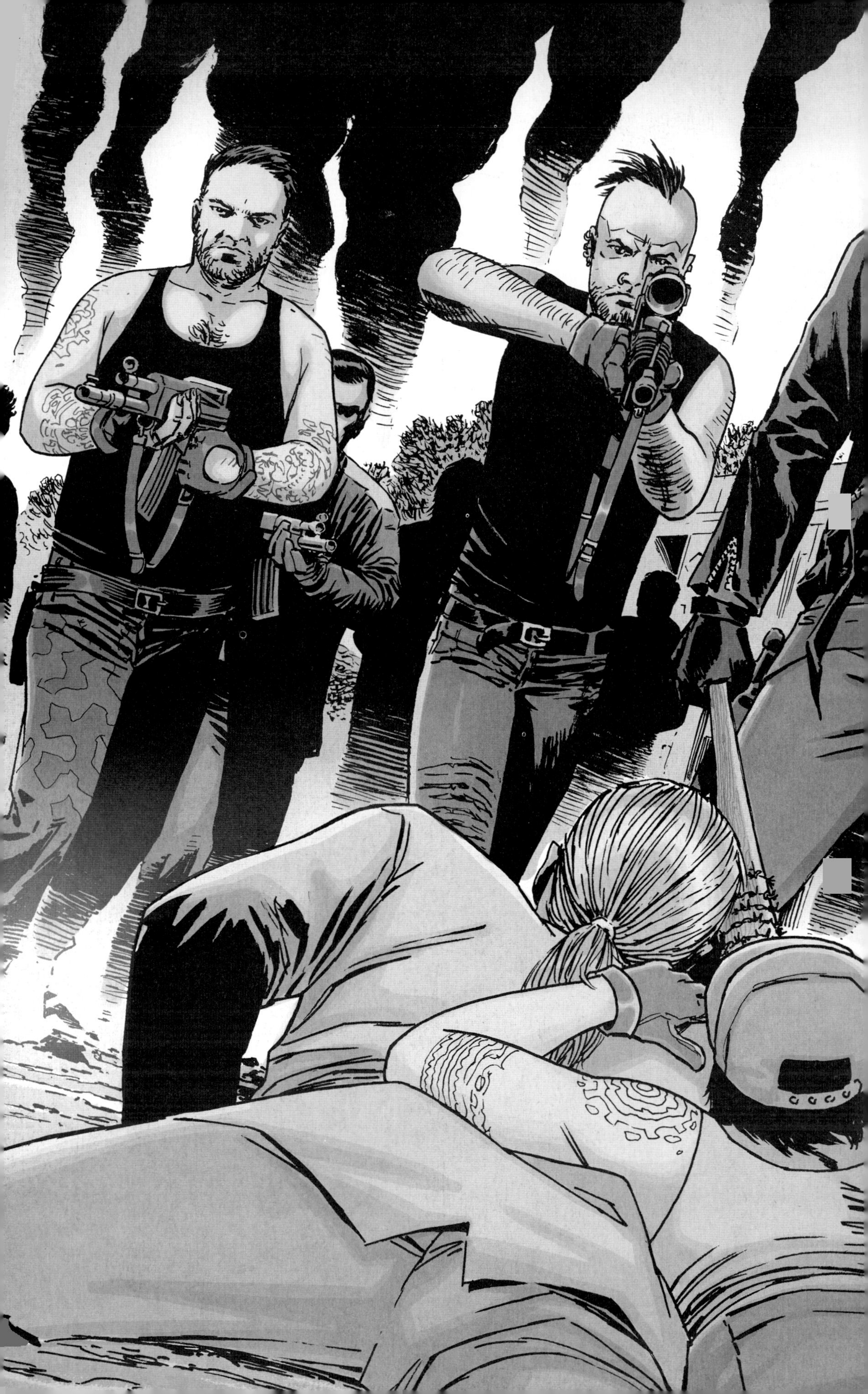

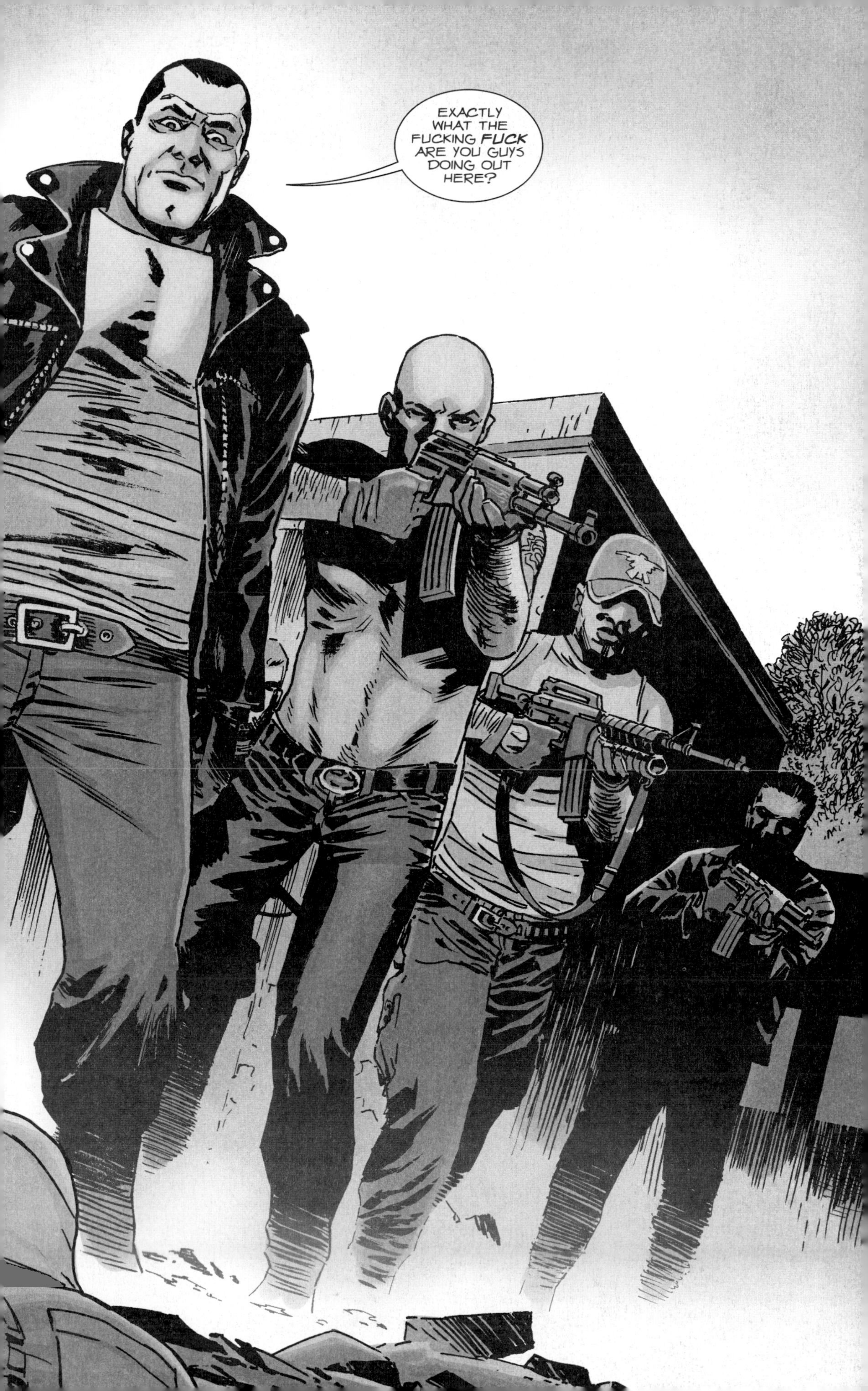
EXACTLY WHAT THE FUCKING FUCK ARE YOU GUYS DOING OUT HERE?

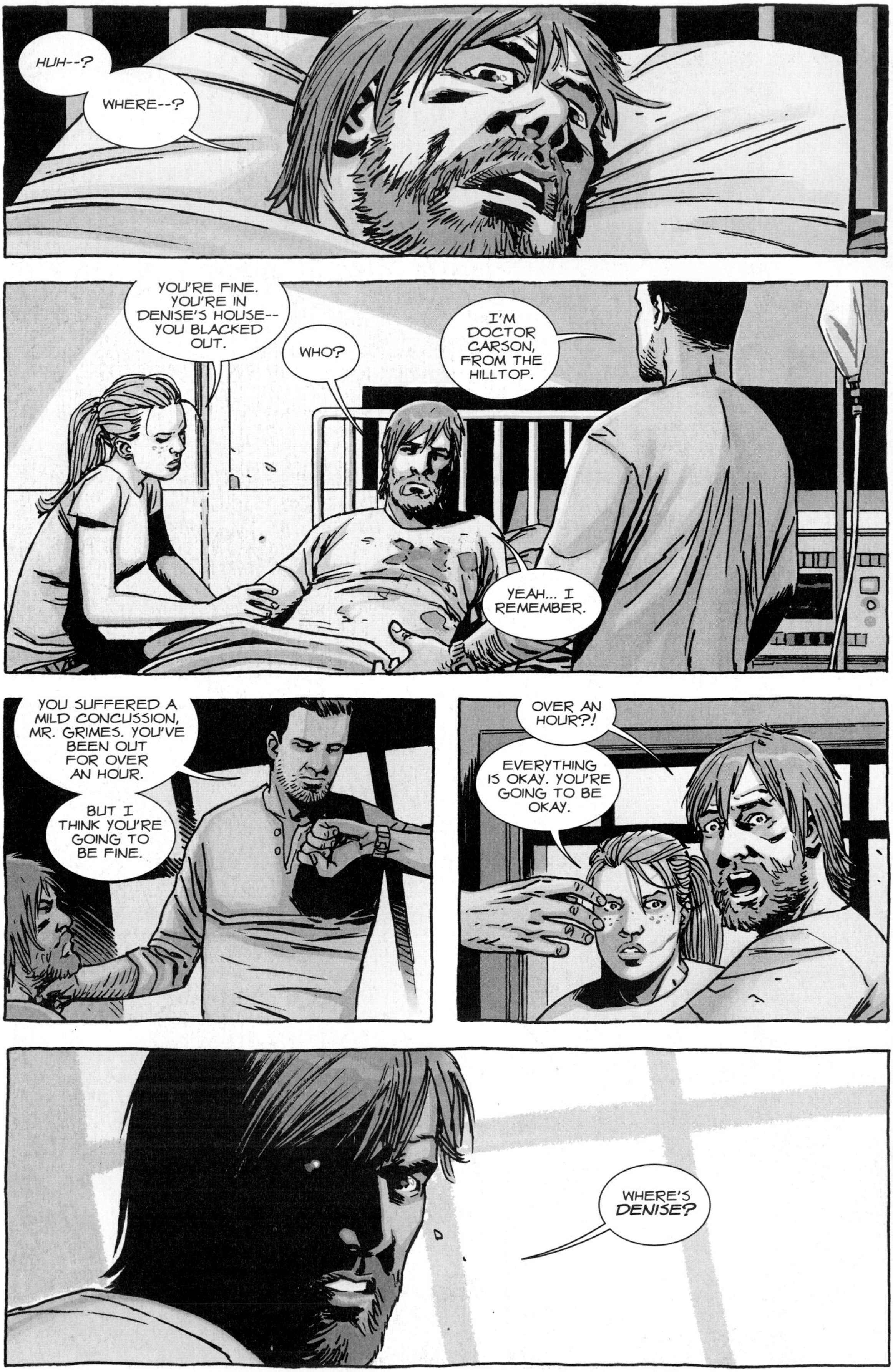
HUH--?
WHERE--?
YOU'RE FINE. YOU'RE IN DENISE'S HOUSE-- YOU BLACKED OUT.
WHO?
I'M DOCTOR CARSON, FROM THE HILLTOP.
YEAH... I REMEMBER.
YOU SUFFERED A MILD CONCUSSION, MR. GRIMES. YOU'VE BEEN OUT FOR OVER AN HOUR.
BUT I THINK YOU'RE GOING TO BE FINE.
OVER AN HOUR?!
EVERYTHING IS OKAY. YOU'RE GOING TO BE OKAY.
WHERE'S DENISE?

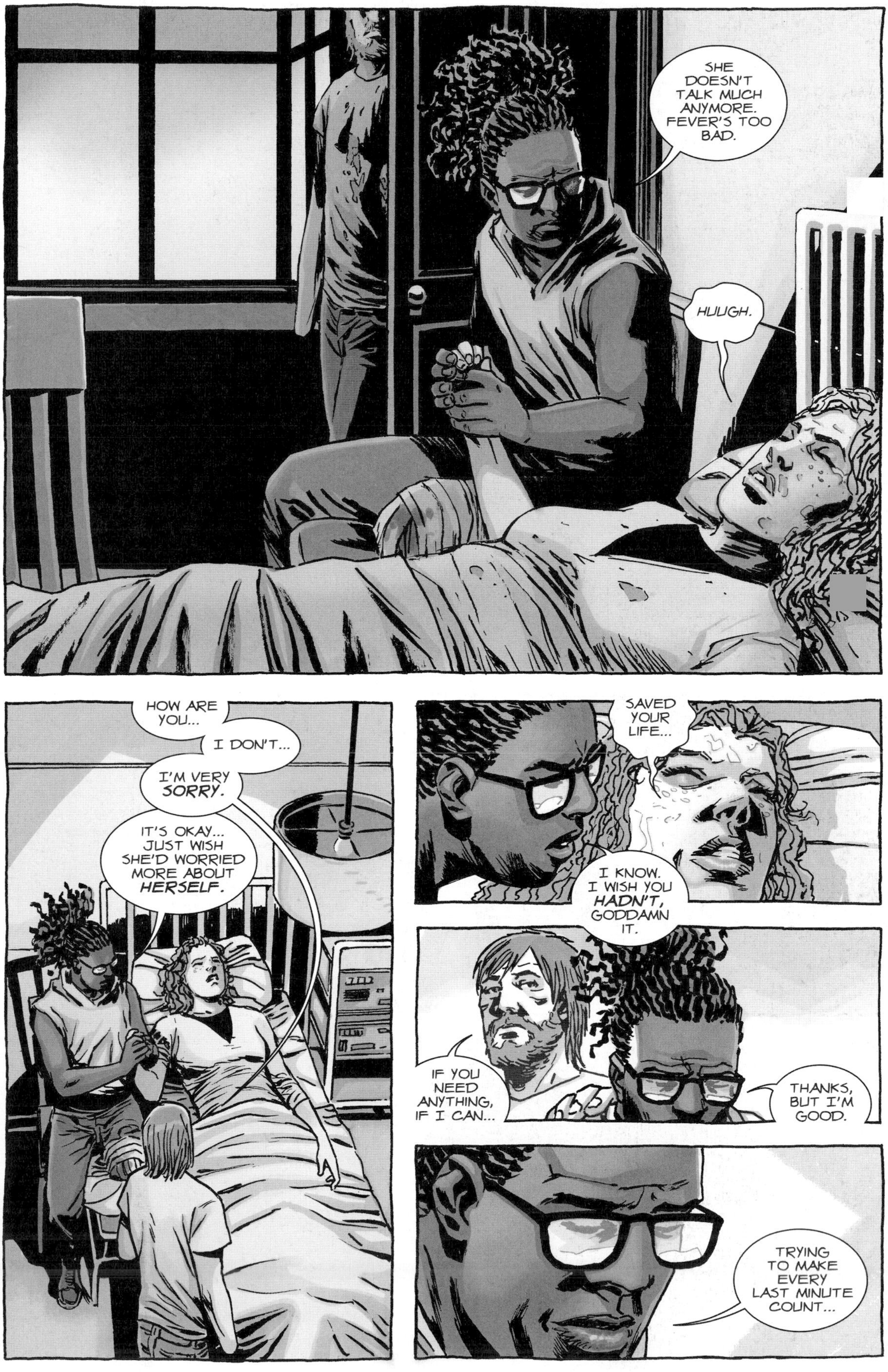
SHE DOESN'T TALK MUCH ANYMORE. FEVER'S TOO BAD.
HUUGH.
HOW ARE YOU...
I DON'T...
I'M VERY SORRY.
IT'S OKAY... JUST WISH SHE'D WORRIED MORE ABOUT HERSELF.
SAVED YOUR LIFE...
I KNOW. I WISH YOU HADN'T, GODDAMN IT.
IF YOU NEED ANYTHING, IF I CAN...
THANKS, BUT I'M GOOD.
TRYING TO MAKE EVERY LAST MINUTE COUNT...

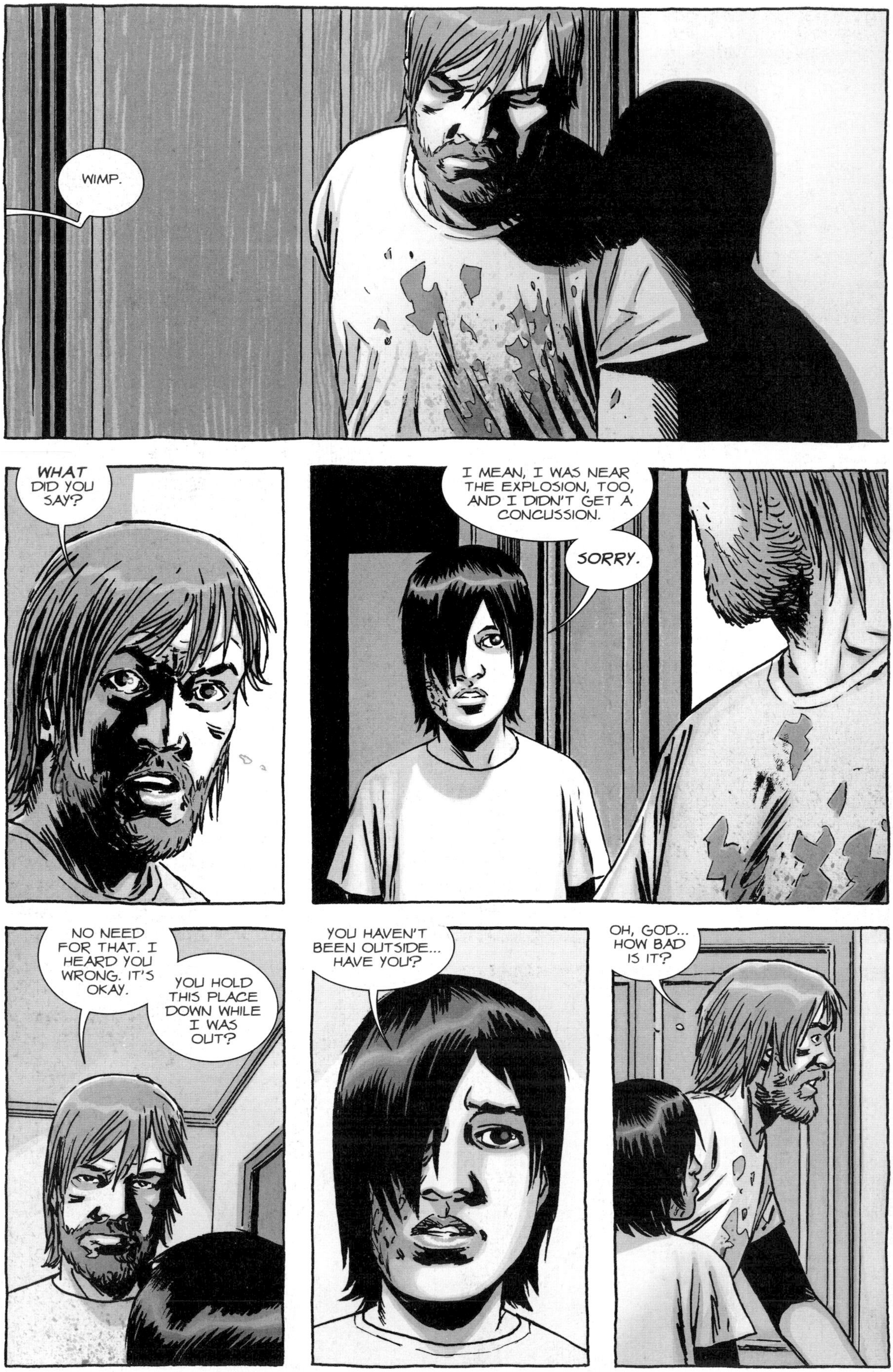
WIMP.
WHAT DID YOU SAY?
I MEAN, I WAS NEAR THE EXPLOSION, TOO, AND I DIDN'T GET A CONCUSSION.
SORRY.
NO NEED FOR THAT. I HEARD YOU WRONG. IT'S OKAY.
YOU HOLD THIS PLACE DOWN WHILE I WAS OUT?
YOU HAVEN'T BEEN OUTSIDE... HAVE YOU?
OH, GOD... HOW BAD IS IT?

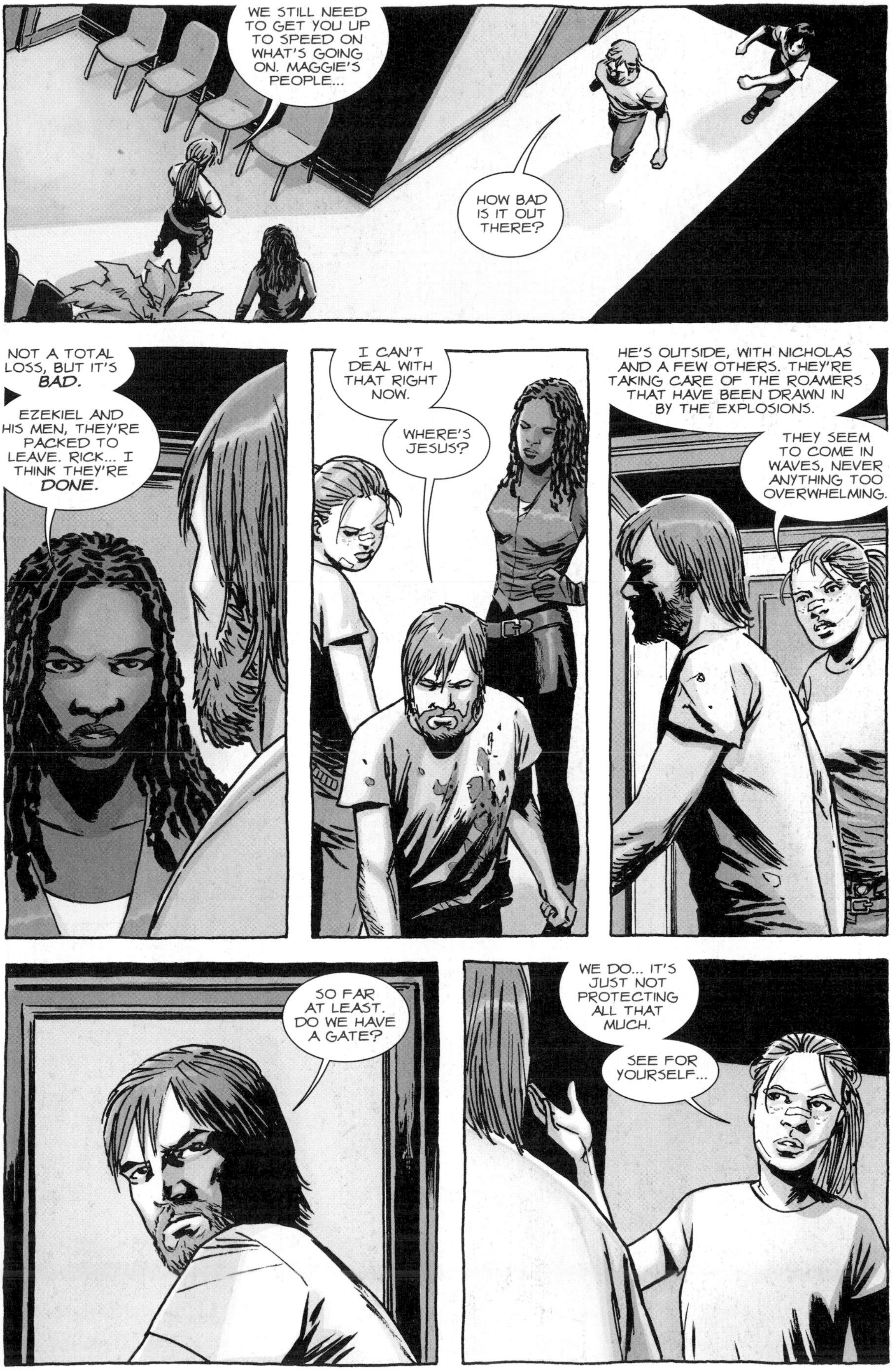
WE STILL NEED TO GET YOU UP TO SPEED ON WHAT'S GOING ON. MAGGIE'S PEOPLE...
HOW BAD IS IT OUT THERE?
NOT A TOTAL LOSS, BUT IT'S BAD.
EZEKIEL AND HIS MEN, THEY'RE PACKED TO LEAVE. RICK... I THINK THEY'RE DONE.
I CAN'T DEAL WITH THAT RIGHT NOW.
WHERE'S JESUS?
HE'S OUTSIDE, WITH NICHOLAS AND A FEW OTHERS. THEY'RE TAKING CARE OF THE ROAMERS THAT HAVE BEEN DRAWN IN BY THE EXPLOSIONS.
THEY SEEM TO COME IN WAVES, NEVER ANYTHING TOO OVERWHELMING.
SO FAR AT LEAST. DO WE HAVE A GATE?
WE DO... IT'S JUST NOT PROTECTING ALL THAT MUCH.
SEE FOR YOURSELF...

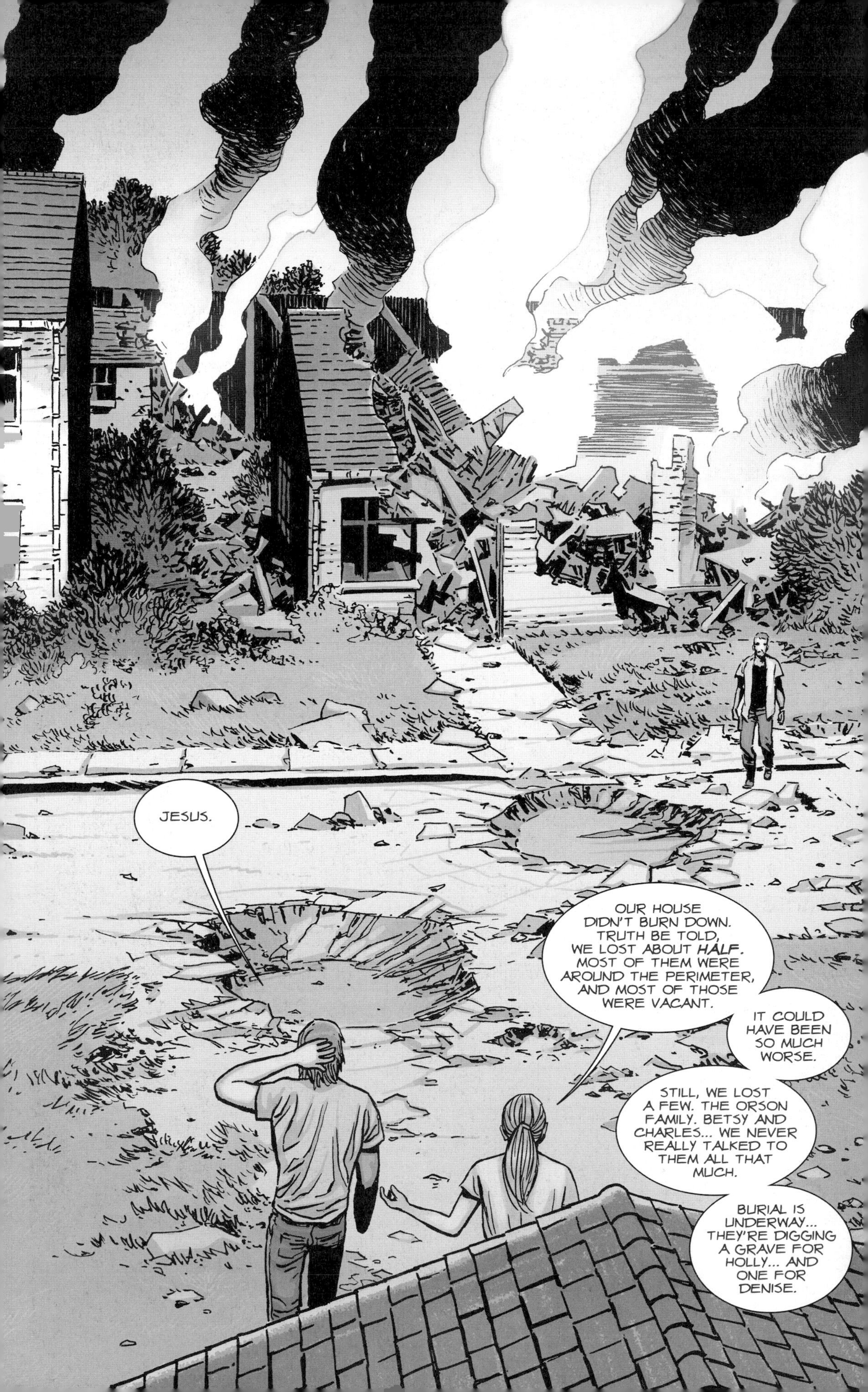
JESUS.
OUR HOUSE DIDN'T BURN DOWN. TRUTH BE TOLD, WE LOST ABOUT HALF. MOST OF THEM WERE AROUND THE PERIMETER, AND MOST OF THOSE WERE VACANT.
IT COULD HAVE BEEN SO MUCH WORSE.
STILL, WE LOST A FEW. THE ORSON FAMILY. BETSY AND CHARLES... WE NEVER REALLY TALKED TO THEM ALL THAT MUCH.
BURIAL IS UNDERWAY... THEY'RE DIGGING A GRAVE FOR HOLLY... AND ONE FOR DENISE.

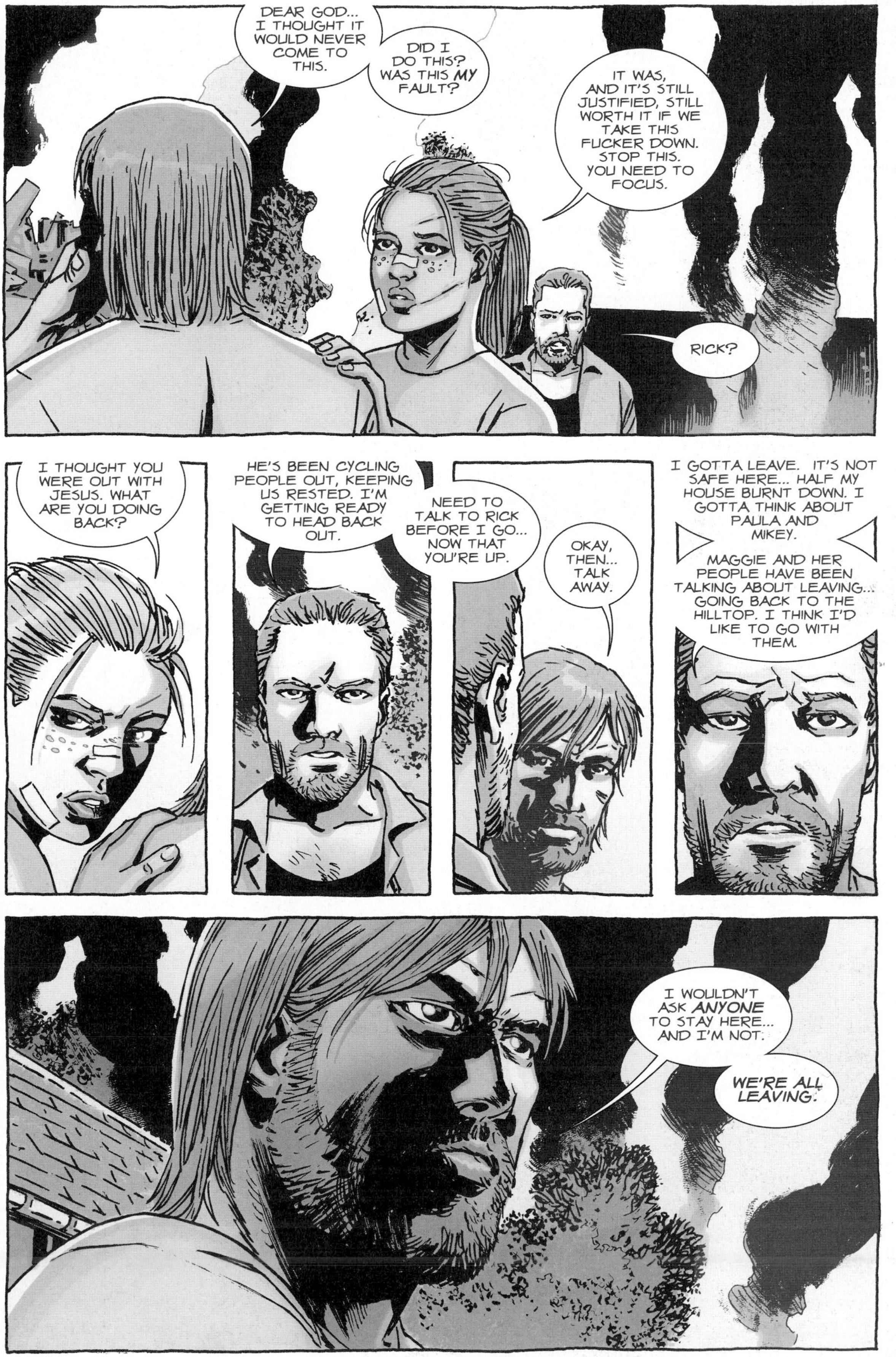
DEAR GOD... I THOUGHT IT WOULD NEVER COME TO THIS.
DID I DO THIS? WAS THIS MY FAULT?
IT WAS, AND IT'S STILL JUSTIFIED, STILL WORTH IT IF WE TAKE THIS FUCKER DOWN. STOP THIS. YOU NEED TO FOCUS.
RICK?
I THOUGHT YOU WERE OUT WITH JESUS. WHAT ARE YOU DOING BACK?
HE'S BEEN CYCLING PEOPLE OUT, KEEPING US RESTED. I'M GETTING READY TO HEAD BACK OUT.
NEED TO TALK TO RICK BEFORE I GO... NOW THAT YOU'RE UP.
OKAY, THEN... TALK AWAY.
I GOTTA LEAVE. IT'S NOT SAFE HERE... HALF MY HOUSE BURNT DOWN. I GOTTA THINK ABOUT PAULA AND MIKEY.
MAGGIE AND HER PEOPLE HAVE BEEN TALKING ABOUT LEAVING... GOING BACK TO THE HILLTOP. I THINK I'D LIKE TO GO WITH THEM.
I WOULDN'T ASK ANYONE TO STAY HERE... AND I'M NOT.
WE'RE ALL LEAVING.

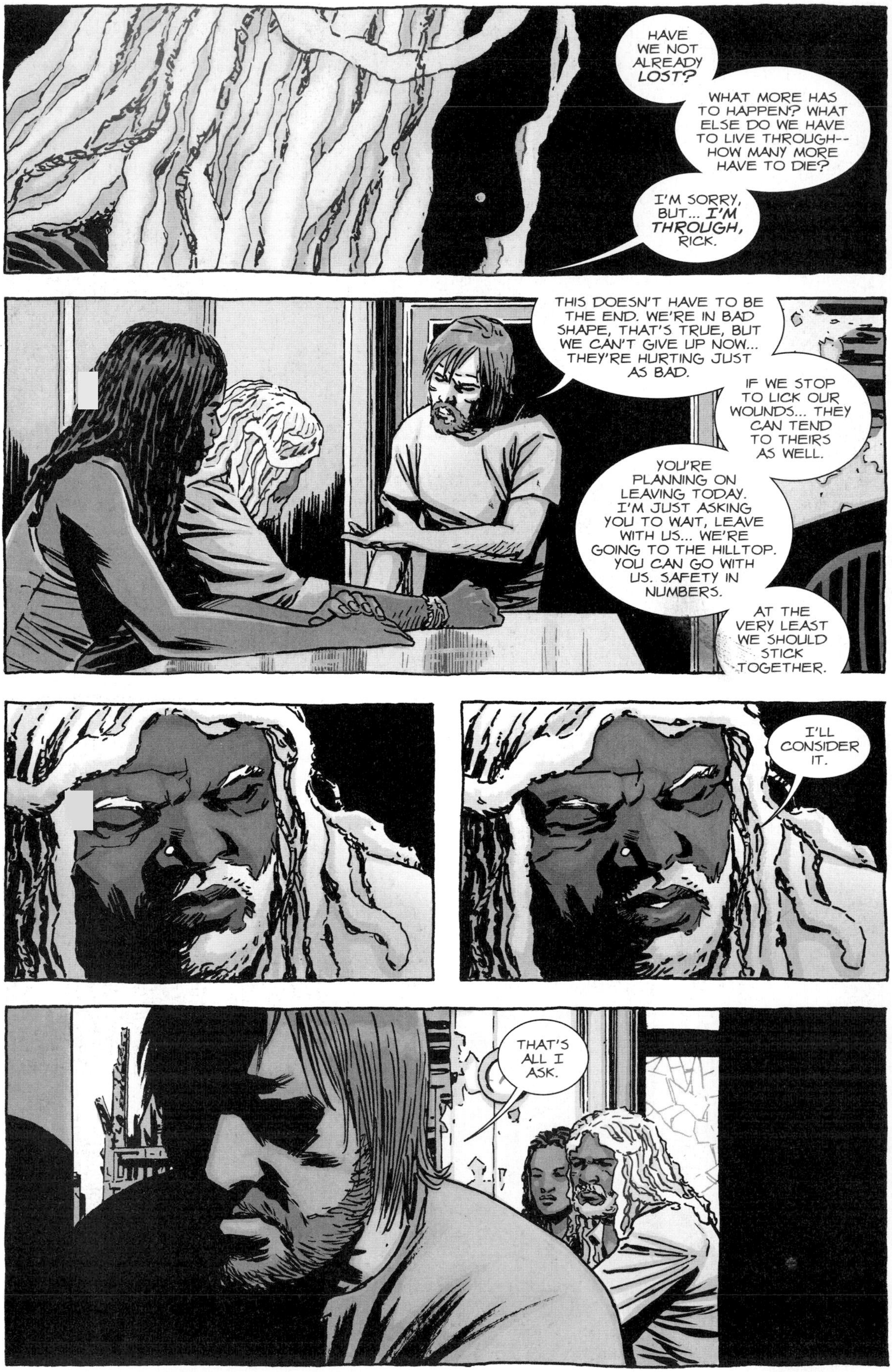
HAVE WE NOT ALREADY *LOST?*
WHAT MORE HAS TO HAPPEN? WHAT ELSE DO WE HAVE TO LIVE THROUGH-- HOW MANY MORE HAVE TO DIE?
I'M SORRY, BUT... *I'M THROUGH,* RICK.
THIS DOESN'T HAVE TO BE THE END. WE'RE IN BAD SHAPE, THAT'S TRUE, BUT WE CAN'T GIVE UP NOW... THEY'RE HURTING JUST AS BAD.
IF WE STOP TO LICK OUR WOUNDS... THEY CAN TEND TO THEIRS AS WELL.
YOU'RE PLANNING ON LEAVING TODAY. I'M JUST ASKING YOU TO WAIT, LEAVE WITH US... WE'RE GOING TO THE HILLTOP. YOU CAN GO WITH US. SAFETY IN NUMBERS.
AT THE VERY LEAST WE SHOULD STICK TOGETHER.
I'LL CONSIDER IT.
THAT'S ALL I ASK.

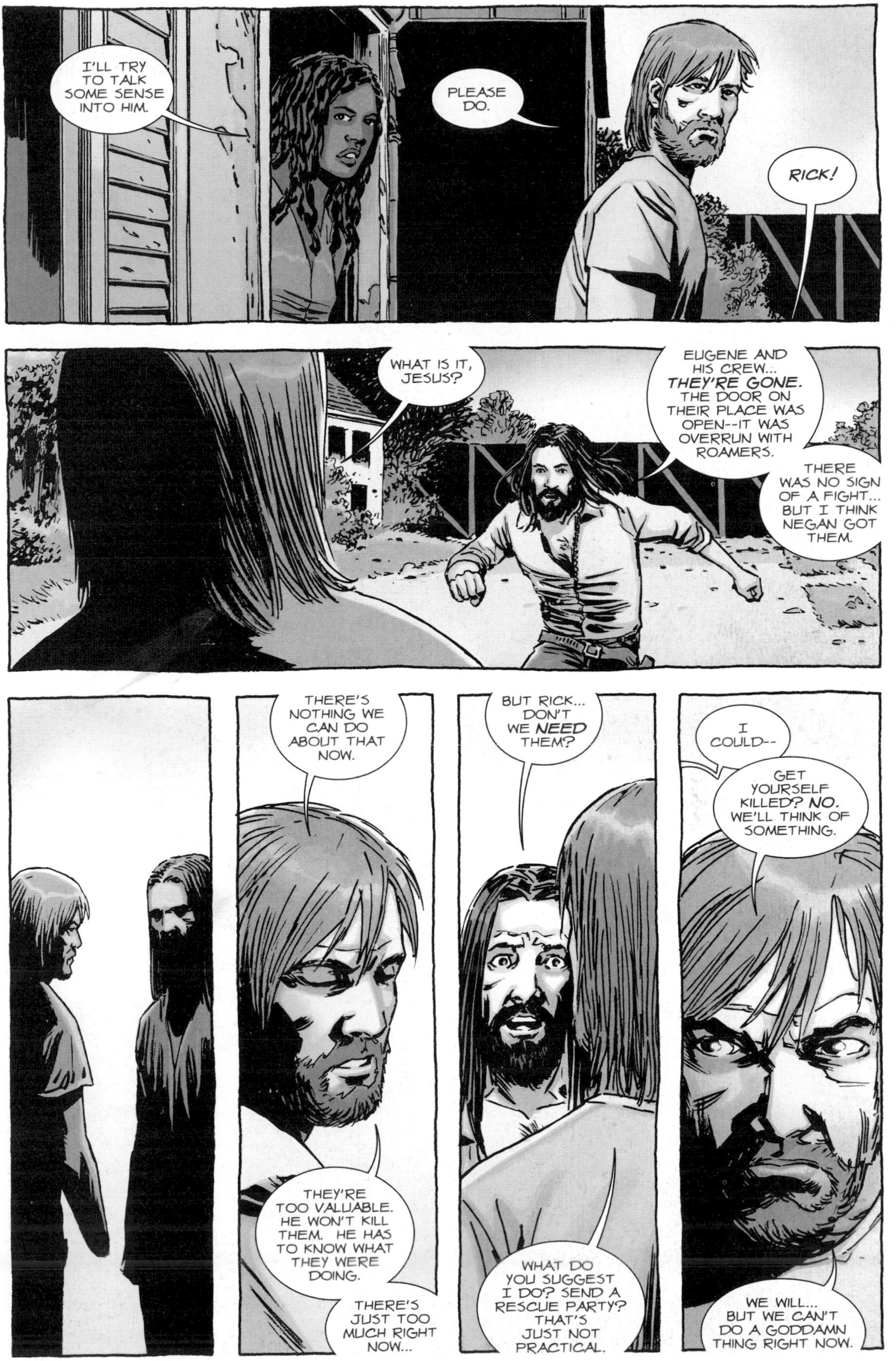
I'LL TRY TO TALK SOME SENSE INTO HIM.
PLEASE DO.
RICK!
WHAT IS IT, JESUS?
EUGENE AND HIS CREW... THEY'RE GONE. THE DOOR ON THEIR PLACE WAS OPEN--IT WAS OVERRUN WITH ROAMERS.
THERE WAS NO SIGN OF A FIGHT... BUT I THINK NEGAN GOT THEM.
THERE'S NOTHING WE CAN DO ABOUT THAT NOW.
THEY'RE TOO VALUABLE. HE WON'T KILL THEM. HE HAS TO KNOW WHAT THEY WERE DOING.
THERE'S JUST TOO MUCH RIGHT NOW...
BUT RICK... DON'T WE NEED THEM?
WHAT DO YOU SUGGEST I DO? SEND A RESCUE PARTY? THAT'S JUST NOT PRACTICAL.
I COULD--
GET YOURSELF KILLED? NO. WE'LL THINK OF SOMETHING.
WE WILL... BUT WE CAN'T DO A GODDAMN THING RIGHT NOW.

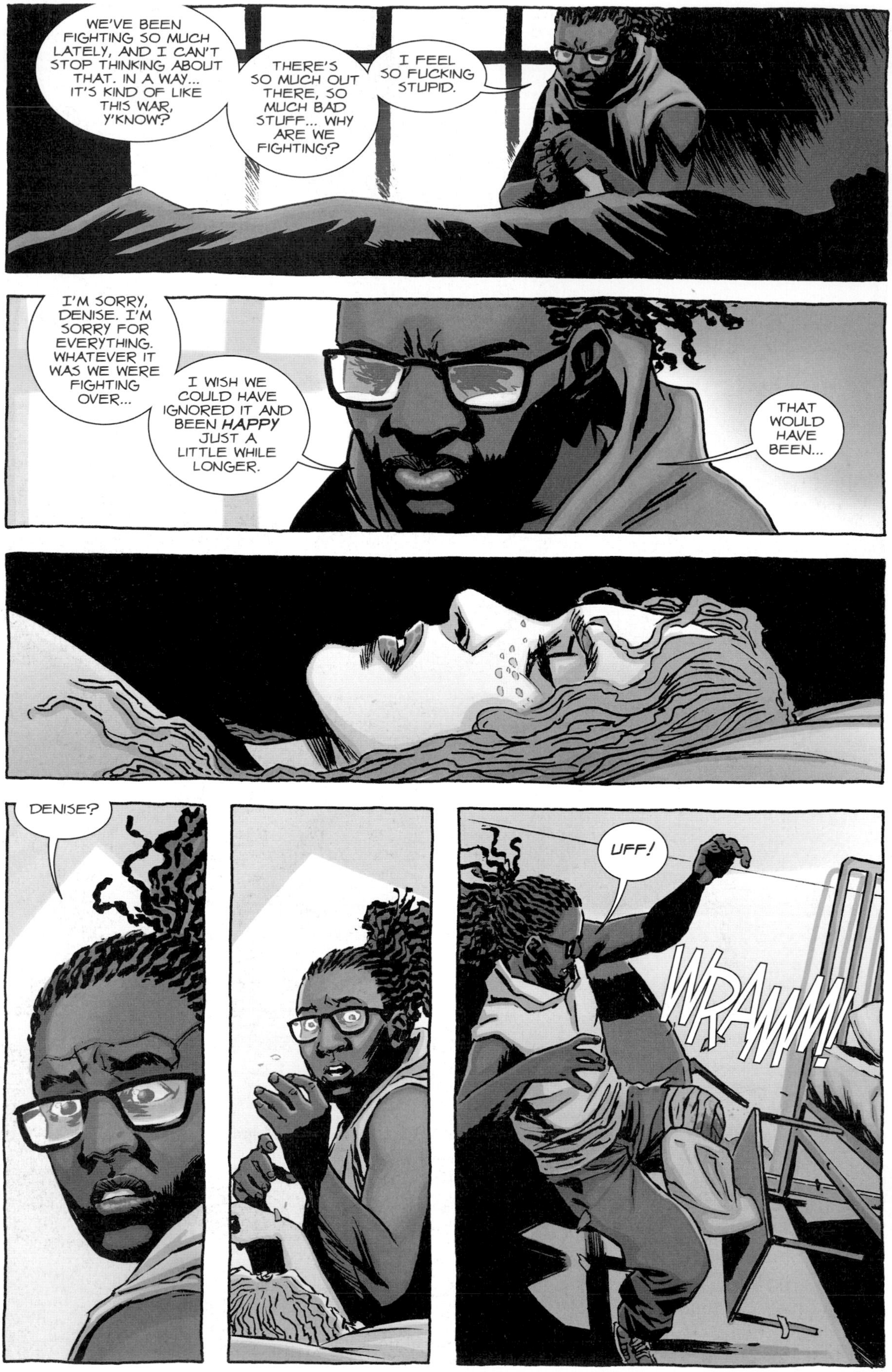
WE'VE BEEN FIGHTING SO MUCH LATELY, AND I CAN'T STOP THINKING ABOUT THAT. IN A WAY... IT'S KIND OF LIKE THIS WAR, Y'KNOW?
THERE'S SO MUCH OUT THERE, SO MUCH BAD STUFF... WHY ARE WE FIGHTING?
I FEEL SO FUCKING STUPID.
I'M SORRY, DENISE. I'M SORRY FOR EVERYTHING. WHATEVER IT WAS WE WERE FIGHTING OVER...
I WISH WE COULD HAVE IGNORED IT AND BEEN *HAPPY* JUST A LITTLE WHILE LONGER.
THAT WOULD HAVE BEEN...
DENISE?
UFF!
WRAMM!

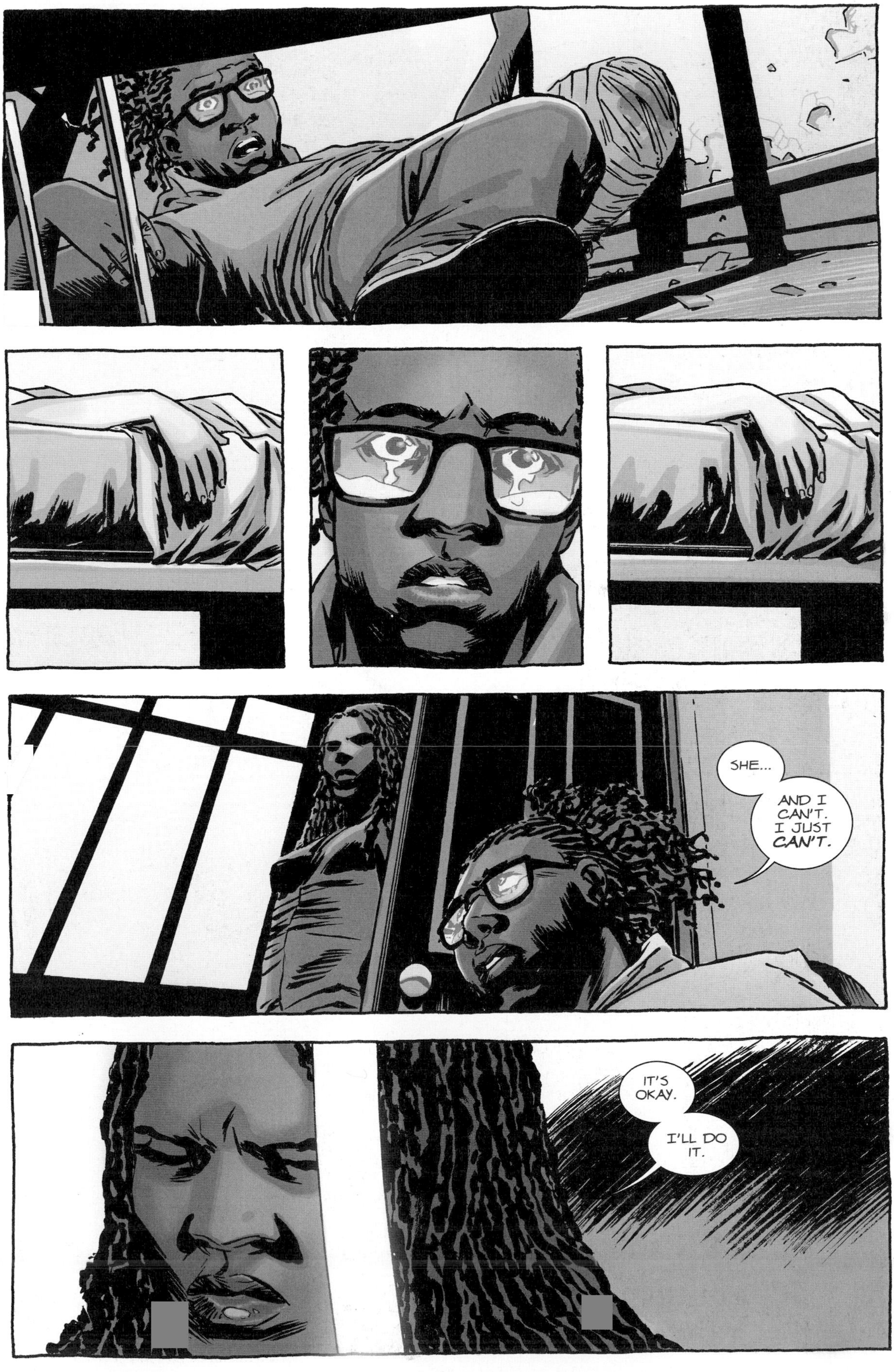
SHE...
AND I CAN'T. I JUST **CAN'T.**
IT'S OKAY.
I'LL DO IT.

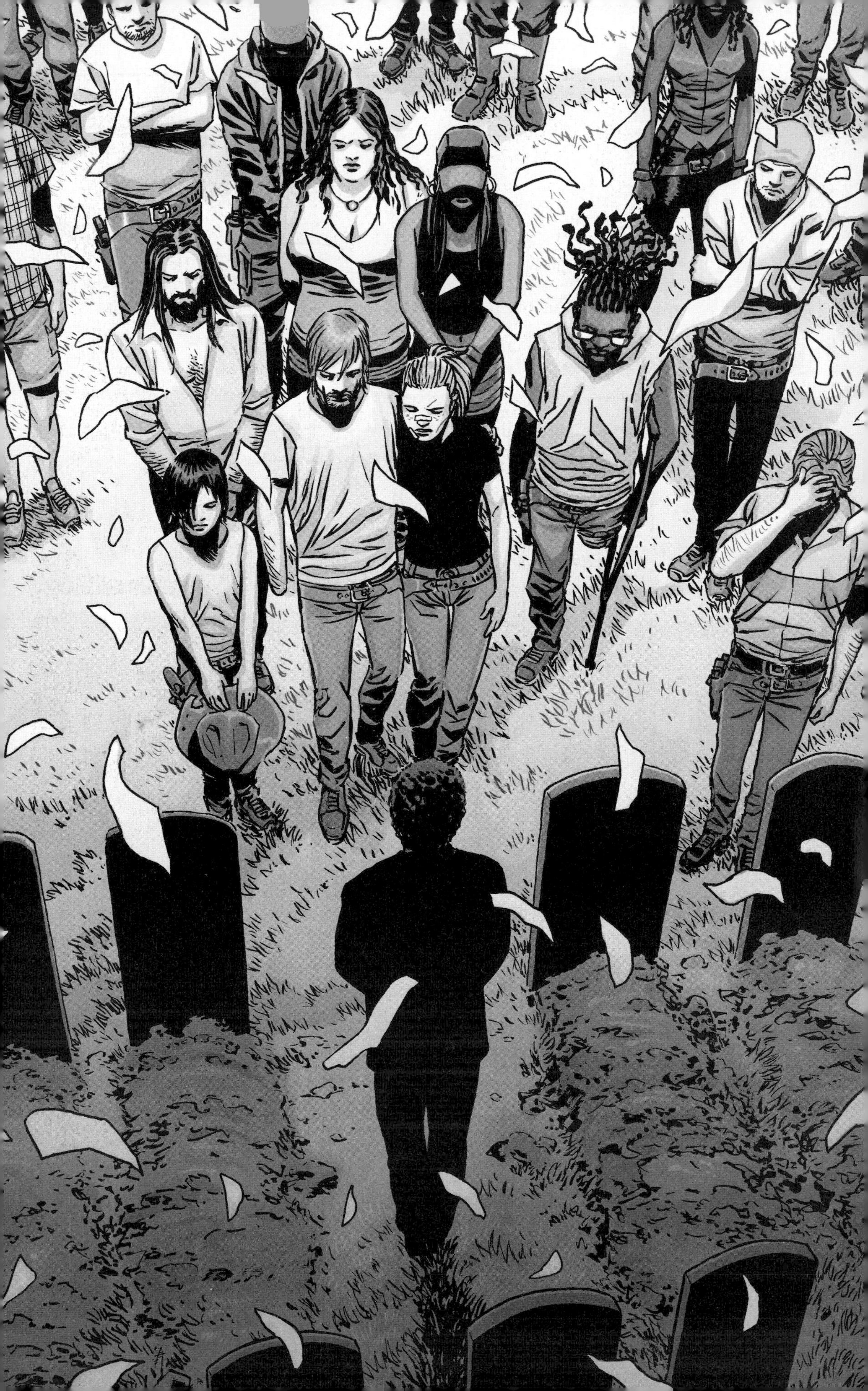

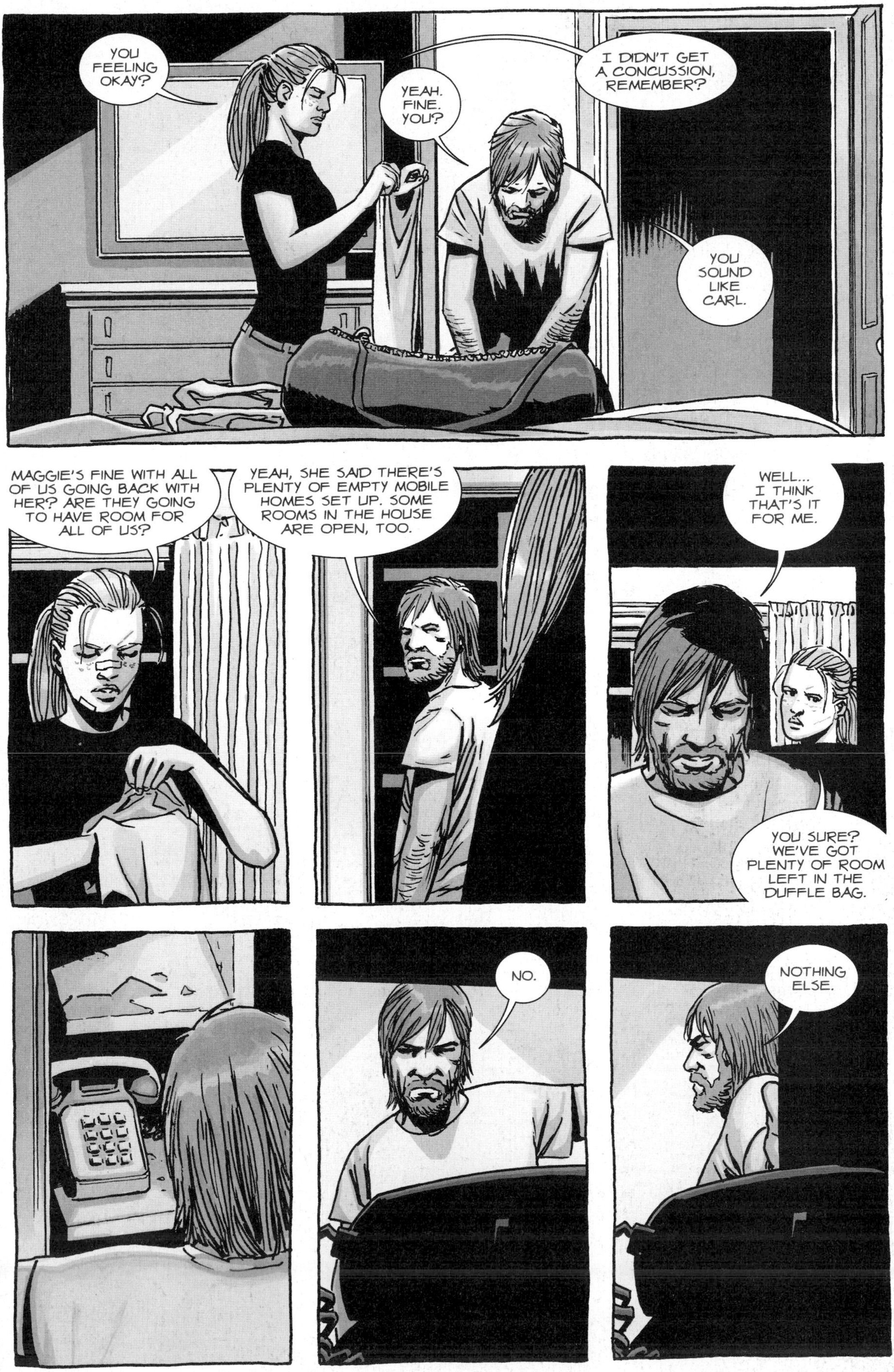
YOU FEELING OKAY?
YEAH. FINE. YOU?
I DIDN'T GET A CONCUSSION, REMEMBER?
YOU SOUND LIKE CARL.
MAGGIE'S FINE WITH ALL OF US GOING BACK WITH HER? ARE THEY GOING TO HAVE ROOM FOR ALL OF US?
YEAH, SHE SAID THERE'S PLENTY OF EMPTY MOBILE HOMES SET UP. SOME ROOMS IN THE HOUSE ARE OPEN, TOO.
WELL... I THINK THAT'S IT FOR ME.
YOU SURE? WE'VE GOT PLENTY OF ROOM LEFT IN THE DUFFLE BAG.
NO.
NOTHING ELSE.

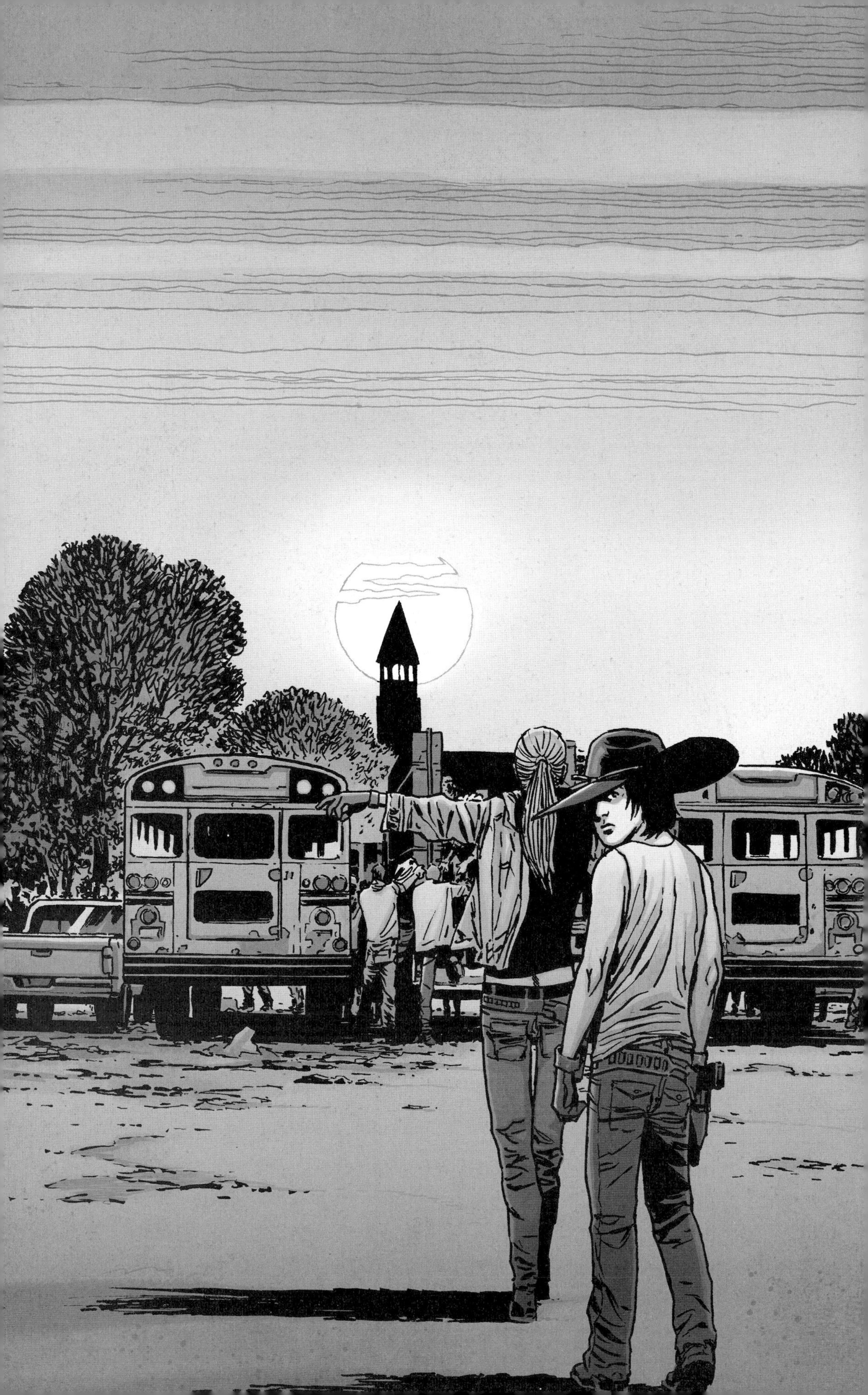

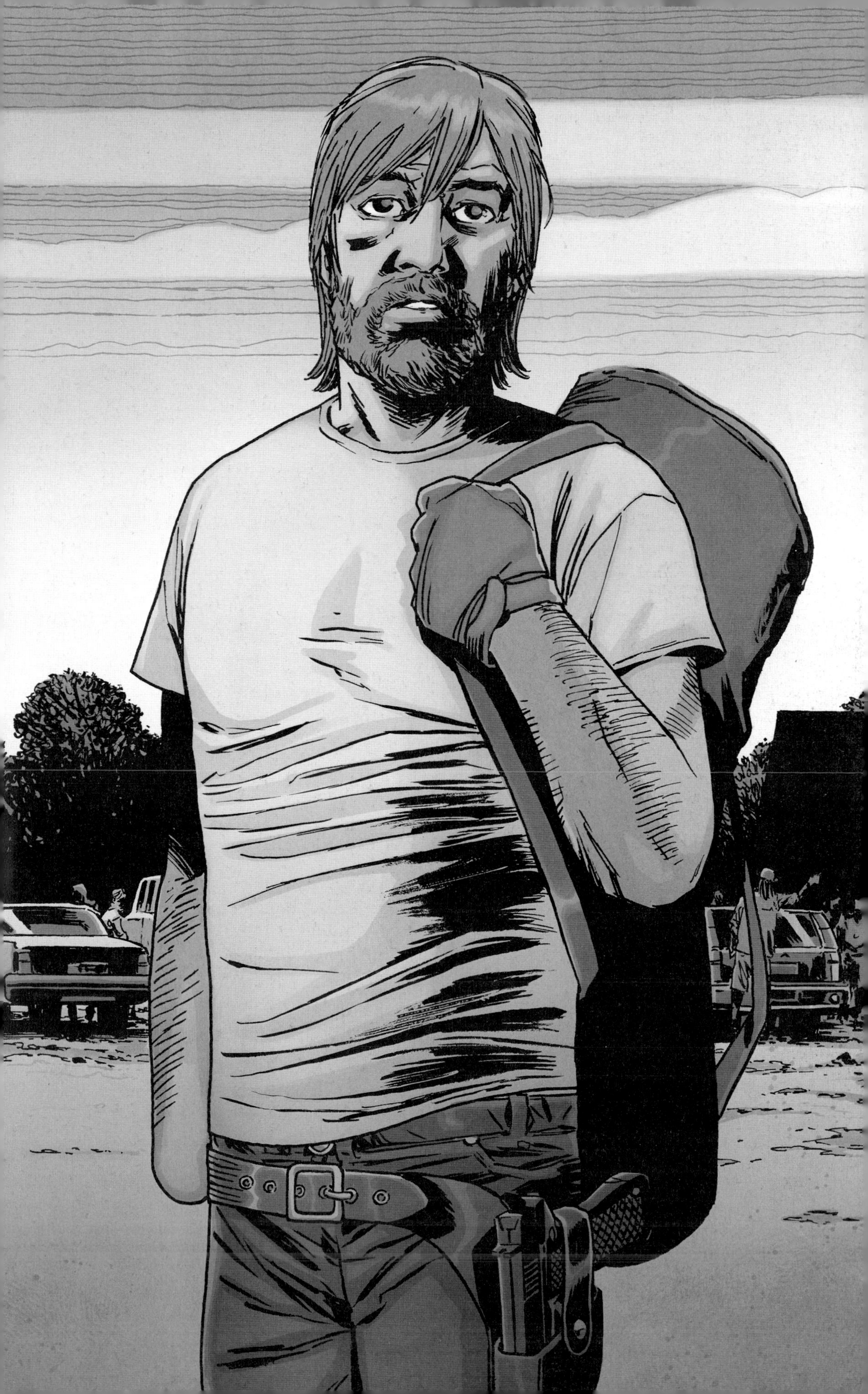

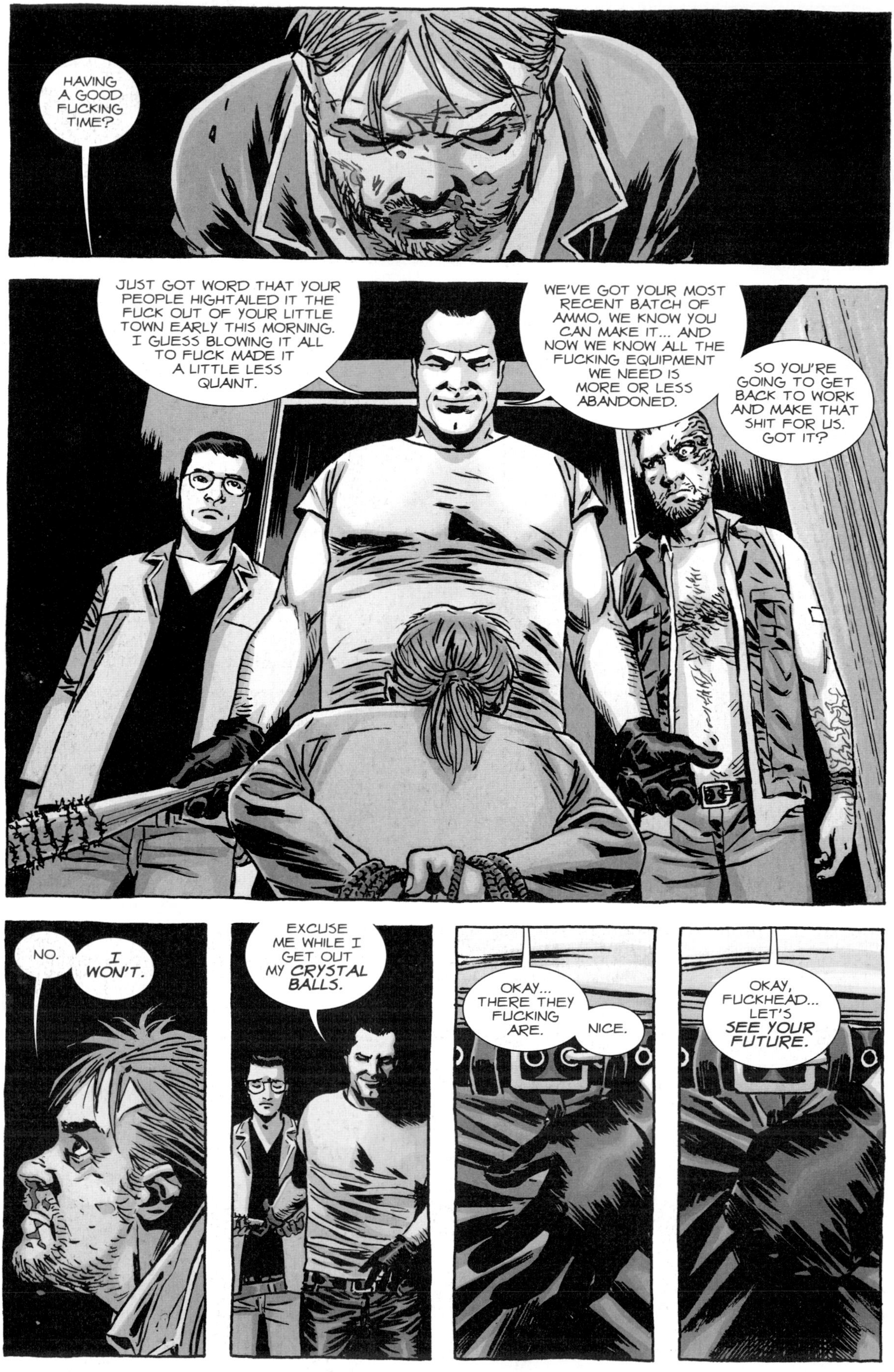
HAVING A GOOD FUCKING TIME?
JUST GOT WORD THAT YOUR PEOPLE HIGHTAILED IT THE FUCK OUT OF YOUR LITTLE TOWN EARLY THIS MORNING. I GUESS BLOWING IT ALL TO FUCK MADE IT A LITTLE LESS QUAINT.
WE'VE GOT YOUR MOST RECENT BATCH OF AMMO, WE KNOW YOU CAN MAKE IT... AND NOW WE KNOW ALL THE FUCKING EQUIPMENT WE NEED IS MORE OR LESS ABANDONED.
SO YOU'RE GOING TO GET BACK TO WORK AND MAKE THAT SHIT FOR US. GOT IT?
NO.
I WON'T.
EXCUSE ME WHILE I GET OUT MY CRYSTAL BALLS.
OKAY... THERE THEY FUCKING ARE.
NICE.
OKAY, FUCKHEAD... LET'S SEE YOUR FUTURE.

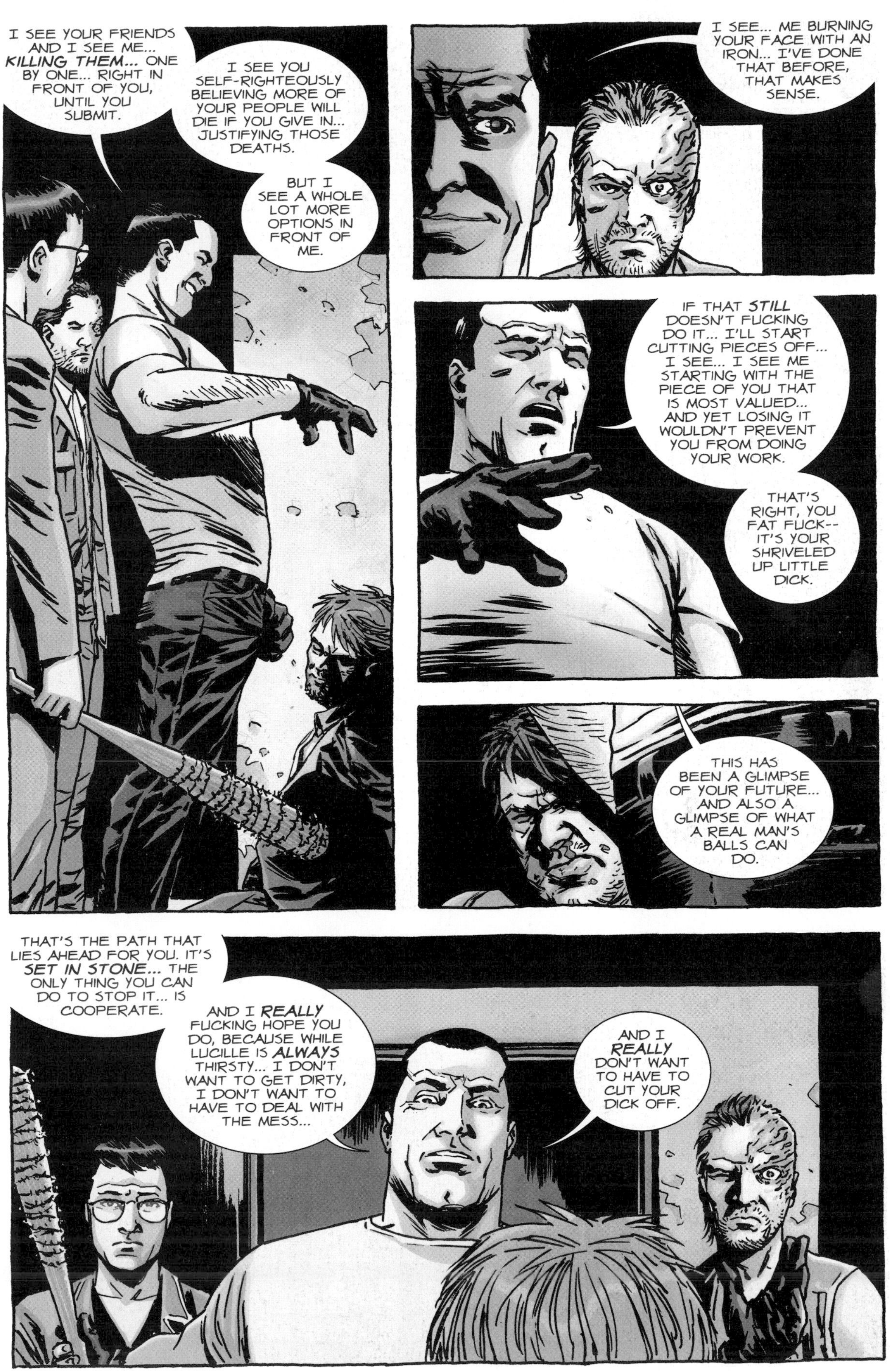

I SEE YOUR FRIENDS AND I SEE ME... KILLING THEM... ONE BY ONE... RIGHT IN FRONT OF YOU, UNTIL YOU SUBMIT.
I SEE YOU SELF-RIGHTEOUSLY BELIEVING MORE OF YOUR PEOPLE WILL DIE IF YOU GIVE IN... JUSTIFYING THOSE DEATHS.
BUT I SEE A WHOLE LOT MORE OPTIONS IN FRONT OF ME.
I SEE... ME BURNING YOUR FACE WITH AN IRON... I'VE DONE THAT BEFORE, THAT MAKES SENSE.
IF THAT STILL DOESN'T FUCKING DO IT... I'LL START CUTTING PIECES OFF... I SEE... I SEE ME STARTING WITH THE PIECE OF YOU THAT IS MOST VALUED... AND YET LOSING IT WOULDN'T PREVENT YOU FROM DOING YOUR WORK.
THAT'S RIGHT, YOU FAT FUCK-- IT'S YOUR SHRIVELED UP LITTLE DICK.
THIS HAS BEEN A GLIMPSE OF YOUR FUTURE... AND ALSO A GLIMPSE OF WHAT A REAL MAN'S BALLS CAN DO.
THAT'S THE PATH THAT LIES AHEAD FOR YOU. IT'S SET IN STONE... THE ONLY THING YOU CAN DO TO STOP IT... IS COOPERATE.
AND I REALLY FUCKING HOPE YOU DO, BECAUSE WHILE LUCILLE IS ALWAYS THIRSTY... I DON'T WANT TO GET DIRTY, I DON'T WANT TO HAVE TO DEAL WITH THE MESS...
AND I REALLY DON'T WANT TO HAVE TO CUT YOUR DICK OFF.

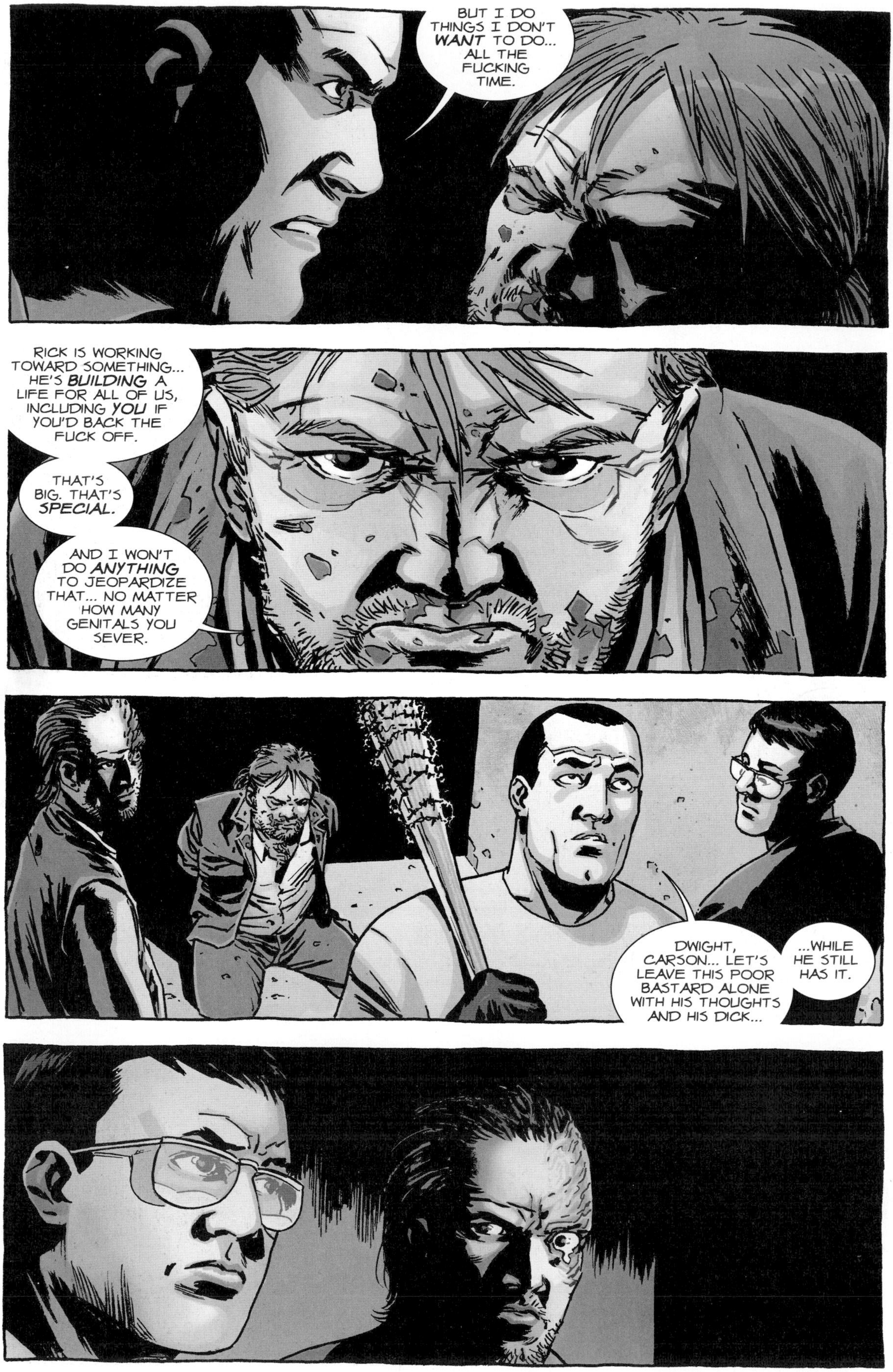
BUT I DO THINGS I DON'T WANT TO DO... ALL THE FUCKING TIME.
RICK IS WORKING TOWARD SOMETHING... HE'S BUILDING A LIFE FOR ALL OF US, INCLUDING YOU IF YOU'D BACK THE FUCK OFF.
THAT'S BIG. THAT'S SPECIAL.
AND I WON'T DO ANYTHING TO JEOPARDIZE THAT... NO MATTER HOW MANY GENITALS YOU SEVER.
DWIGHT, CARSON... LET'S LEAVE THIS POOR BASTARD ALONE WITH HIS THOUGHTS AND HIS DICK...
...WHILE HE STILL HAS IT.

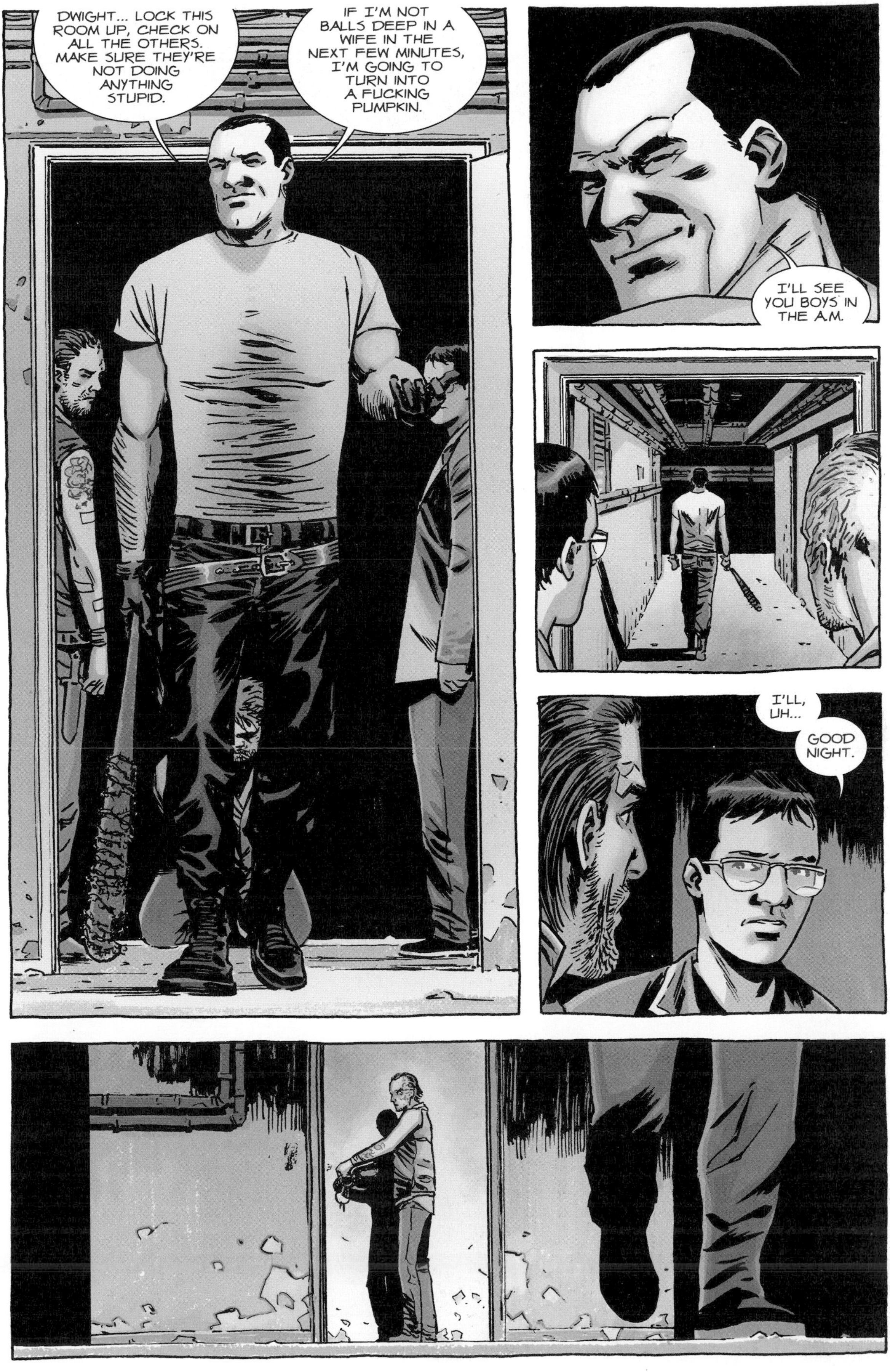

DWIGHT... LOCK THIS ROOM UP, CHECK ON ALL THE OTHERS. MAKE SURE THEY'RE NOT DOING ANYTHING STUPID.
IF I'M NOT BALLS DEEP IN A WIFE IN THE NEXT FEW MINUTES, I'M GOING TO TURN INTO A FUCKING PUMPKIN.
I'LL SEE YOU BOYS IN THE A.M.
I'LL, UH...
GOOD NIGHT.

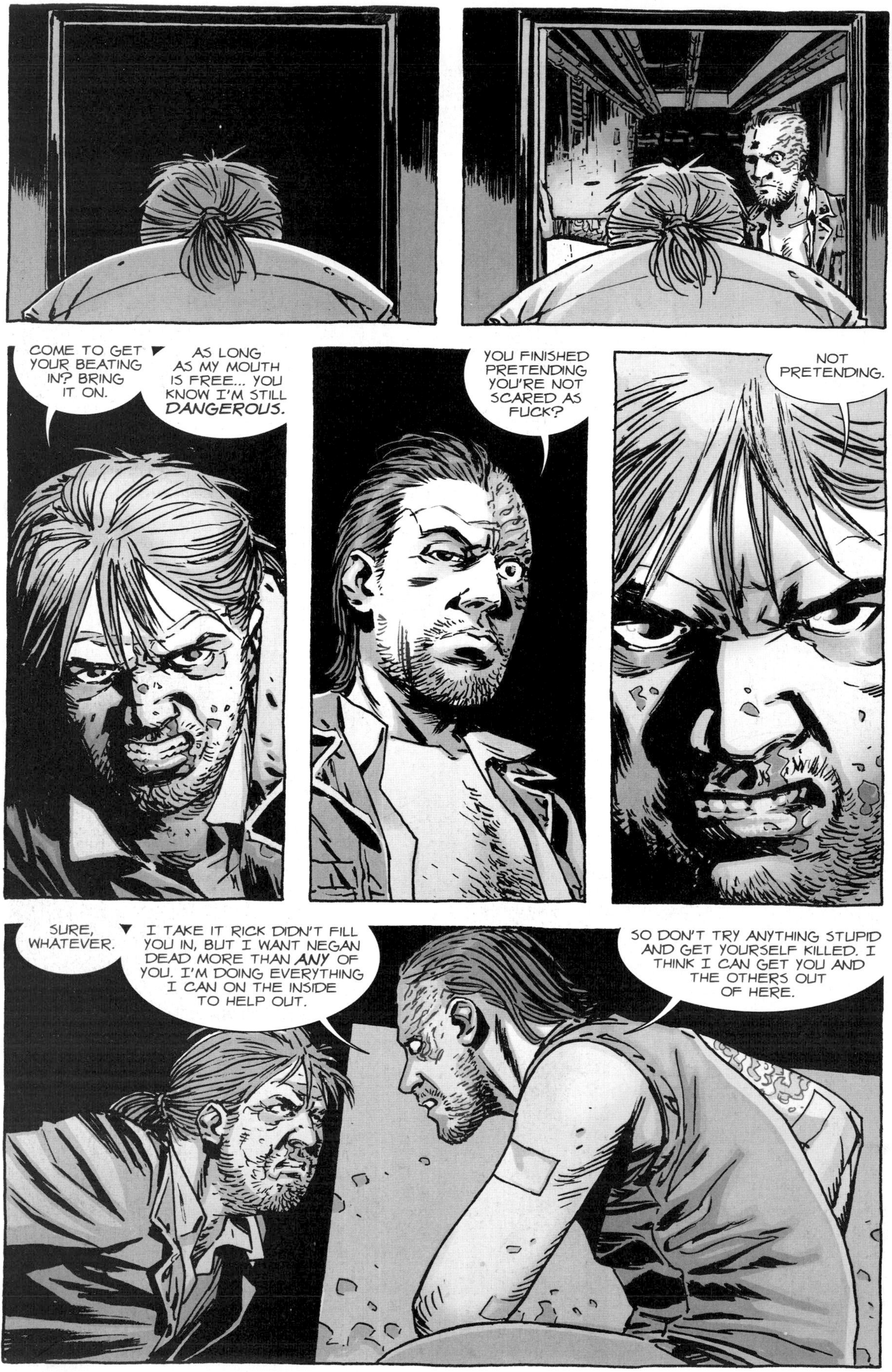
COME TO GET YOUR BEATING IN? BRING IT ON.
AS LONG AS MY MOUTH IS FREE... YOU KNOW I'M STILL *DANGEROUS.*
YOU FINISHED PRETENDING YOU'RE NOT SCARED AS FUCK?
NOT PRETENDING.
SURE, WHATEVER.
I TAKE IT RICK DIDN'T FILL YOU IN, BUT I WANT NEGAN DEAD MORE THAN *ANY* OF YOU. I'M DOING EVERYTHING I CAN ON THE INSIDE TO HELP OUT.
SO DON'T TRY ANYTHING STUPID AND GET YOURSELF KILLED. I THINK I CAN GET YOU AND THE OTHERS OUT OF HERE.

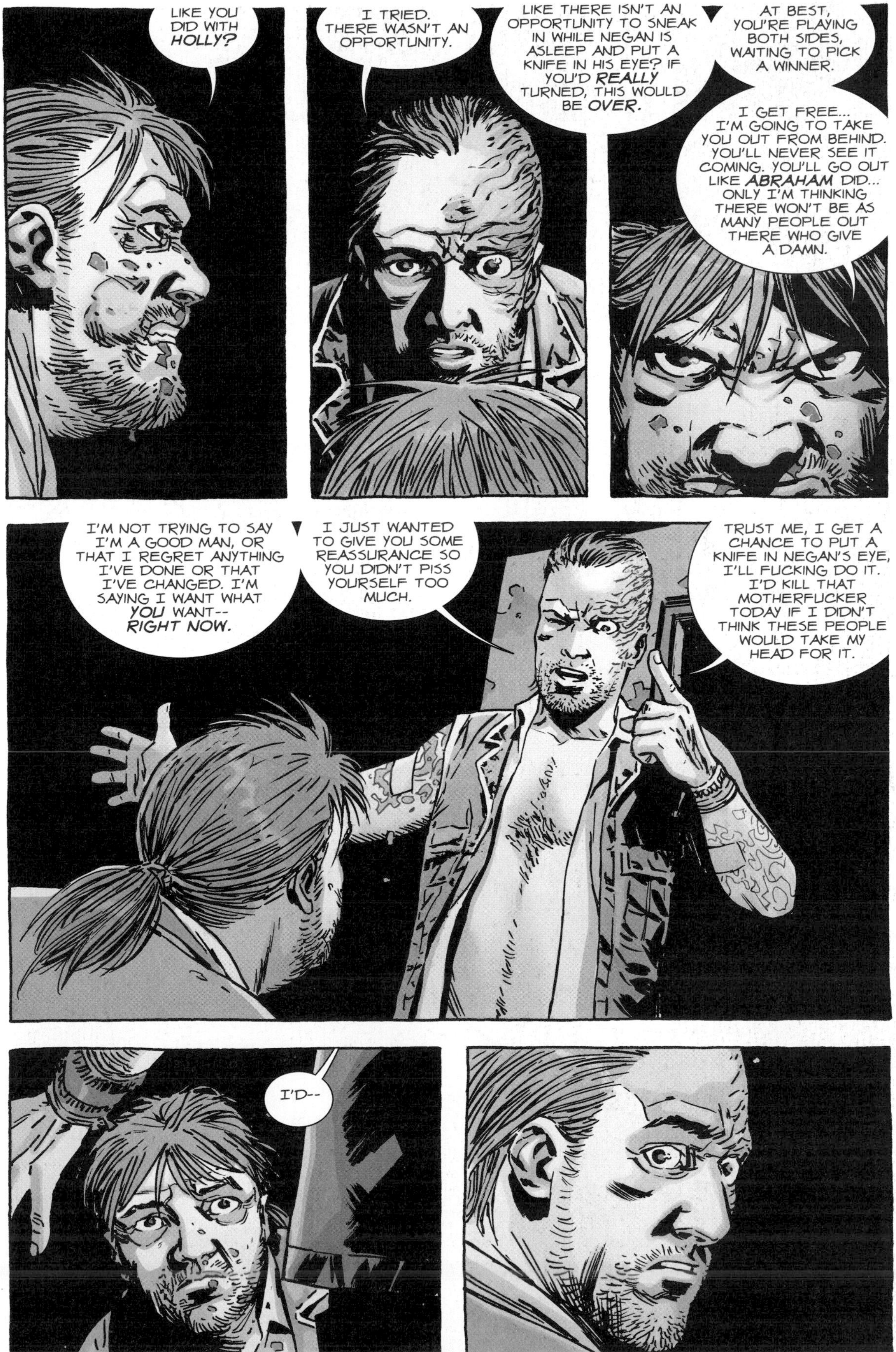
LIKE YOU DID WITH HOLLY?
I TRIED. THERE WASN'T AN OPPORTUNITY.
LIKE THERE ISN'T AN OPPORTUNITY TO SNEAK IN WHILE NEGAN IS ASLEEP AND PUT A KNIFE IN HIS EYE? IF YOU'D REALLY TURNED, THIS WOULD BE OVER.
AT BEST, YOU'RE PLAYING BOTH SIDES, WAITING TO PICK A WINNER.
I GET FREE... I'M GOING TO TAKE YOU OUT FROM BEHIND. YOU'LL NEVER SEE IT COMING. YOU'LL GO OUT LIKE ABRAHAM DID... ONLY I'M THINKING THERE WON'T BE AS MANY PEOPLE OUT THERE WHO GIVE A DAMN.
I'M NOT TRYING TO SAY I'M A GOOD MAN, OR THAT I REGRET ANYTHING I'VE DONE OR THAT I'VE CHANGED. I'M SAYING I WANT WHAT YOU WANT-- RIGHT NOW.
I JUST WANTED TO GIVE YOU SOME REASSURANCE SO YOU DIDN'T PISS YOURSELF TOO MUCH.
TRUST ME, I GET A CHANCE TO PUT A KNIFE IN NEGAN'S EYE, I'LL FUCKING DO IT. I'D KILL THAT MOTHERFUCKER TODAY IF I DIDN'T THINK THESE PEOPLE WOULD TAKE MY HEAD FOR IT.
I'D--

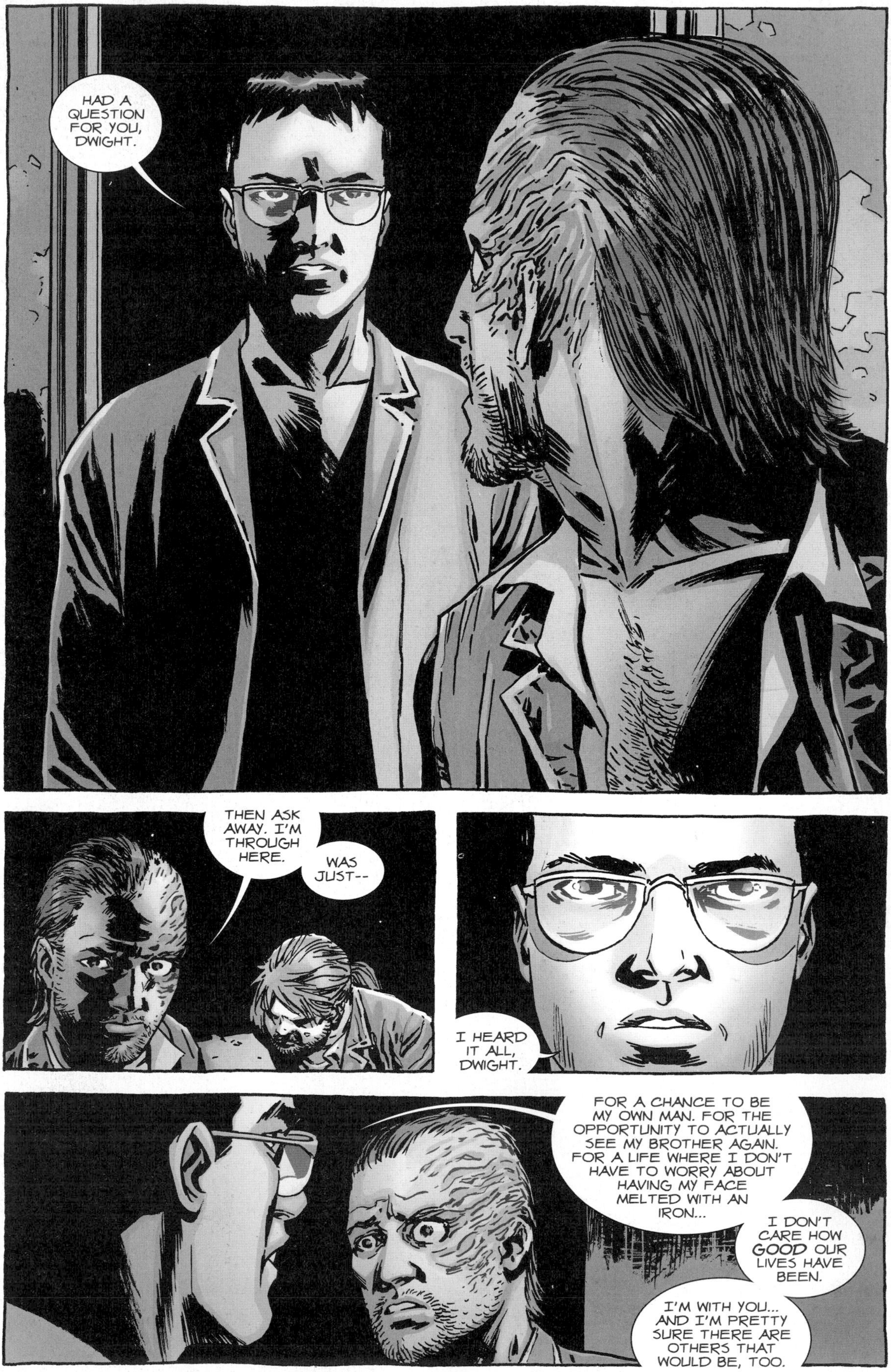
HAD A QUESTION FOR YOU, DWIGHT.
THEN ASK AWAY. I'M THROUGH HERE.
WAS JUST--
I HEARD IT ALL, DWIGHT.
FOR A CHANCE TO BE MY OWN MAN. FOR THE OPPORTUNITY TO ACTUALLY SEE MY BROTHER AGAIN. FOR A LIFE WHERE I DON'T HAVE TO WORRY ABOUT HAVING MY FACE MELTED WITH AN IRON...
I DON'T CARE HOW GOOD OUR LIVES HAVE BEEN.
I'M WITH YOU... AND I'M PRETTY SURE THERE ARE OTHERS THAT WOULD BE, TOO.

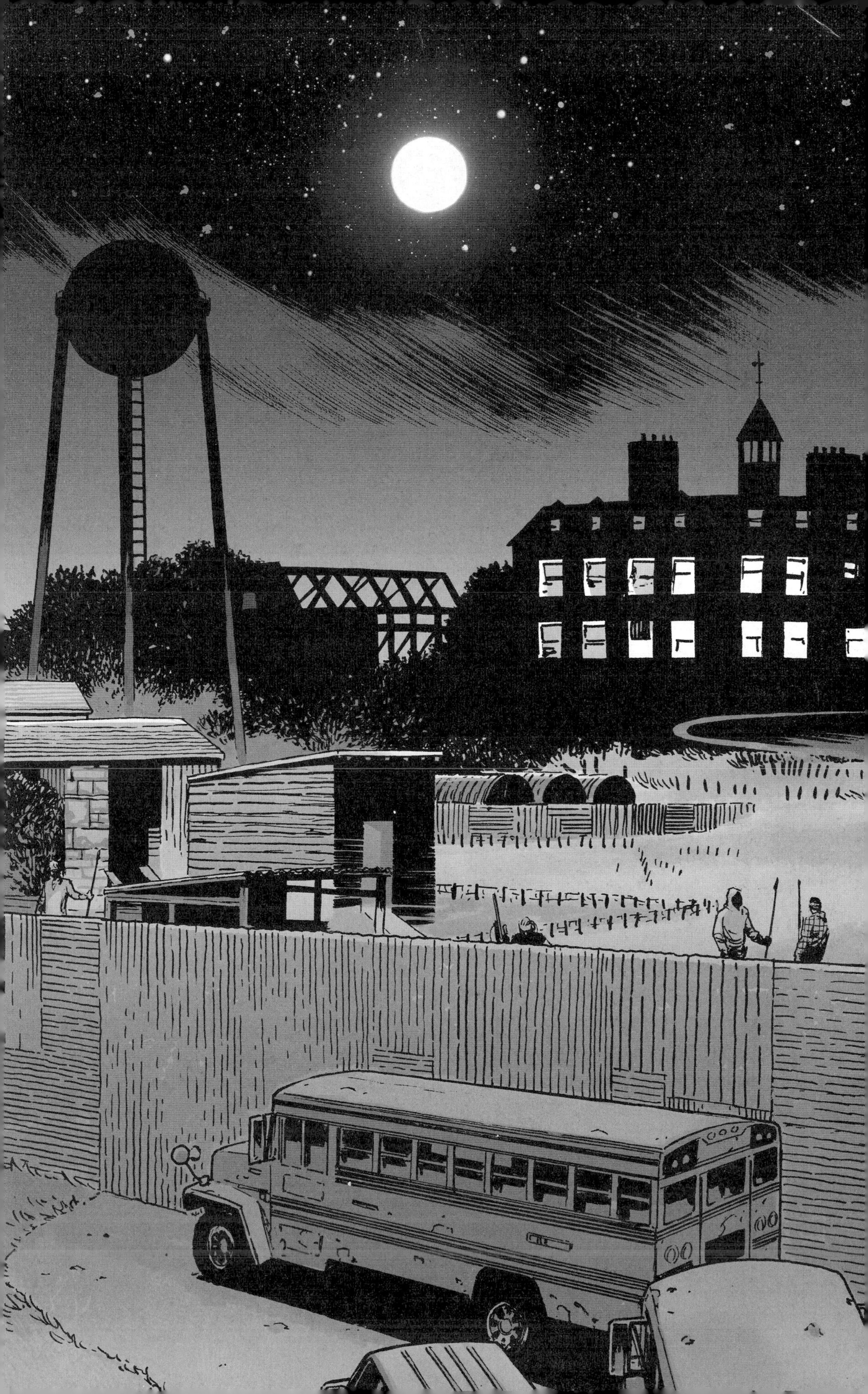

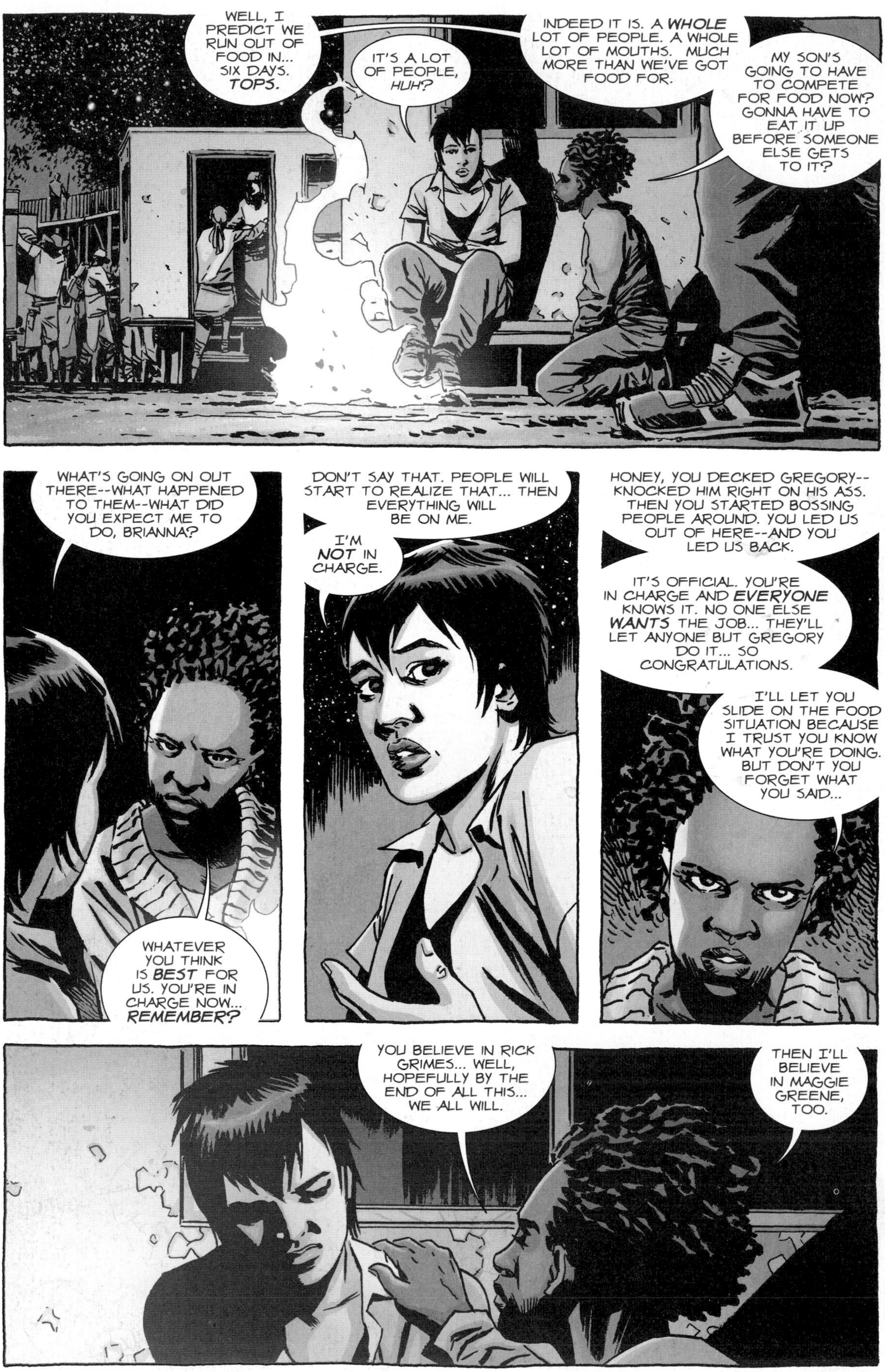

WELL, I PREDICT WE RUN OUT OF FOOD IN... SIX DAYS. TOPS.
IT'S A LOT OF PEOPLE, HUH?
INDEED IT IS. A WHOLE LOT OF PEOPLE. A WHOLE LOT OF MOUTHS. MUCH MORE THAN WE'VE GOT FOOD FOR.
MY SON'S GOING TO HAVE TO COMPETE FOR FOOD NOW? GONNA HAVE TO EAT IT UP BEFORE SOMEONE ELSE GETS TO IT?
WHAT'S GOING ON OUT THERE--WHAT HAPPENED TO THEM--WHAT DID YOU EXPECT ME TO DO, BRIANNA?
WHATEVER YOU THINK IS BEST FOR US. YOU'RE IN CHARGE NOW... REMEMBER?
I'M NOT IN CHARGE.
DON'T SAY THAT. PEOPLE WILL START TO REALIZE THAT... THEN EVERYTHING WILL BE ON ME.
HONEY, YOU DECKED GREGORY--KNOCKED HIM RIGHT ON HIS ASS. THEN YOU STARTED BOSSING PEOPLE AROUND. YOU LED US OUT OF HERE--AND YOU LED US BACK.
IT'S OFFICIAL. YOU'RE IN CHARGE AND EVERYONE KNOWS IT. NO ONE ELSE WANTS THE JOB... THEY'LL LET ANYONE BUT GREGORY DO IT... SO CONGRATULATIONS.
I'LL LET YOU SLIDE ON THE FOOD SITUATION BECAUSE I TRUST YOU KNOW WHAT YOU'RE DOING. BUT DON'T YOU FORGET WHAT YOU SAID...
YOU BELIEVE IN RICK GRIMES... WELL, HOPEFULLY BY THE END OF ALL THIS... WE ALL WILL.
THEN I'LL BELIEVE IN MAGGIE GREENE, TOO.

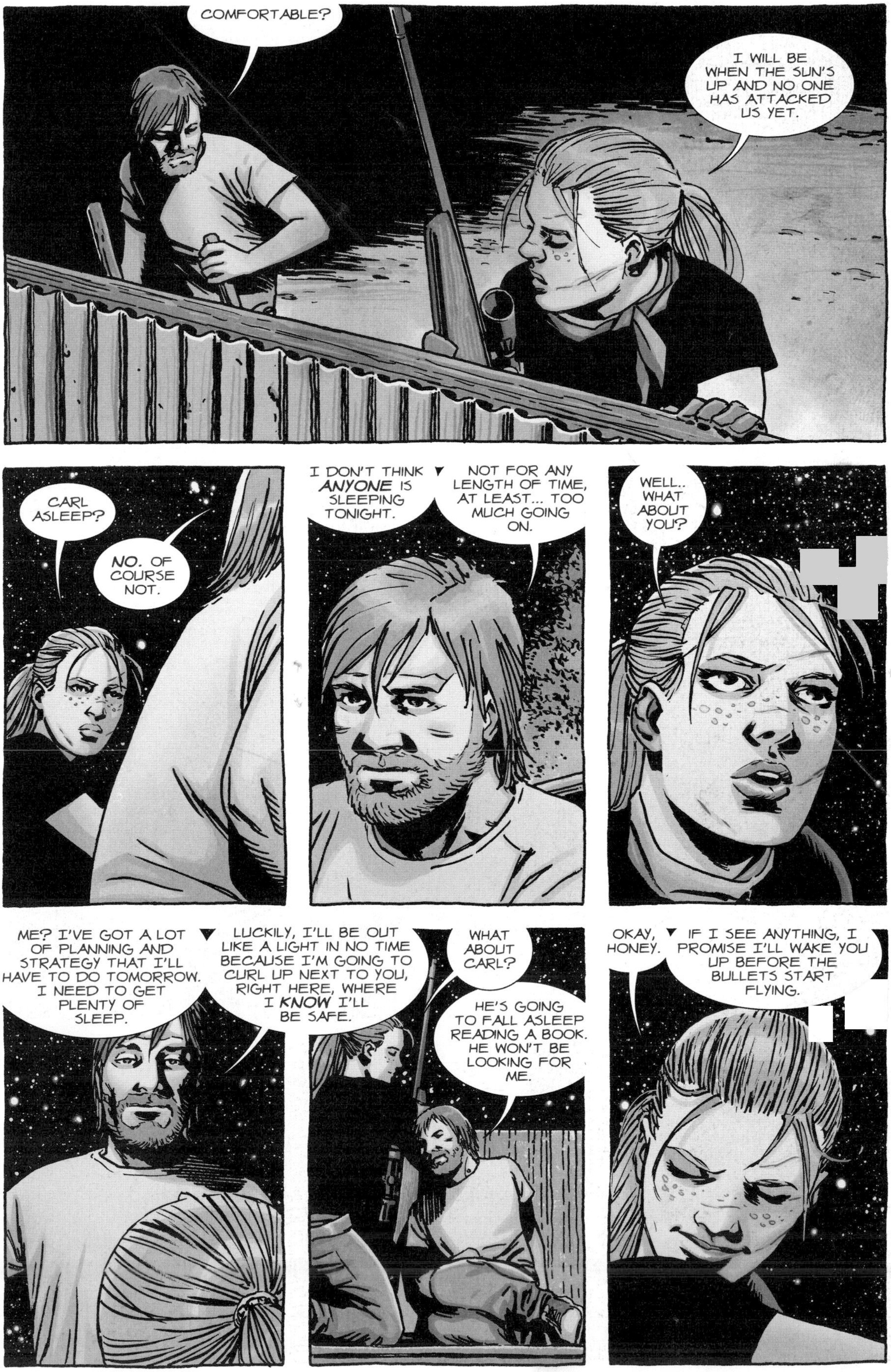
COMFORTABLE?
I WILL BE WHEN THE SUN'S UP AND NO ONE HAS ATTACKED US YET.
CARL ASLEEP?
NO. OF COURSE NOT.
I DON'T THINK ANYONE IS SLEEPING TONIGHT.
NOT FOR ANY LENGTH OF TIME, AT LEAST... TOO MUCH GOING ON.
WELL.. WHAT ABOUT YOU?
ME? I'VE GOT A LOT OF PLANNING AND STRATEGY THAT I'LL HAVE TO DO TOMORROW. I NEED TO GET PLENTY OF SLEEP.
LUCKILY, I'LL BE OUT LIKE A LIGHT IN NO TIME BECAUSE I'M GOING TO CURL UP NEXT TO YOU, RIGHT HERE, WHERE I KNOW I'LL BE SAFE.
WHAT ABOUT CARL?
HE'S GOING TO FALL ASLEEP READING A BOOK. HE WON'T BE LOOKING FOR ME.
OKAY, HONEY.
IF I SEE ANYTHING, I PROMISE I'LL WAKE YOU UP BEFORE THE BULLETS START FLYING.

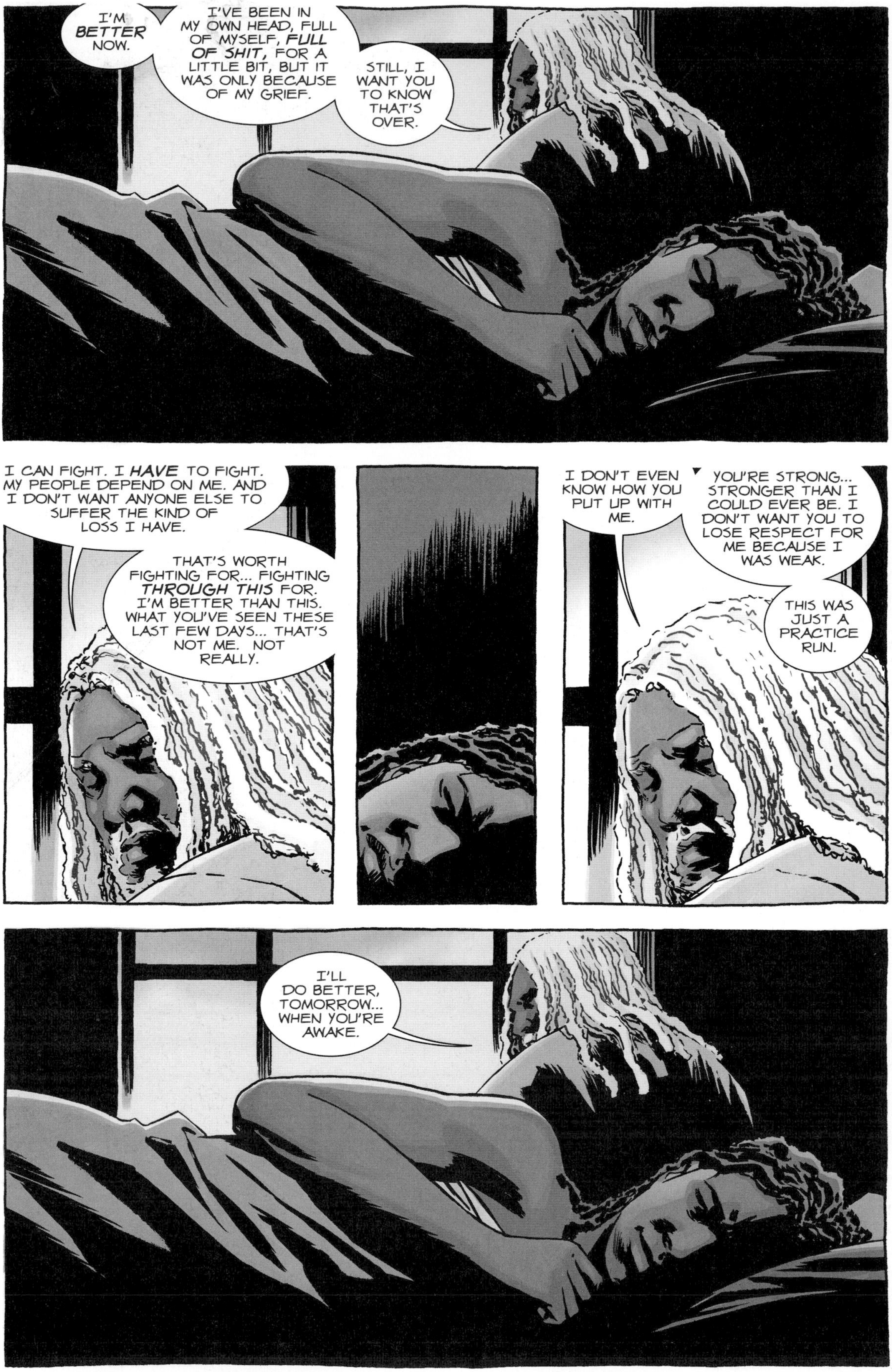
I'M BETTER NOW.
I'VE BEEN IN MY OWN HEAD, FULL OF MYSELF, FULL OF SHIT, FOR A LITTLE BIT, BUT IT WAS ONLY BECAUSE OF MY GRIEF.
STILL, I WANT YOU TO KNOW THAT'S OVER.
I CAN FIGHT. I HAVE TO FIGHT. MY PEOPLE DEPEND ON ME. AND I DON'T WANT ANYONE ELSE TO SUFFER THE KIND OF LOSS I HAVE.
THAT'S WORTH FIGHTING FOR... FIGHTING THROUGH THIS FOR. I'M BETTER THAN THIS. WHAT YOU'VE SEEN THESE LAST FEW DAYS... THAT'S NOT ME. NOT REALLY.
I DON'T EVEN KNOW HOW YOU PUT UP WITH ME.
YOU'RE STRONG... STRONGER THAN I COULD EVER BE. I DON'T WANT YOU TO LOSE RESPECT FOR ME BECAUSE I WAS WEAK.
THIS WAS JUST A PRACTICE RUN.
I'LL DO BETTER, TOMORROW... WHEN YOU'RE AWAKE.

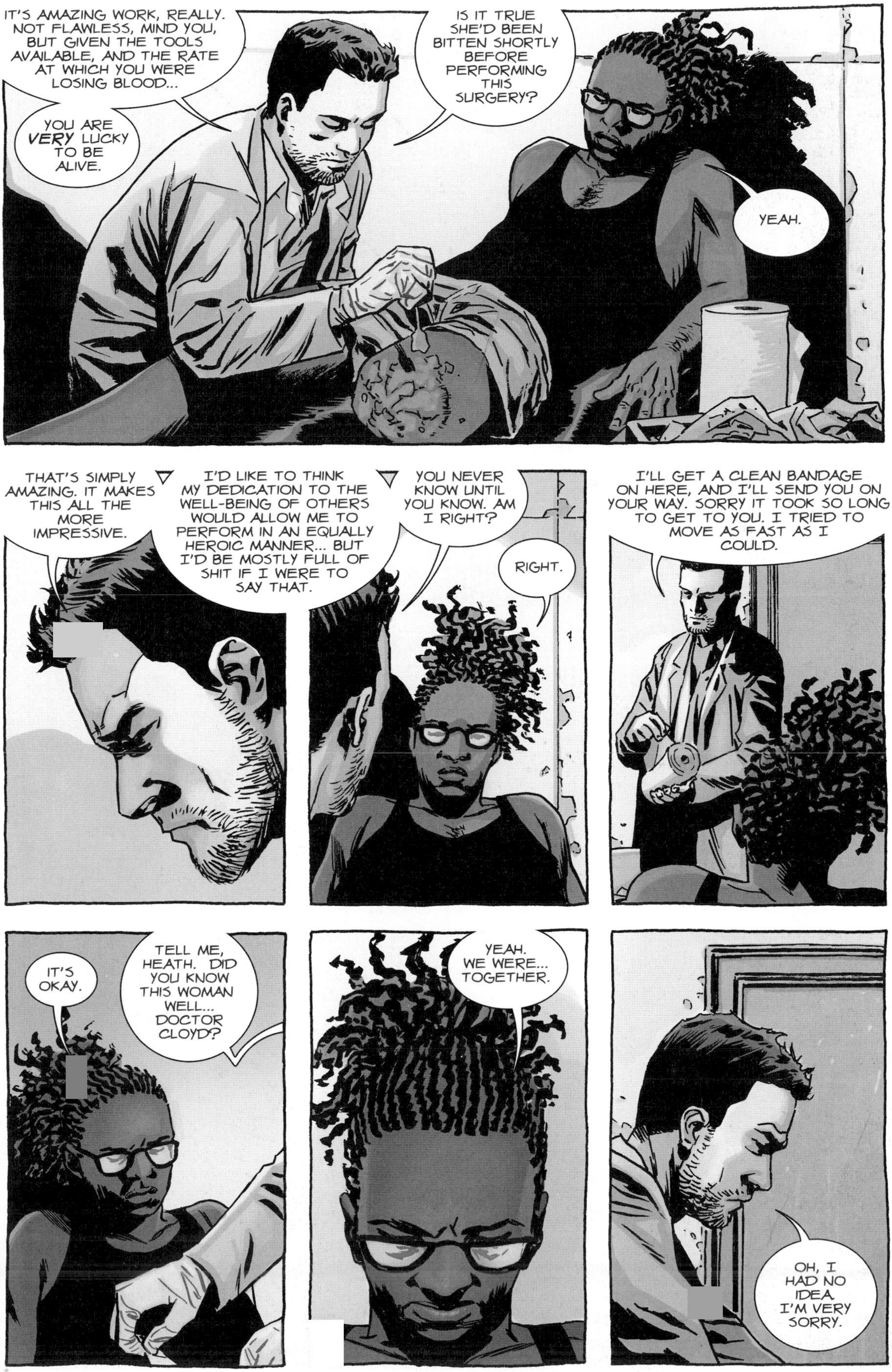
IT'S AMAZING WORK, REALLY. NOT FLAWLESS, MIND YOU, BUT GIVEN THE TOOLS AVAILABLE, AND THE RATE AT WHICH YOU WERE LOSING BLOOD...
YOU ARE VERY LUCKY TO BE ALIVE.
IS IT TRUE SHE'D BEEN BITTEN SHORTLY BEFORE PERFORMING THIS SURGERY?
YEAH.
THAT'S SIMPLY AMAZING. IT MAKES THIS ALL THE MORE IMPRESSIVE.
I'D LIKE TO THINK MY DEDICATION TO THE WELL-BEING OF OTHERS WOULD ALLOW ME TO PERFORM IN AN EQUALLY HEROIC MANNER... BUT I'D BE MOSTLY FULL OF SHIT IF I WERE TO SAY THAT.
YOU NEVER KNOW UNTIL YOU KNOW. AM I RIGHT?
RIGHT.
I'LL GET A CLEAN BANDAGE ON HERE, AND I'LL SEND YOU ON YOUR WAY. SORRY IT TOOK SO LONG TO GET TO YOU. I TRIED TO MOVE AS FAST AS I COULD.
IT'S OKAY.
TELL ME, HEATH. DID YOU KNOW THIS WOMAN WELL... DOCTOR CLOYD?
YEAH. WE WERE... TOGETHER.
OH, I HAD NO IDEA. I'M VERY SORRY.

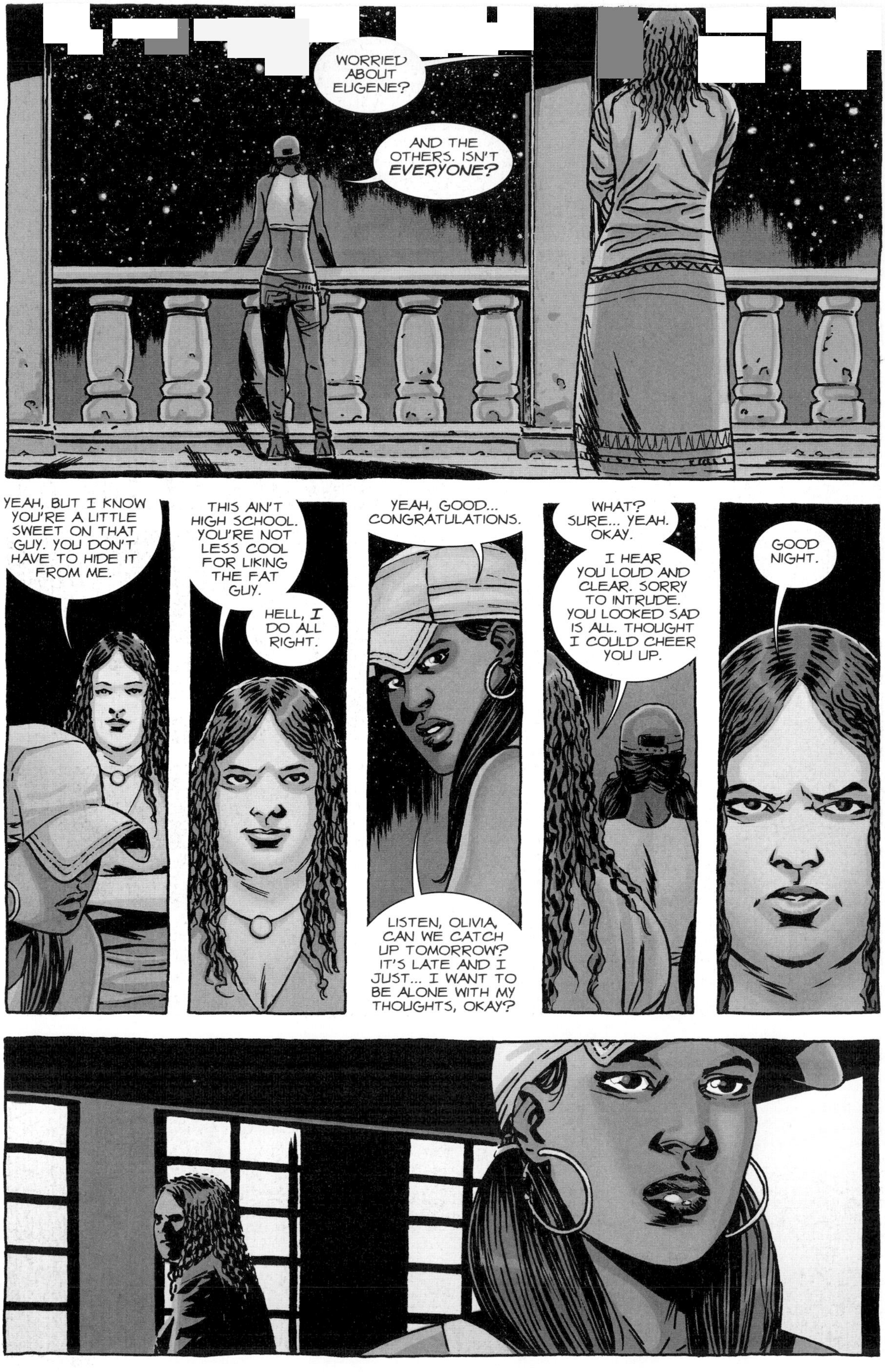
WORRIED ABOUT EUGENE?
AND THE OTHERS. ISN'T EVERYONE?
YEAH, BUT I KNOW YOU'RE A LITTLE SWEET ON THAT GUY. YOU DON'T HAVE TO HIDE IT FROM ME.
THIS AIN'T HIGH SCHOOL. YOU'RE NOT LESS COOL FOR LIKING THE FAT GUY.
HELL, I DO ALL RIGHT.
YEAH, GOOD... CONGRATULATIONS.
LISTEN, OLIVIA, CAN WE CATCH UP TOMORROW? IT'S LATE AND I JUST... I WANT TO BE ALONE WITH MY THOUGHTS, OKAY?
WHAT? SURE... YEAH. OKAY.
I HEAR YOU LOUD AND CLEAR. SORRY TO INTRUDE. YOU LOOKED SAD IS ALL. THOUGHT I COULD CHEER YOU UP.
GOOD NIGHT.

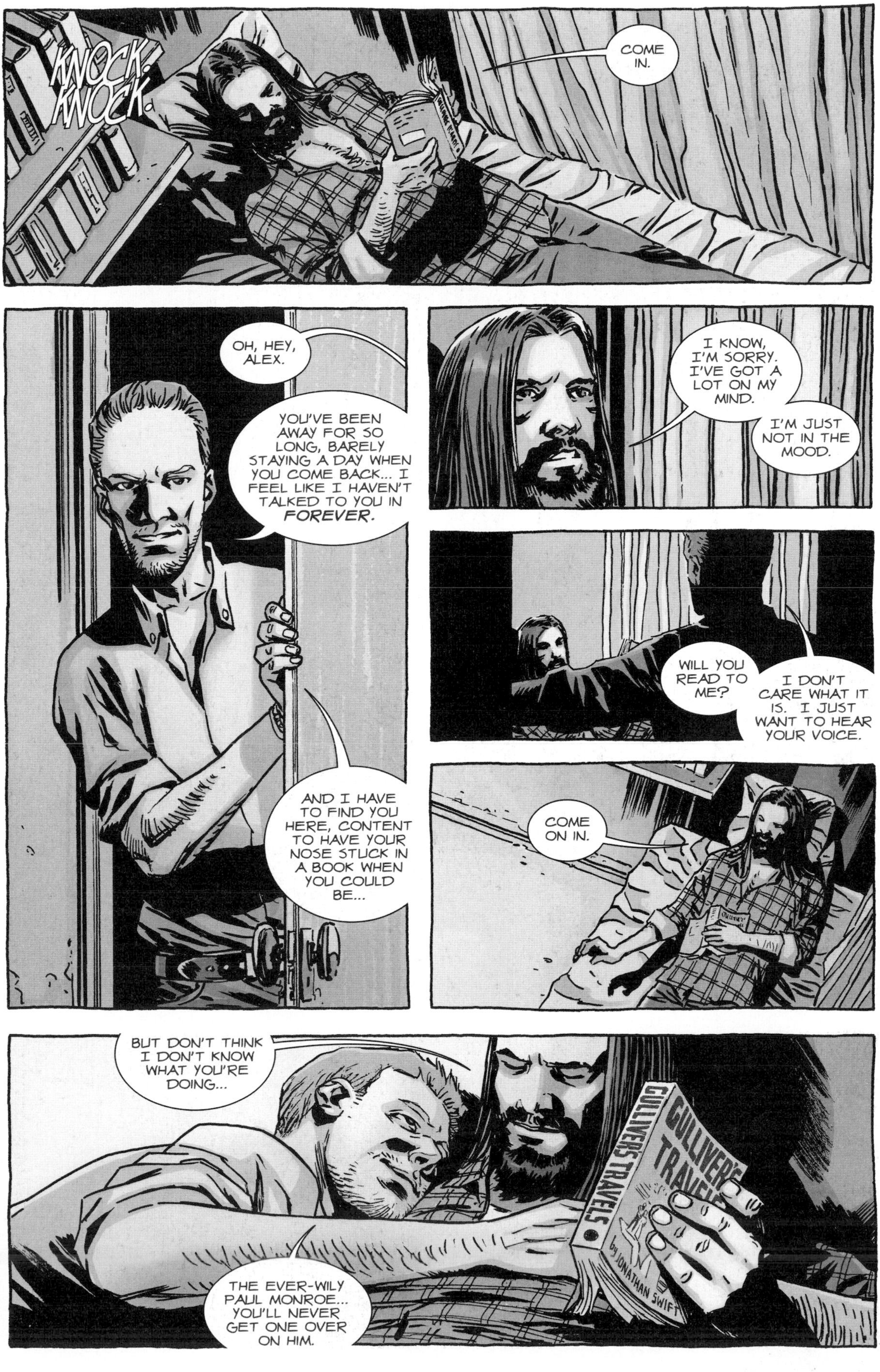

KNOCK. KNOCK.
COME IN.
OH, HEY, ALEX.
YOU'VE BEEN AWAY FOR SO LONG, BARELY STAYING A DAY WHEN YOU COME BACK... I FEEL LIKE I HAVEN'T TALKED TO YOU IN FOREVER.
AND I HAVE TO FIND YOU HERE, CONTENT TO HAVE YOUR NOSE STUCK IN A BOOK WHEN YOU COULD BE...
I KNOW, I'M SORRY. I'VE GOT A LOT ON MY MIND.
I'M JUST NOT IN THE MOOD.
WILL YOU READ TO ME?
I DON'T CARE WHAT IT IS. I JUST WANT TO HEAR YOUR VOICE.
COME ON IN.
BUT DON'T THINK I DON'T KNOW WHAT YOU'RE DOING...
GULLIVER'S TRAVELS
by JONATHAN SWIFT
THE EVER-WILY PAUL MONROE... YOU'LL NEVER GET ONE OVER ON HIM.

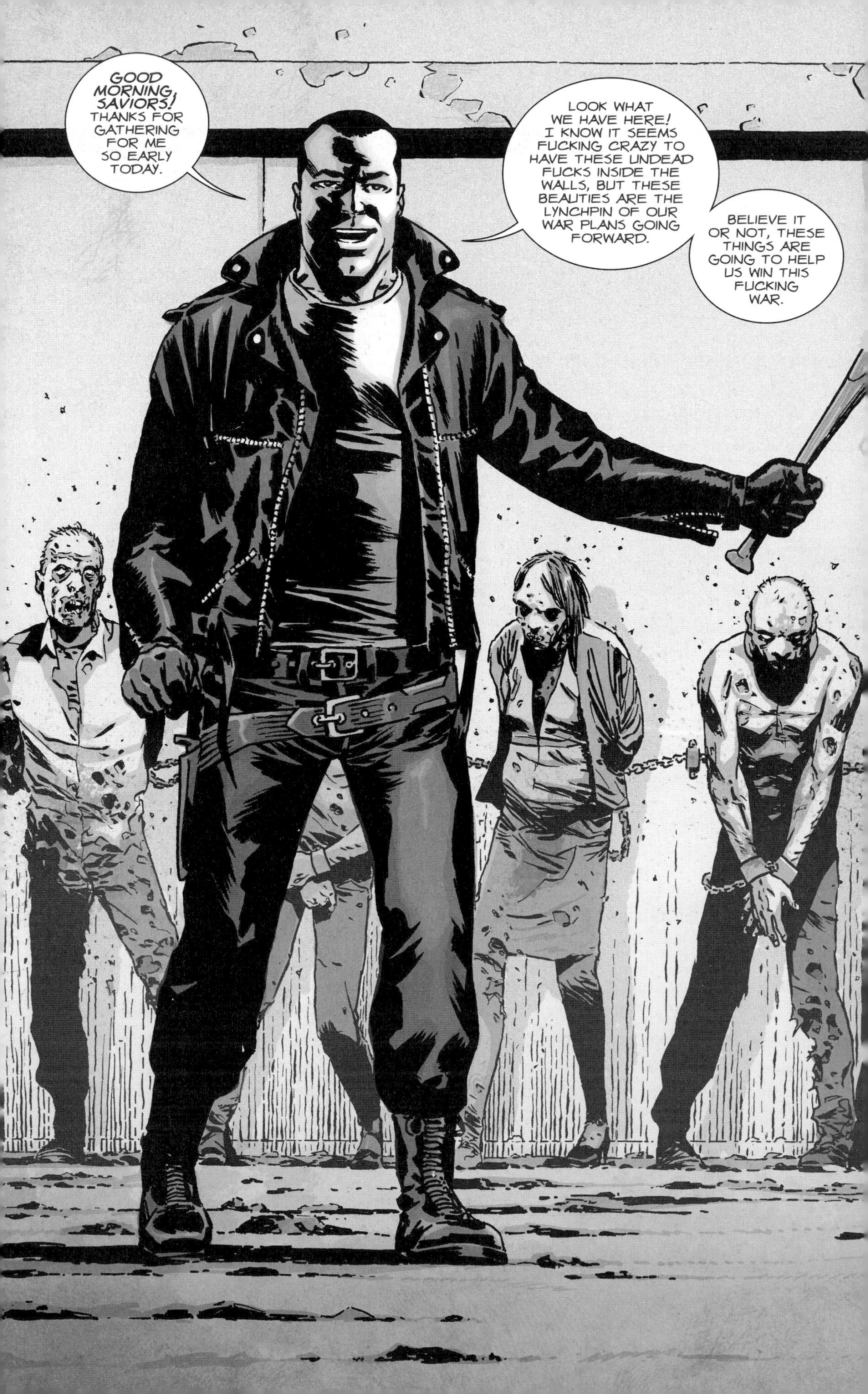
GOOD MORNING, SAVIORS! THANKS FOR GATHERING FOR ME SO EARLY TODAY.
LOOK WHAT WE HAVE HERE! I KNOW IT SEEMS FUCKING CRAZY TO HAVE THESE UNDEAD FUCKS INSIDE THE WALLS, BUT THESE BEAUTIES ARE THE LYNCHPIN OF OUR WAR PLANS GOING FORWARD.
BELIEVE IT OR NOT, THESE THINGS ARE GOING TO HELP US WIN THIS FUCKING WAR.

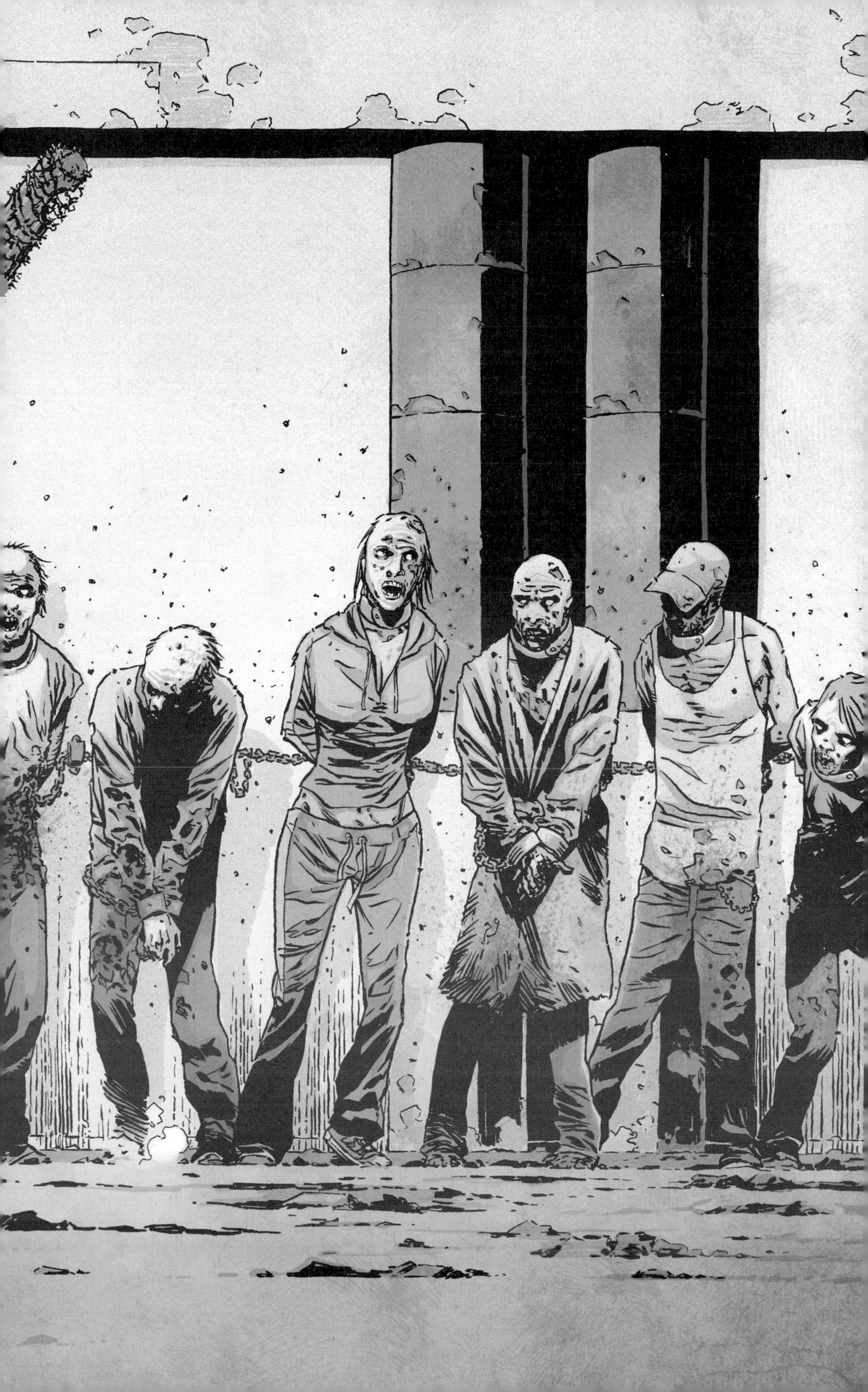

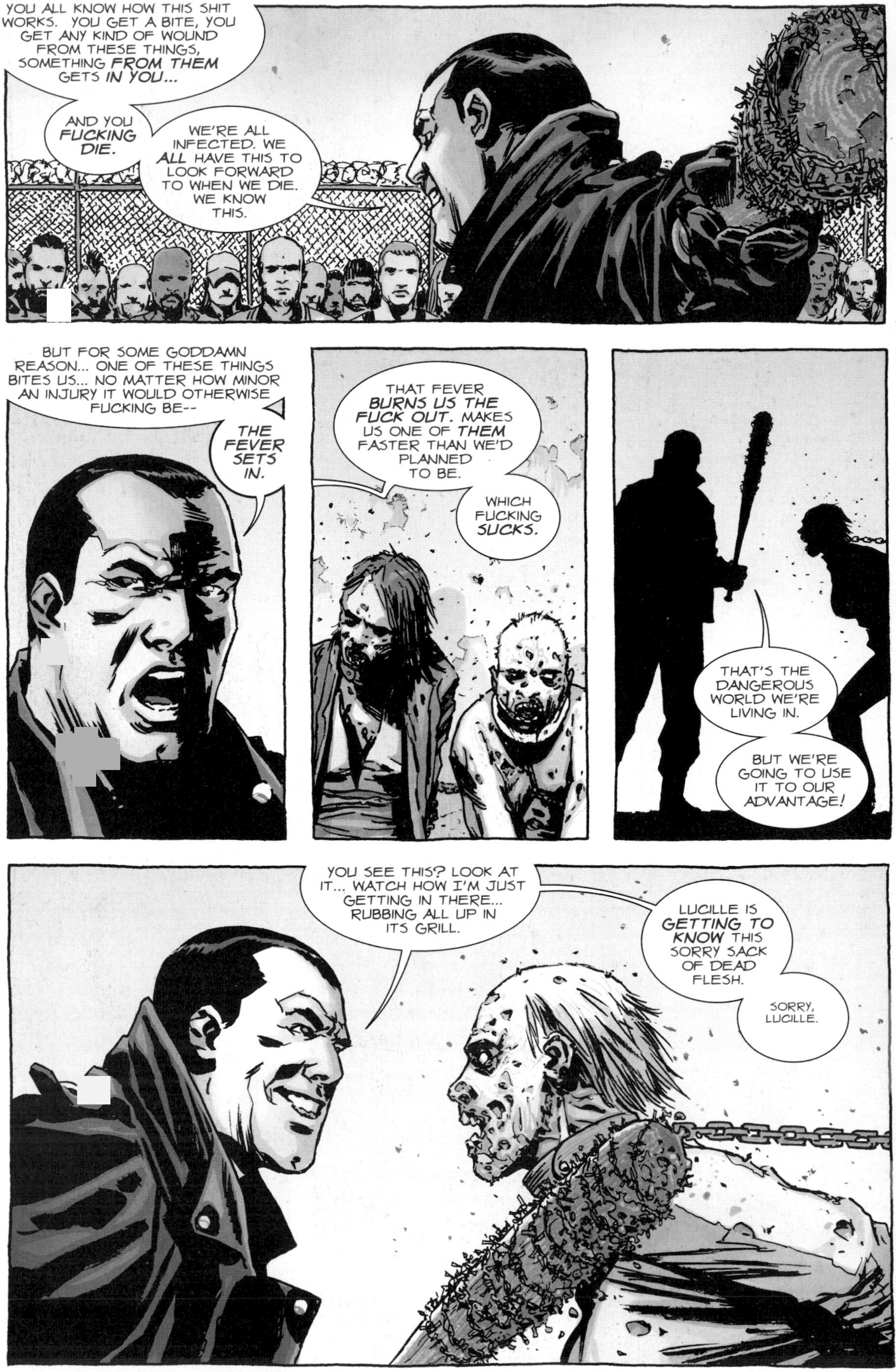
YOU ALL KNOW HOW THIS SHIT WORKS. YOU GET A BITE, YOU GET ANY KIND OF WOUND FROM THESE THINGS, SOMETHING FROM THEM GETS IN YOU...
AND YOU FUCKING DIE.
WE'RE ALL INFECTED. WE ALL HAVE THIS TO LOOK FORWARD TO WHEN WE DIE. WE KNOW THIS.
BUT FOR SOME GODDAMN REASON... ONE OF THESE THINGS BITES US... NO MATTER HOW MINOR AN INJURY IT WOULD OTHERWISE FUCKING BE--
THE FEVER SETS IN.
THAT FEVER BURNS US THE FUCK OUT. MAKES US ONE OF THEM FASTER THAN WE'D PLANNED TO BE.
WHICH FUCKING SUCKS.
THAT'S THE DANGEROUS WORLD WE'RE LIVING IN.
BUT WE'RE GOING TO USE IT TO OUR ADVANTAGE!
YOU SEE THIS? LOOK AT IT... WATCH HOW I'M JUST GETTING IN THERE... RUBBING ALL UP IN ITS GRILL.
LUCILLE IS GETTING TO KNOW THIS SORRY SACK OF DEAD FLESH.
SORRY, LUCILLE.

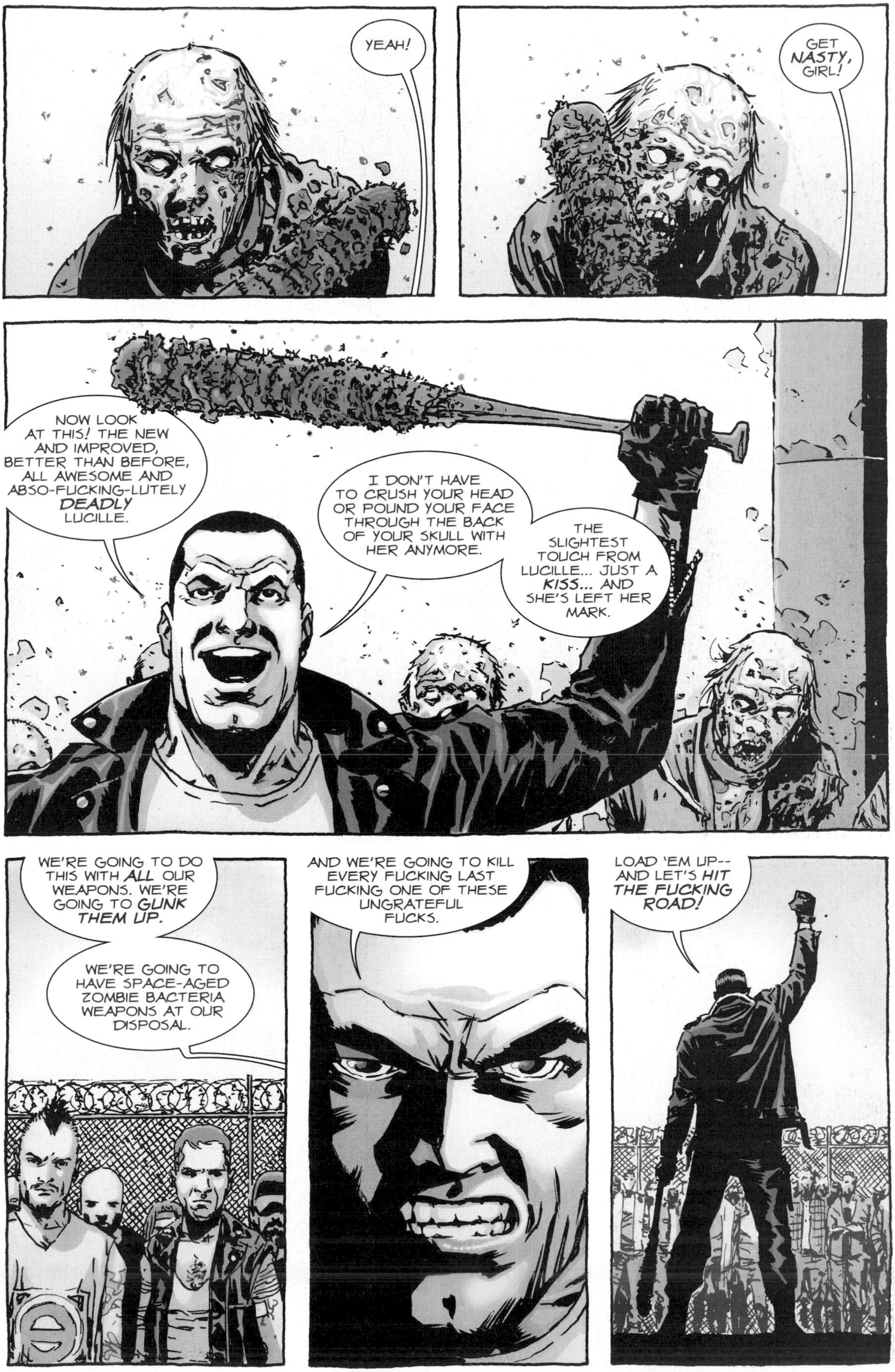
YEAH!
GET NASTY, GIRL!
NOW LOOK AT THIS! THE NEW AND IMPROVED, BETTER THAN BEFORE, ALL AWESOME AND ABSO-FUCKING-LUTELY DEADLY LUCILLE.
I DON'T HAVE TO CRUSH YOUR HEAD OR POUND YOUR FACE THROUGH THE BACK OF YOUR SKULL WITH HER ANYMORE.
THE SLIGHTEST TOUCH FROM LUCILLE... JUST A KISS... AND SHE'S LEFT HER MARK.
WE'RE GOING TO DO THIS WITH ALL OUR WEAPONS. WE'RE GOING TO GUNK THEM UP.
WE'RE GOING TO HAVE SPACE-AGED ZOMBIE BACTERIA WEAPONS AT OUR DISPOSAL.
AND WE'RE GOING TO KILL EVERY FUCKING LAST FUCKING ONE OF THESE UNGRATEFUL FUCKS.
LOAD 'EM UP-- AND LET'S HIT THE FUCKING ROAD!

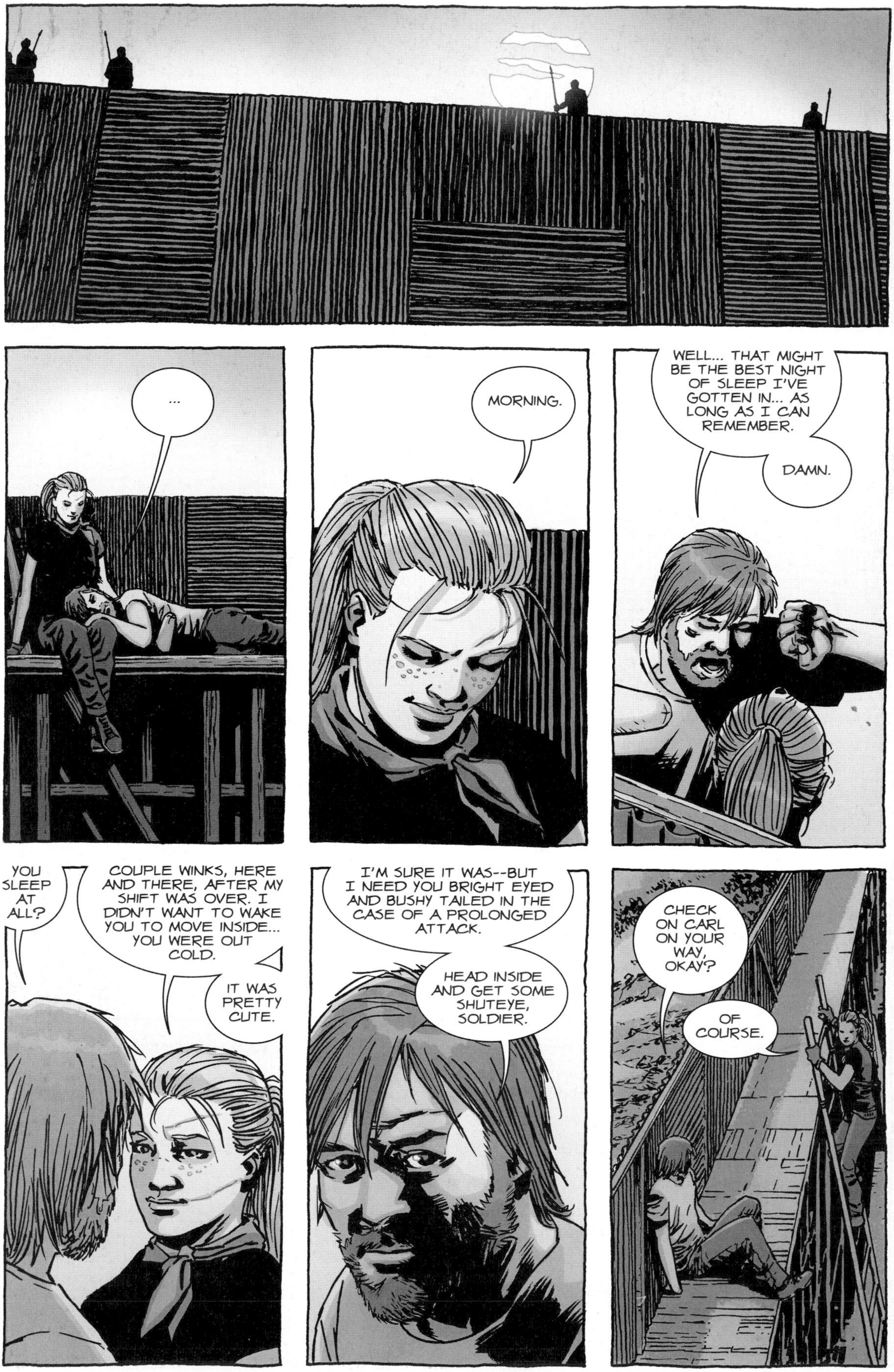
...
MORNING.
WELL... THAT MIGHT BE THE BEST NIGHT OF SLEEP I'VE GOTTEN IN... AS LONG AS I CAN REMEMBER.
DAMN.
YOU SLEEP AT ALL?
COUPLE WINKS, HERE AND THERE, AFTER MY SHIFT WAS OVER. I DIDN'T WANT TO WAKE YOU TO MOVE INSIDE... YOU WERE OUT COLD.
IT WAS PRETTY CUTE.
I'M SURE IT WAS--BUT I NEED YOU BRIGHT EYED AND BUSHY TAILED IN THE CASE OF A PROLONGED ATTACK.
HEAD INSIDE AND GET SOME SHUTEYE, SOLDIER.
CHECK ON CARL ON YOUR WAY, OKAY?
OF COURSE.

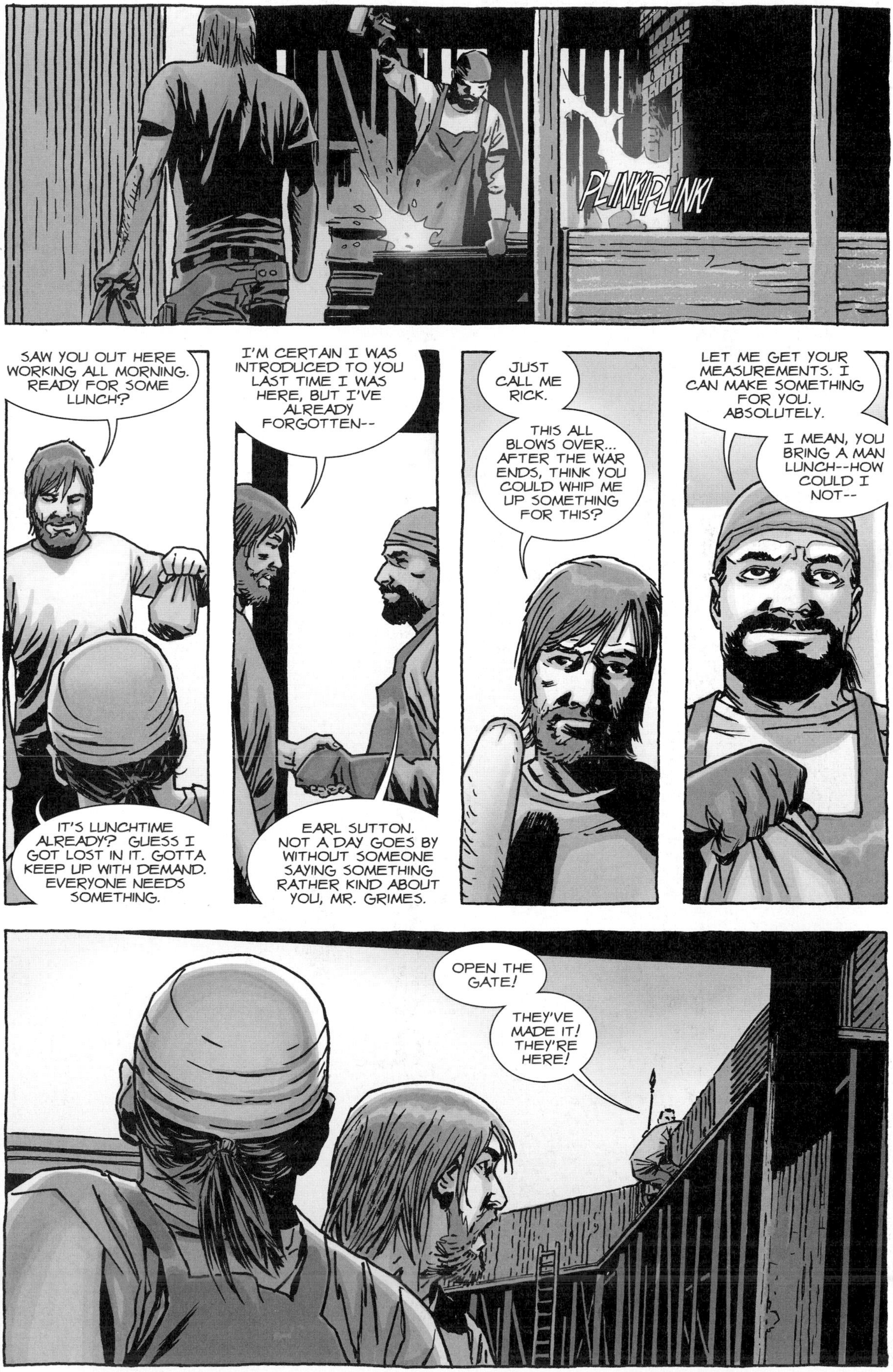
PLINK! PLINK!
SAW YOU OUT HERE WORKING ALL MORNING. READY FOR SOME LUNCH?
IT'S LUNCHTIME ALREADY? GUESS I GOT LOST IN IT. GOTTA KEEP UP WITH DEMAND. EVERYONE NEEDS SOMETHING.
I'M CERTAIN I WAS INTRODUCED TO YOU LAST TIME I WAS HERE, BUT I'VE ALREADY FORGOTTEN--
EARL SUTTON. NOT A DAY GOES BY WITHOUT SOMEONE SAYING SOMETHING RATHER KIND ABOUT YOU, MR. GRIMES.
JUST CALL ME RICK.
THIS ALL BLOWS OVER... AFTER THE WAR ENDS, THINK YOU COULD WHIP ME UP SOMETHING FOR THIS?
LET ME GET YOUR MEASUREMENTS. I CAN MAKE SOMETHING FOR YOU. ABSOLUTELY.
I MEAN, YOU BRING A MAN LUNCH--HOW COULD I NOT--
OPEN THE GATE!
THEY'VE MADE IT! THEY'RE HERE!

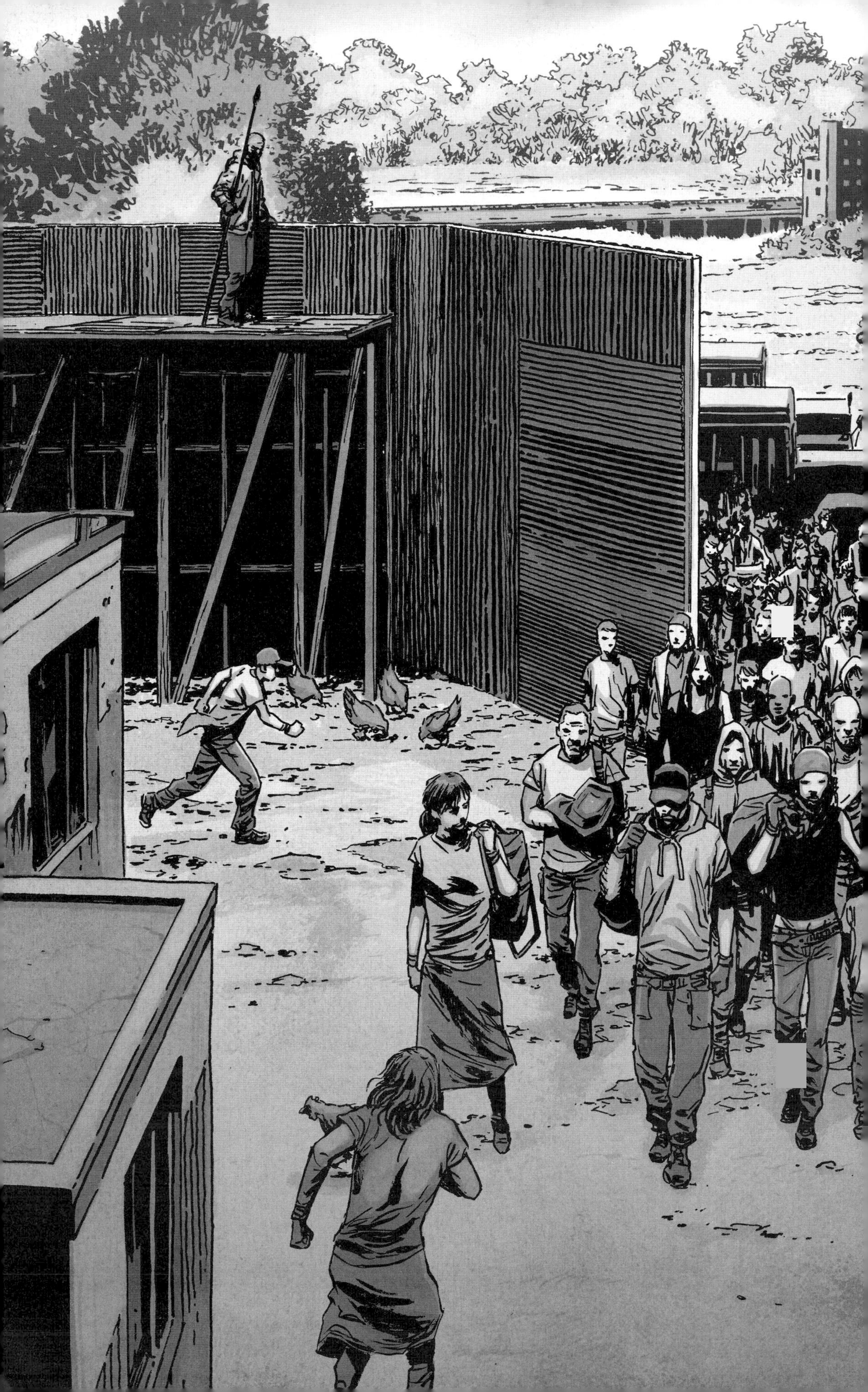

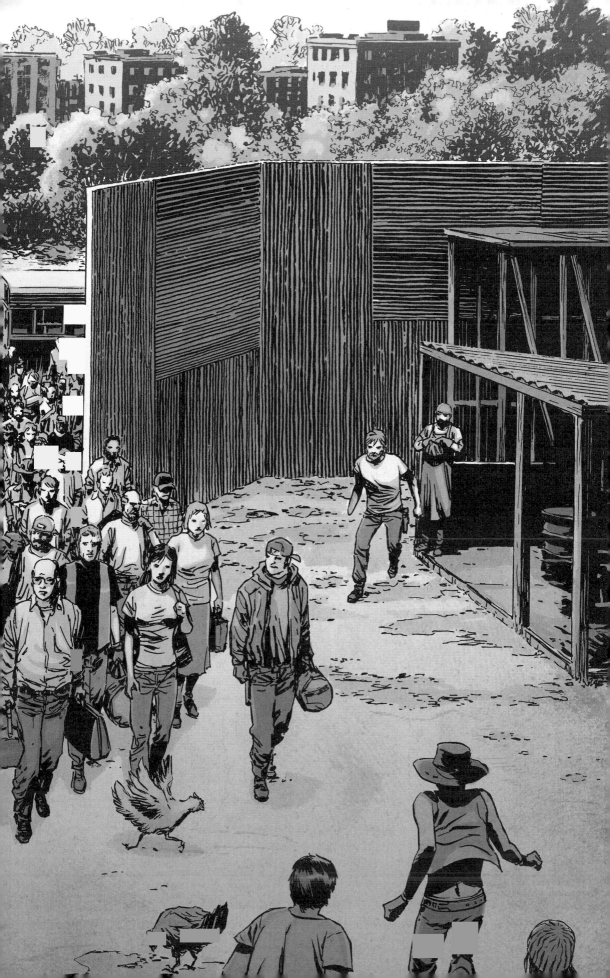

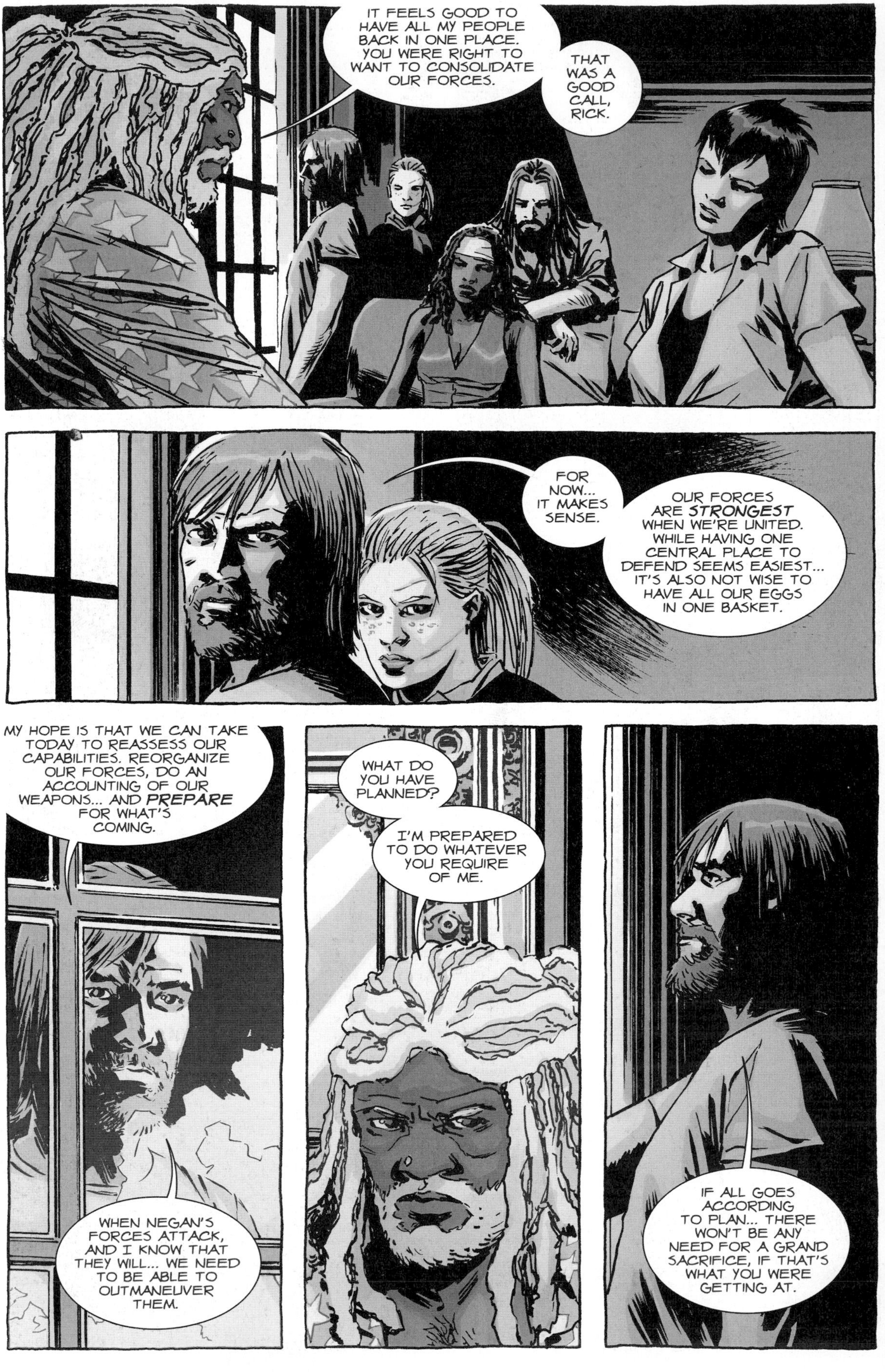
IT FEELS GOOD TO HAVE ALL MY PEOPLE BACK IN ONE PLACE. YOU WERE RIGHT TO WANT TO CONSOLIDATE OUR FORCES.
THAT WAS A GOOD CALL, RICK.
FOR NOW... IT MAKES SENSE.
OUR FORCES ARE STRONGEST WHEN WE'RE UNITED. WHILE HAVING ONE CENTRAL PLACE TO DEFEND SEEMS EASIEST... IT'S ALSO NOT WISE TO HAVE ALL OUR EGGS IN ONE BASKET.
MY HOPE IS THAT WE CAN TAKE TODAY TO REASSESS OUR CAPABILITIES. REORGANIZE OUR FORCES, DO AN ACCOUNTING OF OUR WEAPONS... AND PREPARE FOR WHAT'S COMING.
WHEN NEGAN'S FORCES ATTACK, AND I KNOW THAT THEY WILL... WE NEED TO BE ABLE TO OUTMANEUVER THEM.
WHAT DO YOU HAVE PLANNED?
I'M PREPARED TO DO WHATEVER YOU REQUIRE OF ME.
IF ALL GOES ACCORDING TO PLAN... THERE WON'T BE ANY NEED FOR A GRAND SACRIFICE, IF THAT'S WHAT YOU WERE GETTING AT.

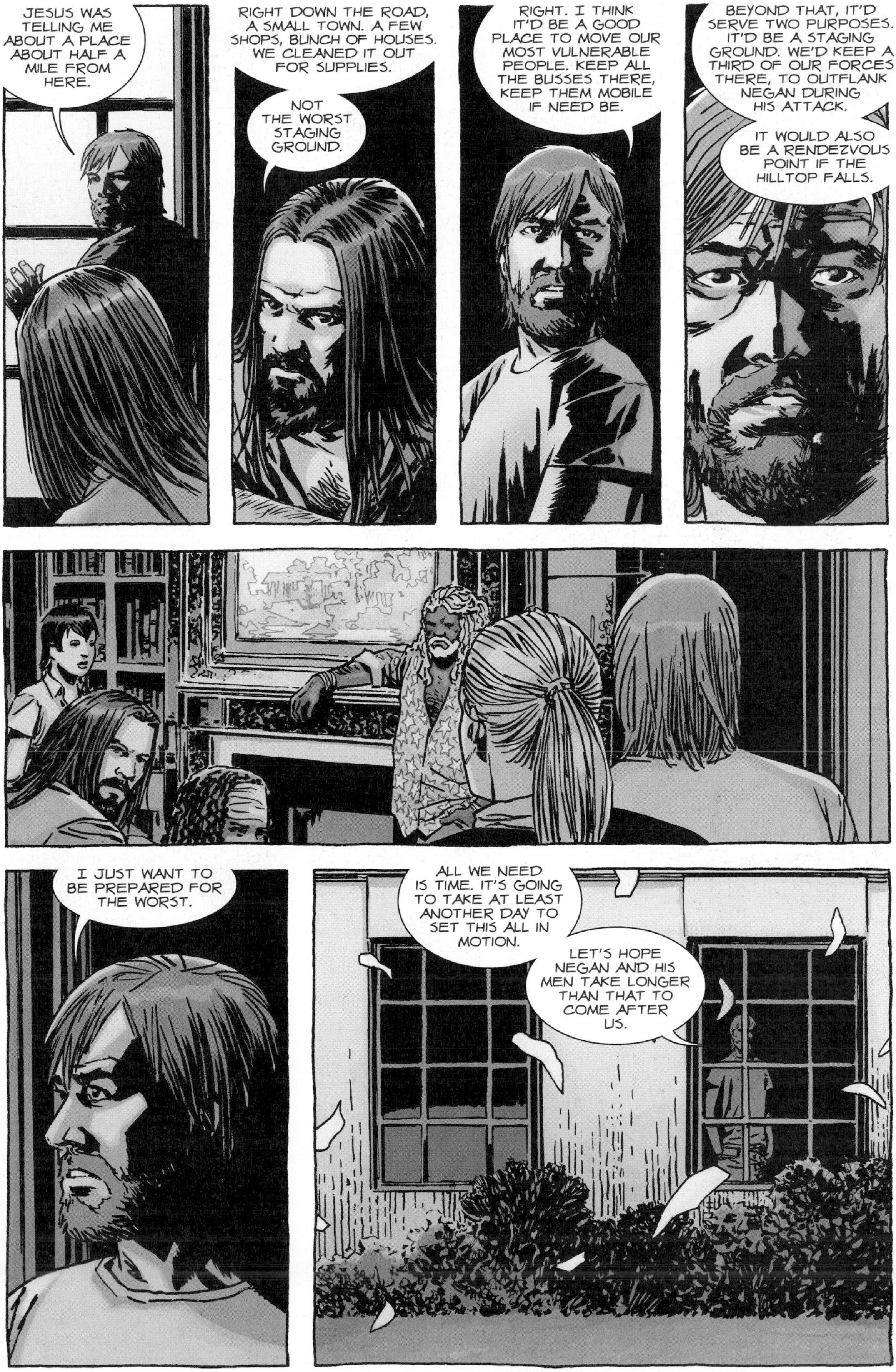
JESUS WAS TELLING ME ABOUT A PLACE ABOUT HALF A MILE FROM HERE.
RIGHT DOWN THE ROAD, A SMALL TOWN. A FEW SHOPS, BUNCH OF HOUSES. WE CLEANED IT OUT FOR SUPPLIES.
NOT THE WORST STAGING GROUND.
RIGHT. I THINK IT'D BE A GOOD PLACE TO MOVE OUR MOST VULNERABLE PEOPLE. KEEP ALL THE BUSSES THERE, KEEP THEM MOBILE IF NEED BE.
BEYOND THAT, IT'D SERVE TWO PURPOSES. IT'D BE A STAGING GROUND. WE'D KEEP A THIRD OF OUR FORCES THERE, TO OUTFLANK NEGAN DURING HIS ATTACK.
IT WOULD ALSO BE A RENDEZVOUS POINT IF THE HILLTOP FALLS.
I JUST WANT TO BE PREPARED FOR THE WORST.
ALL WE NEED IS TIME. IT'S GOING TO TAKE AT LEAST ANOTHER DAY TO SET THIS ALL IN MOTION.
LET'S HOPE NEGAN AND HIS MEN TAKE LONGER THAN THAT TO COME AFTER US.

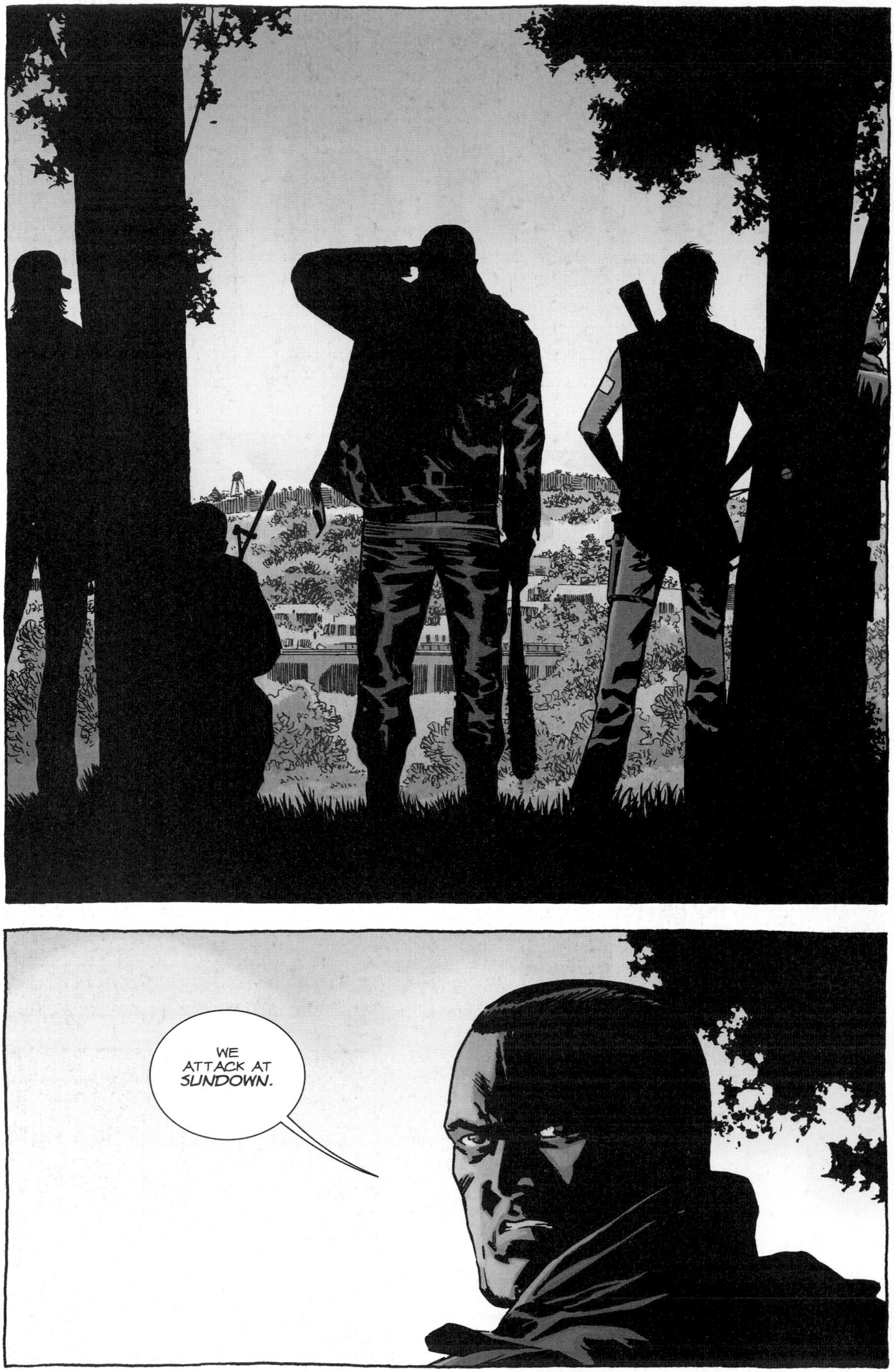
WE ATTACK AT SUNDOWN.

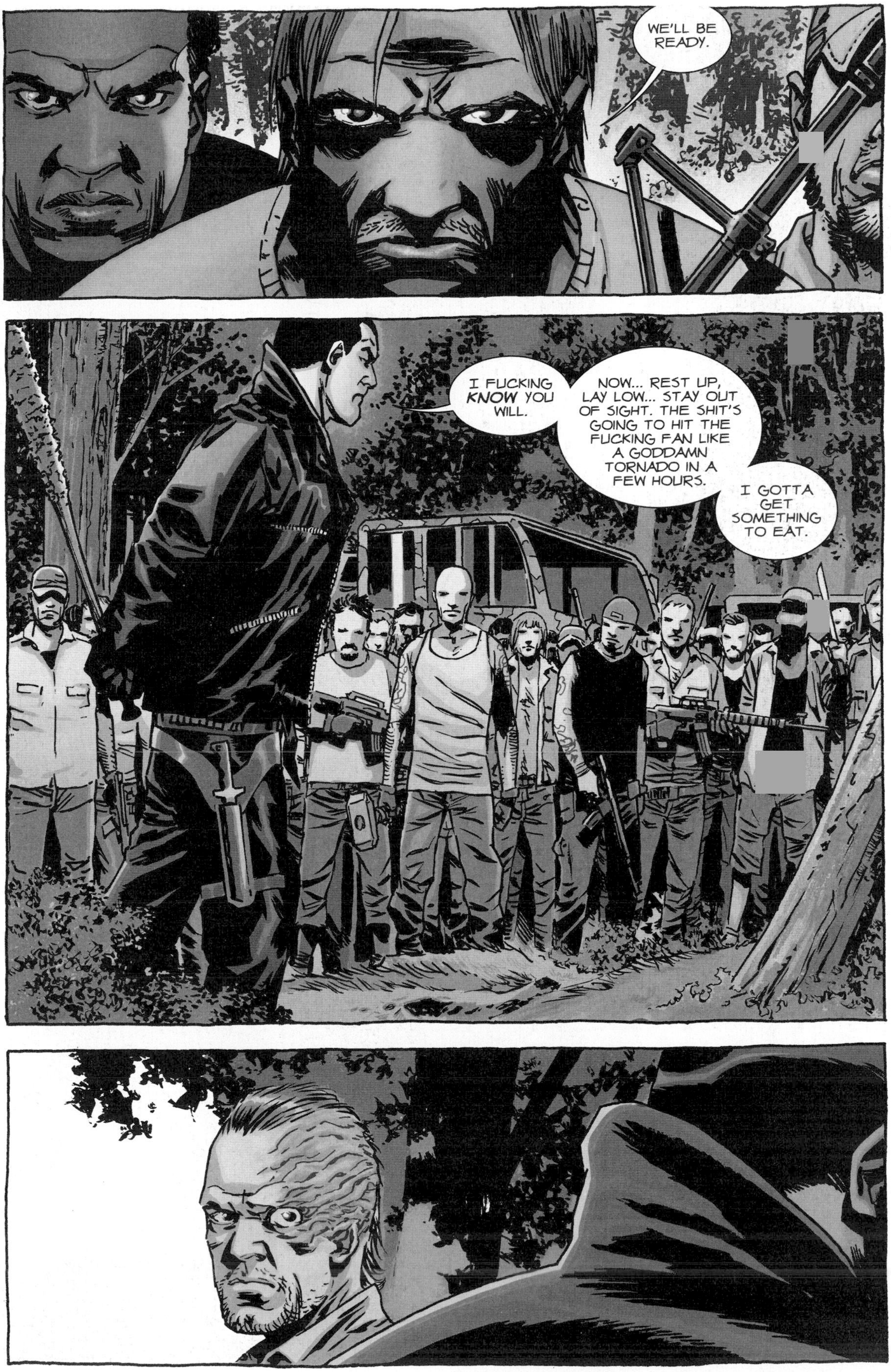
WE'LL BE READY.
I FUCKING KNOW YOU WILL.
NOW... REST UP, LAY LOW... STAY OUT OF SIGHT. THE SHIT'S GOING TO HIT THE FUCKING FAN LIKE A GODDAMN TORNADO IN A FEW HOURS.
I GOTTA GET SOMETHING TO EAT.

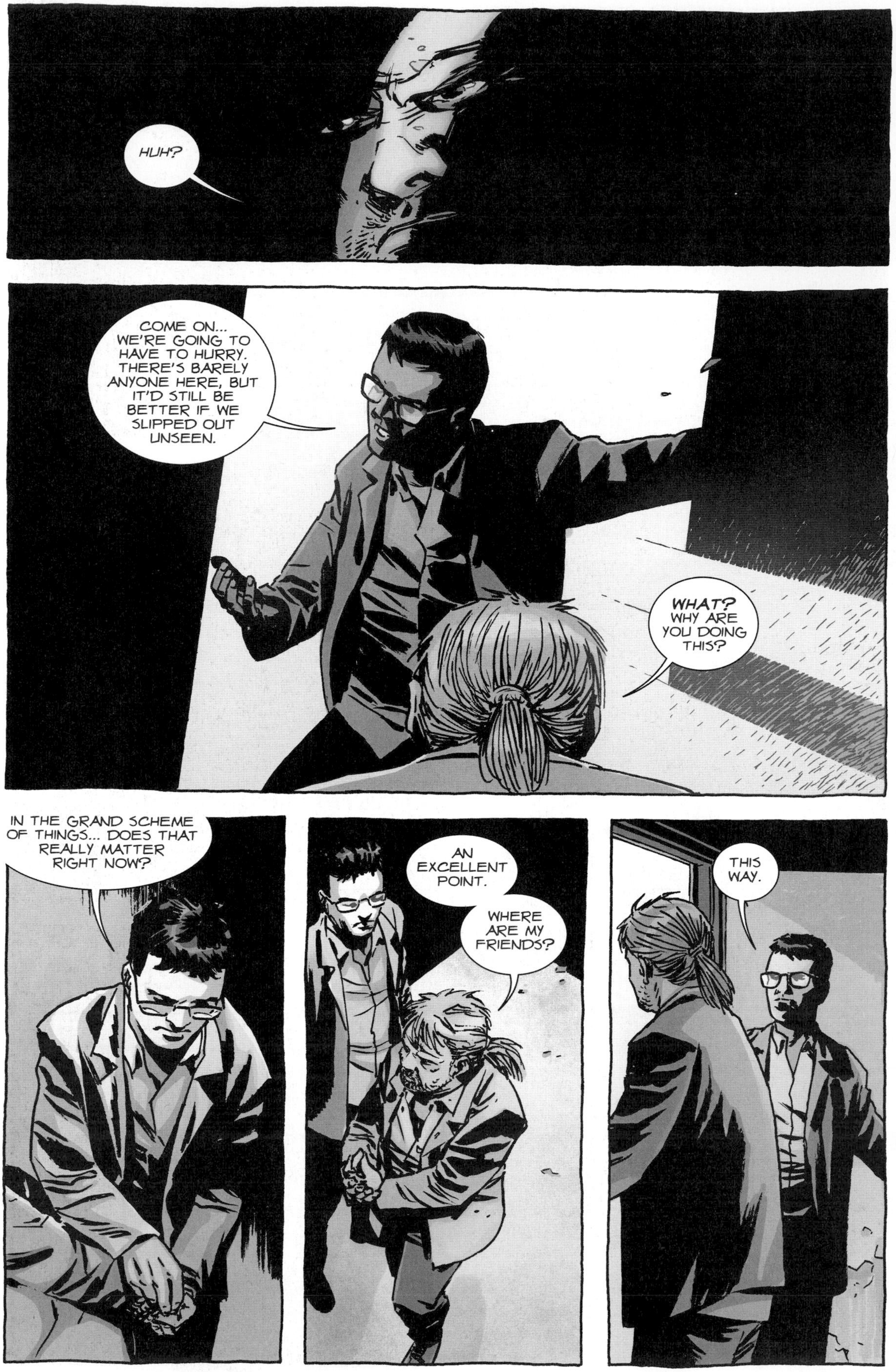
HUH?
COME ON... WE'RE GOING TO HAVE TO HURRY. THERE'S BARELY ANYONE HERE, BUT IT'D STILL BE BETTER IF WE SLIPPED OUT UNSEEN.
WHAT? WHY ARE YOU DOING THIS?
IN THE GRAND SCHEME OF THINGS... DOES THAT REALLY MATTER RIGHT NOW?
AN EXCELLENT POINT.
WHERE ARE MY FRIENDS?
THIS WAY.

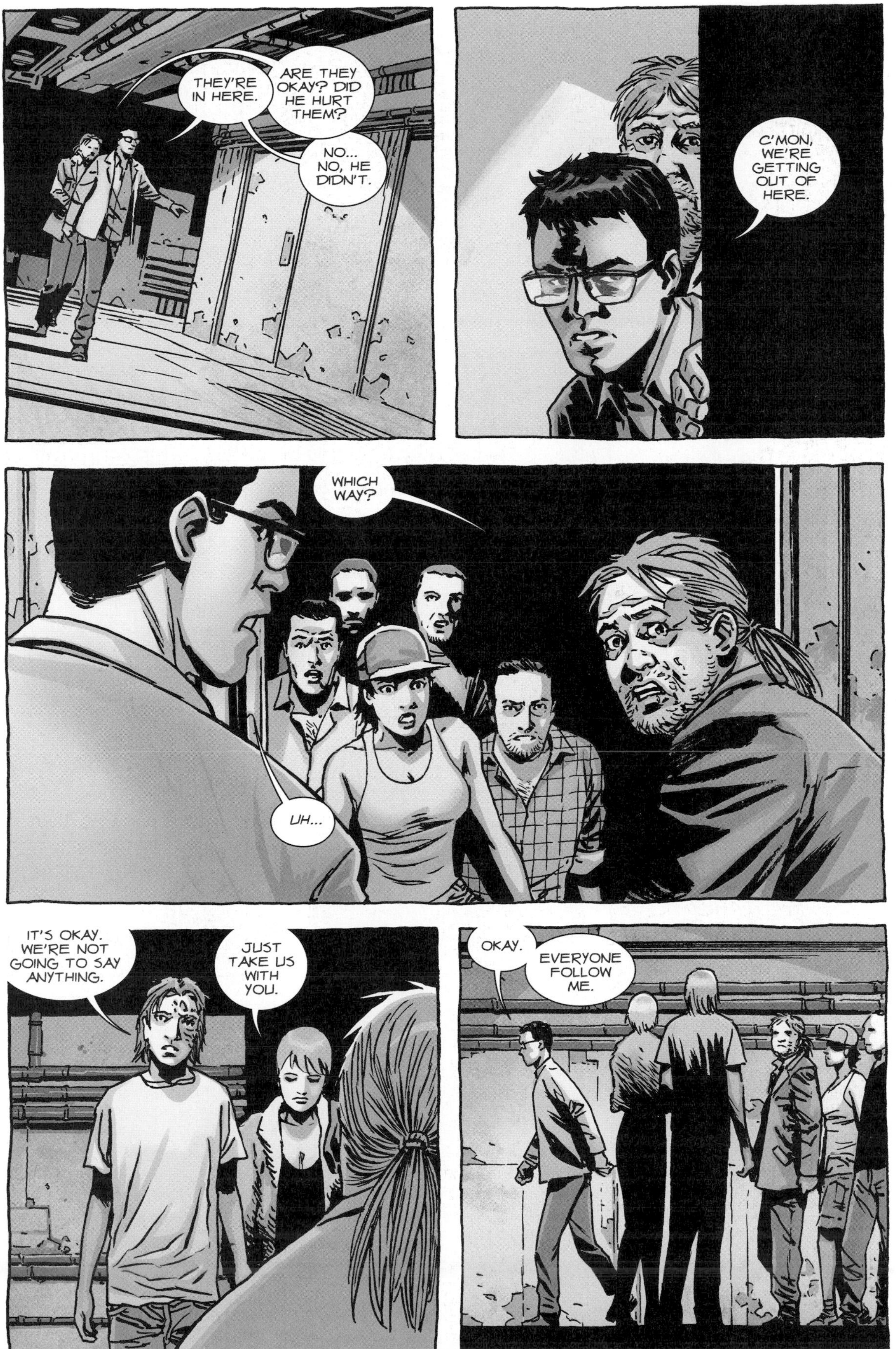
THEY'RE IN HERE.
ARE THEY OKAY? DID HE HURT THEM?
NO... NO, HE DIDN'T.
C'MON, WE'RE GETTING OUT OF HERE.
WHICH WAY?
UH...
IT'S OKAY. WE'RE NOT GOING TO SAY ANYTHING.
JUST TAKE US WITH YOU.
OKAY.
EVERYONE FOLLOW ME.

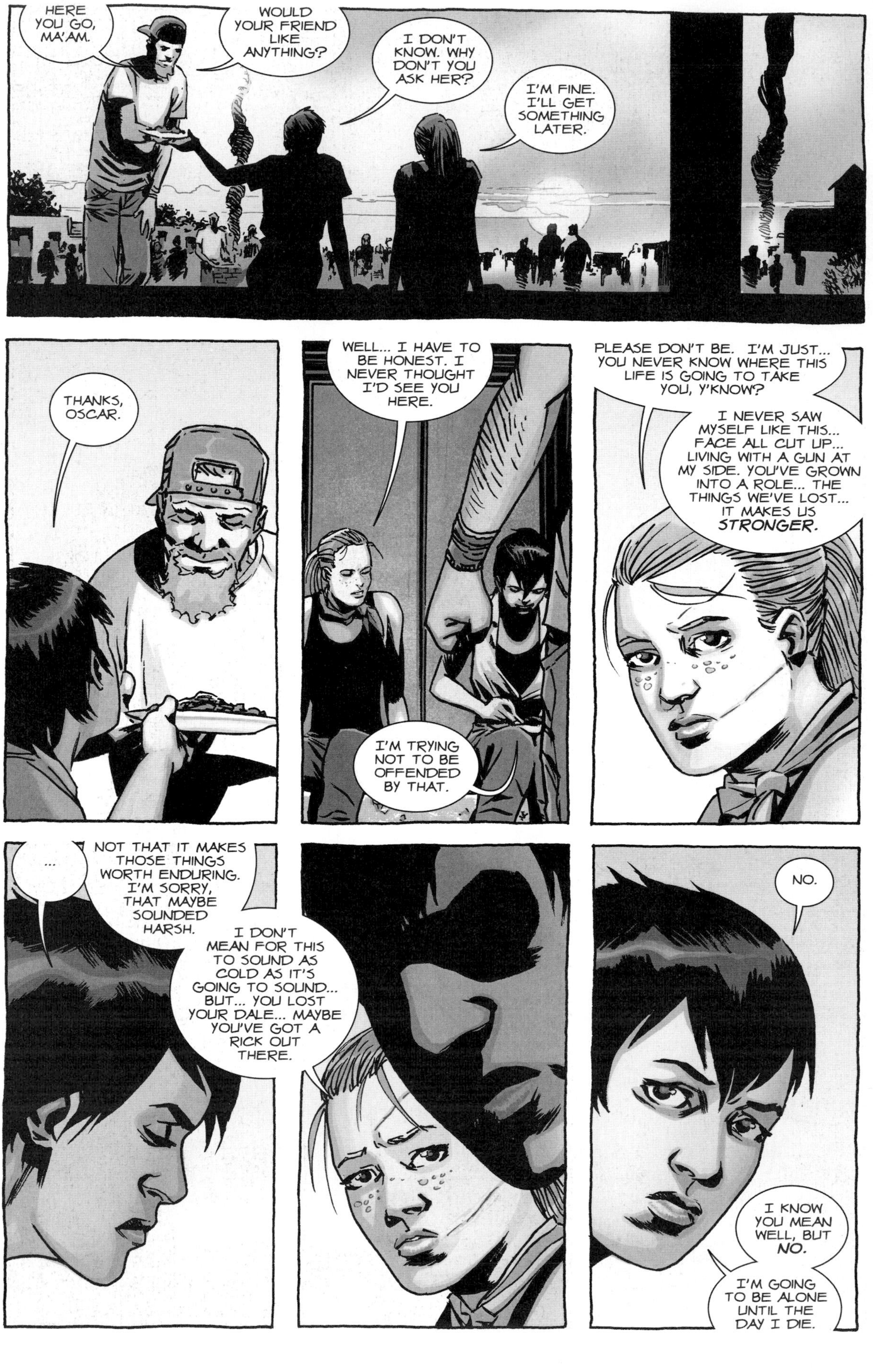
HERE YOU GO, MA'AM.
WOULD YOUR FRIEND LIKE ANYTHING?
I DON'T KNOW. WHY DON'T YOU ASK HER?
I'M FINE. I'LL GET SOMETHING LATER.
THANKS, OSCAR.
WELL... I HAVE TO BE HONEST. I NEVER THOUGHT I'D SEE YOU HERE.
I'M TRYING NOT TO BE OFFENDED BY THAT.
PLEASE DON'T BE. I'M JUST... YOU NEVER KNOW WHERE THIS LIFE IS GOING TO TAKE YOU, Y'KNOW?
I NEVER SAW MYSELF LIKE THIS... FACE ALL CUT UP... LIVING WITH A GUN AT MY SIDE. YOU'VE GROWN INTO A ROLE... THE THINGS WE'VE LOST... IT MAKES US STRONGER.
...
NOT THAT IT MAKES THOSE THINGS WORTH ENDURING. I'M SORRY, THAT MAYBE SOUNDED HARSH.
I DON'T MEAN FOR THIS TO SOUND AS COLD AS IT'S GOING TO SOUND... BUT... YOU LOST YOUR DALE... MAYBE YOU'VE GOT A RICK OUT THERE.
NO.
I KNOW YOU MEAN WELL, BUT NO.
I'M GOING TO BE ALONE UNTIL THE DAY I DIE.

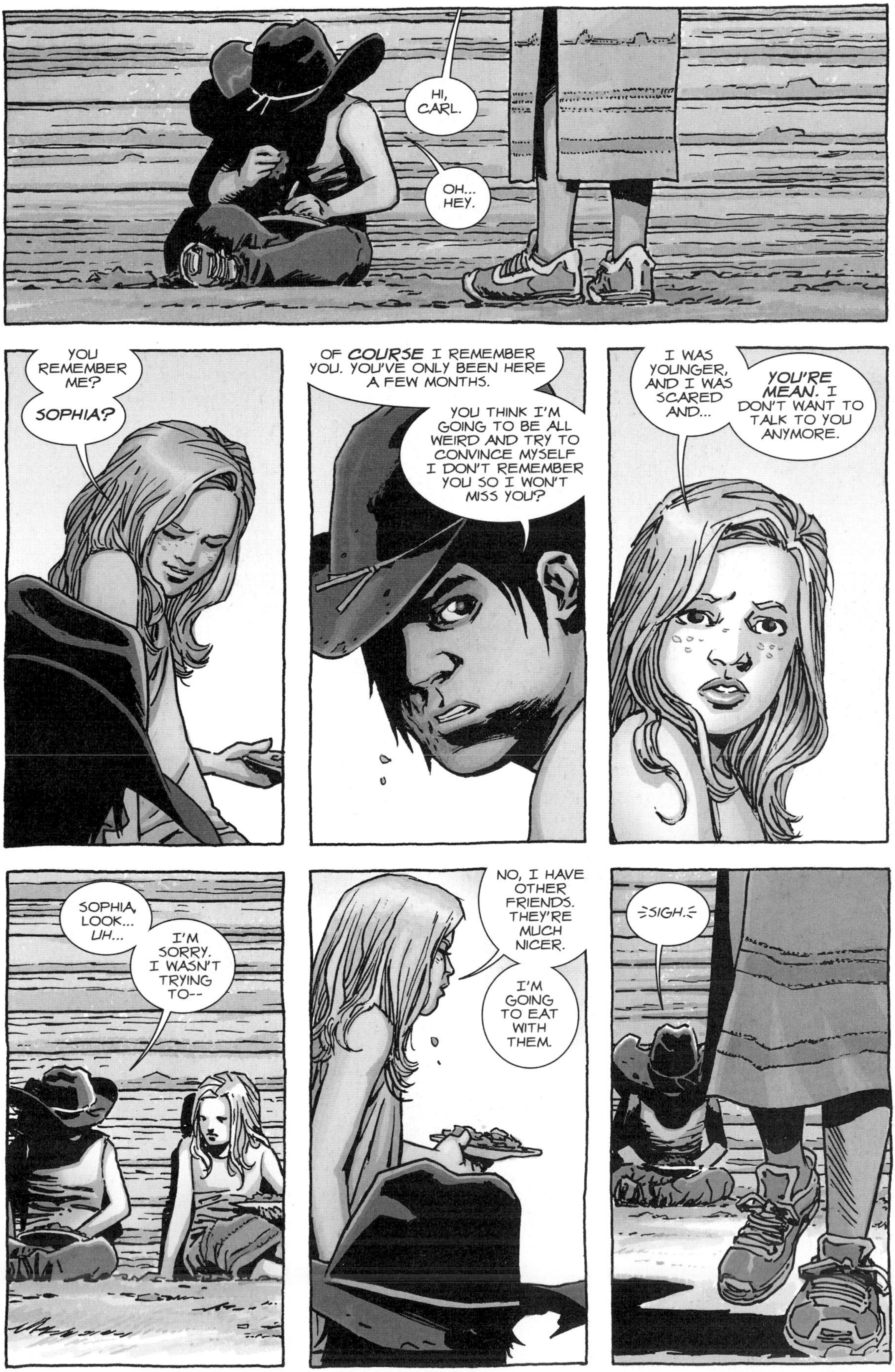
HI, CARL.
OH... HEY.
YOU REMEMBER ME?
SOPHIA?
OF COURSE I REMEMBER YOU. YOU'VE ONLY BEEN HERE A FEW MONTHS.
YOU THINK I'M GOING TO BE ALL WEIRD AND TRY TO CONVINCE MYSELF I DON'T REMEMBER YOU SO I WON'T MISS YOU?
I WAS YOUNGER, AND I WAS SCARED AND...
YOU'RE MEAN. I DON'T WANT TO TALK TO YOU ANYMORE.
SOPHIA, LOOK... UH...
I'M SORRY. I WASN'T TRYING TO--
NO, I HAVE OTHER FRIENDS. THEY'RE MUCH NICER.
I'M GOING TO EAT WITH THEM.
SIGH.

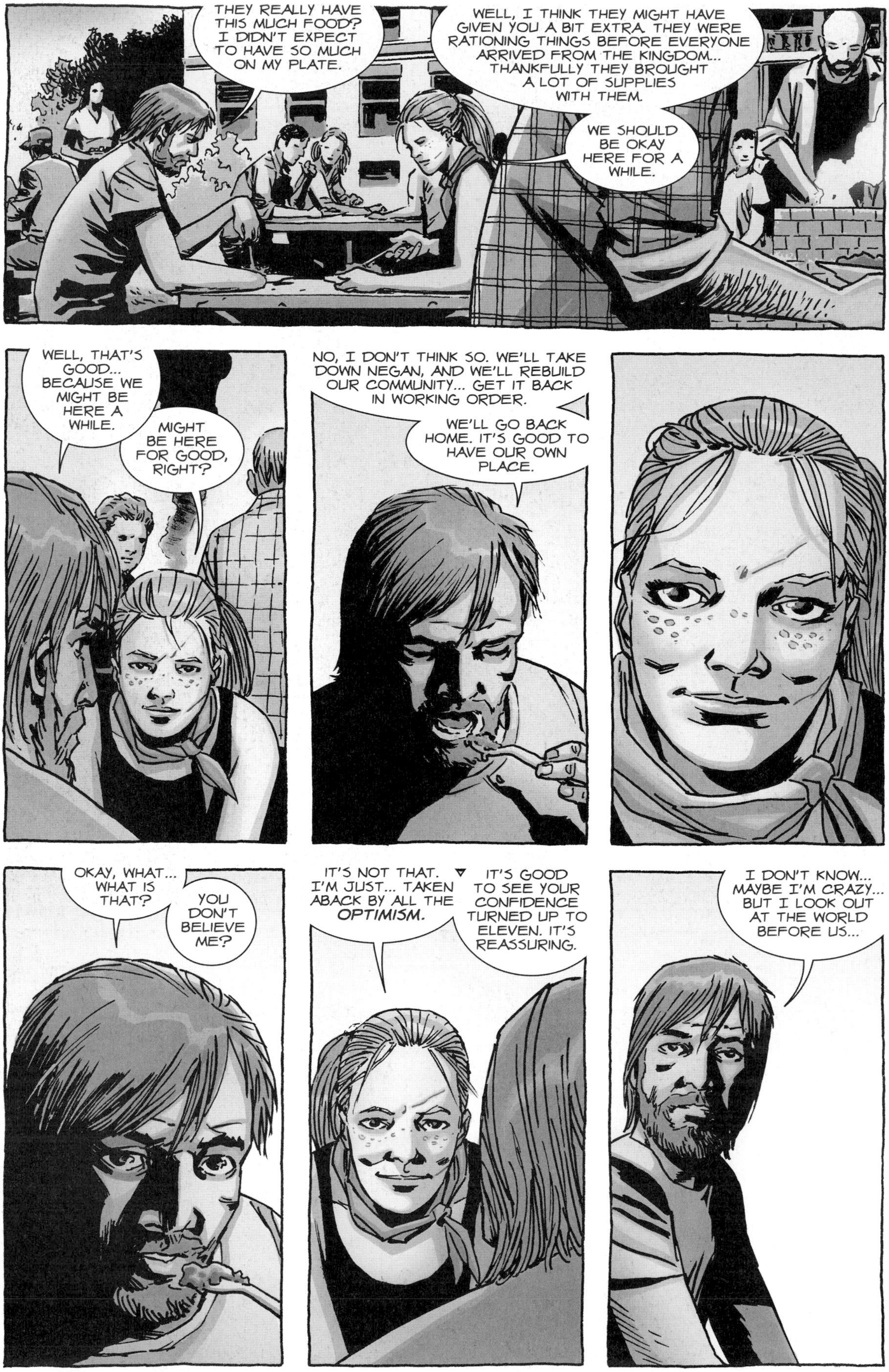
THEY REALLY HAVE THIS MUCH FOOD? I DIDN'T EXPECT TO HAVE SO MUCH ON MY PLATE.
WELL, I THINK THEY MIGHT HAVE GIVEN YOU A BIT EXTRA. THEY WERE RATIONING THINGS BEFORE EVERYONE ARRIVED FROM THE KINGDOM... THANKFULLY THEY BROUGHT A LOT OF SUPPLIES WITH THEM.
WE SHOULD BE OKAY HERE FOR A WHILE.
WELL, THAT'S GOOD... BECAUSE WE MIGHT BE HERE A WHILE.
MIGHT BE HERE FOR GOOD, RIGHT?
NO, I DON'T THINK SO. WE'LL TAKE DOWN NEGAN, AND WE'LL REBUILD OUR COMMUNITY... GET IT BACK IN WORKING ORDER.
WE'LL GO BACK HOME. IT'S GOOD TO HAVE OUR OWN PLACE.
OKAY, WHAT... WHAT IS THAT?
YOU DON'T BELIEVE ME?
IT'S NOT THAT. I'M JUST... TAKEN ABACK BY ALL THE *OPTIMISM.*
IT'S GOOD TO SEE YOUR CONFIDENCE TURNED UP TO ELEVEN. IT'S REASSURING.
I DON'T KNOW... MAYBE I'M CRAZY... BUT I LOOK OUT AT THE WORLD BEFORE US...

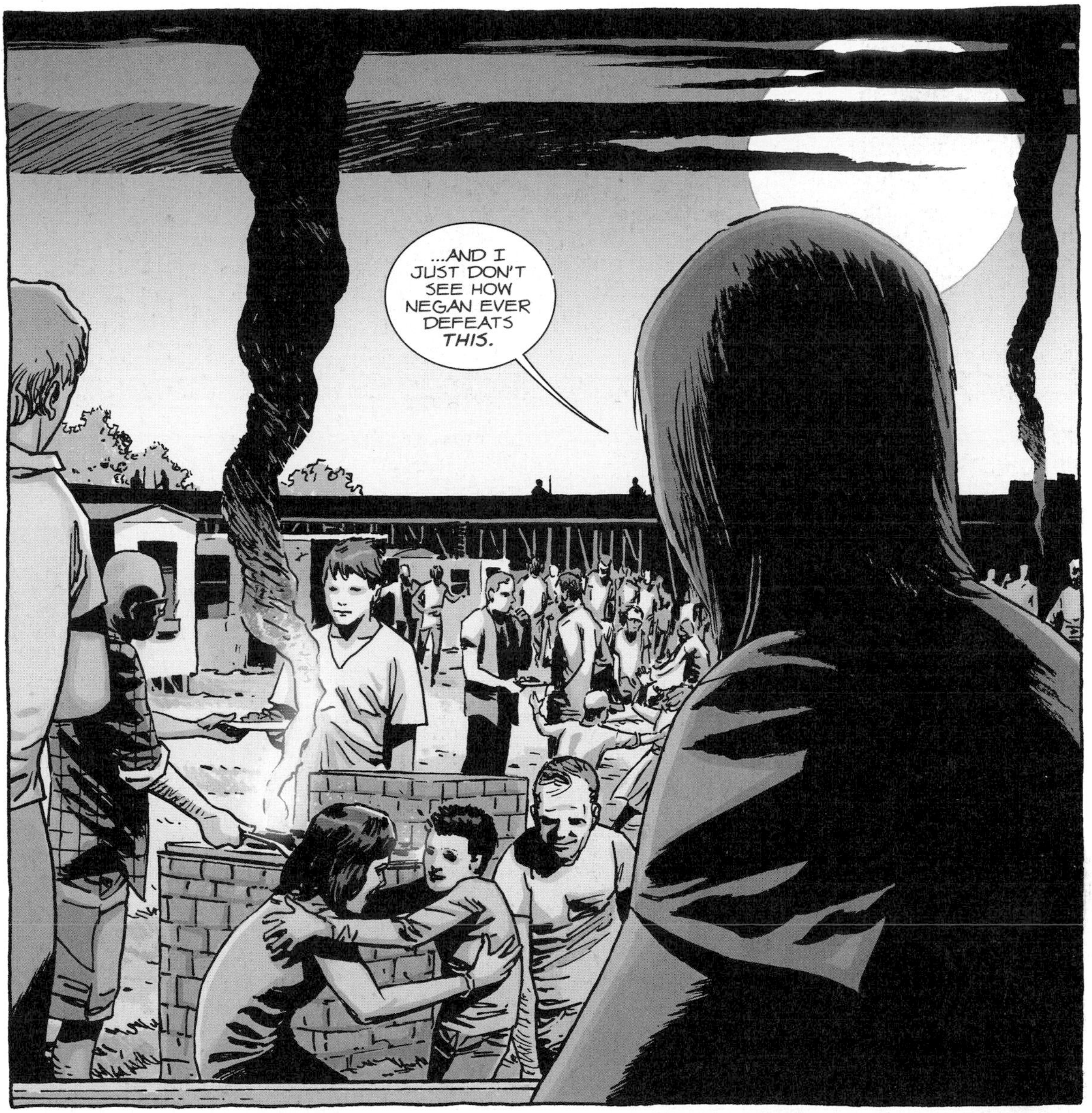
...AND I JUST DON'T SEE HOW NEGAN EVER DEFEATS *THIS.*

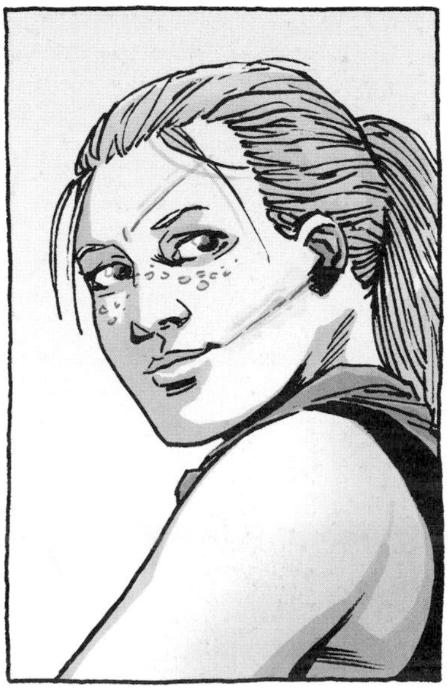

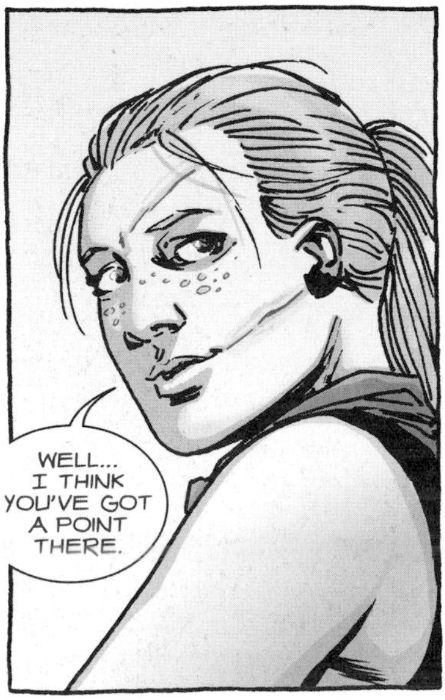
WELL... I THINK YOU'VE GOT A POINT THERE.

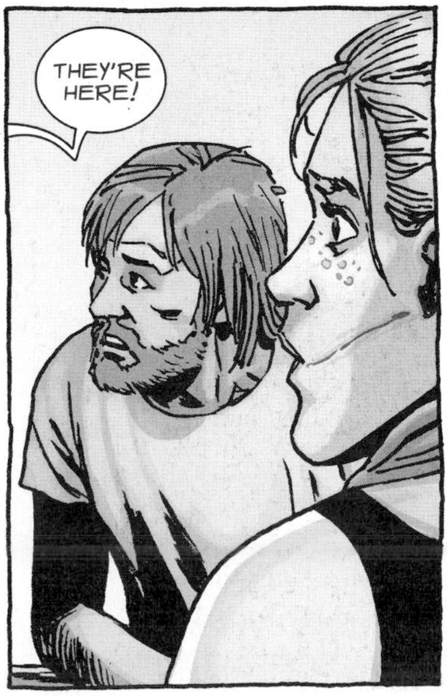
THEY'RE HERE!

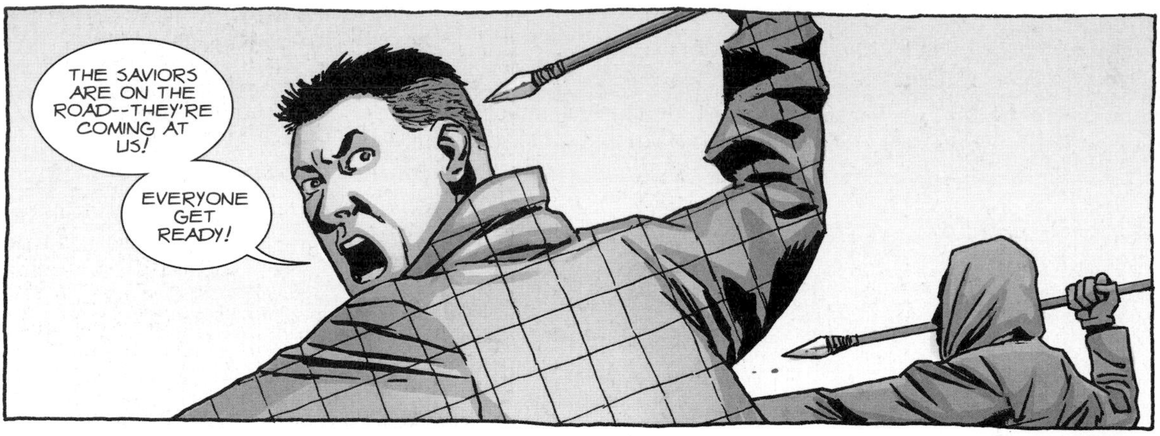
THE SAVIORS ARE ON THE ROAD--THEY'RE COMING AT US!
EVERYONE GET READY!

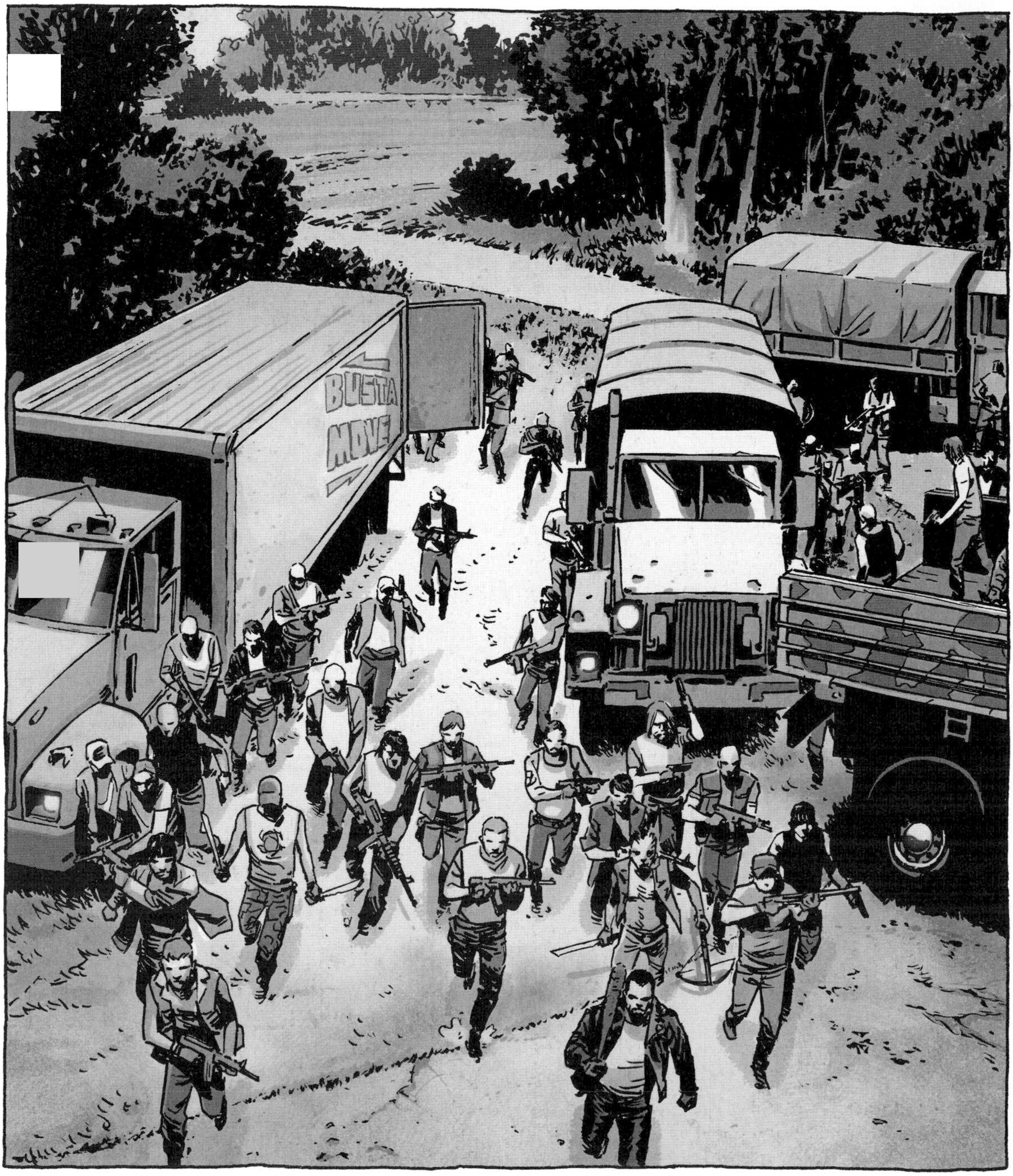
BUSTA MOVE

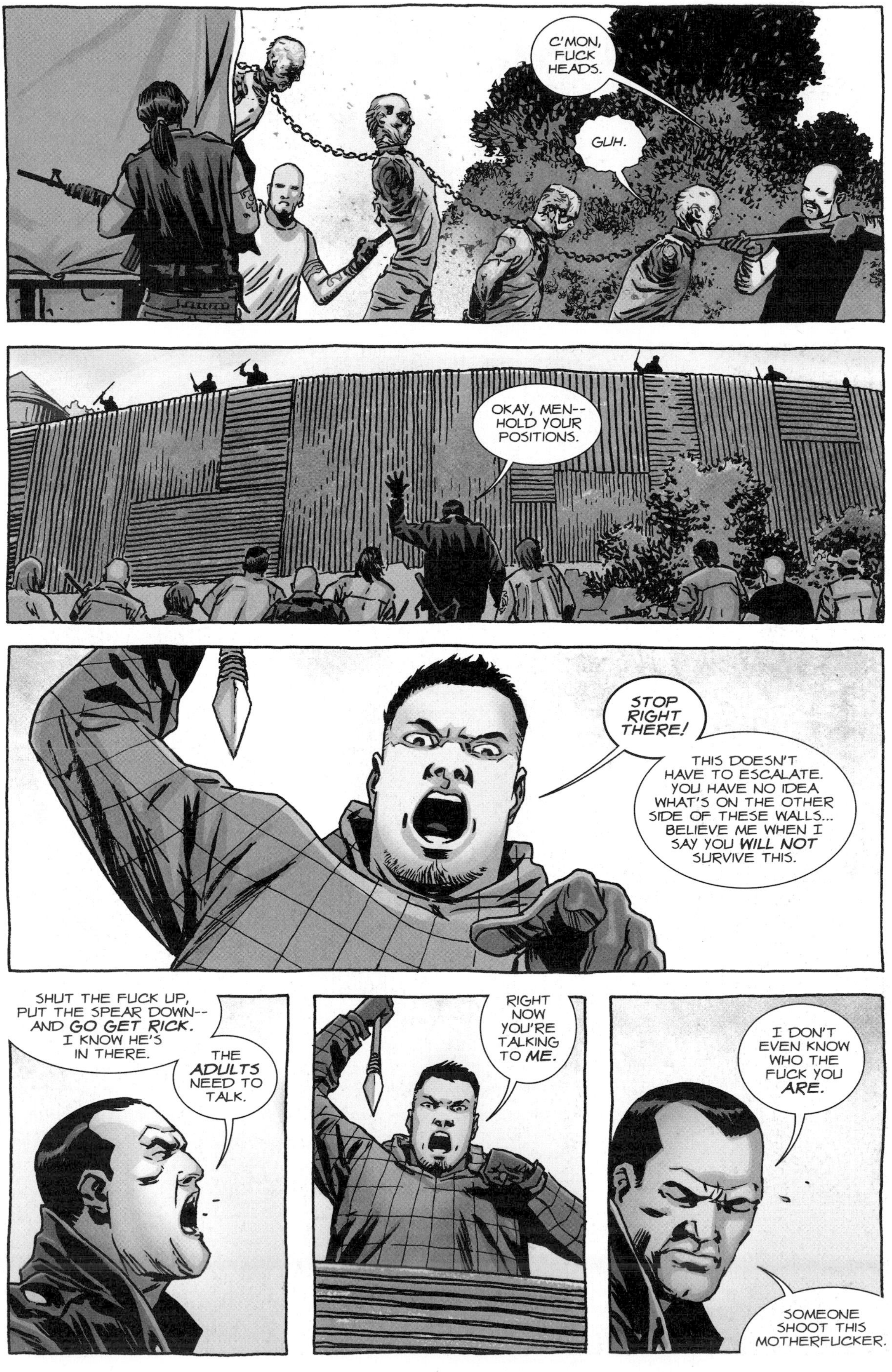

C'MON, FUCK HEADS.
GUH.
OKAY, MEN-- HOLD YOUR POSITIONS.
STOP RIGHT THERE!
THIS DOESN'T HAVE TO ESCALATE. YOU HAVE NO IDEA WHAT'S ON THE OTHER SIDE OF THESE WALLS... BELIEVE ME WHEN I SAY YOU WILL NOT SURVIVE THIS.
SHUT THE FUCK UP, PUT THE SPEAR DOWN-- AND GO GET RICK. I KNOW HE'S IN THERE.
THE ADULTS NEED TO TALK.
RIGHT NOW YOU'RE TALKING TO ME.
I DON'T EVEN KNOW WHO THE FUCK YOU ARE.
SOMEONE SHOOT THIS MOTHERFUCKER.

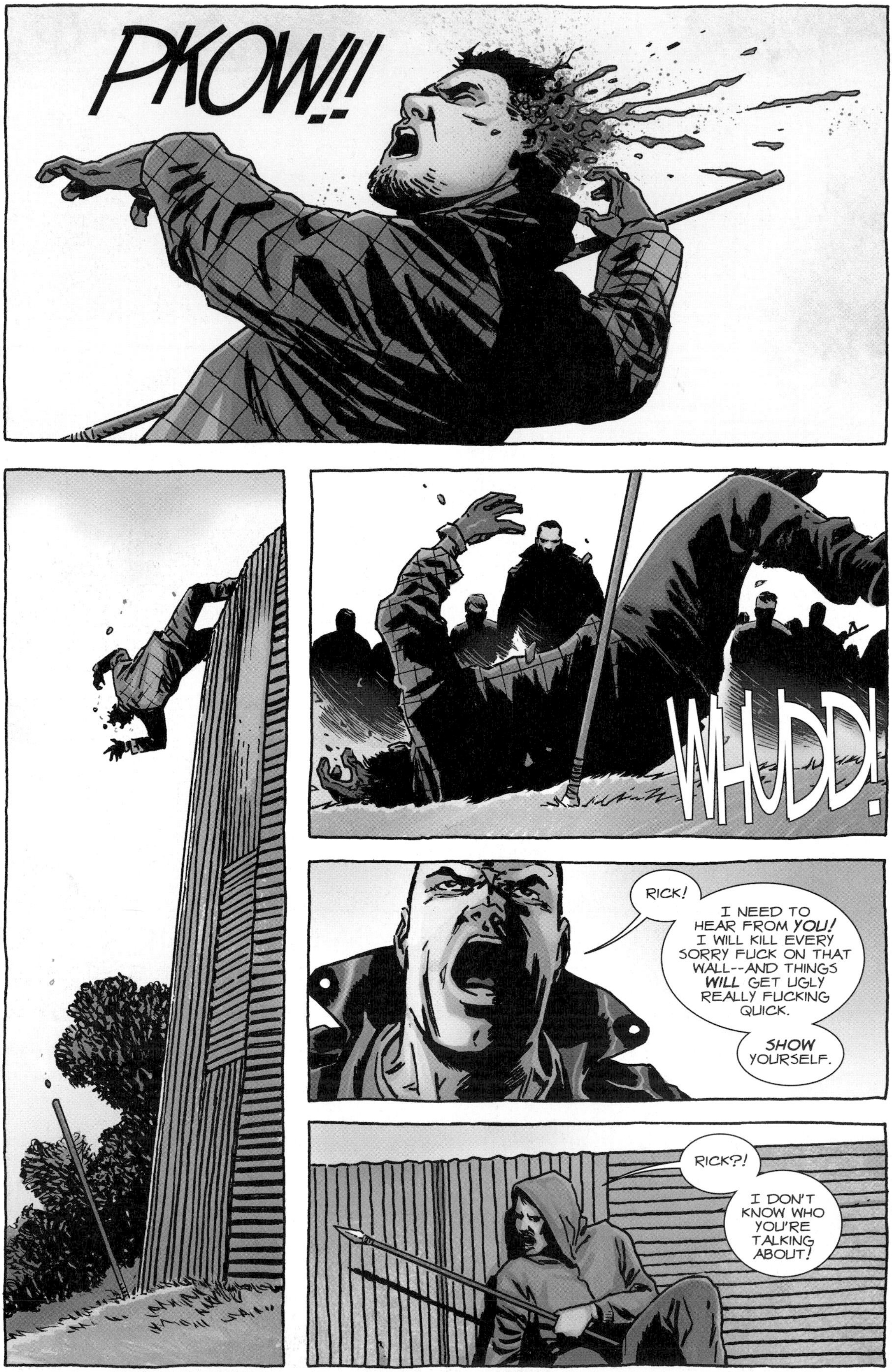
PKOW!!
WHUDD!
RICK!
I NEED TO HEAR FROM YOU! I WILL KILL EVERY SORRY FUCK ON THAT WALL--AND THINGS WILL GET UGLY REALLY FUCKING QUICK.
SHOW YOURSELF.
RICK?!
I DON'T KNOW WHO YOU'RE TALKING ABOUT!

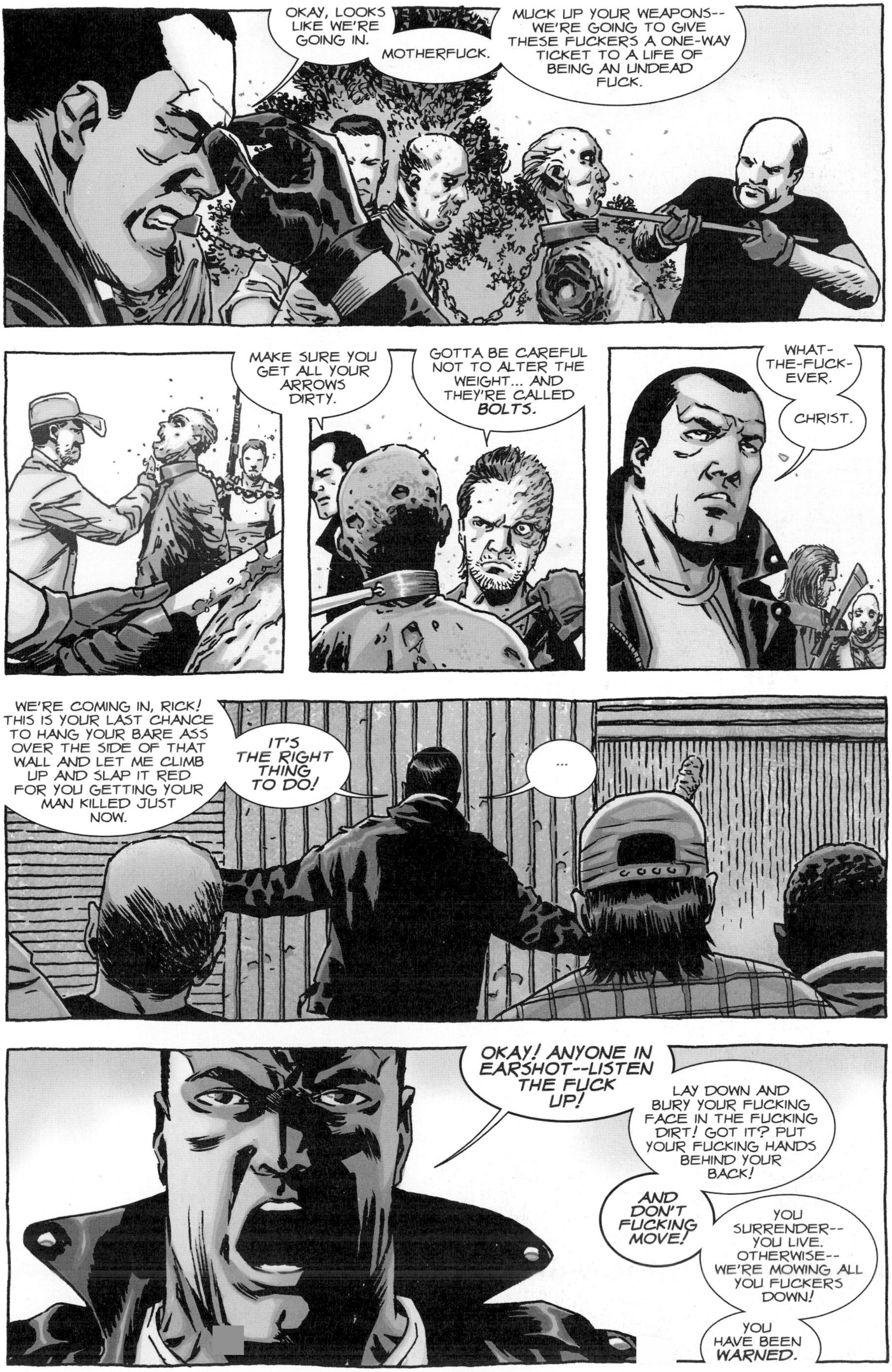
OKAY, LOOKS LIKE WE'RE GOING IN.
MOTHERFUCK.
MUCK UP YOUR WEAPONS-- WE'RE GOING TO GIVE THESE FUCKERS A ONE-WAY TICKET TO A LIFE OF BEING AN UNDEAD FUCK.
MAKE SURE YOU GET ALL YOUR ARROWS DIRTY.
GOTTA BE CAREFUL NOT TO ALTER THE WEIGHT... AND THEY'RE CALLED BOLTS.
WHAT-THE-FUCK-EVER.
CHRIST.
WE'RE COMING IN, RICK! THIS IS YOUR LAST CHANCE TO HANG YOUR BARE ASS OVER THE SIDE OF THAT WALL AND LET ME CLIMB UP AND SLAP IT RED FOR YOU GETTING YOUR MAN KILLED JUST NOW.
IT'S THE RIGHT THING TO DO!
...
OKAY! ANYONE IN EARSHOT--LISTEN THE FUCK UP!
LAY DOWN AND BURY YOUR FUCKING FACE IN THE FUCKING DIRT! GOT IT? PUT YOUR FUCKING HANDS BEHIND YOUR BACK!
AND DON'T FUCKING MOVE!
YOU SURRENDER-- YOU LIVE. OTHERWISE-- WE'RE MOWING ALL YOU FUCKERS DOWN!
YOU HAVE BEEN WARNED.

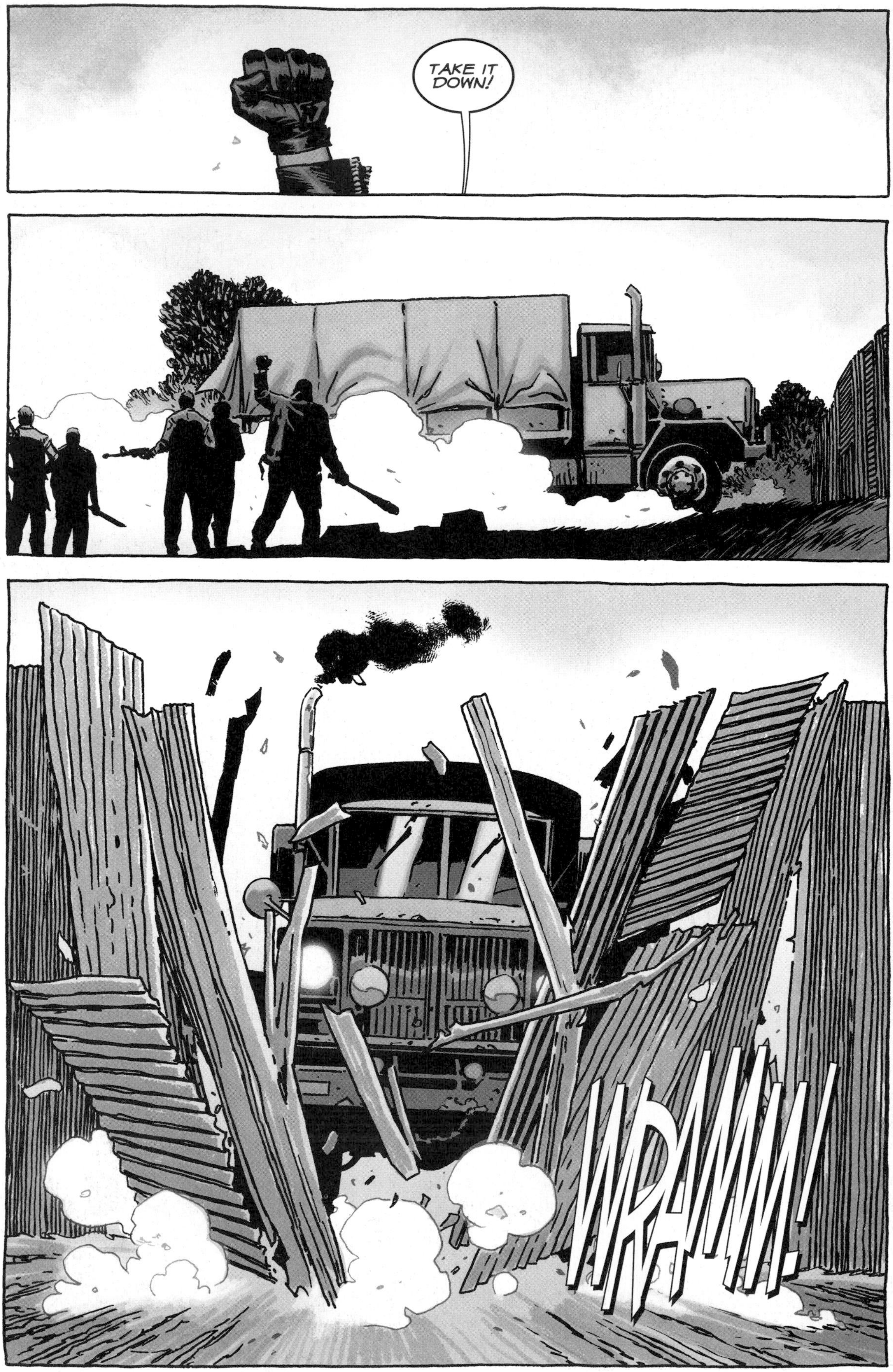
TAKE IT DOWN!
WRAMM!

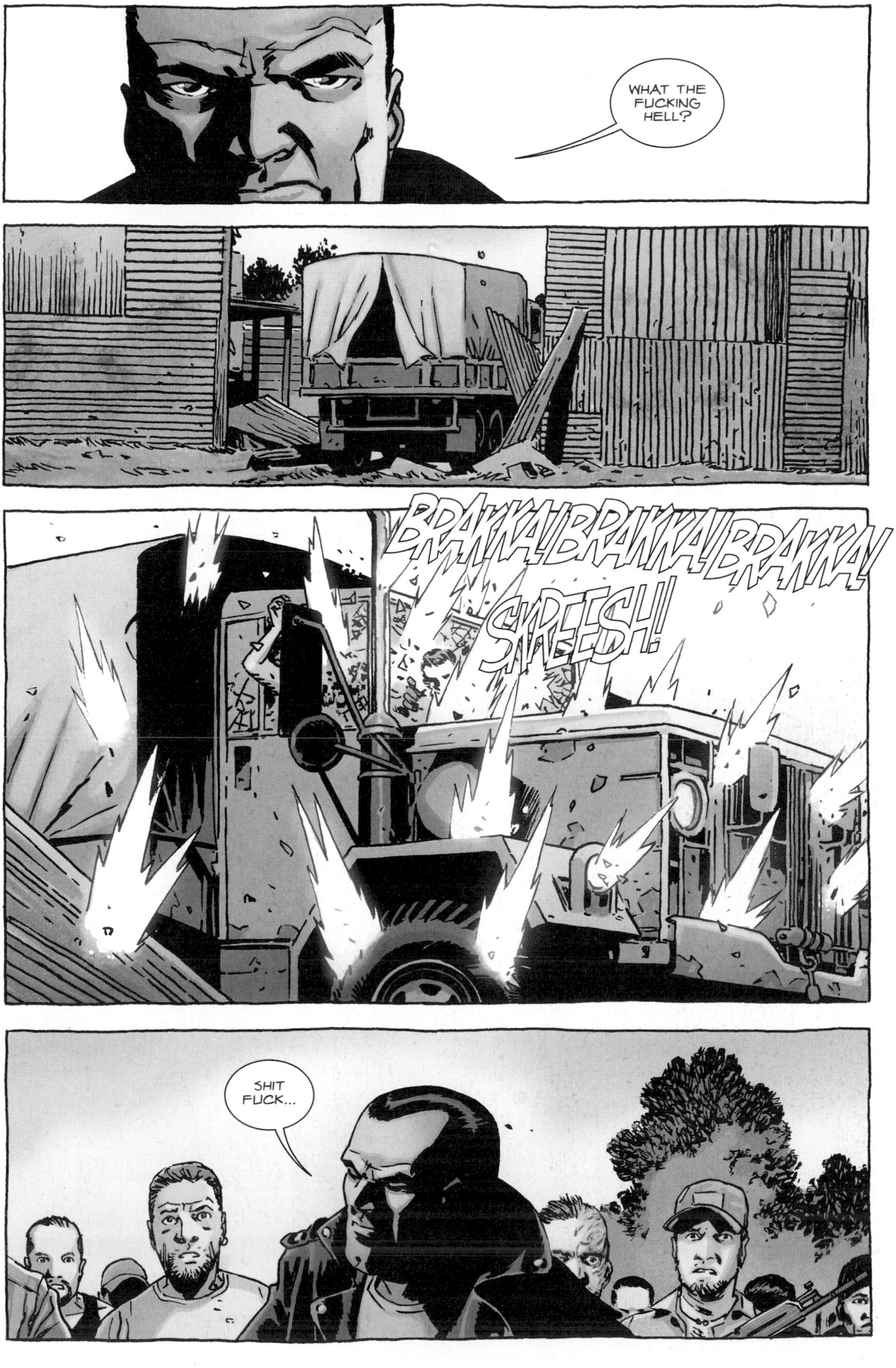
WHAT THE FUCKING HELL?
BRAKKA! BRAKKA! BRAKKA!
SKREEESH!
SHIT FUCK...

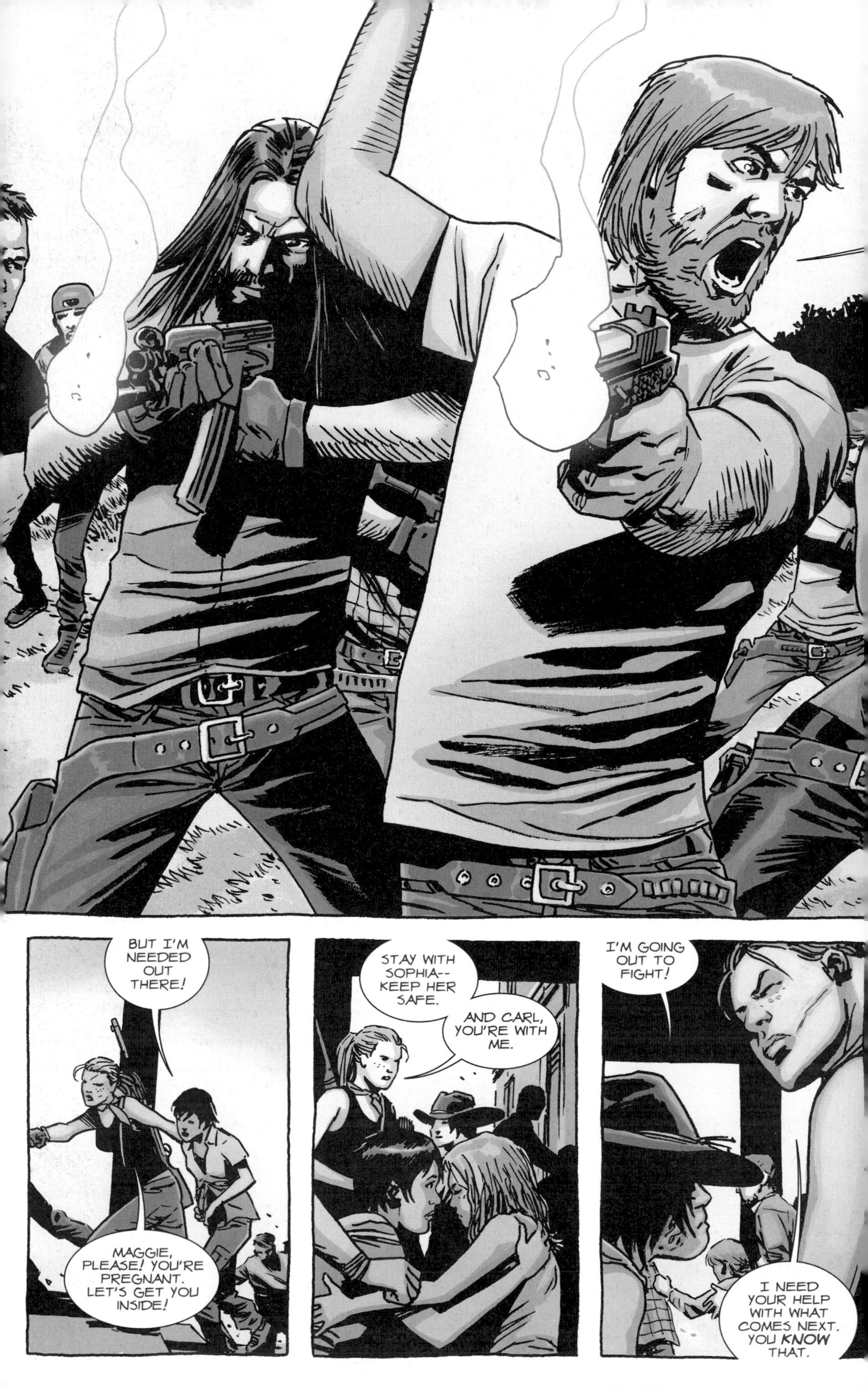
BUT I'M NEEDED OUT THERE!
MAGGIE, PLEASE! YOU'RE PREGNANT. LET'S GET YOU INSIDE!
STAY WITH SOPHIA-- KEEP HER SAFE.
AND CARL, YOU'RE WITH ME.
I'M GOING OUT TO FIGHT!
I NEED YOUR HELP WITH WHAT COMES NEXT. YOU KNOW THAT.

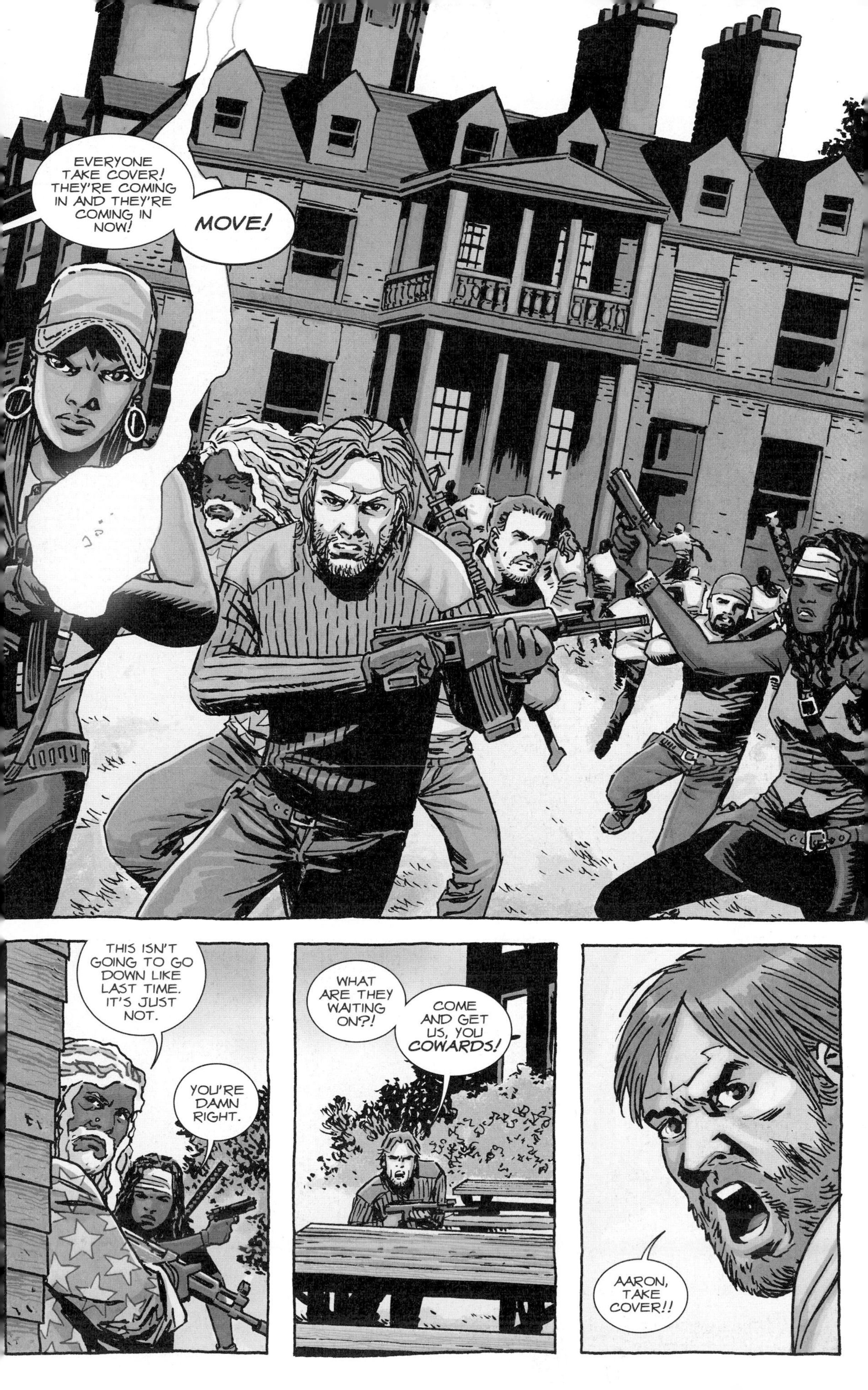
EVERYONE TAKE COVER! THEY'RE COMING IN AND THEY'RE COMING IN NOW!
MOVE!
THIS ISN'T GOING TO GO DOWN LIKE LAST TIME. IT'S JUST NOT.
YOU'RE DAMN RIGHT.
WHAT ARE THEY WAITING ON?!
COME AND GET US, YOU COWARDS!
AARON, TAKE COVER!!

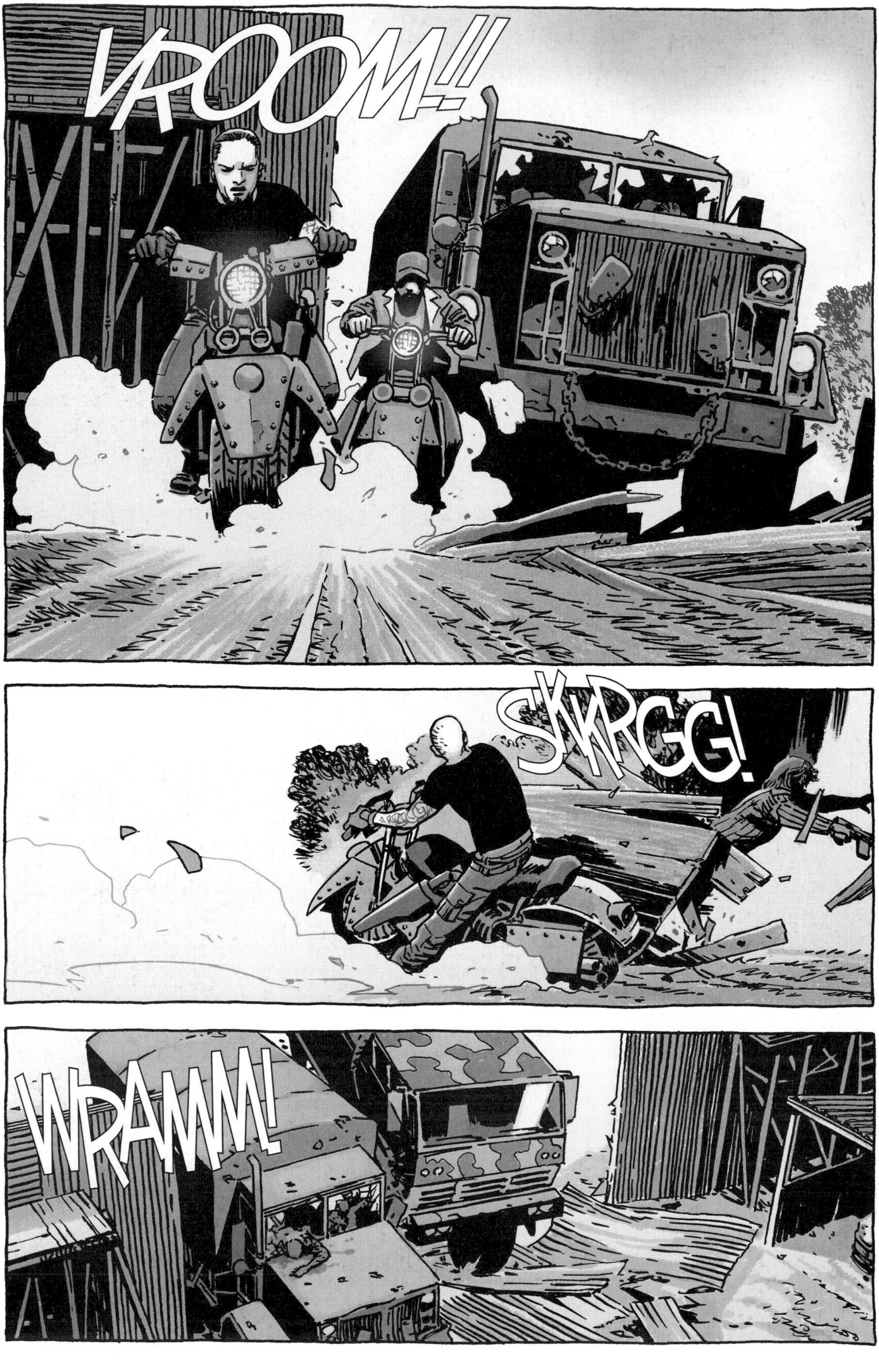
VROOM!!
SKKRGG!
WRAMM!

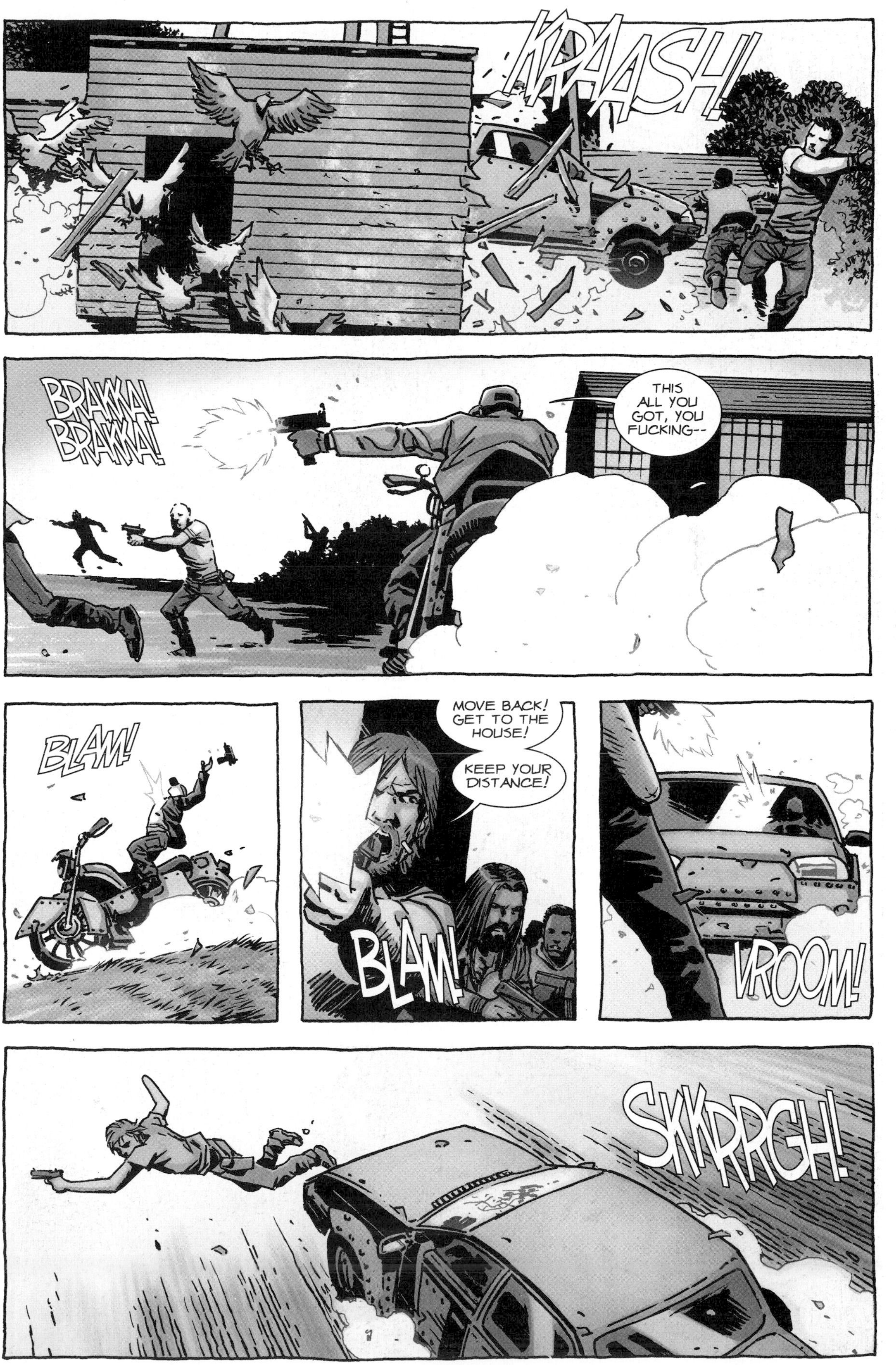
KRAASH!
BRAKKA! BRAKKA!
THIS ALL YOU GOT, YOU FUCKING--
BLAM!
MOVE BACK! GET TO THE HOUSE!
KEEP YOUR DISTANCE!
BLAM!
VROOM!
SKKRRGH!

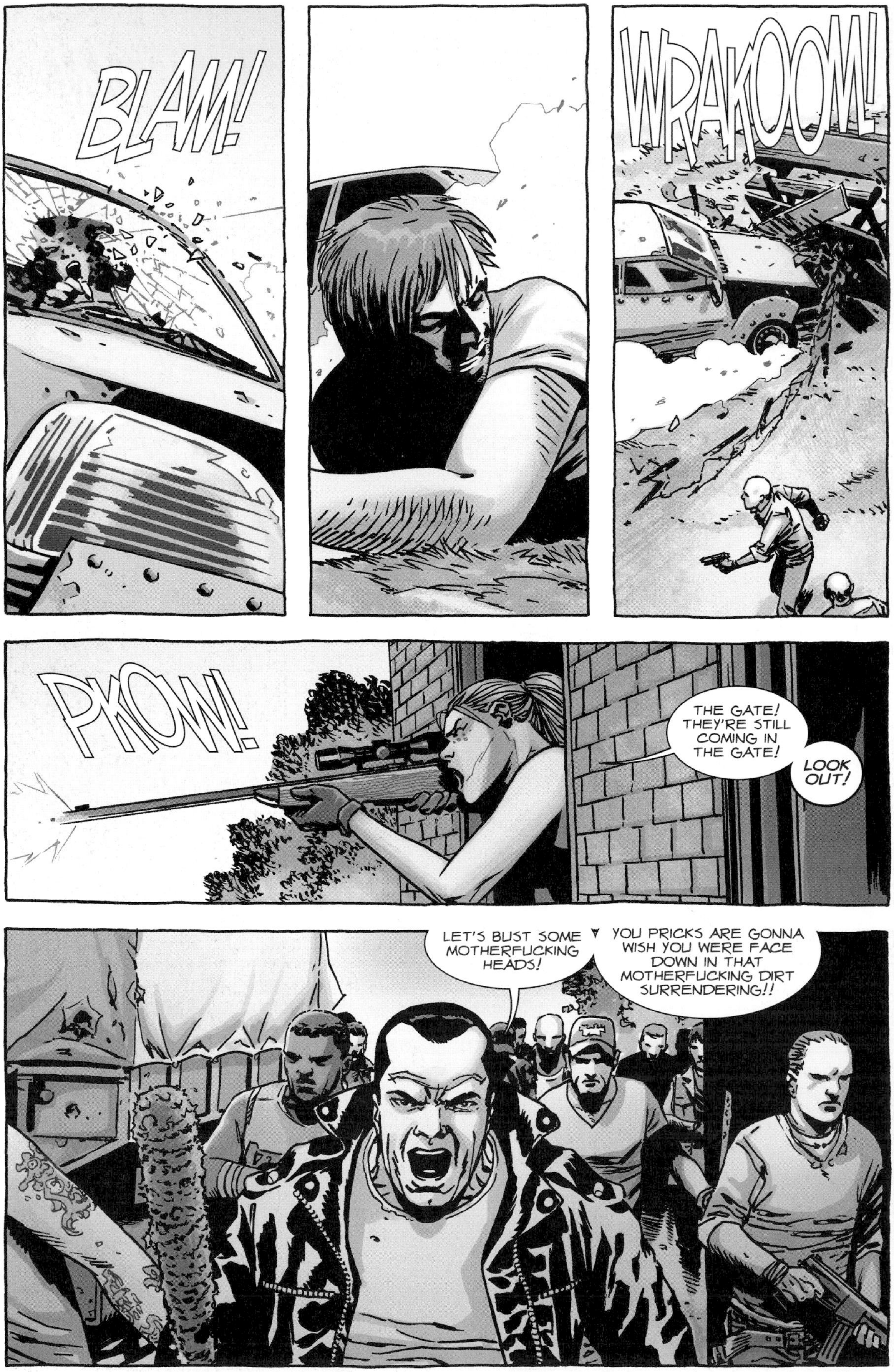
BLAM!
WRAKOOM!
PKOW!
THE GATE! THEY'RE STILL COMING IN THE GATE!
LOOK OUT!
LET'S BUST SOME MOTHERFUCKING HEADS!
YOU PRICKS ARE GONNA WISH YOU WERE FACE DOWN IN THAT MOTHERFUCKING DIRT SURRENDERING!!

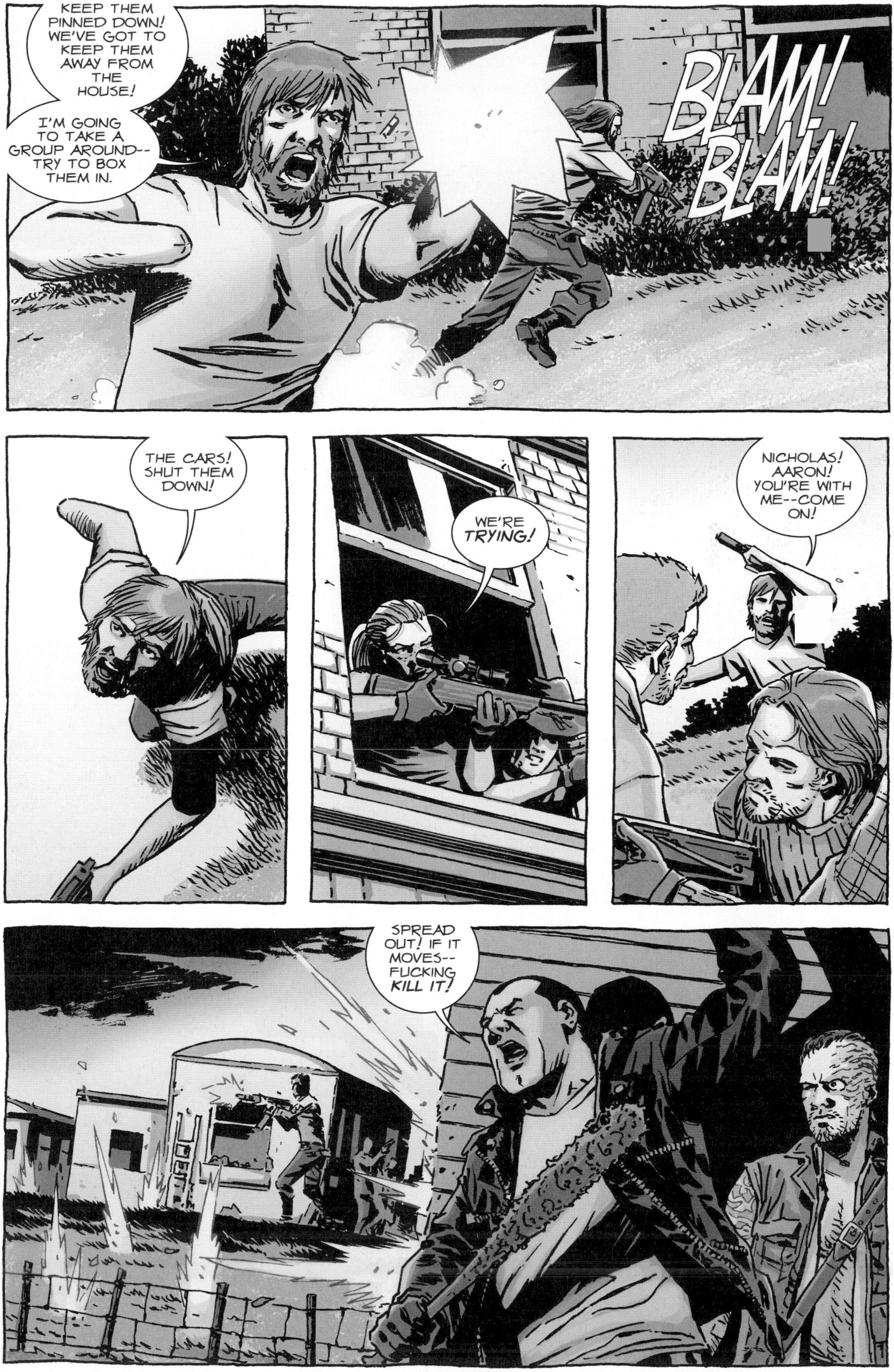
KEEP THEM PINNED DOWN! WE'VE GOT TO KEEP THEM AWAY FROM THE HOUSE!
I'M GOING TO TAKE A GROUP AROUND-- TRY TO BOX THEM IN.
BLAM! BLAM!
THE CARS! SHUT THEM DOWN!
WE'RE TRYING!
NICHOLAS! AARON! YOU'RE WITH ME--COME ON!
SPREAD OUT! IF IT MOVES-- FUCKING KILL IT!

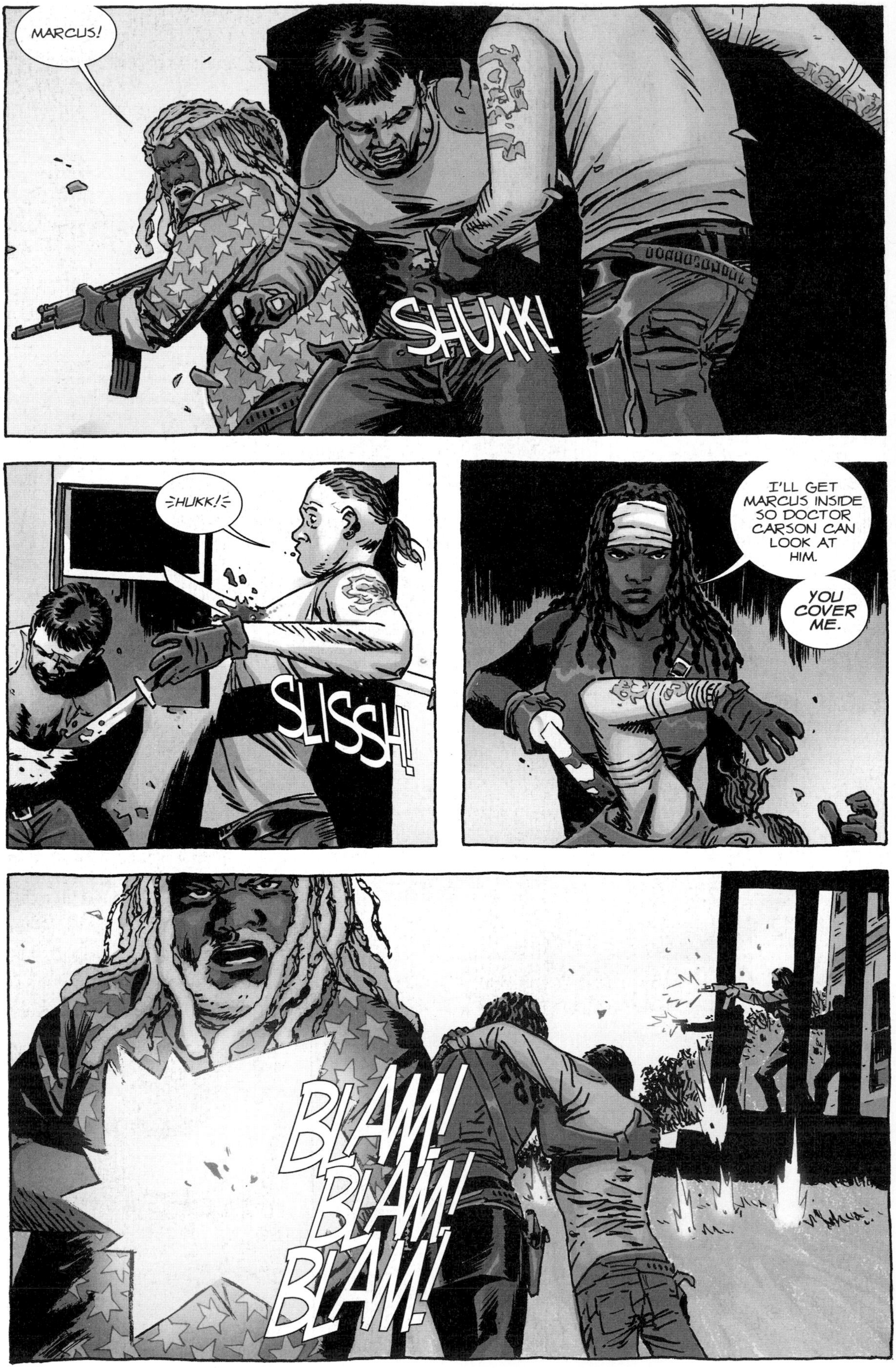
MARCUS!
SHUKK!
HUKK!
SLISSH!
I'LL GET MARCUS INSIDE SO DOCTOR CARSON CAN LOOK AT HIM.
YOU COVER ME.
BLAM! BLAM! BLAM!

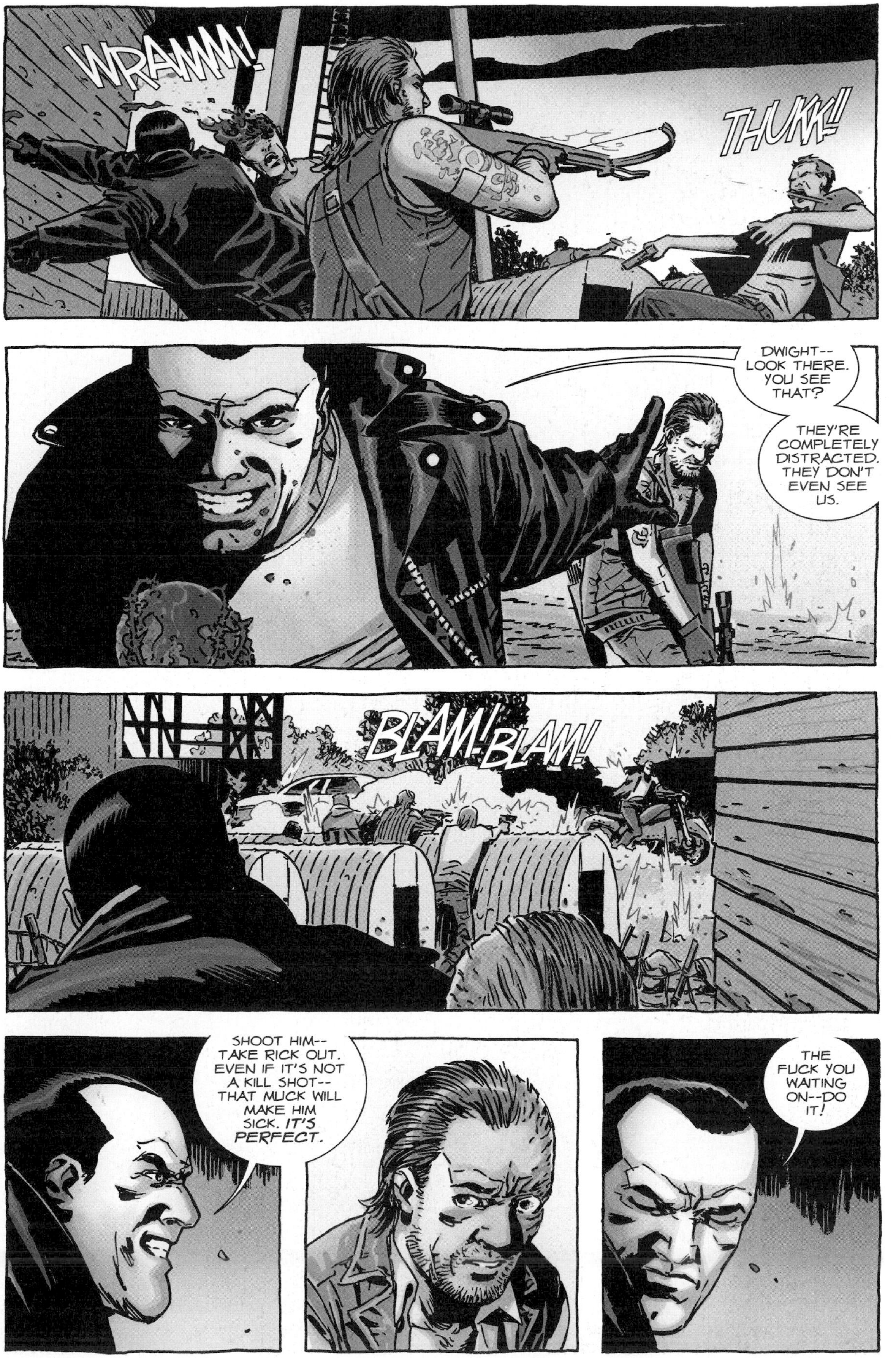
WRAMM!
THUKK!!
DWIGHT-- LOOK THERE. YOU SEE THAT?
THEY'RE COMPLETELY DISTRACTED. THEY DON'T EVEN SEE US.
BLAM! BLAM!
SHOOT HIM-- TAKE RICK OUT. EVEN IF IT'S NOT A KILL SHOT-- THAT MUCK WILL MAKE HIM SICK. IT'S PERFECT.
THE FUCK YOU WAITING ON--DO IT!

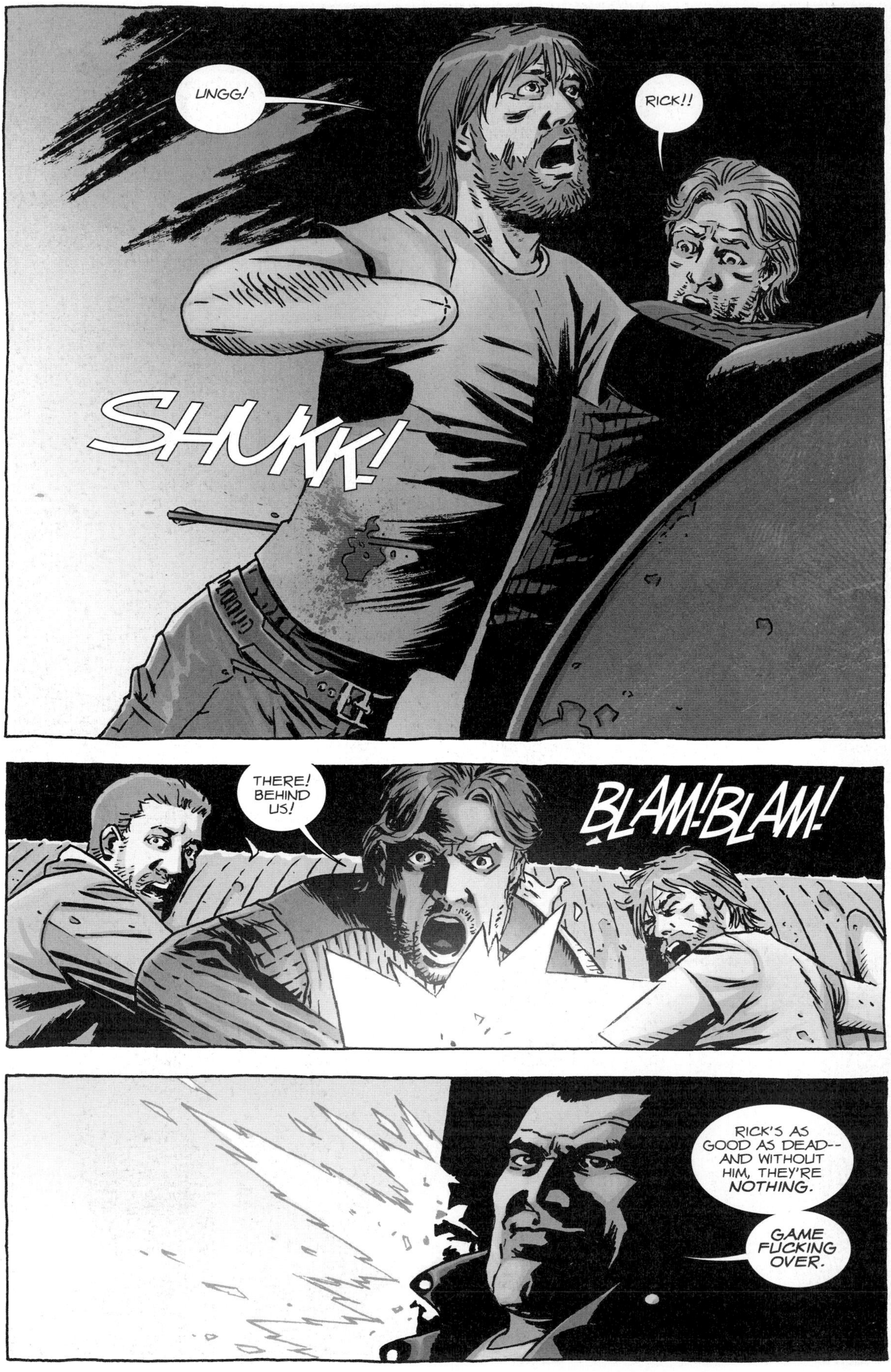
UNGG!
RICK!!
SHUKK!
THERE! BEHIND US!
BLAM!BLAM!
RICK'S AS GOOD AS DEAD-- AND WITHOUT HIM, THEY'RE NOTHING.
GAME FUCKING OVER.

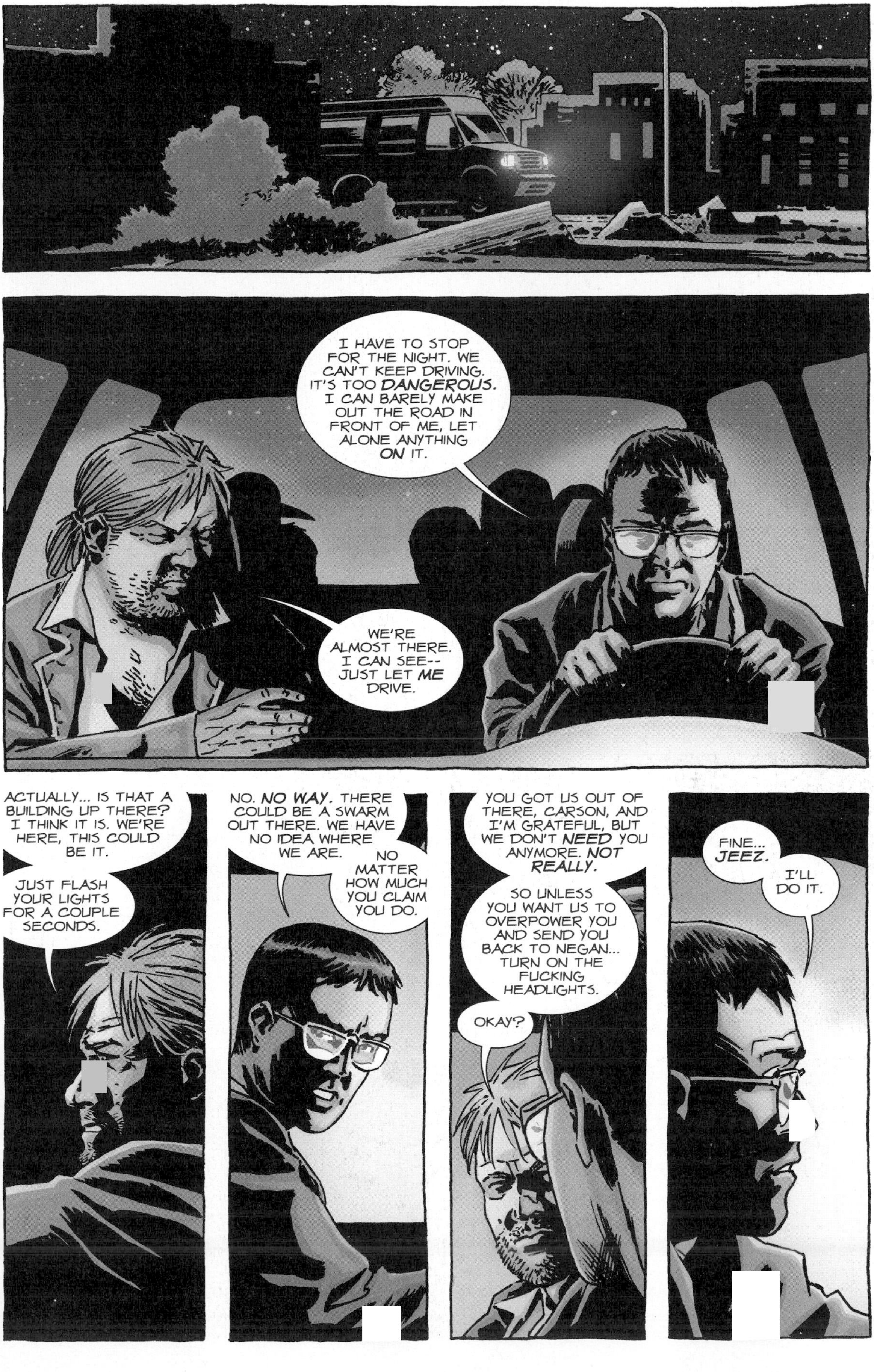
I HAVE TO STOP FOR THE NIGHT. WE CAN'T KEEP DRIVING. IT'S TOO DANGEROUS. I CAN BARELY MAKE OUT THE ROAD IN FRONT OF ME, LET ALONE ANYTHING ON IT.
WE'RE ALMOST THERE. I CAN SEE-- JUST LET ME DRIVE.
ACTUALLY... IS THAT A BUILDING UP THERE? I THINK IT IS. WE'RE HERE, THIS COULD BE IT.
JUST FLASH YOUR LIGHTS FOR A COUPLE SECONDS.
NO. NO WAY. THERE COULD BE A SWARM OUT THERE. WE HAVE NO IDEA WHERE WE ARE.
NO MATTER HOW MUCH YOU CLAIM YOU DO.
YOU GOT US OUT OF THERE, CARSON, AND I'M GRATEFUL, BUT WE DON'T NEED YOU ANYMORE. NOT REALLY.
SO UNLESS YOU WANT US TO OVERPOWER YOU AND SEND YOU BACK TO NEGAN... TURN ON THE FUCKING HEADLIGHTS.
OKAY?
FINE... JEEZ.
I'LL DO IT.

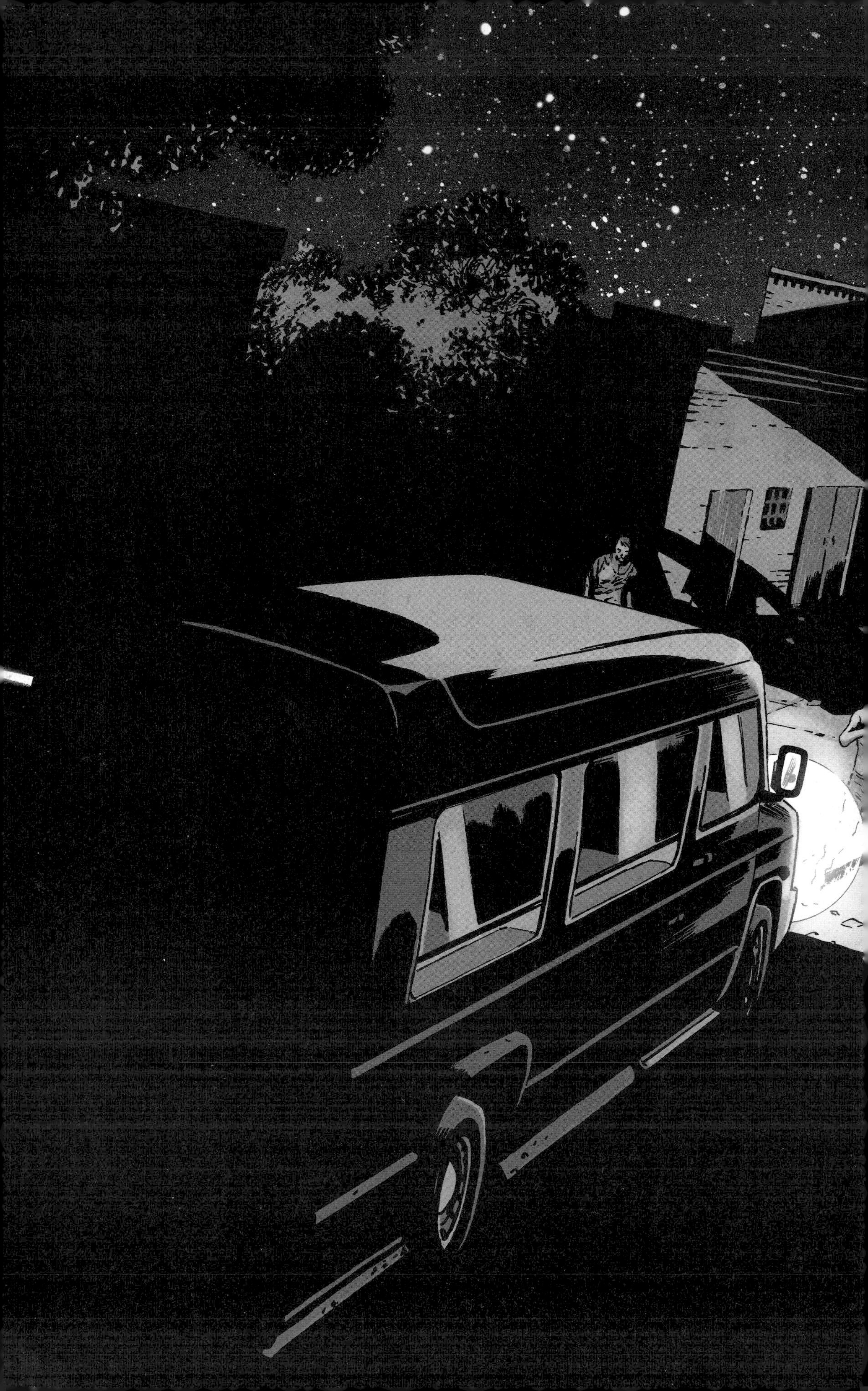

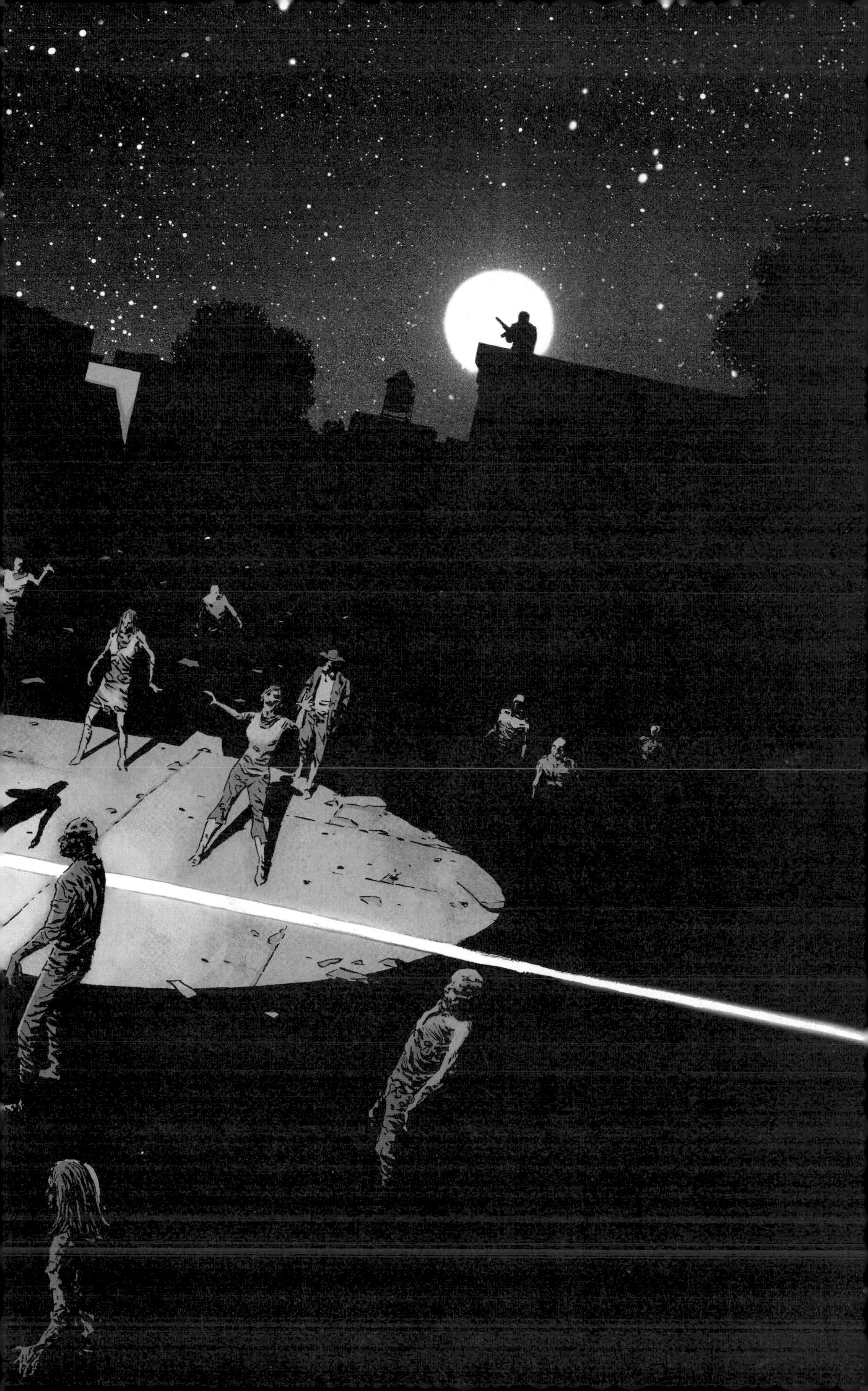

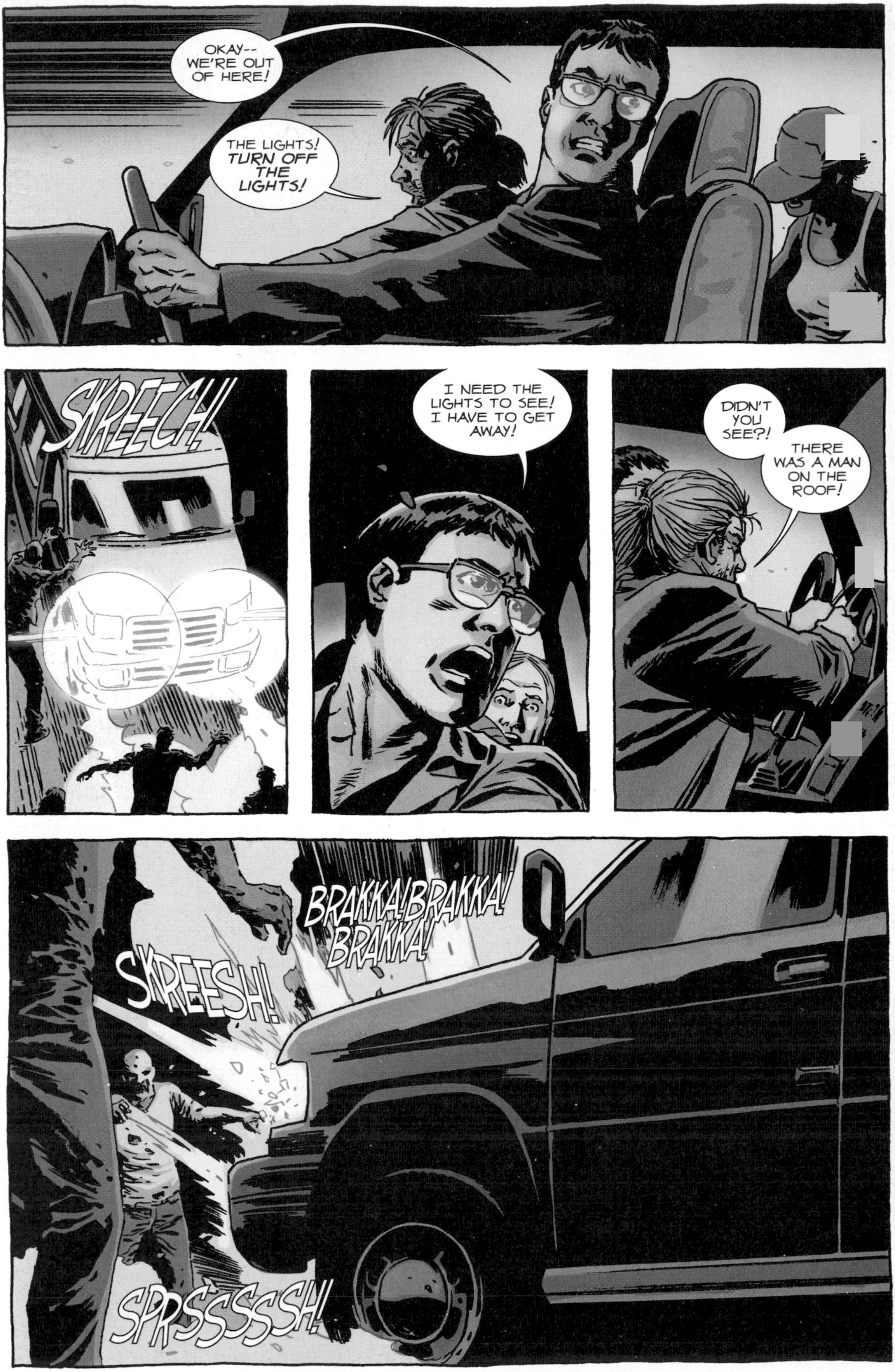
OKAY-- WE'RE OUT OF HERE!
THE LIGHTS! TURN OFF THE LIGHTS!
SKREECH!
I NEED THE LIGHTS TO SEE! I HAVE TO GET AWAY!
DIDN'T YOU SEE?!
THERE WAS A MAN ON THE ROOF!
BRAKKA! BRAKKA! BRAKKA!
SKREESH!
SPRSSSSSH!

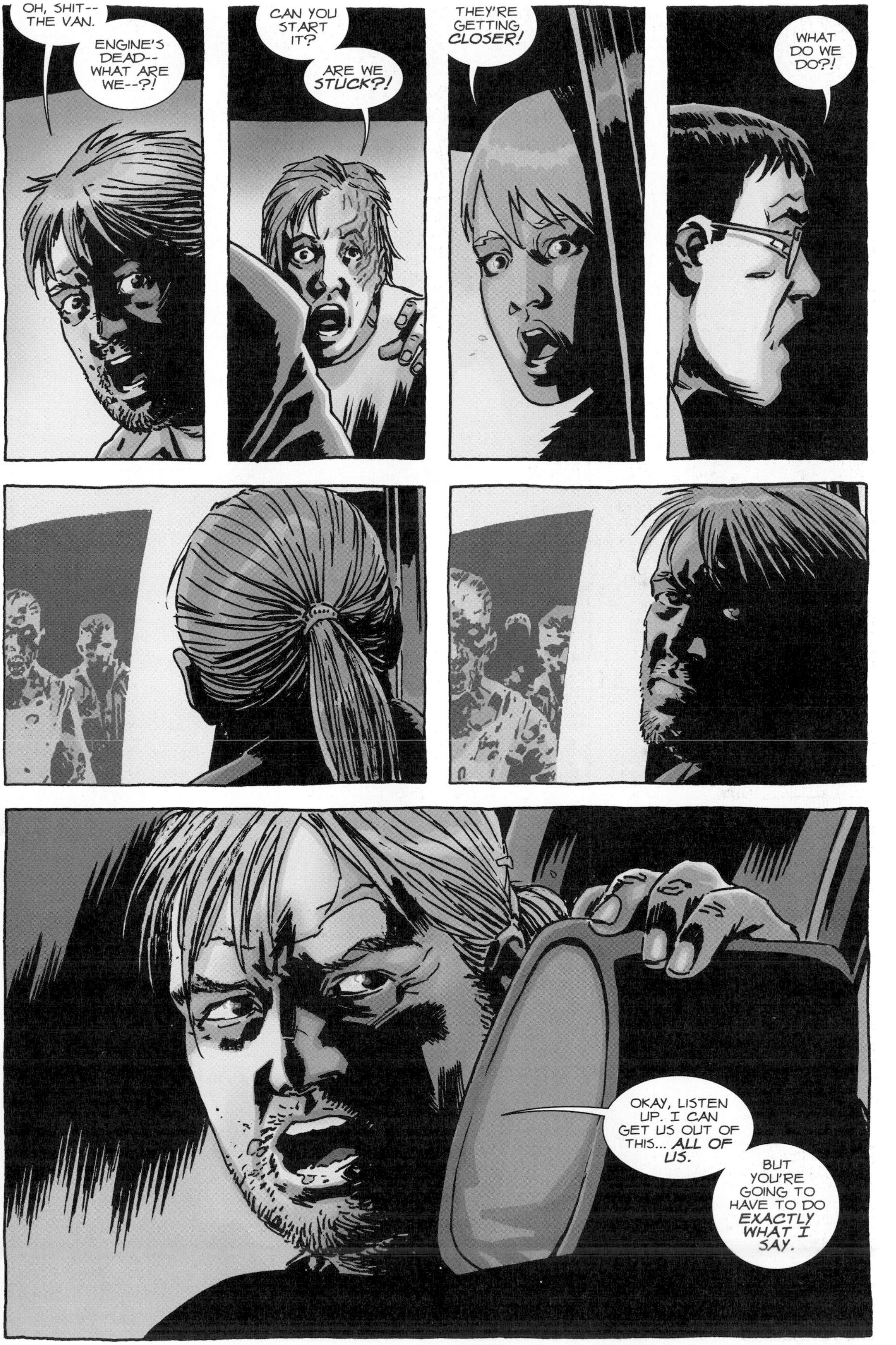

OH, SHIT-- THE VAN.
ENGINE'S DEAD-- WHAT ARE WE--?!
CAN YOU START IT?
ARE WE STUCK?!
THEY'RE GETTING CLOSER!
WHAT DO WE DO?!
OKAY, LISTEN UP. I CAN GET US OUT OF THIS... ALL OF US.
BUT YOU'RE GOING TO HAVE TO DO EXACTLY WHAT I SAY.

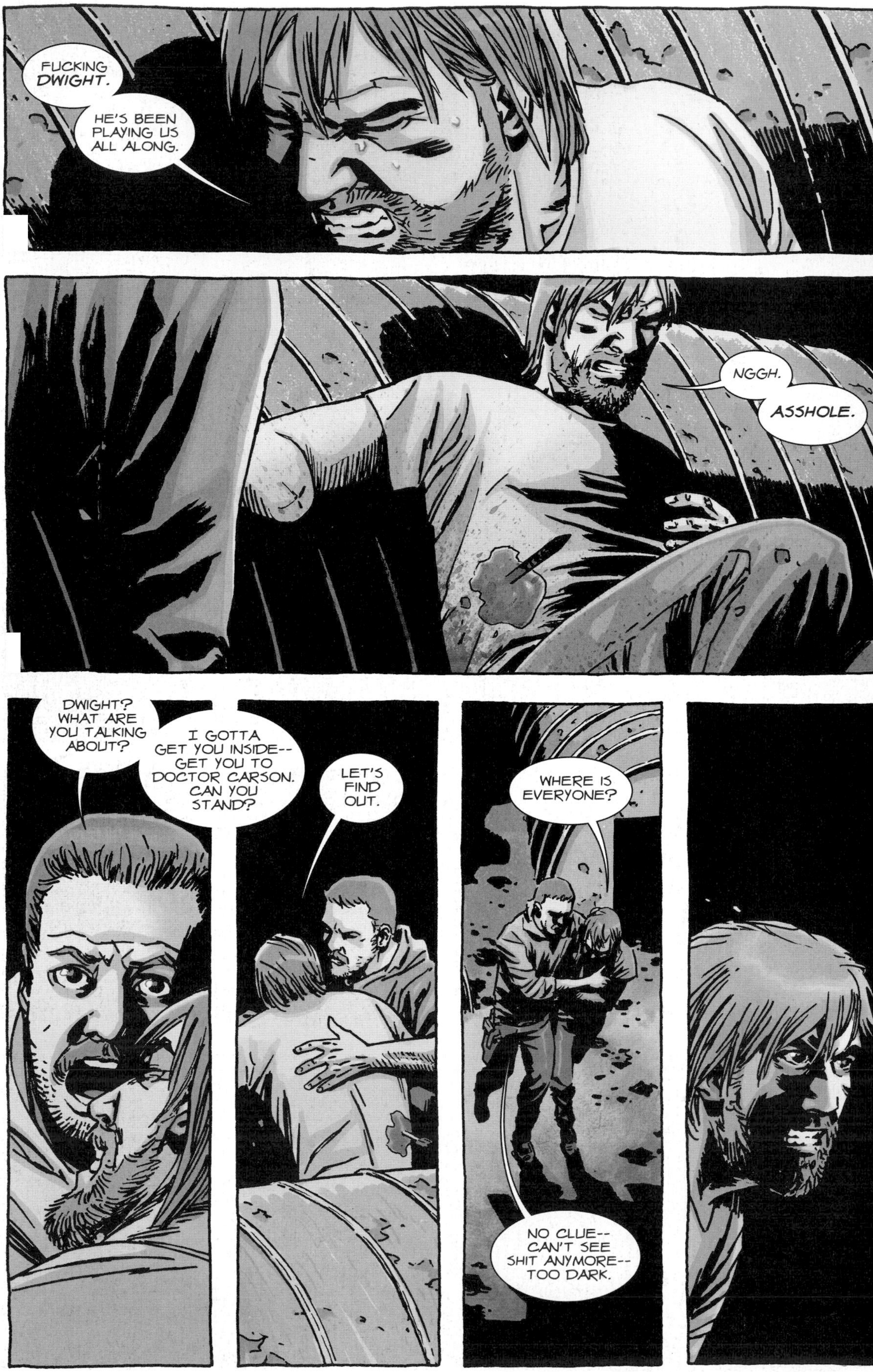
FUCKING DWIGHT.
HE'S BEEN PLAYING US ALL ALONG.
NGGH.
ASSHOLE.
DWIGHT? WHAT ARE YOU TALKING ABOUT?
I GOTTA GET YOU INSIDE-- GET YOU TO DOCTOR CARSON. CAN YOU STAND?
LET'S FIND OUT.
WHERE IS EVERYONE?
NO CLUE-- CAN'T SEE SHIT ANYMORE-- TOO DARK.

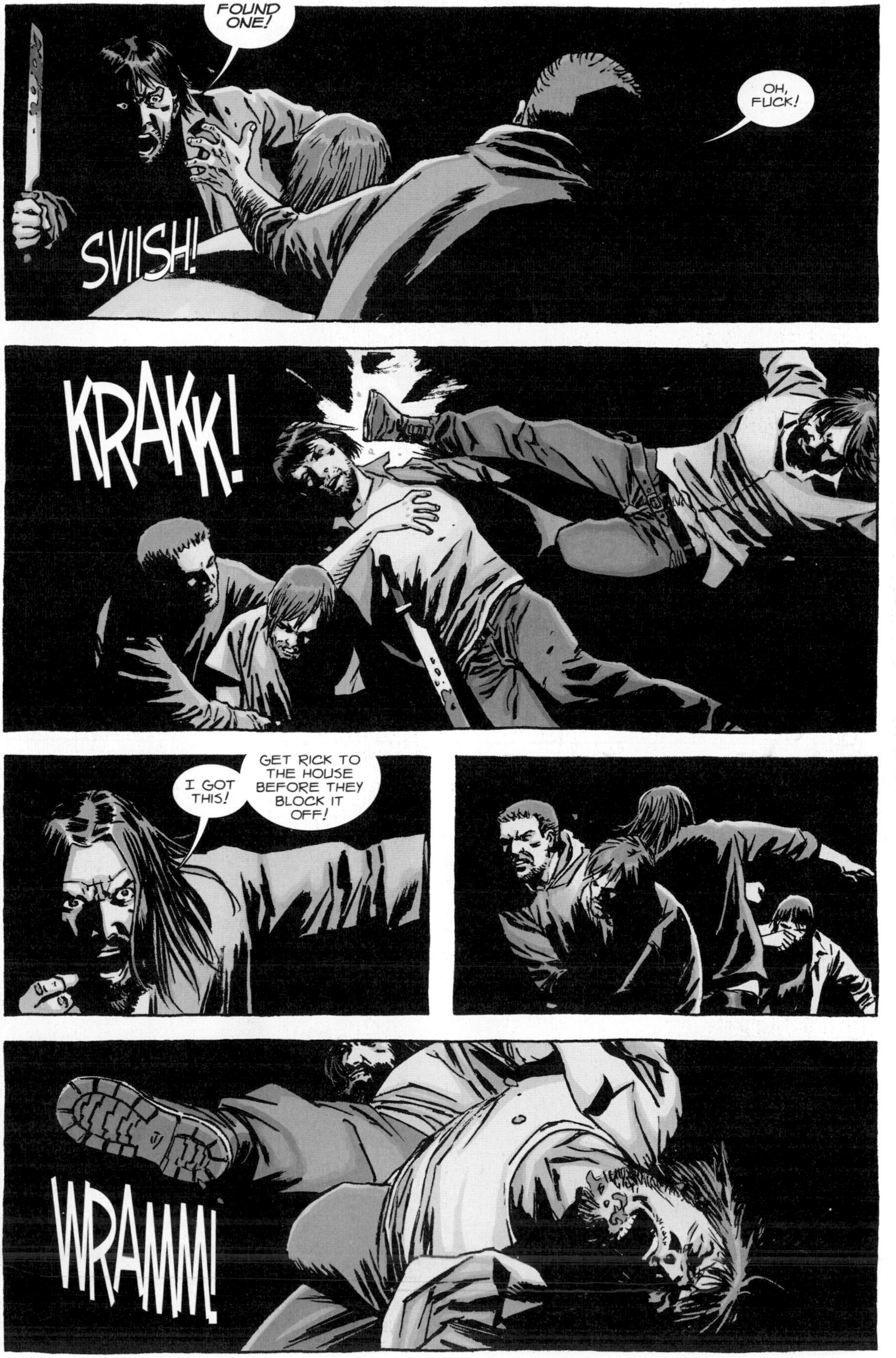
FOUND ONE!
OH, FUCK!
SVIISH!
KRAKK!
I GOT THIS!
GET RICK TO THE HOUSE BEFORE THEY BLOCK IT OFF!
WRAMM!

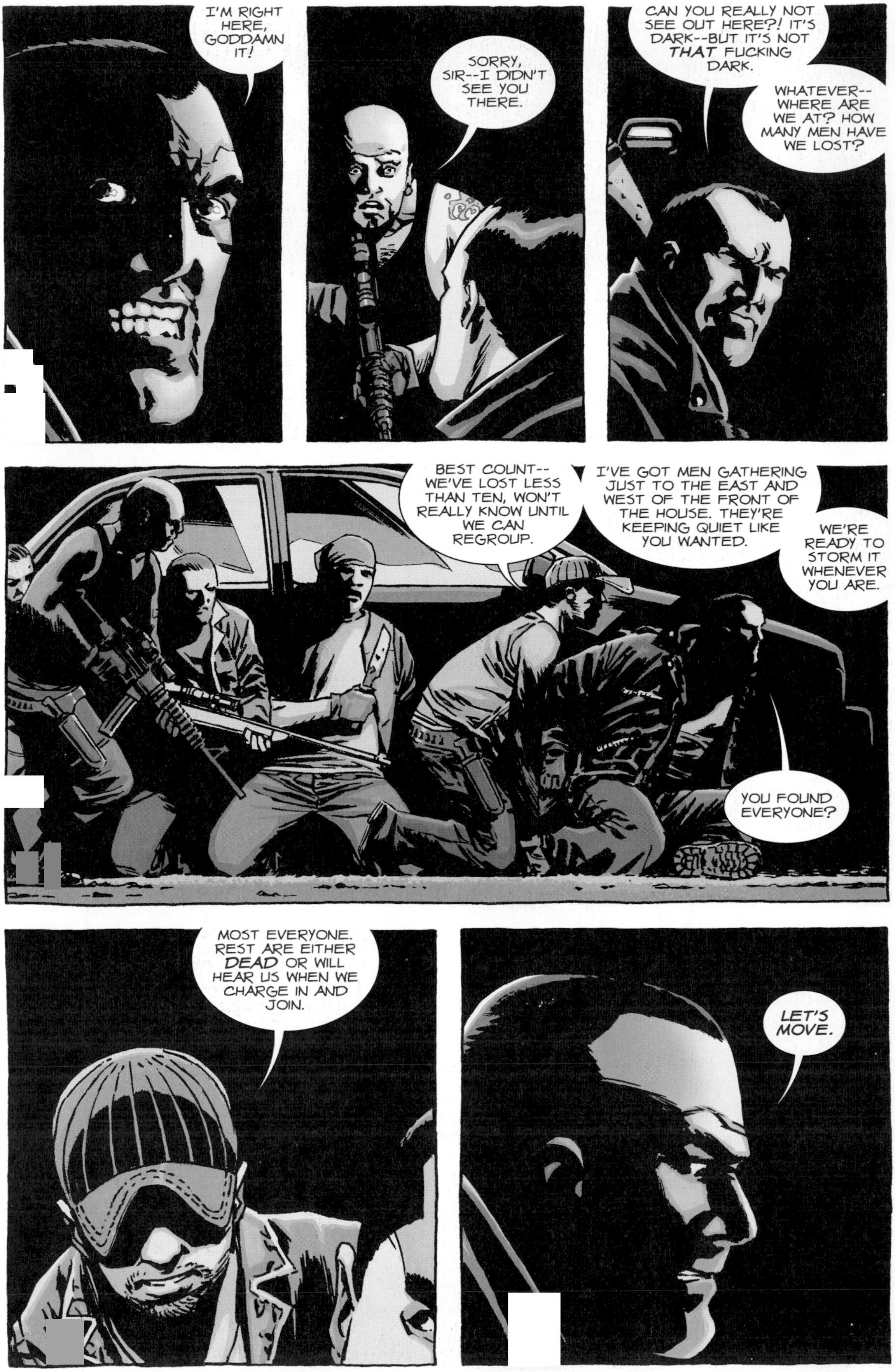
I'M RIGHT HERE, GODDAMN IT!
SORRY, SIR--I DIDN'T SEE YOU THERE.
CAN YOU REALLY NOT SEE OUT HERE?! IT'S DARK--BUT IT'S NOT *THAT* FUCKING DARK.
WHATEVER-- WHERE ARE WE AT? HOW MANY MEN HAVE WE LOST?
BEST COUNT-- WE'VE LOST LESS THAN TEN, WON'T REALLY KNOW UNTIL WE CAN REGROUP.
I'VE GOT MEN GATHERING JUST TO THE EAST AND WEST OF THE FRONT OF THE HOUSE. THEY'RE KEEPING QUIET LIKE YOU WANTED.
WE'RE READY TO STORM IT WHENEVER YOU ARE.
YOU FOUND EVERYONE?
MOST EVERYONE. REST ARE EITHER *DEAD* OR WILL HEAR US WHEN WE CHARGE IN AND JOIN.
LET'S MOVE.

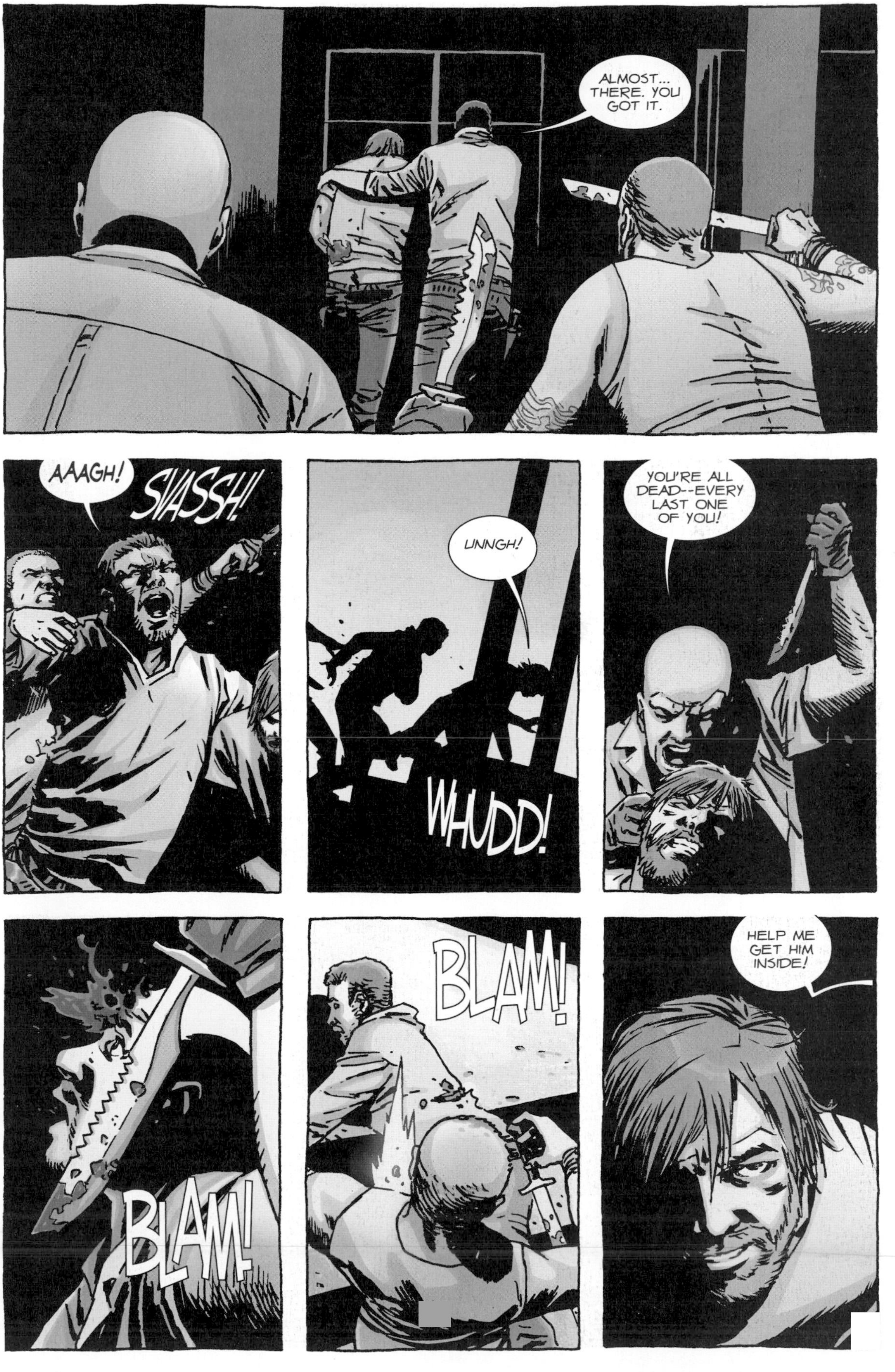
ALMOST... THERE. YOU GOT IT.
AAAGH!
SVASSH!
UNNGH!
WHUDD!
YOU'RE ALL DEAD--EVERY LAST ONE OF YOU!
BLAM!
BLAM!
HELP ME GET HIM INSIDE!

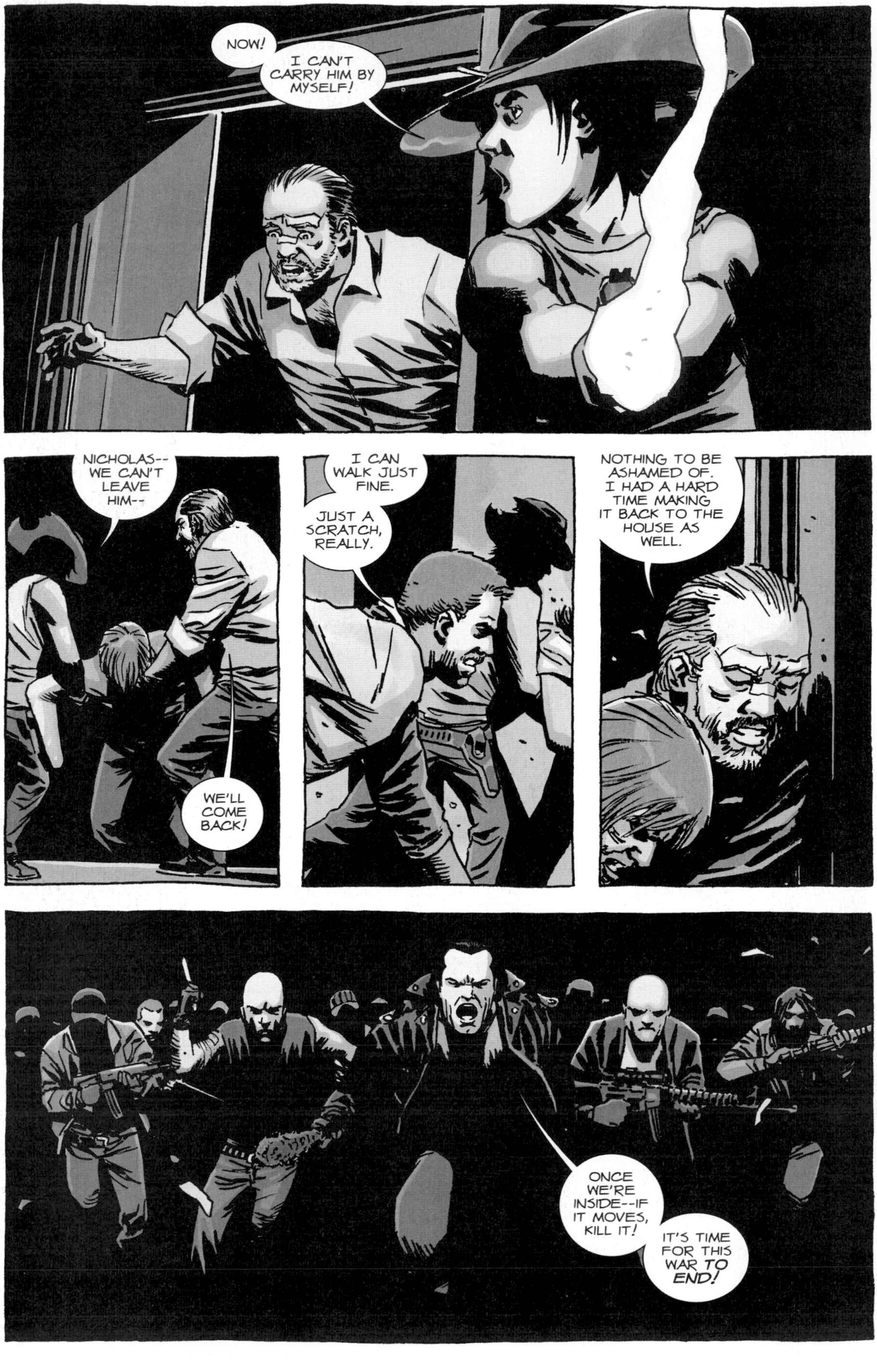
NOW!
I CAN'T CARRY HIM BY MYSELF!
NICHOLAS-- WE CAN'T LEAVE HIM--
WE'LL COME BACK!
I CAN WALK JUST FINE.
JUST A SCRATCH, REALLY.
NOTHING TO BE ASHAMED OF. I HAD A HARD TIME MAKING IT BACK TO THE HOUSE AS WELL.
ONCE WE'RE INSIDE--IF IT MOVES, KILL IT!
IT'S TIME FOR THIS WAR TO END!

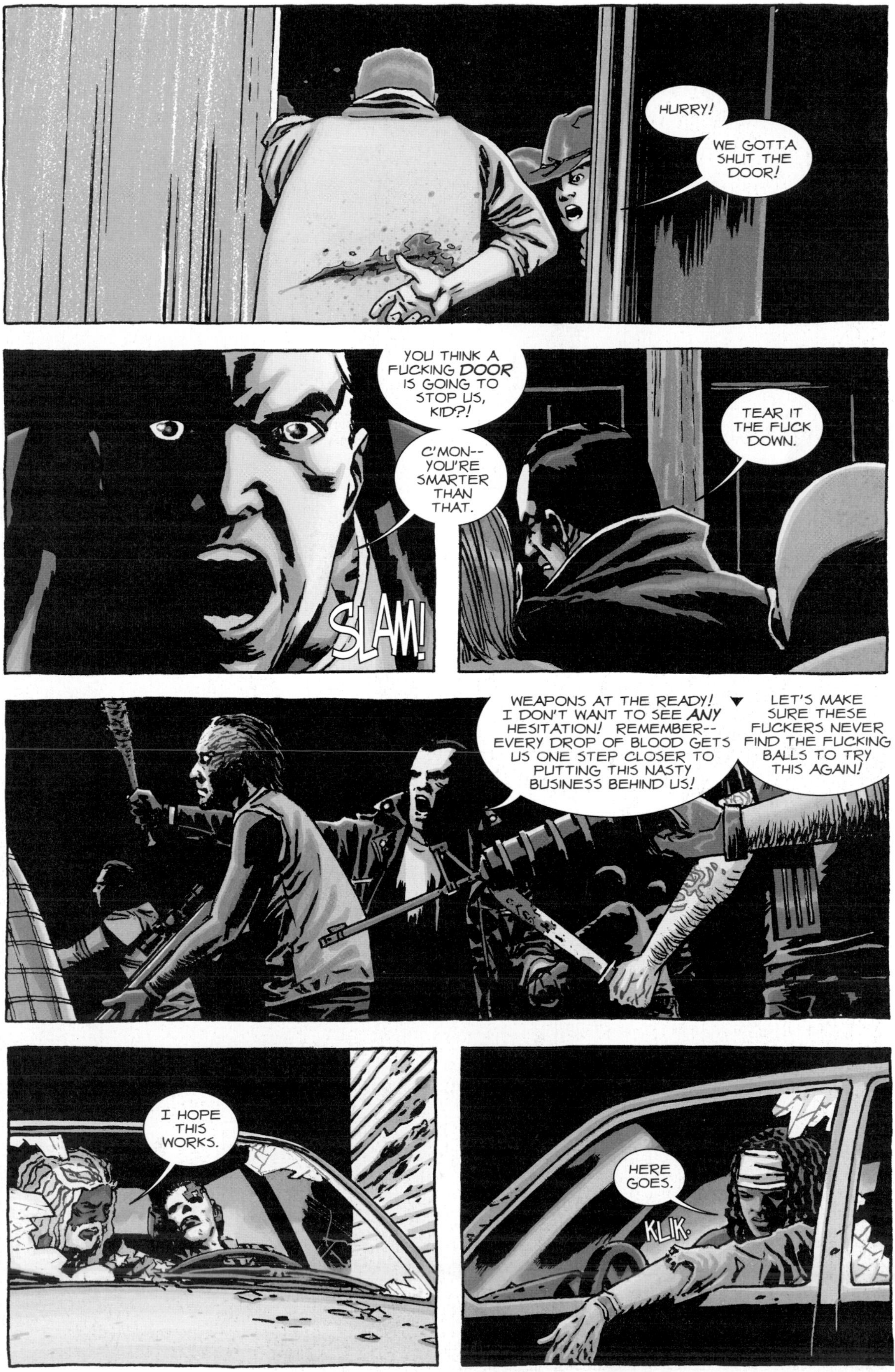
HURRY!
WE GOTTA SHUT THE DOOR!
YOU THINK A FUCKING DOOR IS GOING TO STOP US, KID?!
C'MON-- YOU'RE SMARTER THAN THAT.
SLAM!
TEAR IT THE FUCK DOWN.
WEAPONS AT THE READY! I DON'T WANT TO SEE ANY HESITATION! REMEMBER-- EVERY DROP OF BLOOD GETS US ONE STEP CLOSER TO PUTTING THIS NASTY BUSINESS BEHIND US!
LET'S MAKE SURE THESE FUCKERS NEVER FIND THE FUCKING BALLS TO TRY THIS AGAIN!
I HOPE THIS WORKS.
HERE GOES.
KLIK.

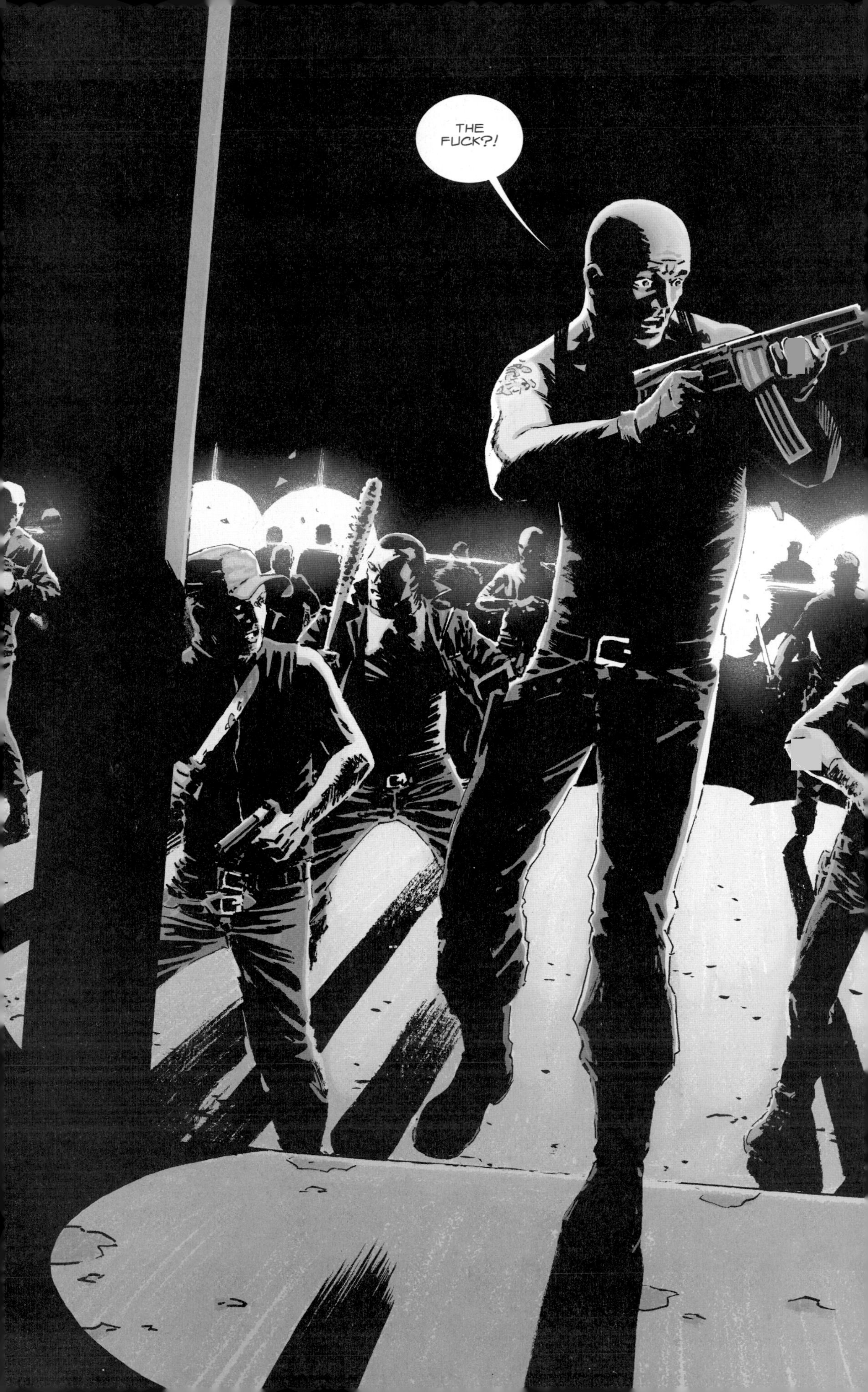
THE FUCK?!

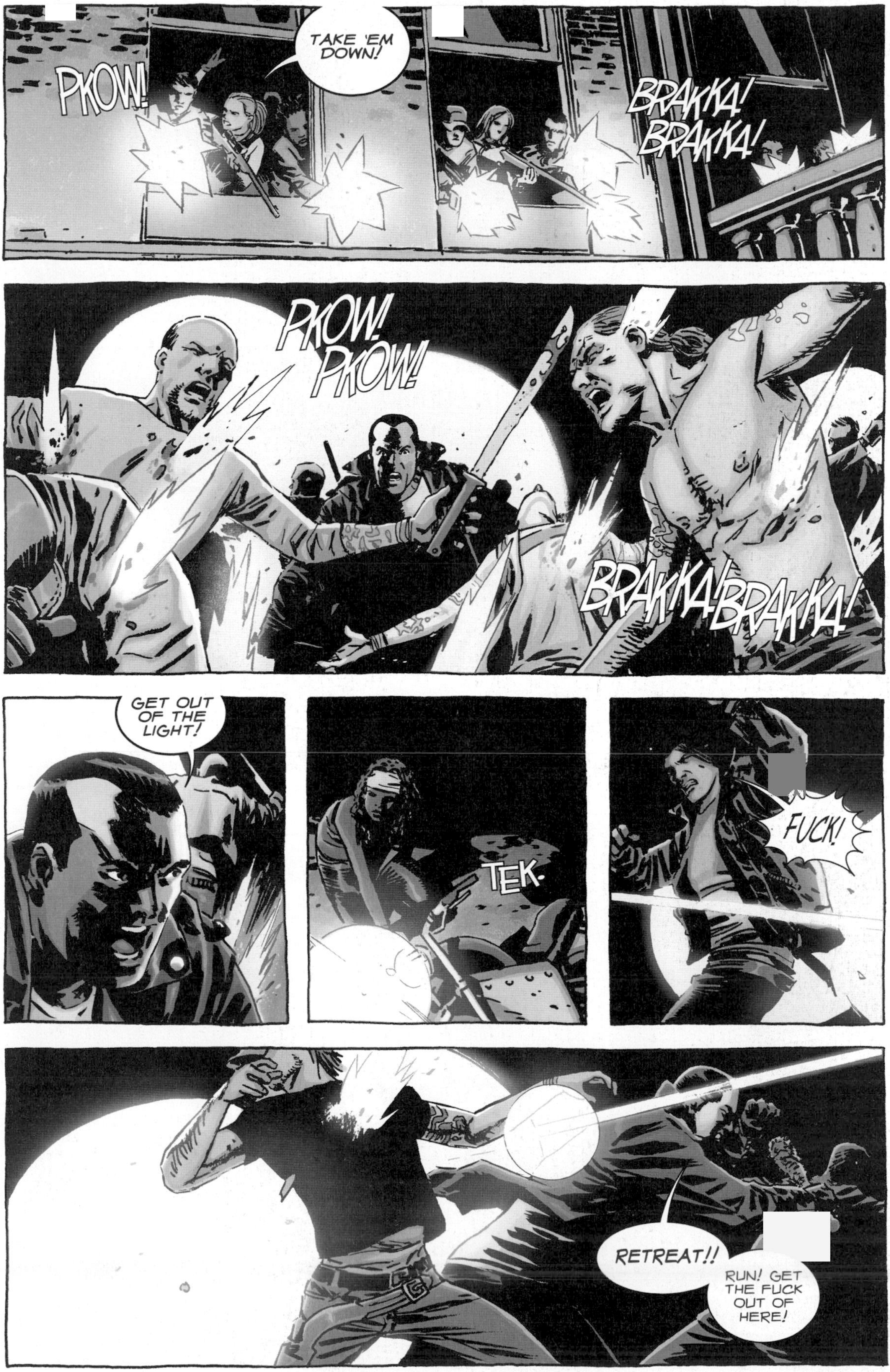
PKOW!
TAKE 'EM DOWN!
BRAKKA! BRAKKA!
PKOW! PKOW!
BRAKKA! BRAKKA!
GET OUT OF THE LIGHT!
TEK.
FUCK!
RETREAT!!
RUN! GET THE FUCK OUT OF HERE!

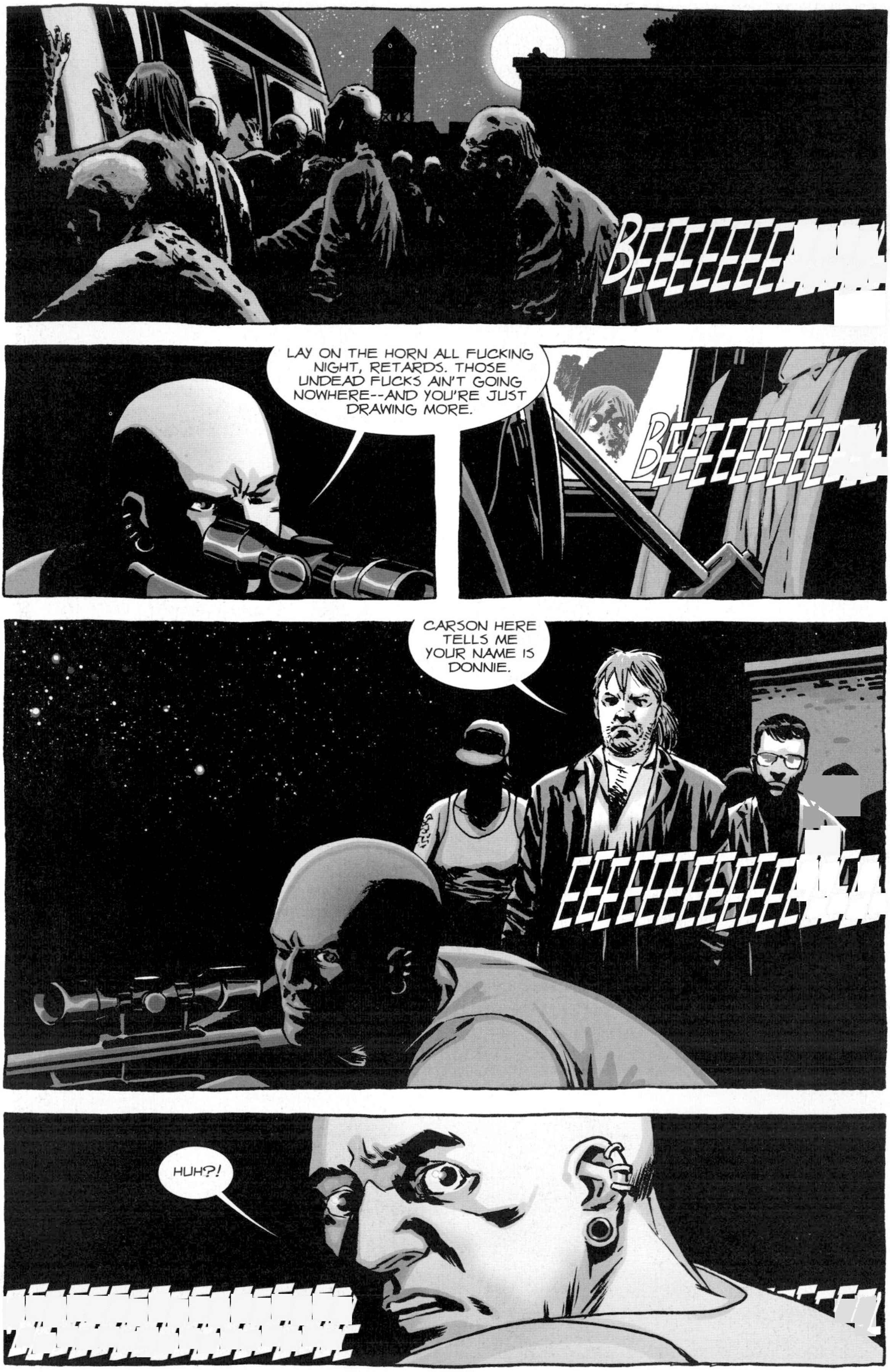
BEEEEEEEE
LAY ON THE HORN ALL FUCKING NIGHT, RETARDS. THOSE UNDEAD FUCKS AIN'T GOING NOWHERE--AND YOU'RE JUST DRAWING MORE.
BEEEEEEEEE
CARSON HERE TELLS ME YOUR NAME IS DONNIE.
EEEEEEEEEEE
HUH?!

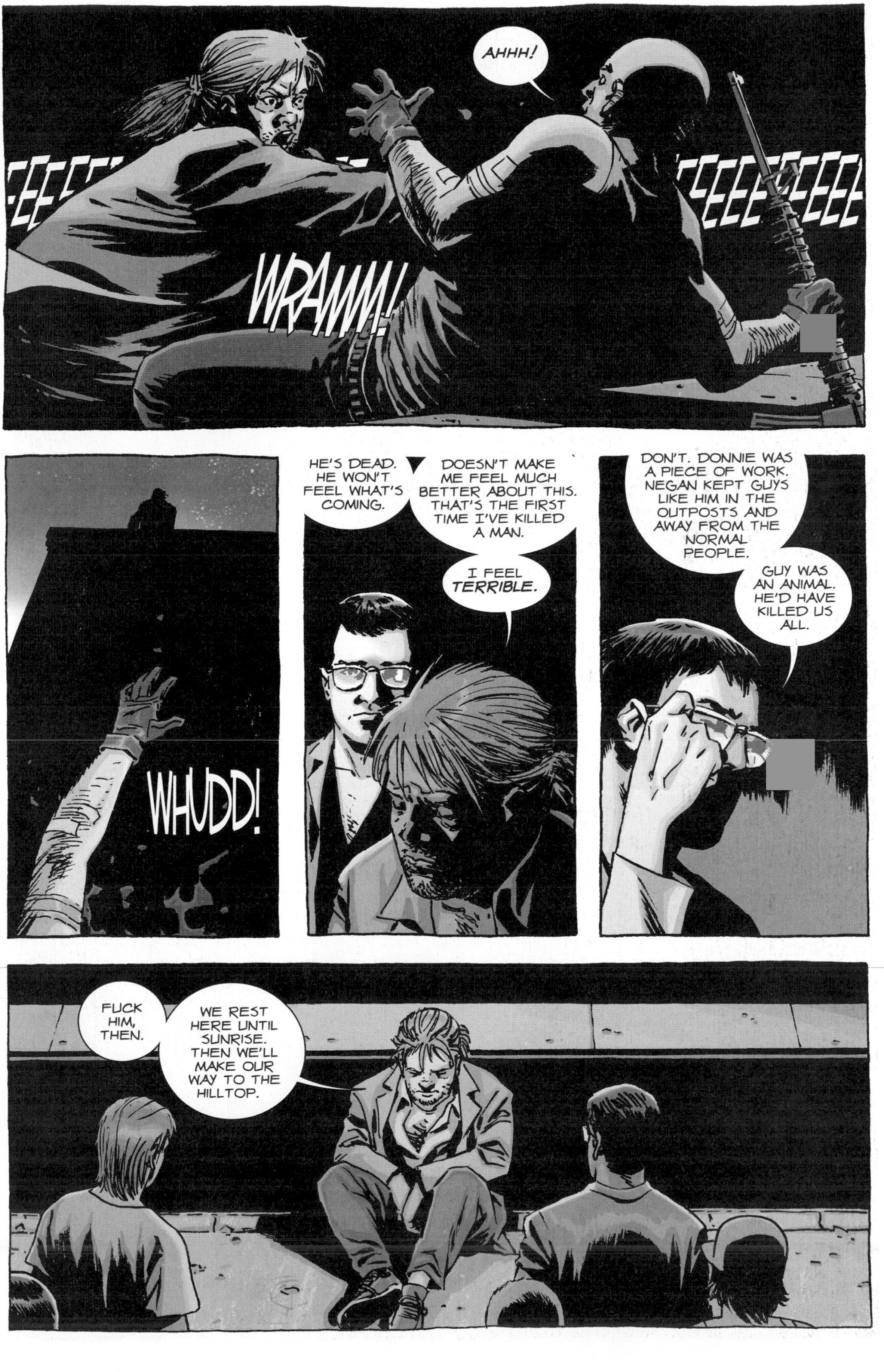
AHHH!
WRAMM!
WHUDD!
HE'S DEAD. HE WON'T FEEL WHAT'S COMING.
DOESN'T MAKE ME FEEL MUCH BETTER ABOUT THIS. THAT'S THE FIRST TIME I'VE KILLED A MAN.
I FEEL *TERRIBLE*.
DON'T. DONNIE WAS A PIECE OF WORK. NEGAN KEPT GUYS LIKE HIM IN THE OUTPOSTS AND AWAY FROM THE NORMAL PEOPLE.
GUY WAS AN ANIMAL. HE'D HAVE KILLED US ALL.
FUCK HIM, THEN.
WE REST HERE UNTIL SUNRISE. THEN WE'LL MAKE OUR WAY TO THE HILLTOP.

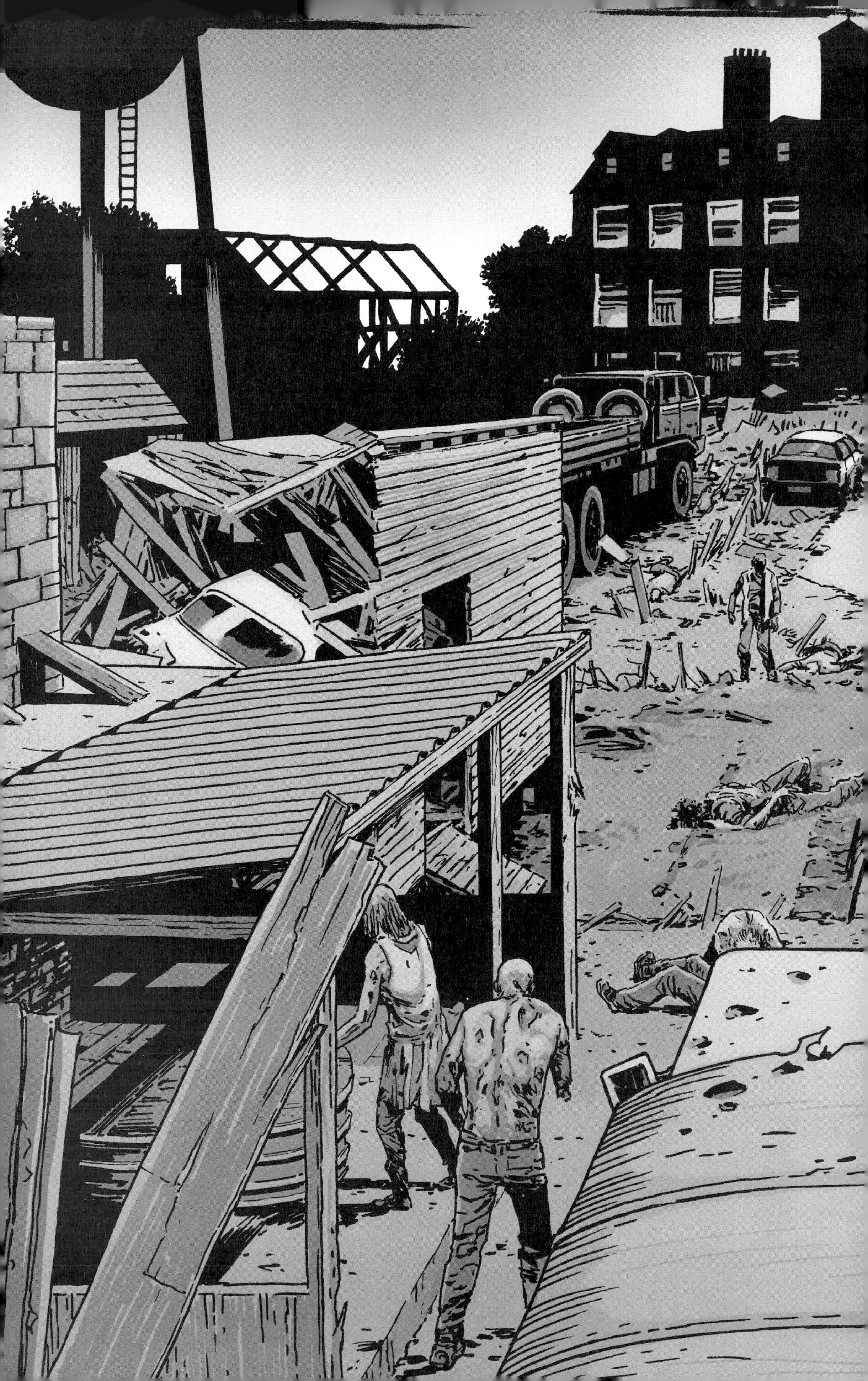

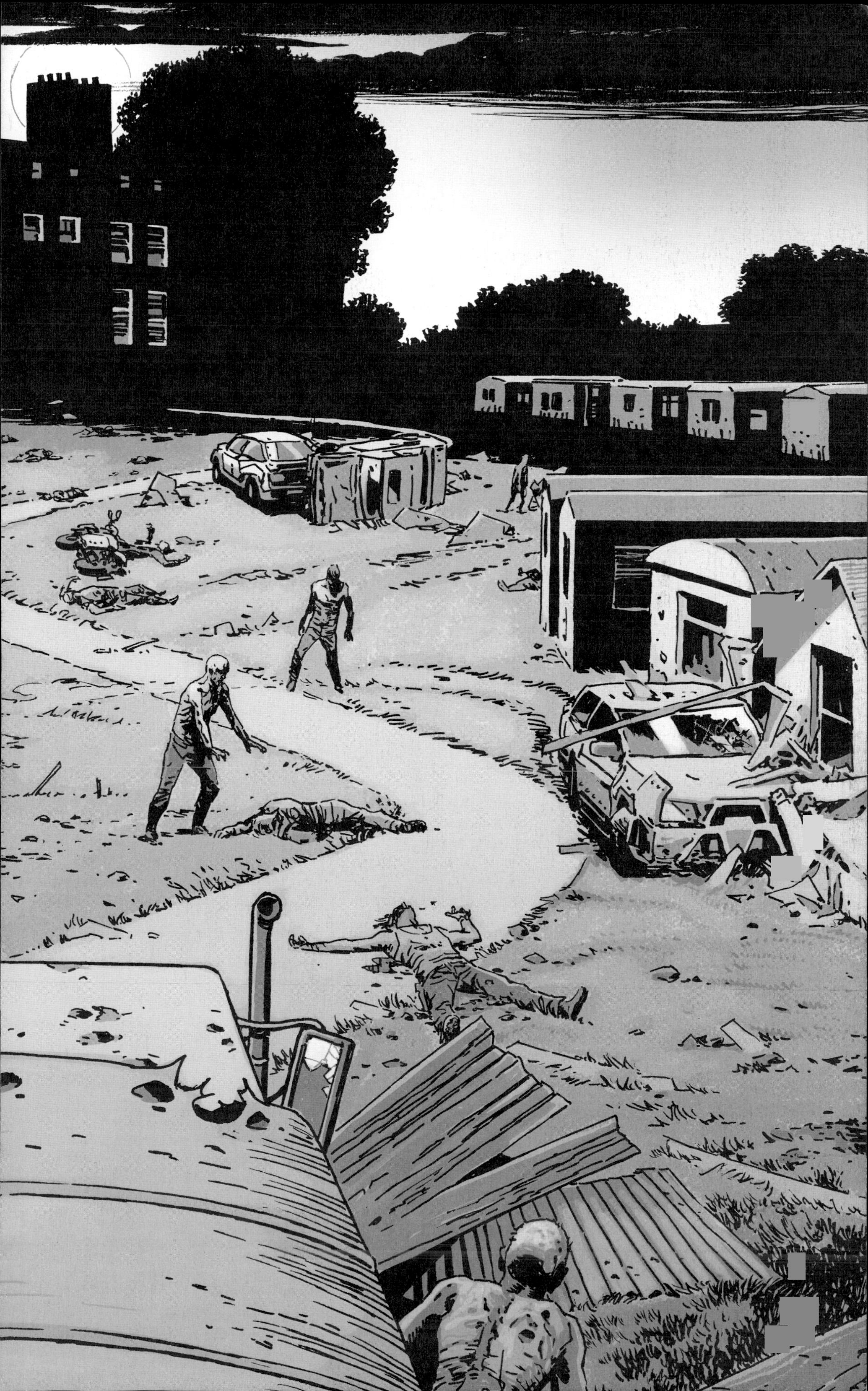

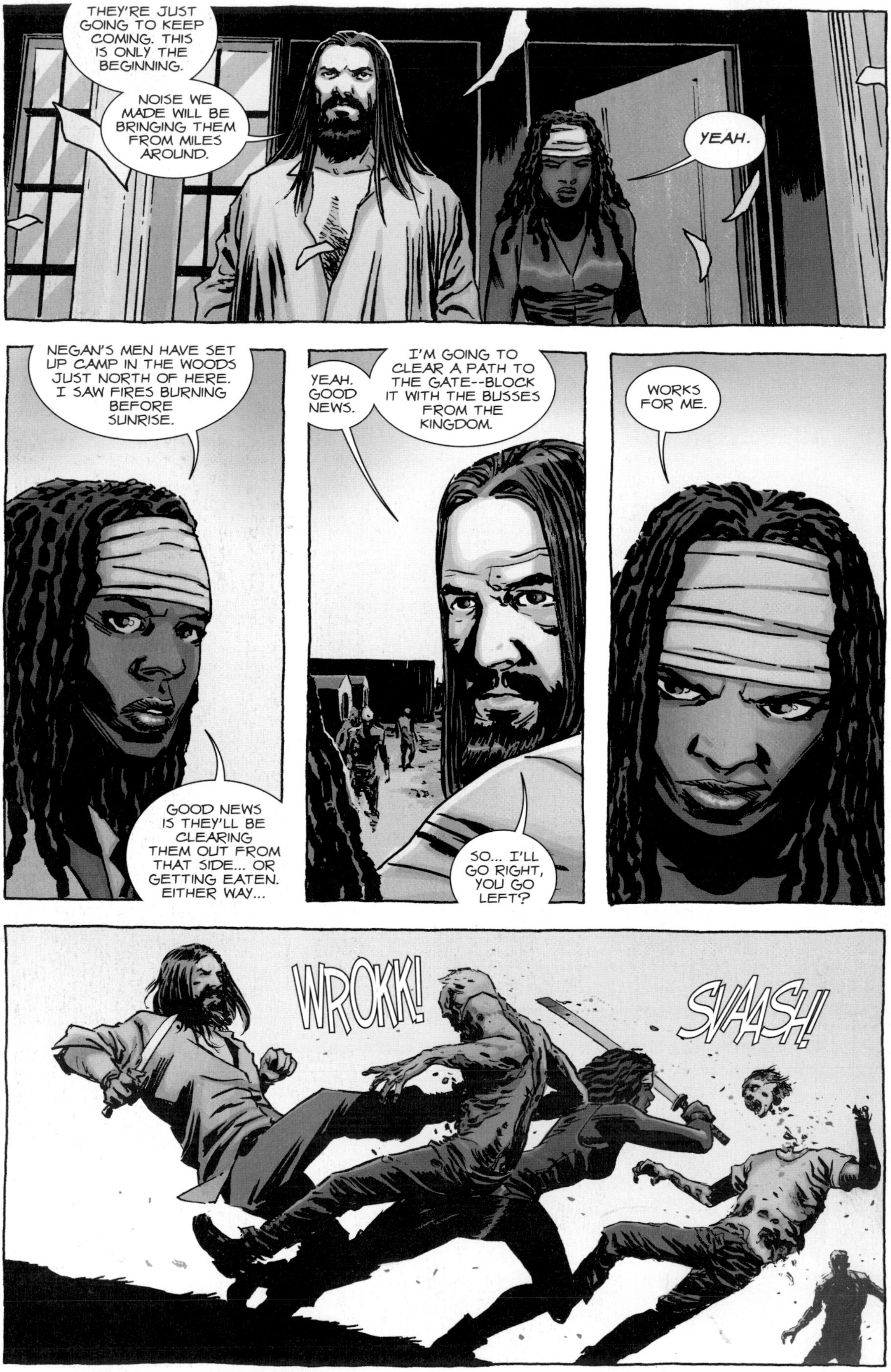
THEY'RE JUST GOING TO KEEP COMING. THIS IS ONLY THE BEGINNING.
NOISE WE MADE WILL BE BRINGING THEM FROM MILES AROUND.
YEAH.
NEGAN'S MEN HAVE SET UP CAMP IN THE WOODS JUST NORTH OF HERE. I SAW FIRES BURNING BEFORE SUNRISE.
GOOD NEWS IS THEY'LL BE CLEARING THEM OUT FROM THAT SIDE... OR GETTING EATEN. EITHER WAY...
YEAH. GOOD NEWS.
I'M GOING TO CLEAR A PATH TO THE GATE--BLOCK IT WITH THE BUSSES FROM THE KINGDOM.
SO... I'LL GO RIGHT, YOU GO LEFT?
WORKS FOR ME.
WROKK!
SVAASH!

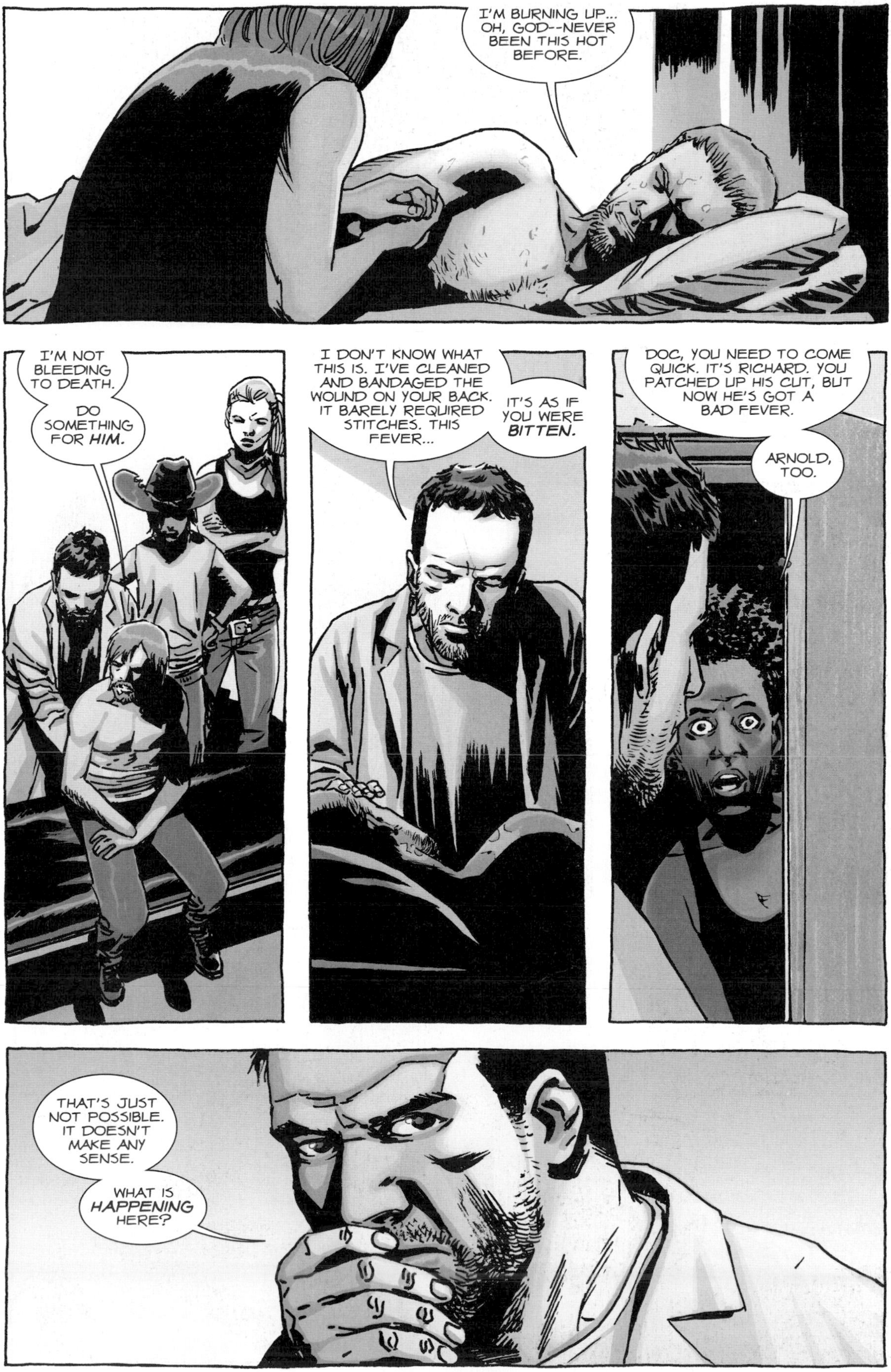
I'M BURNING UP... OH, GOD--NEVER BEEN THIS HOT BEFORE.
I'M NOT BLEEDING TO DEATH.
DO SOMETHING FOR *HIM*.
I DON'T KNOW WHAT THIS IS. I'VE CLEANED AND BANDAGED THE WOUND ON YOUR BACK. IT BARELY REQUIRED STITCHES. THIS FEVER...
IT'S AS IF YOU WERE *BITTEN*.
DOC, YOU NEED TO COME QUICK. IT'S RICHARD. YOU PATCHED UP HIS CUT, BUT NOW HE'S GOT A BAD FEVER.
ARNOLD, TOO.
THAT'S JUST NOT POSSIBLE. IT DOESN'T MAKE ANY SENSE.
WHAT IS *HAPPENING* HERE?

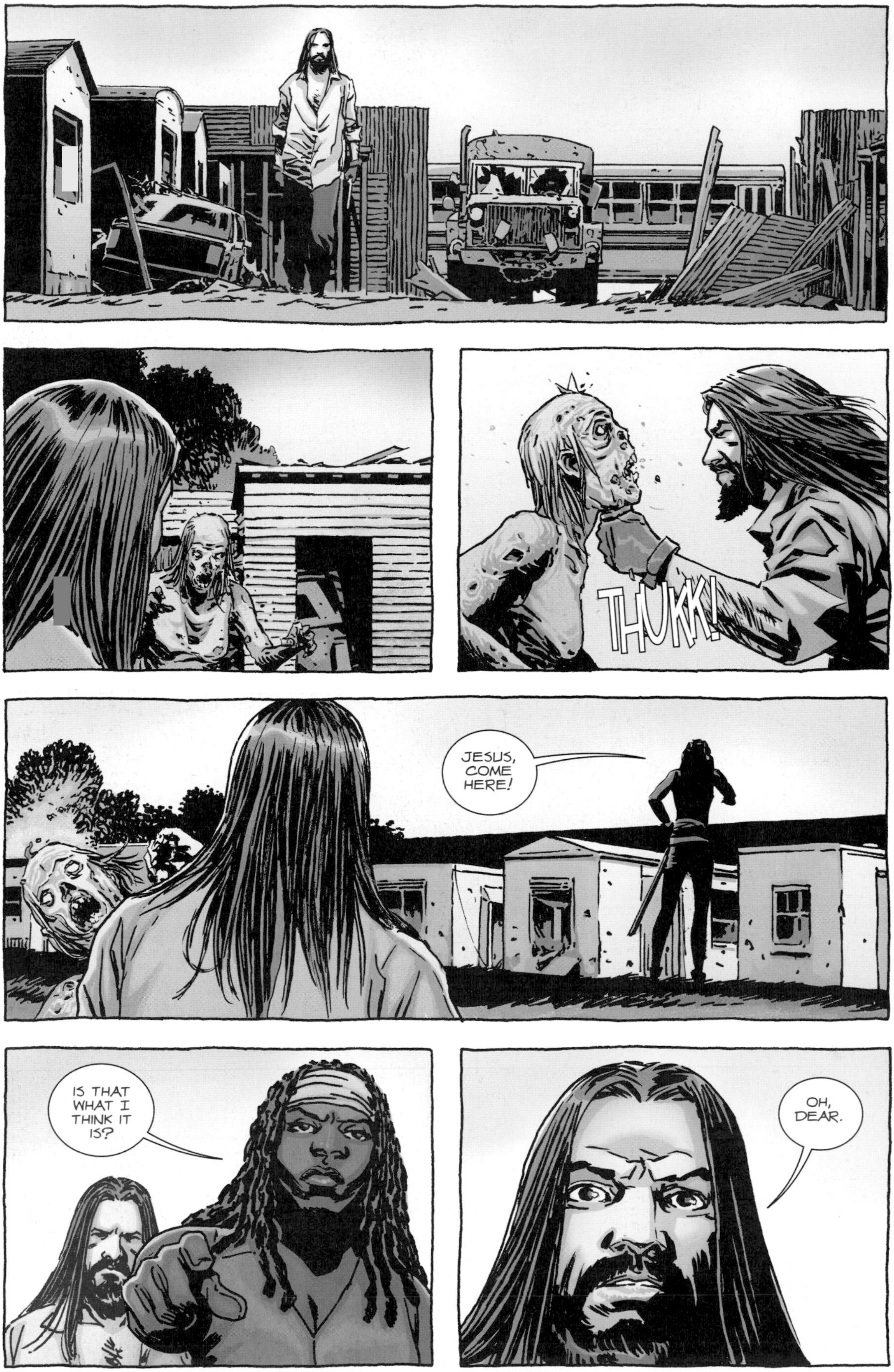
THUKK!
JESUS, COME HERE!
IS THAT WHAT I THINK IT IS?
OH, DEAR.

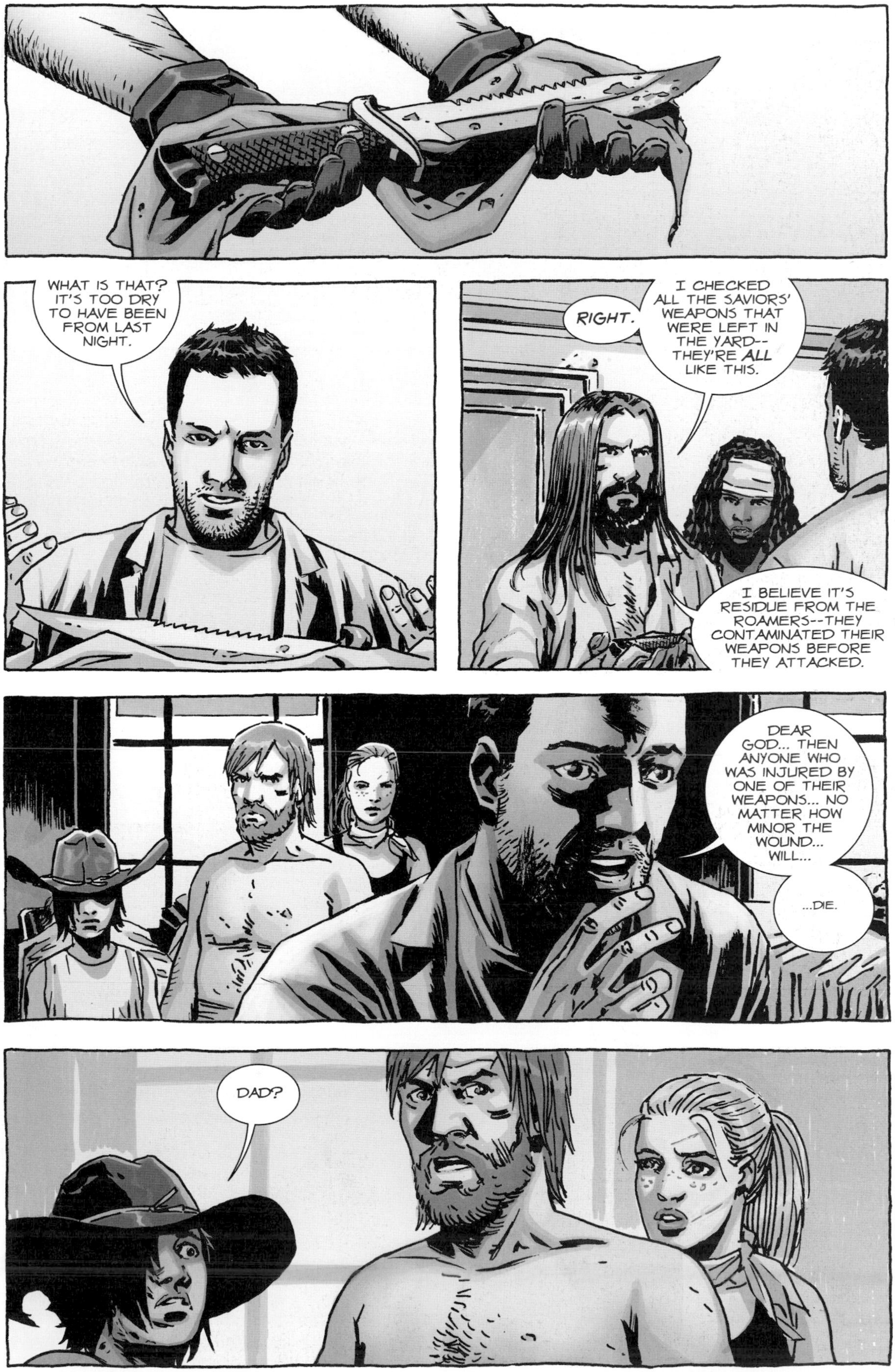
WHAT IS THAT? IT'S TOO DRY TO HAVE BEEN FROM LAST NIGHT.
RIGHT.
I CHECKED ALL THE SAVIORS' WEAPONS THAT WERE LEFT IN THE YARD-- THEY'RE ALL LIKE THIS.
I BELIEVE IT'S RESIDUE FROM THE ROAMERS--THEY CONTAMINATED THEIR WEAPONS BEFORE THEY ATTACKED.
DEAR GOD... THEN ANYONE WHO WAS INJURED BY ONE OF THEIR WEAPONS... NO MATTER HOW MINOR THE WOUND... WILL...
...DIE.
DAD?

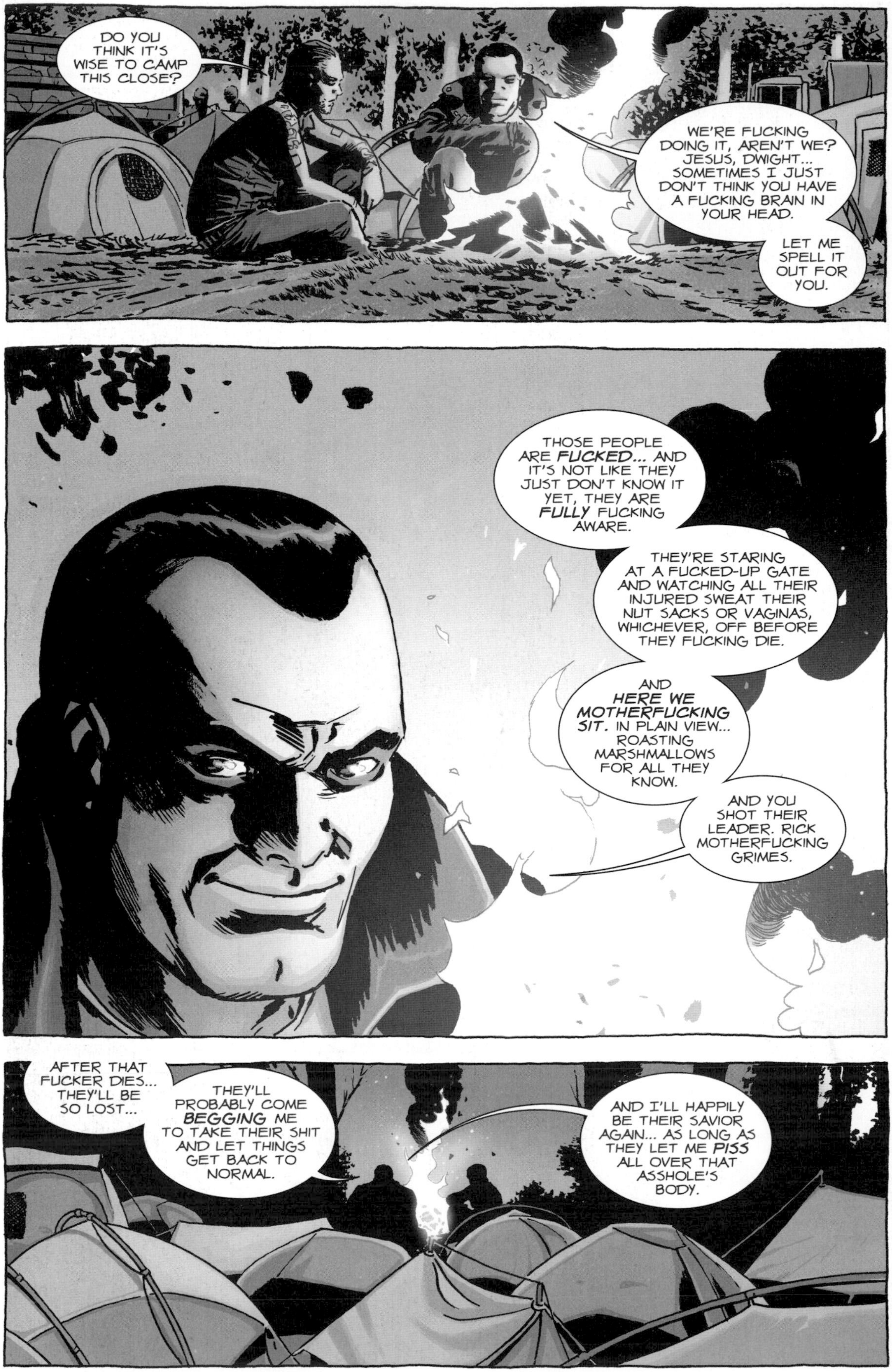
DO YOU THINK IT'S WISE TO CAMP THIS CLOSE?
WE'RE FUCKING DOING IT, AREN'T WE? JESUS, DWIGHT... SOMETIMES I JUST DON'T THINK YOU HAVE A FUCKING BRAIN IN YOUR HEAD.
LET ME SPELL IT OUT FOR YOU.
THOSE PEOPLE ARE FUCKED... AND IT'S NOT LIKE THEY JUST DON'T KNOW IT YET, THEY ARE FULLY FUCKING AWARE.
THEY'RE STARING AT A FUCKED-UP GATE AND WATCHING ALL THEIR INJURED SWEAT THEIR NUT SACKS OR VAGINAS, WHICHEVER, OFF BEFORE THEY FUCKING DIE.
AND HERE WE MOTHERFUCKING SIT. IN PLAIN VIEW... ROASTING MARSHMALLOWS FOR ALL THEY KNOW.
AND YOU SHOT THEIR LEADER. RICK MOTHERFUCKING GRIMES.
AFTER THAT FUCKER DIES... THEY'LL BE SO LOST...
THEY'LL PROBABLY COME BEGGING ME TO TAKE THEIR SHIT AND LET THINGS GET BACK TO NORMAL.
AND I'LL HAPPILY BE THEIR SAVIOR AGAIN... AS LONG AS THEY LET ME PISS ALL OVER THAT ASSHOLE'S BODY.

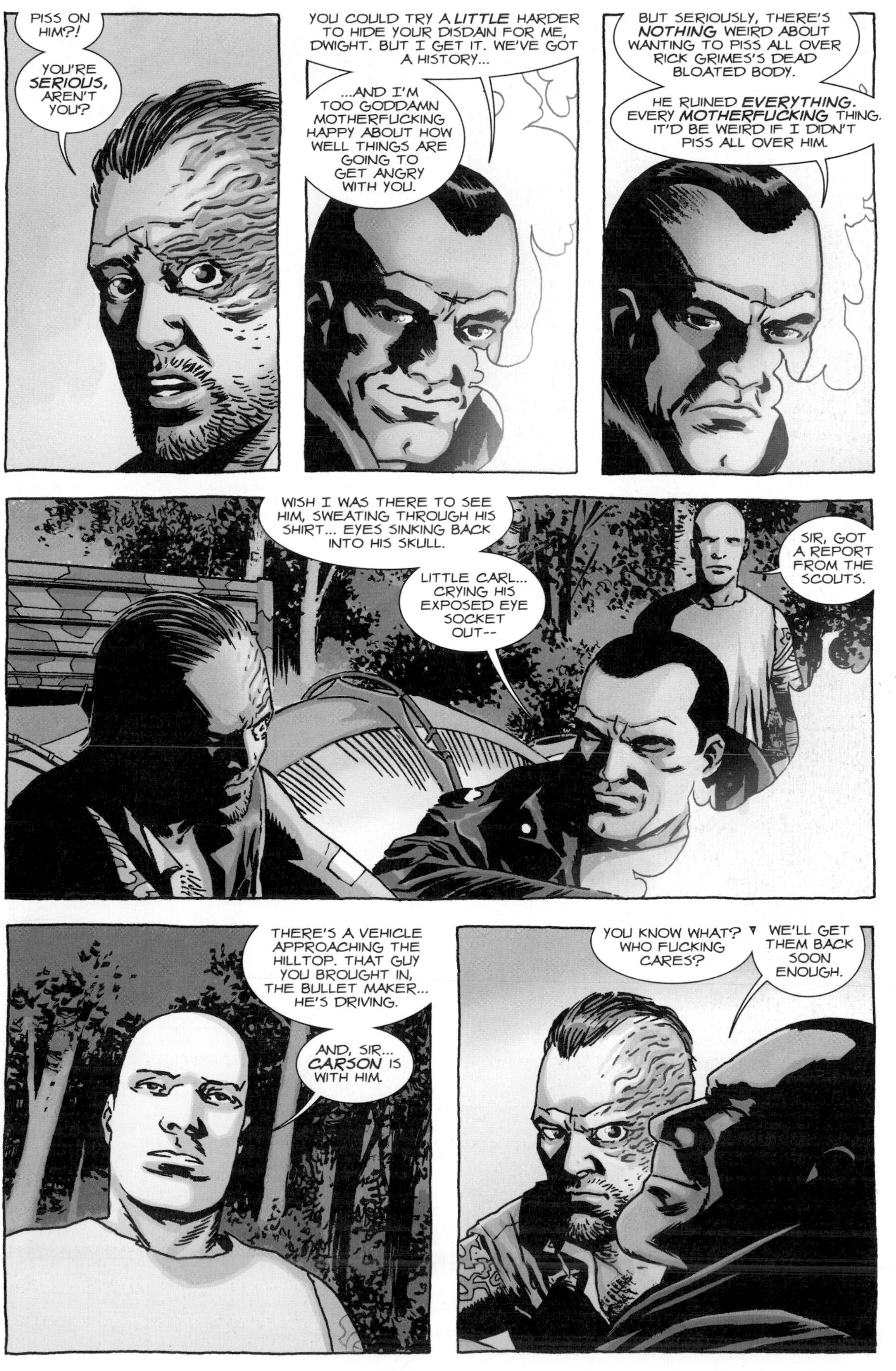
PISS ON HIM?!
YOU'RE SERIOUS, AREN'T YOU?
YOU COULD TRY A LITTLE HARDER TO HIDE YOUR DISDAIN FOR ME, DWIGHT. BUT I GET IT. WE'VE GOT A HISTORY...
...AND I'M TOO GODDAMN MOTHERFUCKING HAPPY ABOUT HOW WELL THINGS ARE GOING TO GET ANGRY WITH YOU.
BUT SERIOUSLY, THERE'S NOTHING WEIRD ABOUT WANTING TO PISS ALL OVER RICK GRIMES'S DEAD BLOATED BODY.
HE RUINED EVERYTHING. EVERY MOTHERFUCKING THING. IT'D BE WEIRD IF I DIDN'T PISS ALL OVER HIM.
WISH I WAS THERE TO SEE HIM, SWEATING THROUGH HIS SHIRT... EYES SINKING BACK INTO HIS SKULL.
LITTLE CARL... CRYING HIS EXPOSED EYE SOCKET OUT--
SIR, GOT A REPORT FROM THE SCOUTS.
THERE'S A VEHICLE APPROACHING THE HILLTOP. THAT GUY YOU BROUGHT IN, THE BULLET MAKER... HE'S DRIVING.
AND, SIR... CARSON IS WITH HIM.
YOU KNOW WHAT? WHO FUCKING CARES?
WE'LL GET THEM BACK SOON ENOUGH.

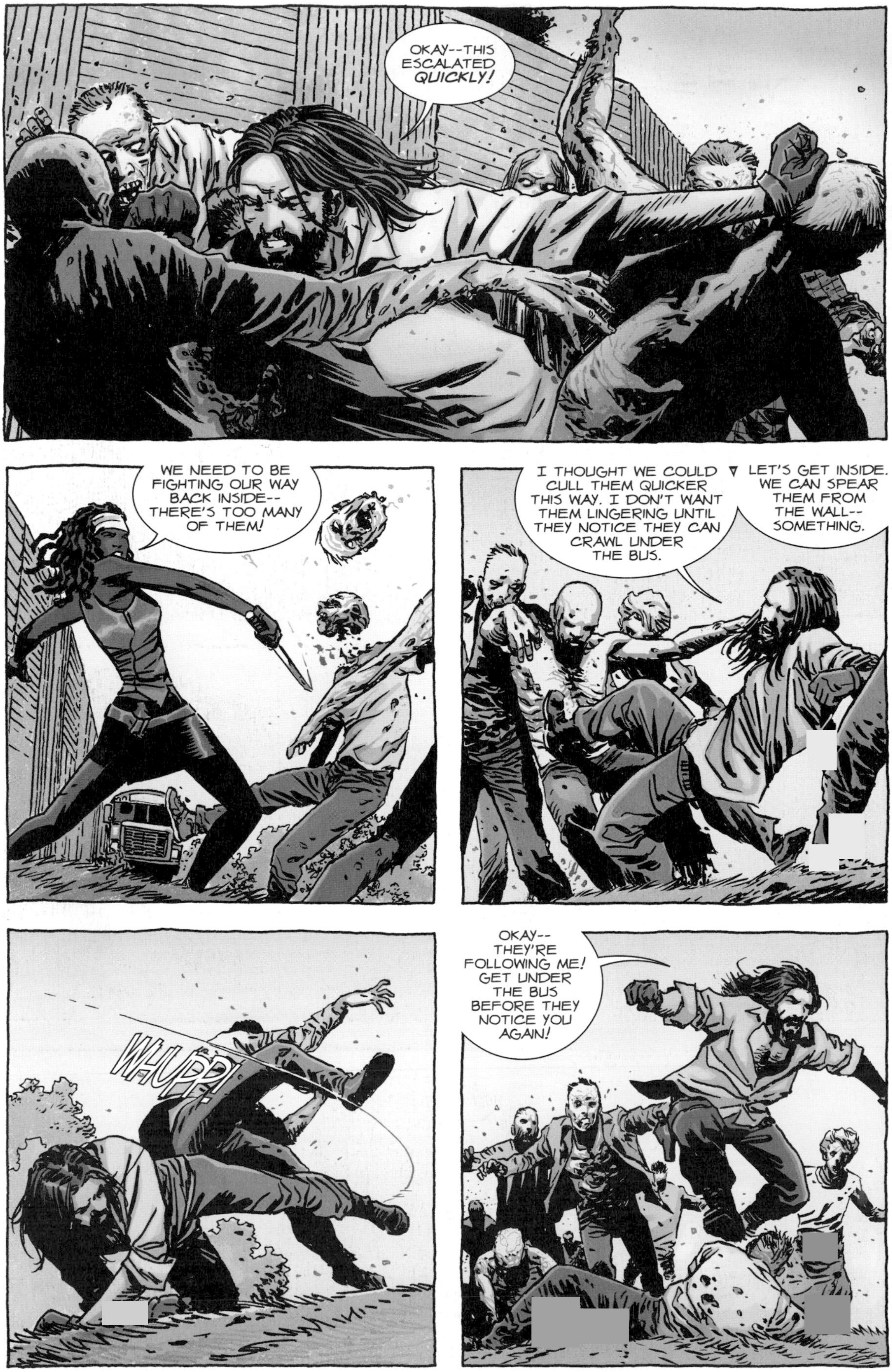
OKAY--THIS ESCALATED QUICKLY!
WE NEED TO BE FIGHTING OUR WAY BACK INSIDE-- THERE'S TOO MANY OF THEM!
I THOUGHT WE COULD CULL THEM QUICKER THIS WAY. I DON'T WANT THEM LINGERING UNTIL THEY NOTICE THEY CAN CRAWL UNDER THE BUS.
LET'S GET INSIDE. WE CAN SPEAR THEM FROM THE WALL-- SOMETHING.
WHUPP!
OKAY-- THEY'RE FOLLOWING ME! GET UNDER THE BUS BEFORE THEY NOTICE YOU AGAIN!

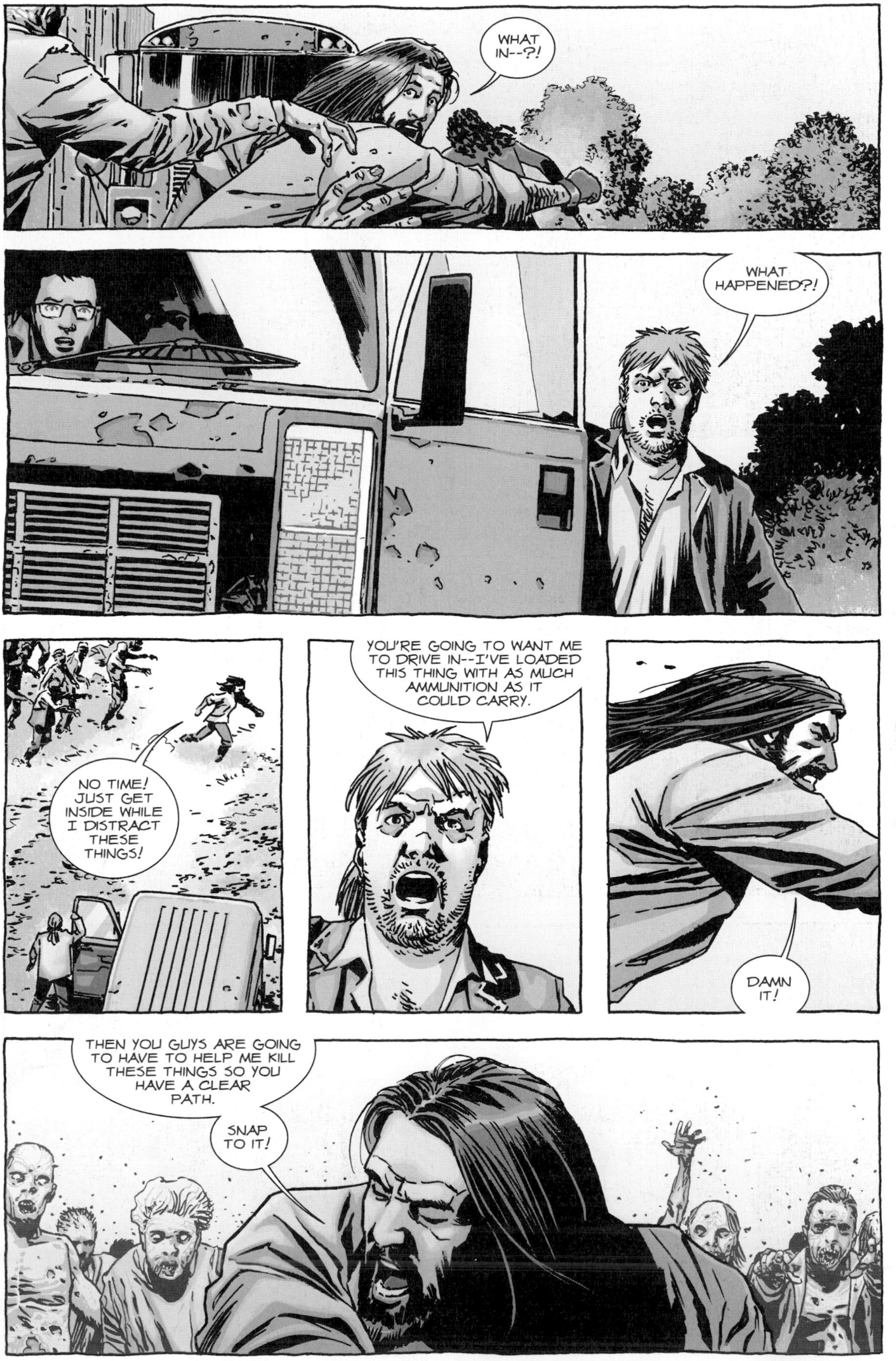

WHAT IN--?!
WHAT HAPPENED?!
NO TIME! JUST GET INSIDE WHILE I DISTRACT THESE THINGS!
YOU'RE GOING TO WANT ME TO DRIVE IN--I'VE LOADED THIS THING WITH AS MUCH AMMUNITION AS IT COULD CARRY.
DAMN IT!
THEN YOU GUYS ARE GOING TO HAVE TO HELP ME KILL THESE THINGS SO YOU HAVE A CLEAR PATH.
SNAP TO IT!

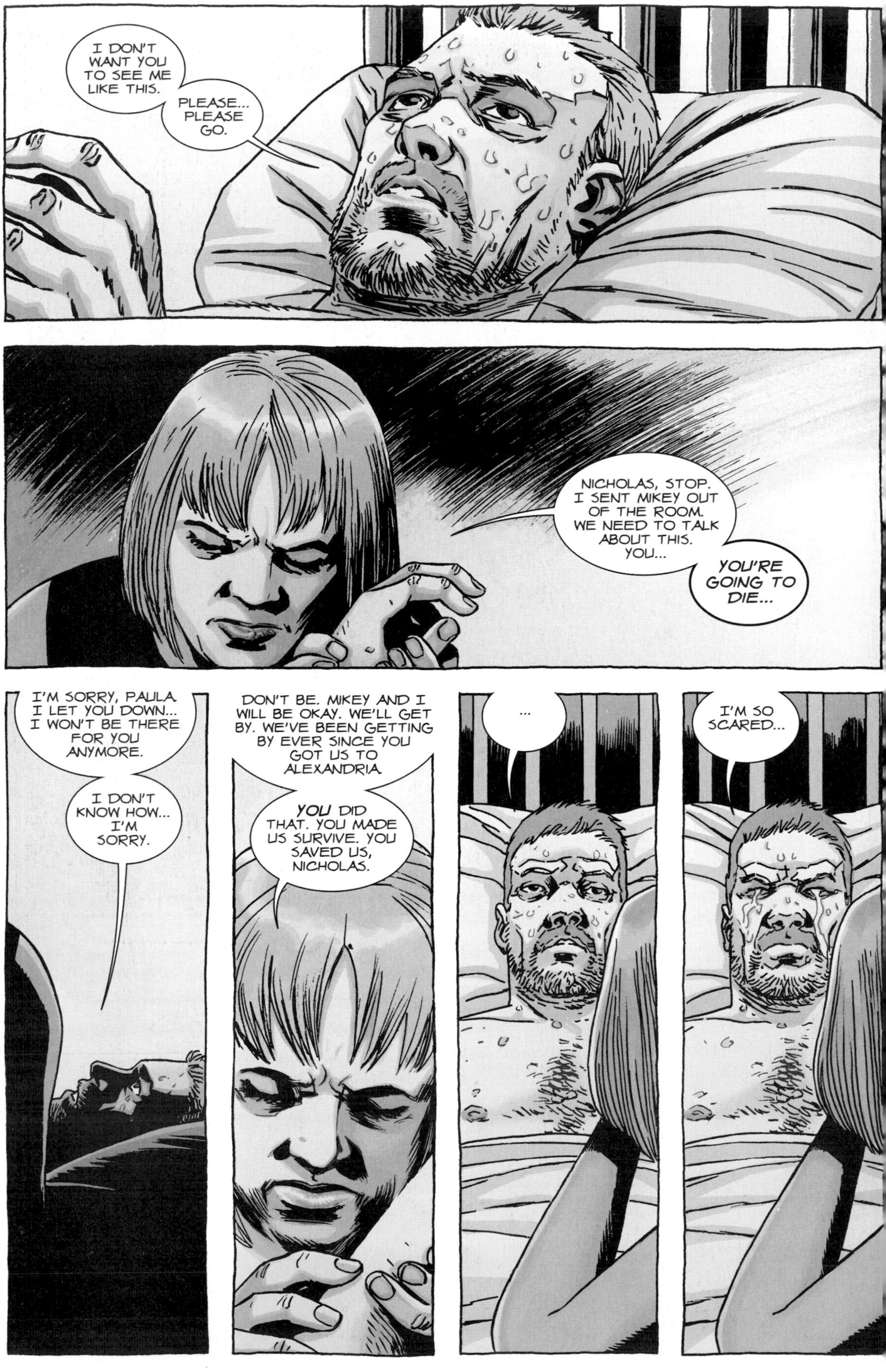
I DON'T WANT YOU TO SEE ME LIKE THIS.
PLEASE... PLEASE GO.
NICHOLAS, STOP. I SENT MIKEY OUT OF THE ROOM. WE NEED TO TALK ABOUT THIS. YOU...
YOU'RE GOING TO DIE...
I'M SORRY, PAULA. I LET YOU DOWN... I WON'T BE THERE FOR YOU ANYMORE.
I DON'T KNOW HOW... I'M SORRY.
DON'T BE. MIKEY AND I WILL BE OKAY. WE'LL GET BY. WE'VE BEEN GETTING BY EVER SINCE YOU GOT US TO ALEXANDRIA.
YOU DID THAT. YOU MADE US SURVIVE. YOU SAVED US, NICHOLAS.
...
I'M SO SCARED...

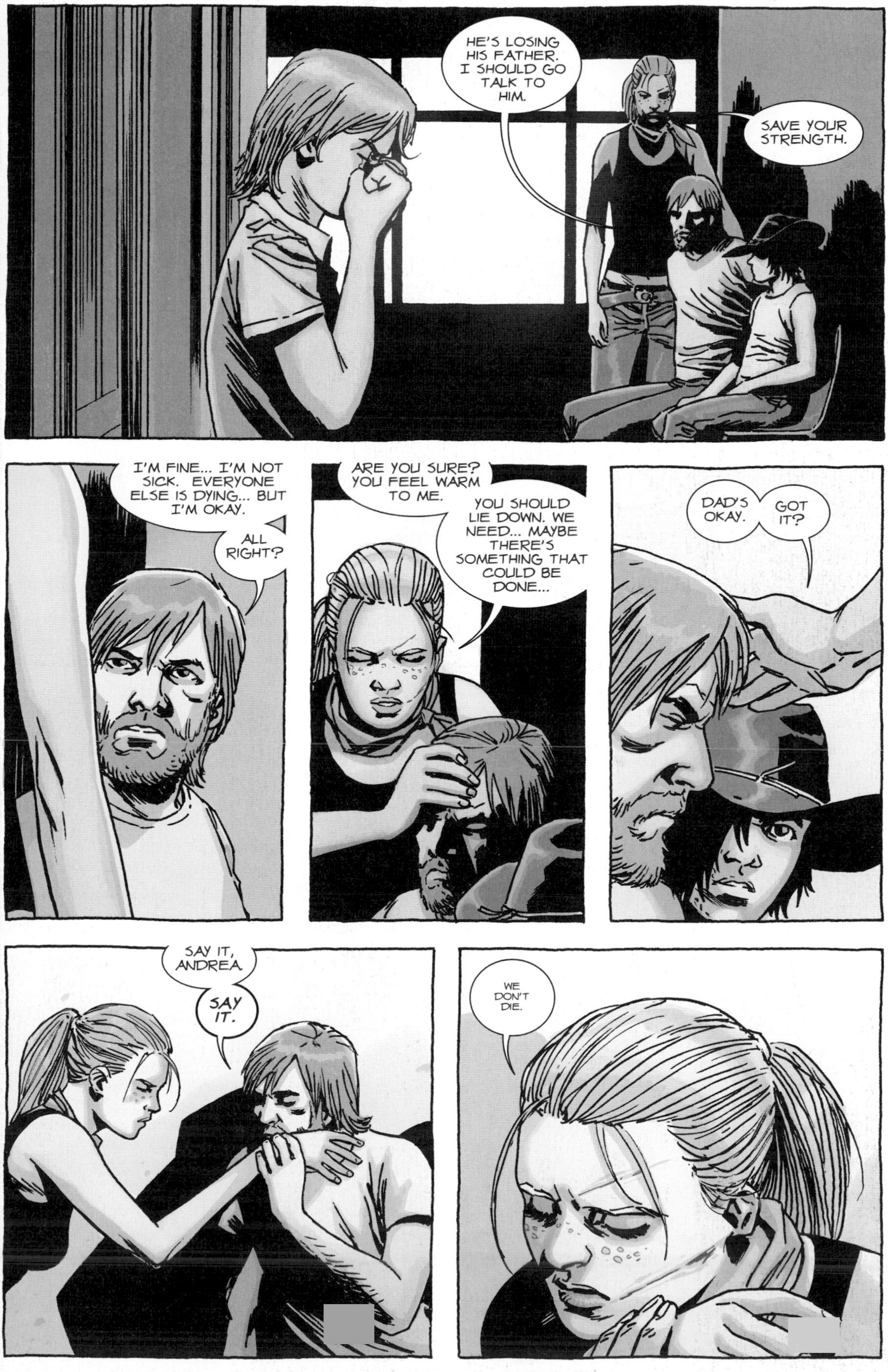
HE'S LOSING HIS FATHER. I SHOULD GO TALK TO HIM.
SAVE YOUR STRENGTH.
I'M FINE... I'M NOT SICK. EVERYONE ELSE IS DYING... BUT I'M OKAY.
ALL RIGHT?
ARE YOU SURE? YOU FEEL WARM TO ME.
YOU SHOULD LIE DOWN. WE NEED... MAYBE THERE'S SOMETHING THAT COULD BE DONE...
DAD'S OKAY.
GOT IT?
SAY IT, ANDREA.
SAY IT.
WE DON'T DIE.

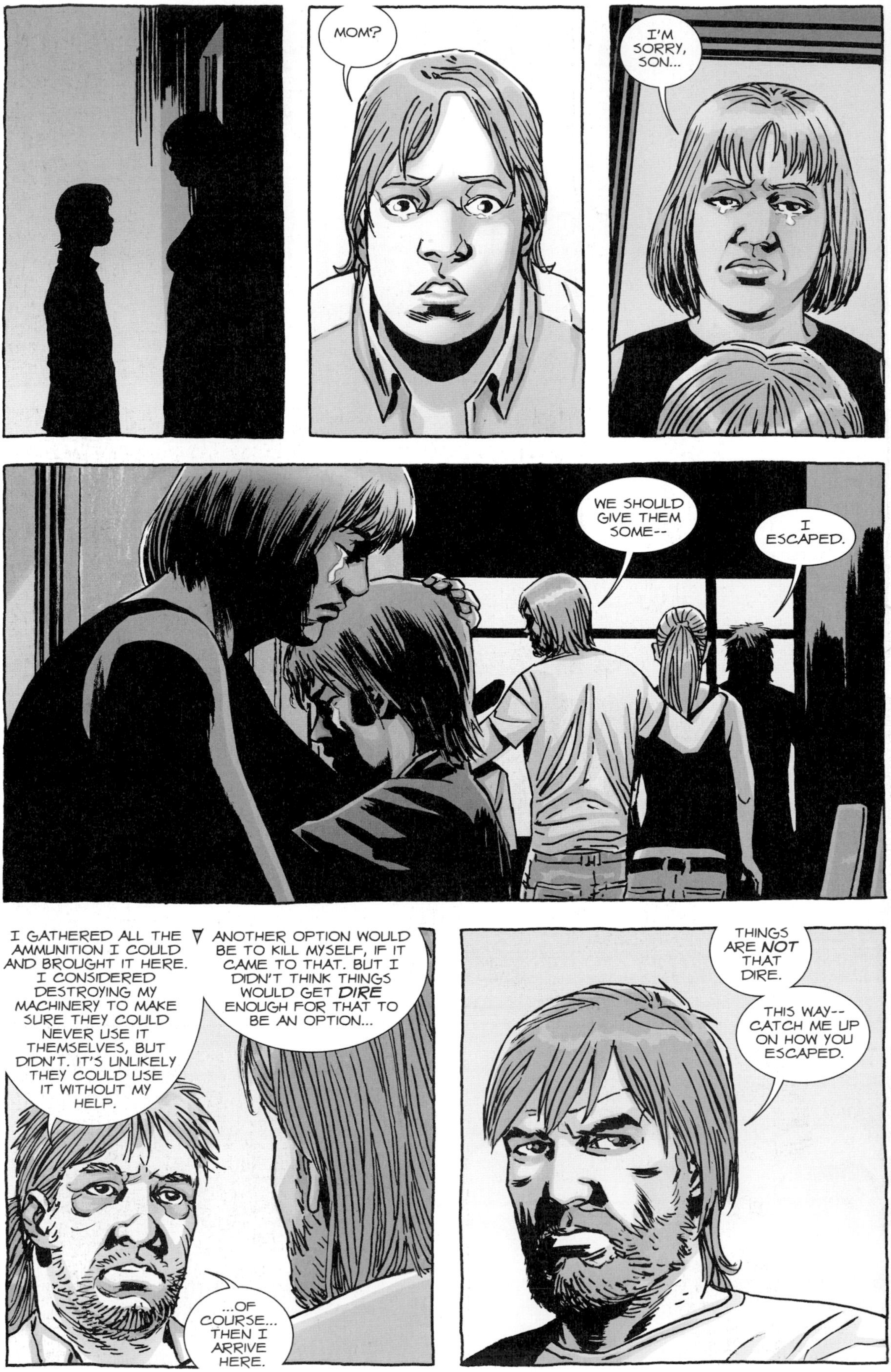
MOM?
I'M SORRY, SON...
WE SHOULD GIVE THEM SOME--
I ESCAPED.
I GATHERED ALL THE AMMUNITION I COULD AND BROUGHT IT HERE. I CONSIDERED DESTROYING MY MACHINERY TO MAKE SURE THEY COULD NEVER USE IT THEMSELVES, BUT DIDN'T. IT'S UNLIKELY THEY COULD USE IT WITHOUT MY HELP.
ANOTHER OPTION WOULD BE TO KILL MYSELF, IF IT CAME TO THAT. BUT I DIDN'T THINK THINGS WOULD GET DIRE ENOUGH FOR THAT TO BE AN OPTION...
...OF COURSE... THEN I ARRIVE HERE.
THINGS ARE NOT THAT DIRE.
THIS WAY-- CATCH ME UP ON HOW YOU ESCAPED.

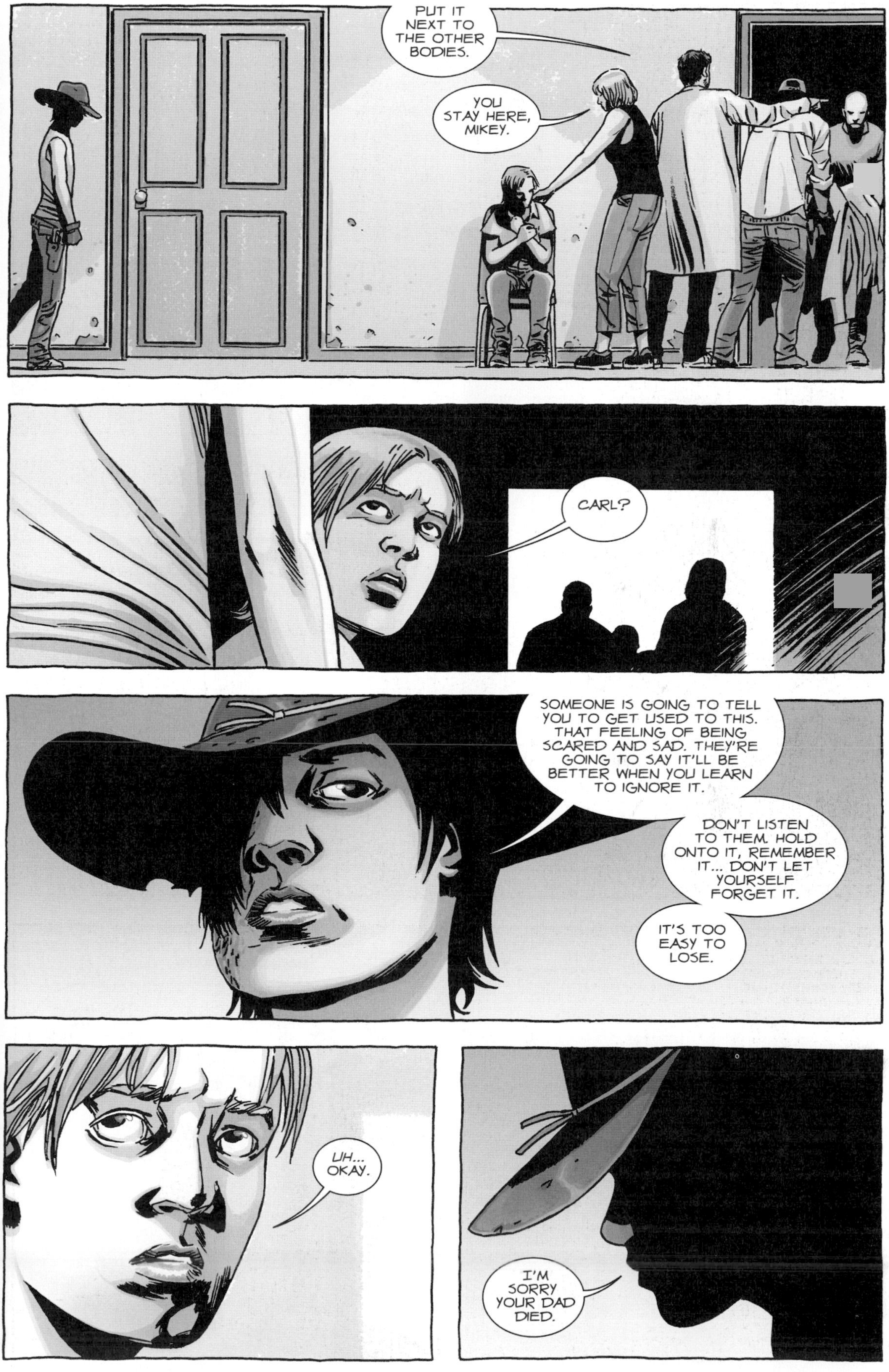
PUT IT NEXT TO THE OTHER BODIES.
YOU STAY HERE, MIKEY.
CARL?
SOMEONE IS GOING TO TELL YOU TO GET USED TO THIS. THAT FEELING OF BEING SCARED AND SAD. THEY'RE GOING TO SAY IT'LL BE BETTER WHEN YOU LEARN TO IGNORE IT.
DON'T LISTEN TO THEM. HOLD ONTO IT, REMEMBER IT... DON'T LET YOURSELF FORGET IT.
IT'S TOO EASY TO LOSE.
UH... OKAY.
I'M SORRY YOUR DAD DIED.

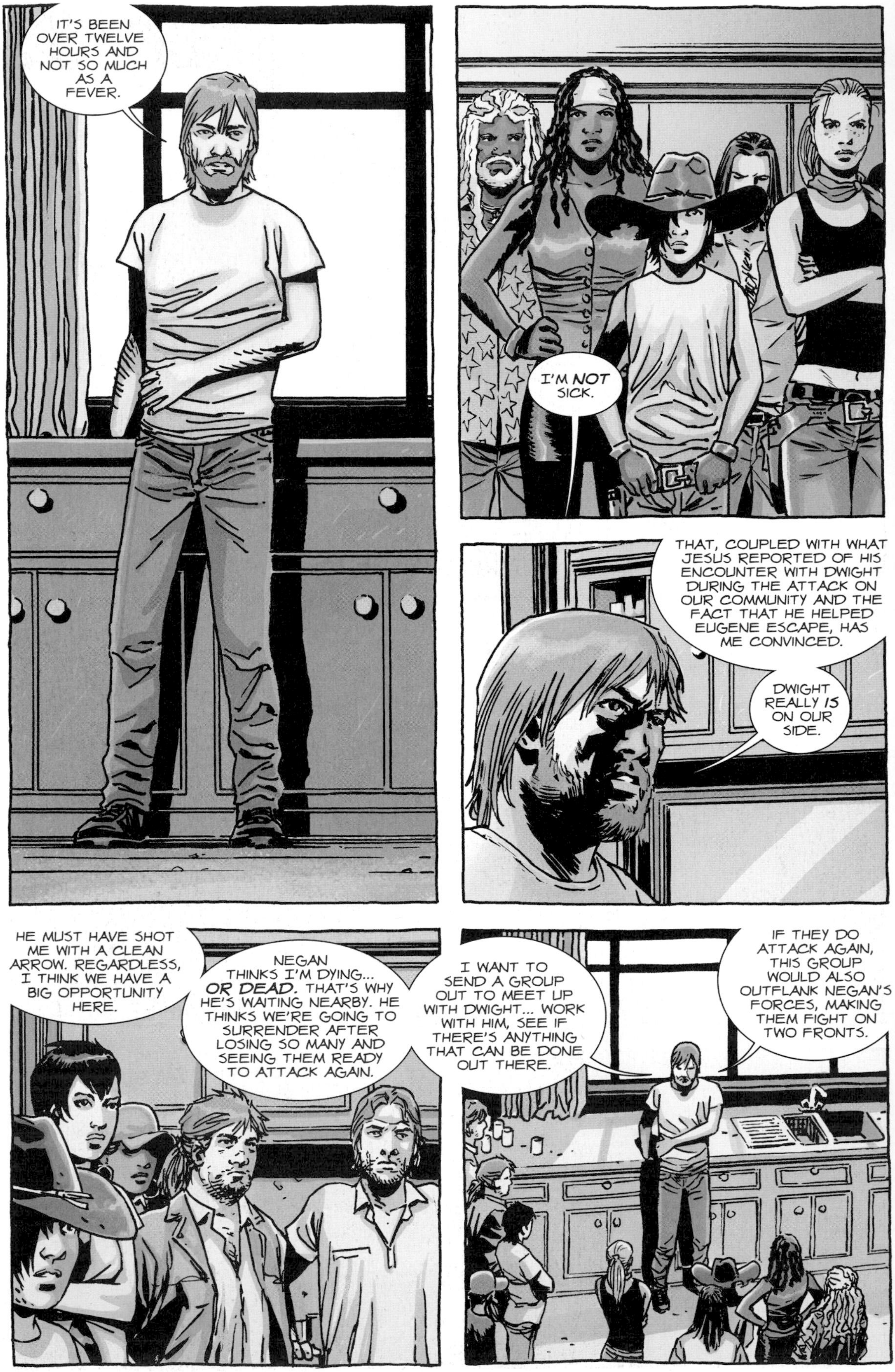
IT'S BEEN OVER TWELVE HOURS AND NOT SO MUCH AS A FEVER.
I'M NOT SICK.
THAT, COUPLED WITH WHAT JESUS REPORTED OF HIS ENCOUNTER WITH DWIGHT DURING THE ATTACK ON OUR COMMUNITY AND THE FACT THAT HE HELPED EUGENE ESCAPE, HAS ME CONVINCED.
DWIGHT REALLY IS ON OUR SIDE.
HE MUST HAVE SHOT ME WITH A CLEAN ARROW. REGARDLESS, I THINK WE HAVE A BIG OPPORTUNITY HERE.
NEGAN THINKS I'M DYING... OR DEAD. THAT'S WHY HE'S WAITING NEARBY. HE THINKS WE'RE GOING TO SURRENDER AFTER LOSING SO MANY AND SEEING THEM READY TO ATTACK AGAIN.
I WANT TO SEND A GROUP OUT TO MEET UP WITH DWIGHT... WORK WITH HIM, SEE IF THERE'S ANYTHING THAT CAN BE DONE OUT THERE.
IF THEY DO ATTACK AGAIN, THIS GROUP WOULD ALSO OUTFLANK NEGAN'S FORCES, MAKING THEM FIGHT ON TWO FRONTS.

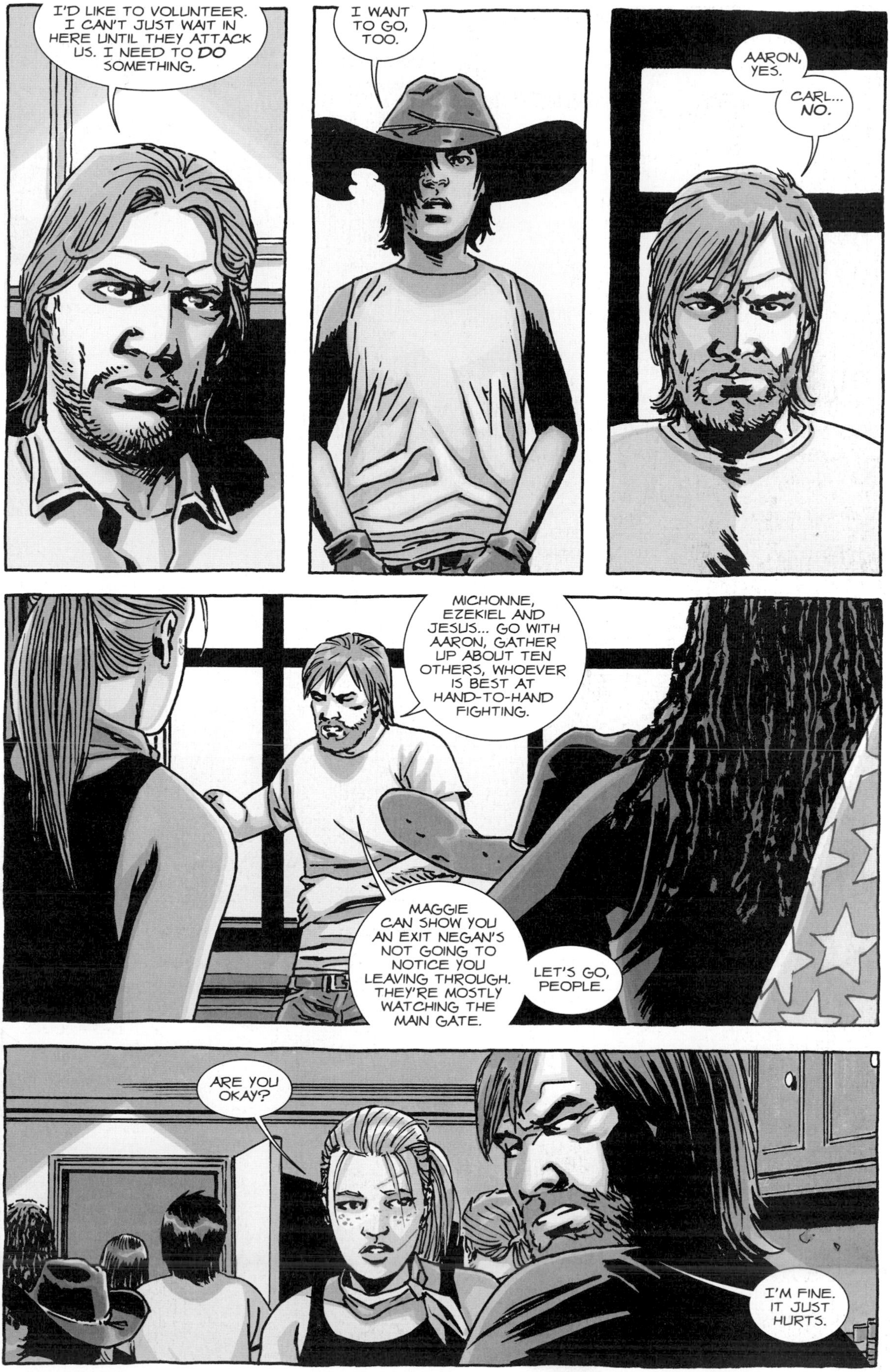
I'D LIKE TO VOLUNTEER. I CAN'T JUST WAIT IN HERE UNTIL THEY ATTACK US. I NEED TO DO SOMETHING.
I WANT TO GO, TOO.
AARON, YES.
CARL... NO.
MICHONNE, EZEKIEL AND JESUS... GO WITH AARON, GATHER UP ABOUT TEN OTHERS, WHOEVER IS BEST AT HAND-TO-HAND FIGHTING.
MAGGIE CAN SHOW YOU AN EXIT NEGAN'S NOT GOING TO NOTICE YOU LEAVING THROUGH. THEY'RE MOSTLY WATCHING THE MAIN GATE.
LET'S GO, PEOPLE.
ARE YOU OKAY?
I'M FINE. IT JUST HURTS.

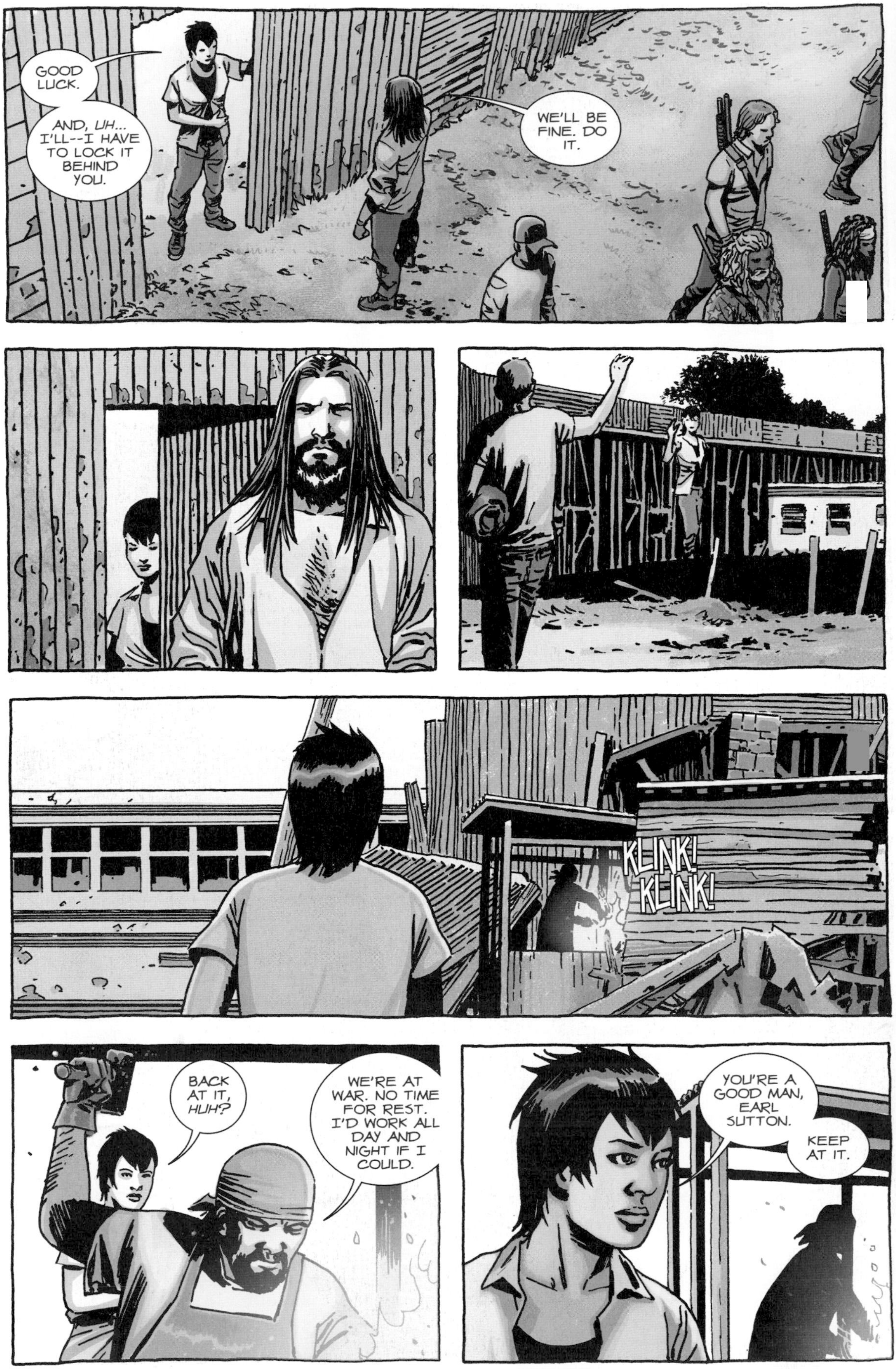
GOOD LUCK.
AND, UH... I'LL--I HAVE TO LOCK IT BEHIND YOU.
WE'LL BE FINE. DO IT.
KLINK! KLINK!
BACK AT IT, HUH?
WE'RE AT WAR. NO TIME FOR REST. I'D WORK ALL DAY AND NIGHT IF I COULD.
YOU'RE A GOOD MAN, EARL SUTTON.
KEEP AT IT.

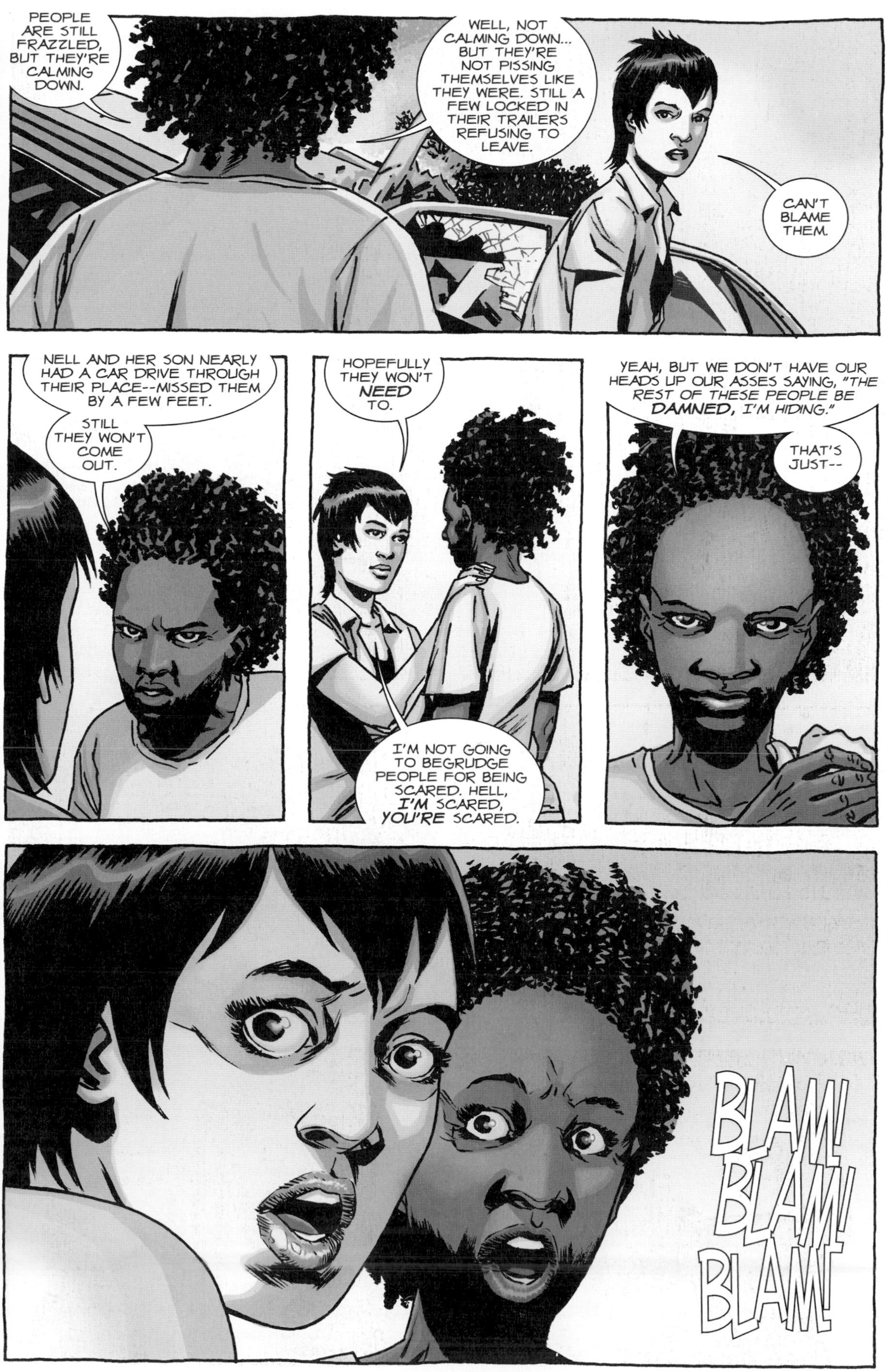
PEOPLE ARE STILL FRAZZLED, BUT THEY'RE CALMING DOWN.
WELL, NOT CALMING DOWN... BUT THEY'RE NOT PISSING THEMSELVES LIKE THEY WERE. STILL A FEW LOCKED IN THEIR TRAILERS REFUSING TO LEAVE.
CAN'T BLAME THEM.
NELL AND HER SON NEARLY HAD A CAR DRIVE THROUGH THEIR PLACE--MISSED THEM BY A FEW FEET.
STILL THEY WON'T COME OUT.
HOPEFULLY THEY WON'T NEED TO.
I'M NOT GOING TO BEGRUDGE PEOPLE FOR BEING SCARED. HELL, I'M SCARED, YOU'RE SCARED.
YEAH, BUT WE DON'T HAVE OUR HEADS UP OUR ASSES SAYING, "THE REST OF THESE PEOPLE BE DAMNED, I'M HIDING."
THAT'S JUST--
BLAM! BLAM! BLAM!

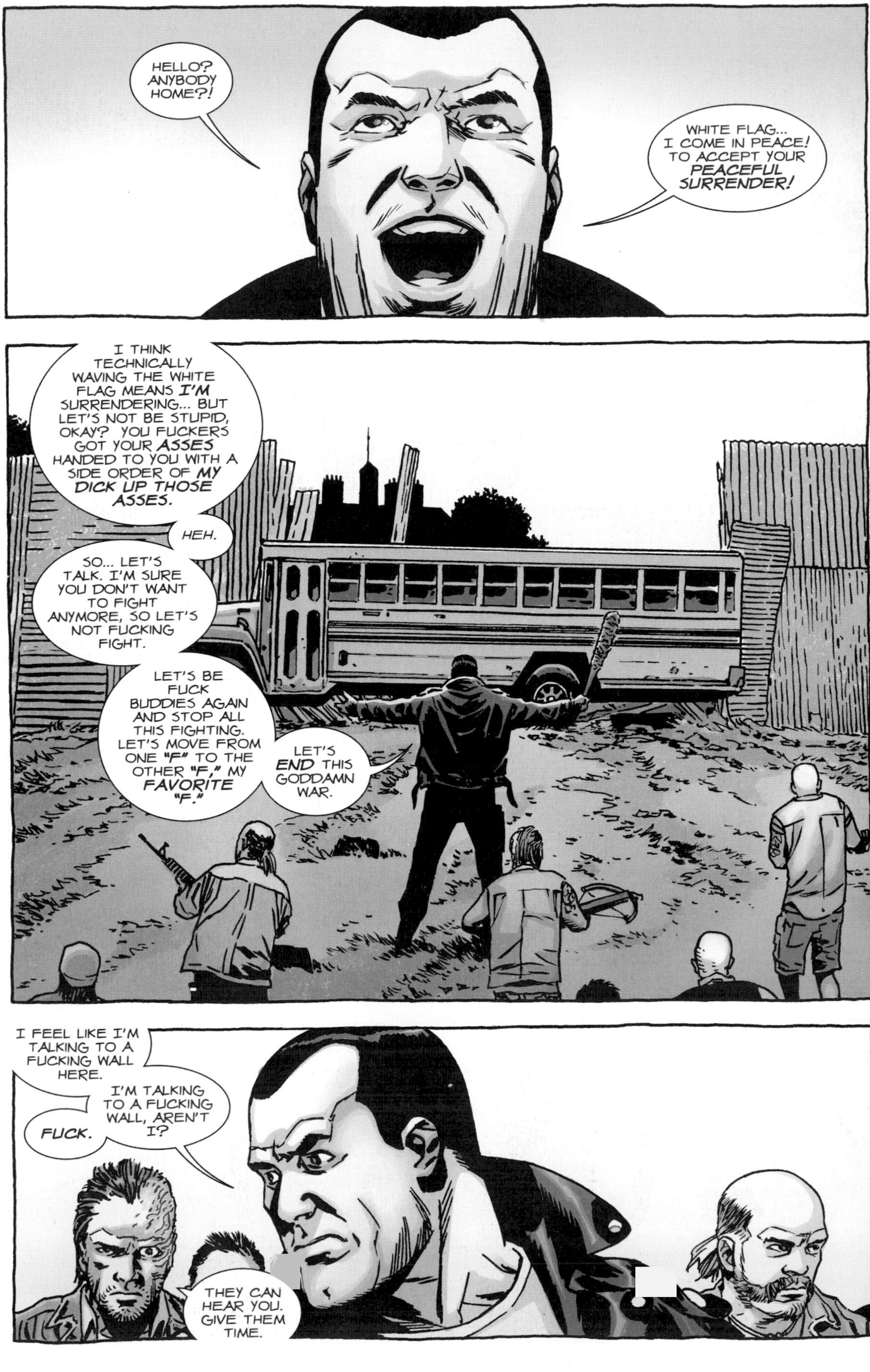
HELLO? ANYBODY HOME?!
WHITE FLAG... I COME IN PEACE! TO ACCEPT YOUR PEACEFUL SURRENDER!
I THINK TECHNICALLY WAVING THE WHITE FLAG MEANS I'M SURRENDERING... BUT LET'S NOT BE STUPID, OKAY? YOU FUCKERS GOT YOUR ASSES HANDED TO YOU WITH A SIDE ORDER OF MY DICK UP THOSE ASSES.
HEH.
SO... LET'S TALK. I'M SURE YOU DON'T WANT TO FIGHT ANYMORE, SO LET'S NOT FUCKING FIGHT.
LET'S BE FUCK BUDDIES AGAIN AND STOP ALL THIS FIGHTING. LET'S MOVE FROM ONE "F" TO THE OTHER "F," MY FAVORITE "F."
LET'S END THIS GODDAMN WAR.
I FEEL LIKE I'M TALKING TO A FUCKING WALL HERE.
FUCK.
I'M TALKING TO A FUCKING WALL, AREN'T I?
THEY CAN HEAR YOU. GIVE THEM TIME.

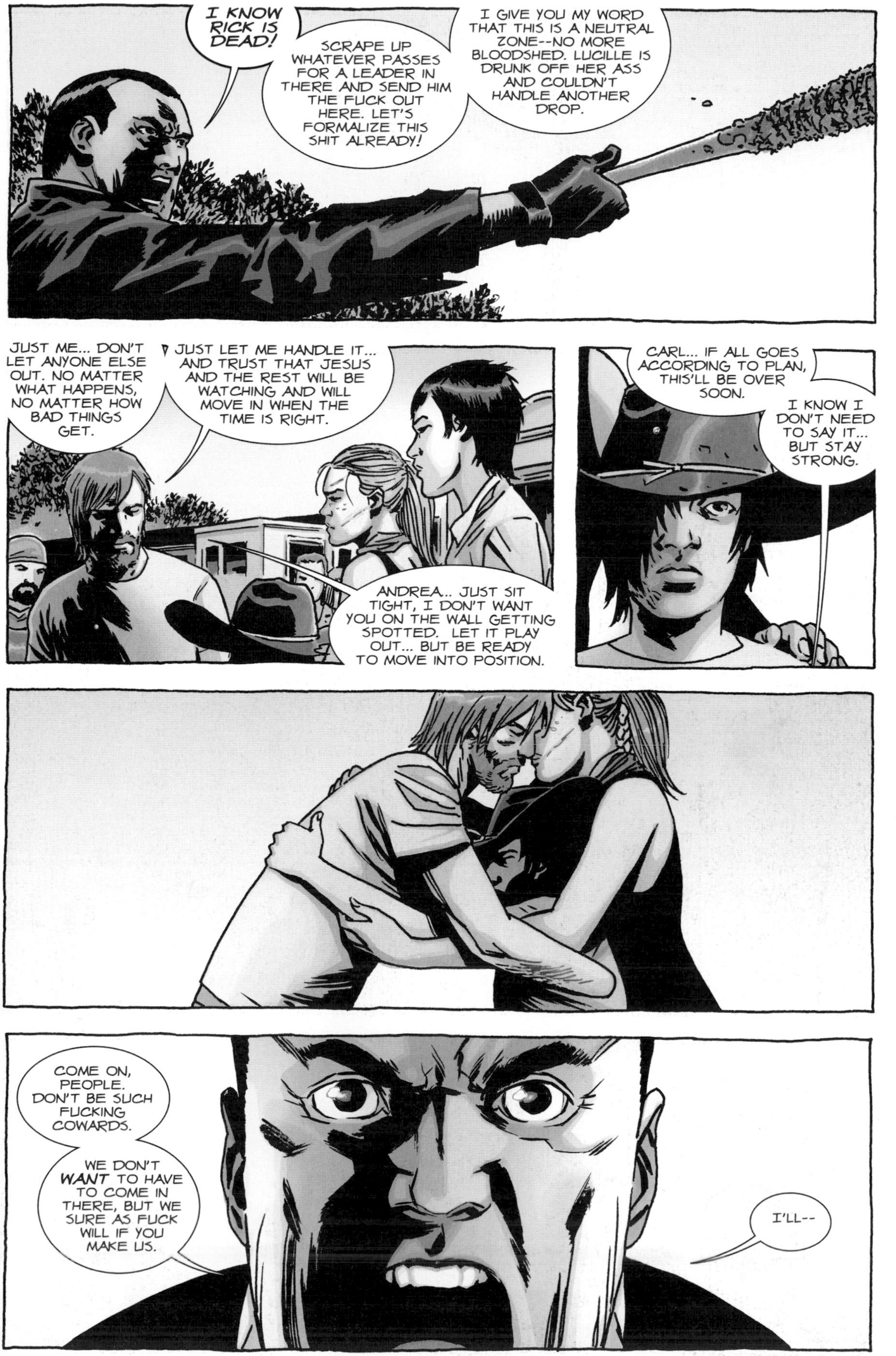
I KNOW RICK IS DEAD!
SCRAPE UP WHATEVER PASSES FOR A LEADER IN THERE AND SEND HIM THE FUCK OUT HERE. LET'S FORMALIZE THIS SHIT ALREADY!
I GIVE YOU MY WORD THAT THIS IS A NEUTRAL ZONE--NO MORE BLOODSHED. LUCILLE IS DRUNK OFF HER ASS AND COULDN'T HANDLE ANOTHER DROP.
JUST ME... DON'T LET ANYONE ELSE OUT. NO MATTER WHAT HAPPENS, NO MATTER HOW BAD THINGS GET.
JUST LET ME HANDLE IT... AND TRUST THAT JESUS AND THE REST WILL BE WATCHING AND WILL MOVE IN WHEN THE TIME IS RIGHT.
ANDREA... JUST SIT TIGHT, I DON'T WANT YOU ON THE WALL GETTING SPOTTED. LET IT PLAY OUT... BUT BE READY TO MOVE INTO POSITION.
CARL... IF ALL GOES ACCORDING TO PLAN, THIS'LL BE OVER SOON.
I KNOW I DON'T NEED TO SAY IT... BUT STAY STRONG.
COME ON, PEOPLE. DON'T BE SUCH FUCKING COWARDS.
WE DON'T WANT TO HAVE TO COME IN THERE, BUT WE SURE AS FUCK WILL IF YOU MAKE US.
I'LL--

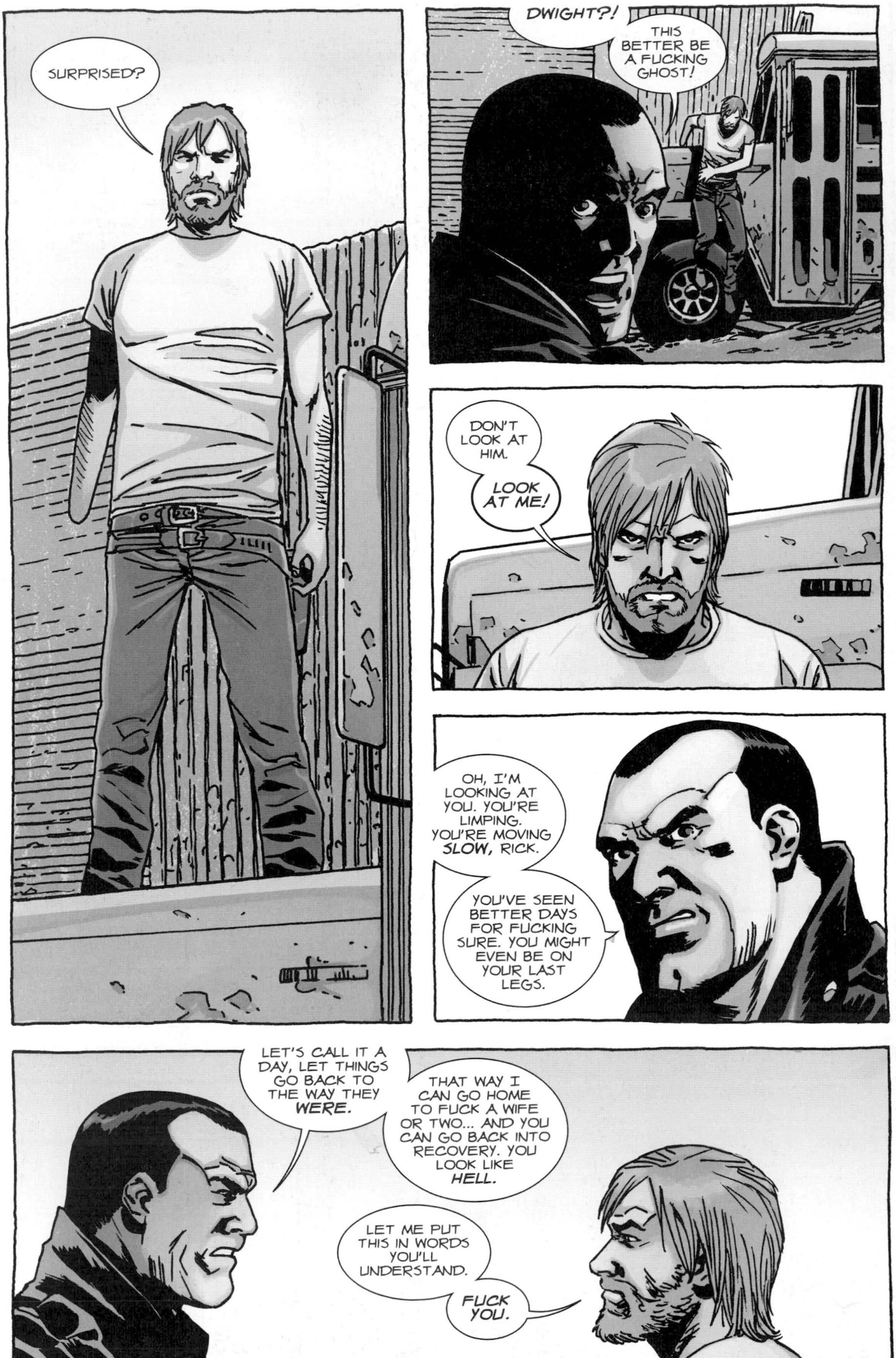
SURPRISED?
DWIGHT?!
THIS BETTER BE A FUCKING GHOST!
DON'T LOOK AT HIM.
LOOK AT ME!
OH, I'M LOOKING AT YOU. YOU'RE LIMPING. YOU'RE MOVING SLOW, RICK.
YOU'VE SEEN BETTER DAYS FOR FUCKING SURE. YOU MIGHT EVEN BE ON YOUR LAST LEGS.
LET'S CALL IT A DAY, LET THINGS GO BACK TO THE WAY THEY WERE.
THAT WAY I CAN GO HOME TO FUCK A WIFE OR TWO... AND YOU CAN GO BACK INTO RECOVERY. YOU LOOK LIKE HELL.
LET ME PUT THIS IN WORDS YOU'LL UNDERSTAND.
FUCK YOU.

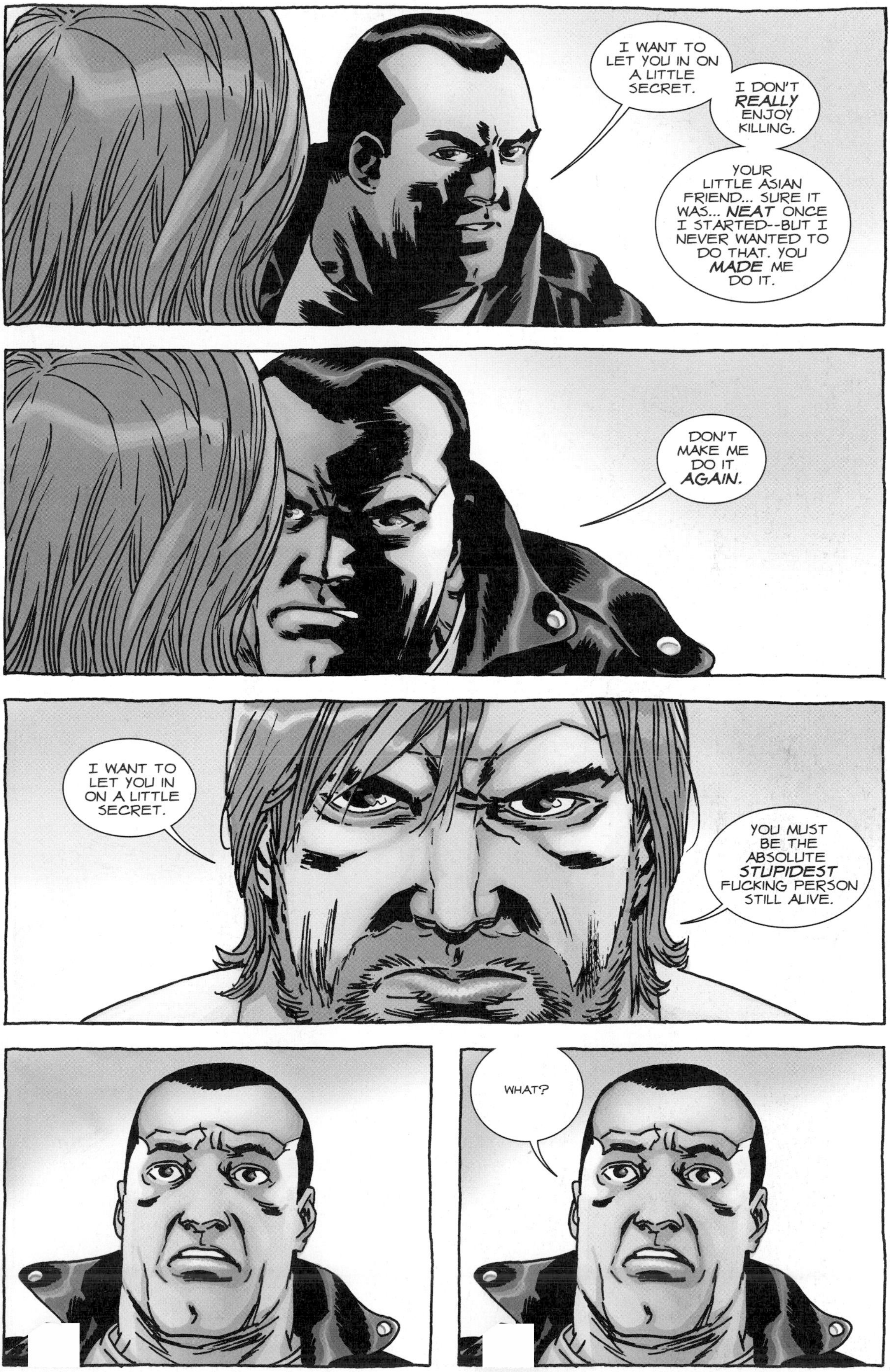
I WANT TO LET YOU IN ON A LITTLE SECRET.
I DON'T REALLY ENJOY KILLING.
YOUR LITTLE ASIAN FRIEND... SURE IT WAS... NEAT ONCE I STARTED--BUT I NEVER WANTED TO DO THAT. YOU MADE ME DO IT.
DON'T MAKE ME DO IT AGAIN.
I WANT TO LET YOU IN ON A LITTLE SECRET.
YOU MUST BE THE ABSOLUTE STUPIDEST FUCKING PERSON STILL ALIVE.
WHAT?

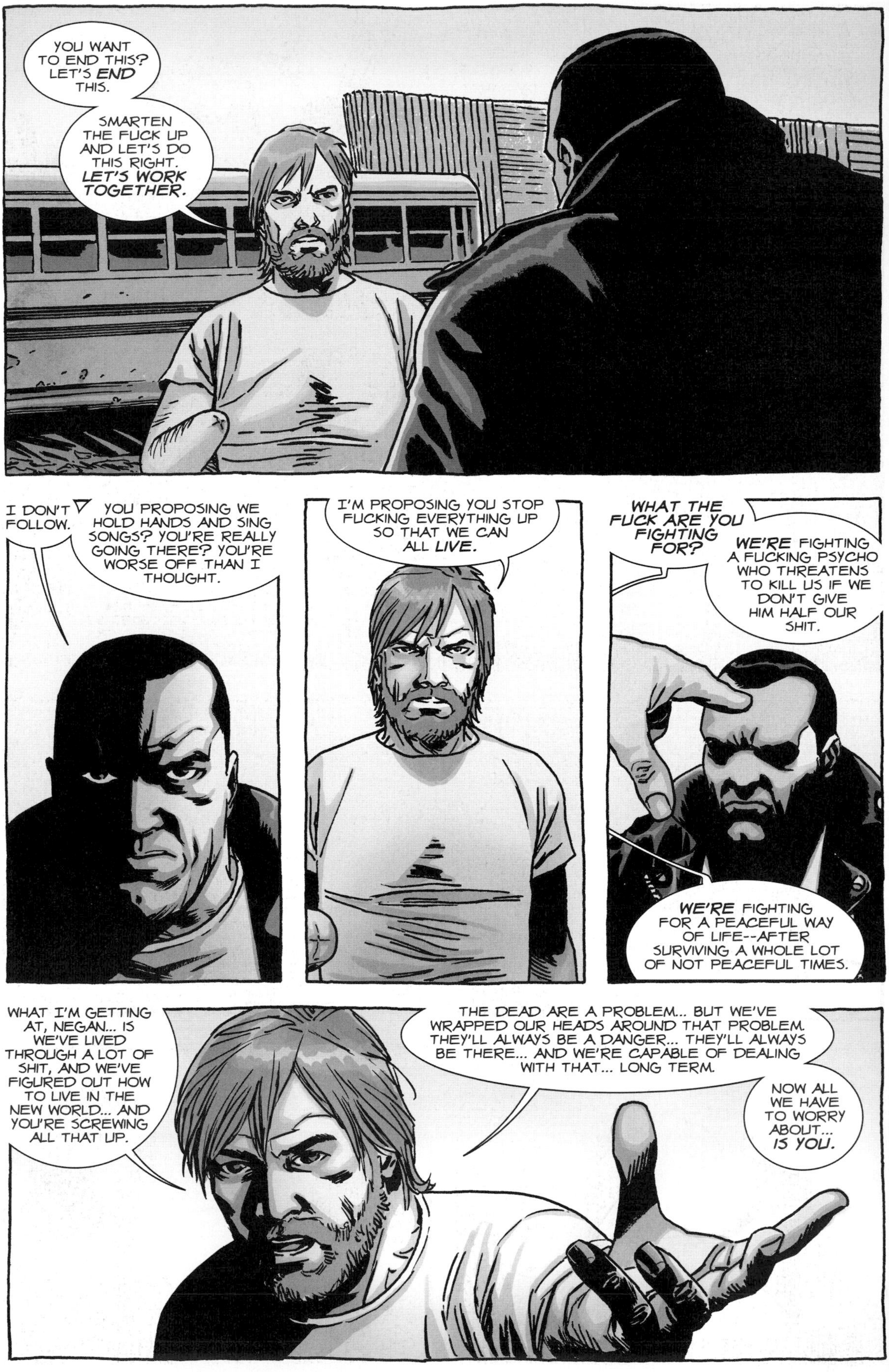
YOU WANT TO END THIS? LET'S END THIS.
SMARTEN THE FUCK UP AND LET'S DO THIS RIGHT. LET'S WORK TOGETHER.
I DON'T FOLLOW.
YOU PROPOSING WE HOLD HANDS AND SING SONGS? YOU'RE REALLY GOING THERE? YOU'RE WORSE OFF THAN I THOUGHT.
I'M PROPOSING YOU STOP FUCKING EVERYTHING UP SO THAT WE CAN ALL LIVE.
WHAT THE FUCK ARE YOU FIGHTING FOR?
WE'RE FIGHTING A FUCKING PSYCHO WHO THREATENS TO KILL US IF WE DON'T GIVE HIM HALF OUR SHIT.
WE'RE FIGHTING FOR A PEACEFUL WAY OF LIFE--AFTER SURVIVING A WHOLE LOT OF NOT PEACEFUL TIMES.
WHAT I'M GETTING AT, NEGAN... IS WE'VE LIVED THROUGH A LOT OF SHIT, AND WE'VE FIGURED OUT HOW TO LIVE IN THE NEW WORLD... AND YOU'RE SCREWING ALL THAT UP.
THE DEAD ARE A PROBLEM... BUT WE'VE WRAPPED OUR HEADS AROUND THAT PROBLEM. THEY'LL ALWAYS BE A DANGER... THEY'LL ALWAYS BE THERE... AND WE'RE CAPABLE OF DEALING WITH THAT... LONG TERM.
NOW ALL WE HAVE TO WORRY ABOUT... IS YOU.

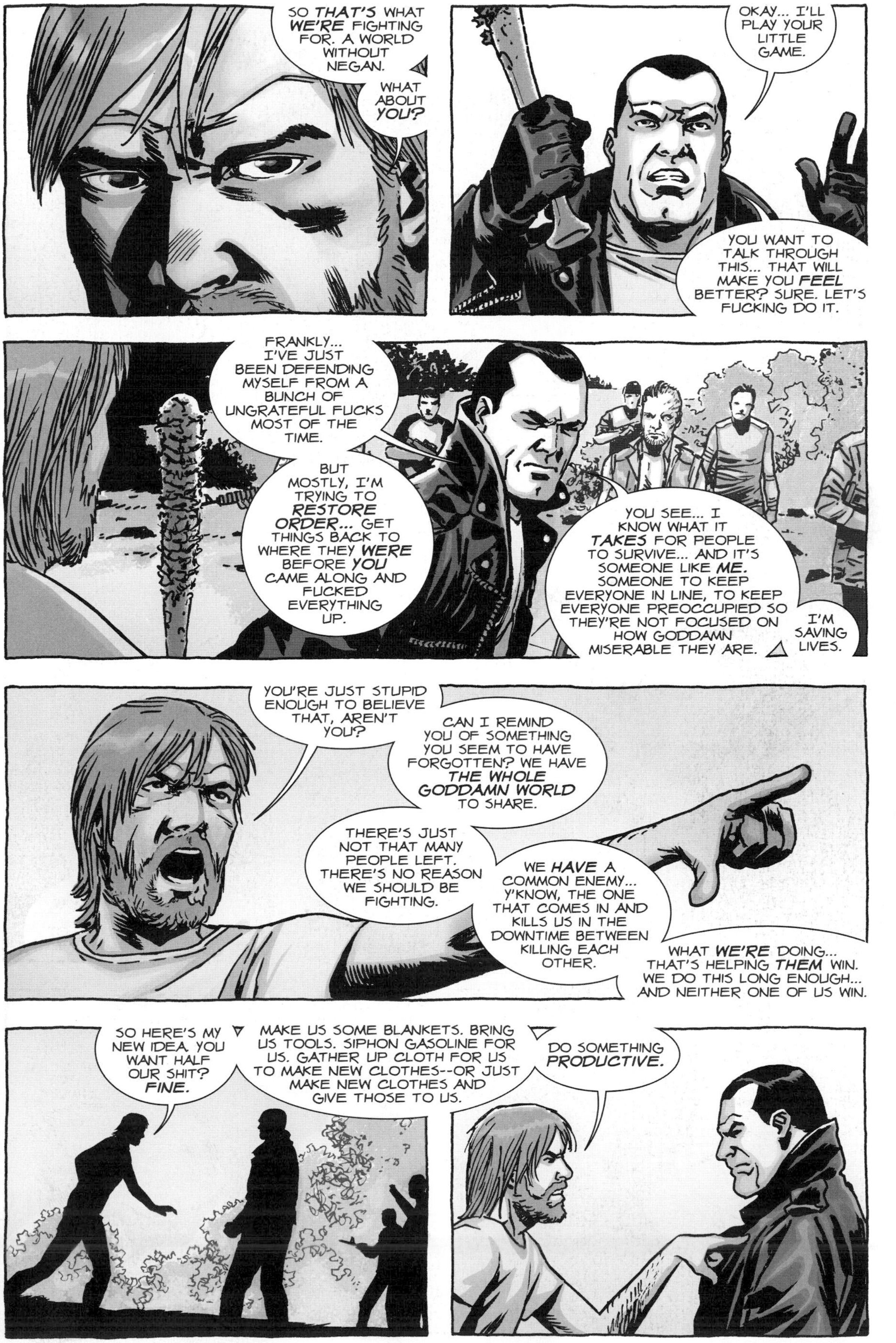
SO THAT'S WHAT WE'RE FIGHTING FOR. A WORLD WITHOUT NEGAN.
WHAT ABOUT YOU?
OKAY... I'LL PLAY YOUR LITTLE GAME.
YOU WANT TO TALK THROUGH THIS... THAT WILL MAKE YOU FEEL BETTER? SURE. LET'S FUCKING DO IT.
FRANKLY... I'VE JUST BEEN DEFENDING MYSELF FROM A BUNCH OF UNGRATEFUL FUCKS MOST OF THE TIME.
BUT MOSTLY, I'M TRYING TO RESTORE ORDER... GET THINGS BACK TO WHERE THEY WERE BEFORE YOU CAME ALONG AND FUCKED EVERYTHING UP.
YOU SEE... I KNOW WHAT IT TAKES FOR PEOPLE TO SURVIVE... AND IT'S SOMEONE LIKE ME. SOMEONE TO KEEP EVERYONE IN LINE, TO KEEP EVERYONE PREOCCUPIED SO THEY'RE NOT FOCUSED ON HOW GODDAMN MISERABLE THEY ARE.
I'M SAVING LIVES.
YOU'RE JUST STUPID ENOUGH TO BELIEVE THAT, AREN'T YOU?
CAN I REMIND YOU OF SOMETHING YOU SEEM TO HAVE FORGOTTEN? WE HAVE THE WHOLE GODDAMN WORLD TO SHARE.
THERE'S JUST NOT THAT MANY PEOPLE LEFT. THERE'S NO REASON WE SHOULD BE FIGHTING.
WE HAVE A COMMON ENEMY... Y'KNOW, THE ONE THAT COMES IN AND KILLS US IN THE DOWNTIME BETWEEN KILLING EACH OTHER.
WHAT WE'RE DOING... THAT'S HELPING THEM WIN. WE DO THIS LONG ENOUGH... AND NEITHER ONE OF US WIN.
SO HERE'S MY NEW IDEA. YOU WANT HALF OUR SHIT? FINE.
MAKE US SOME BLANKETS. BRING US TOOLS. SIPHON GASOLINE FOR US. GATHER UP CLOTH FOR US TO MAKE NEW CLOTHES--OR JUST MAKE NEW CLOTHES AND GIVE THOSE TO US.
DO SOMETHING PRODUCTIVE.

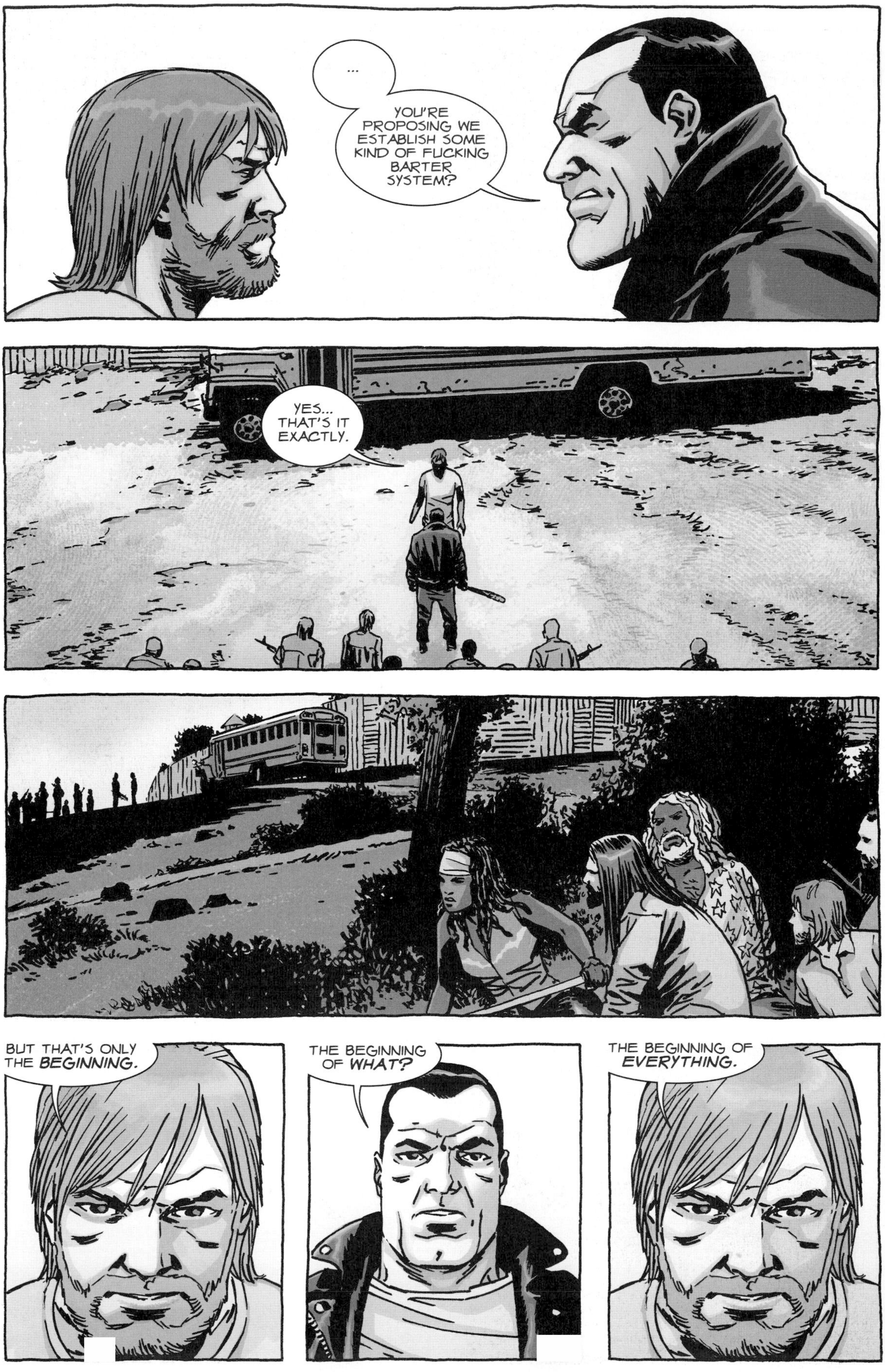
...
YOU'RE PROPOSING WE ESTABLISH SOME KIND OF FUCKING BARTER SYSTEM?
YES... THAT'S IT EXACTLY.
BUT THAT'S ONLY THE *BEGINNING*.
THE BEGINNING OF *WHAT?*
THE BEGINNING OF *EVERYTHING*.

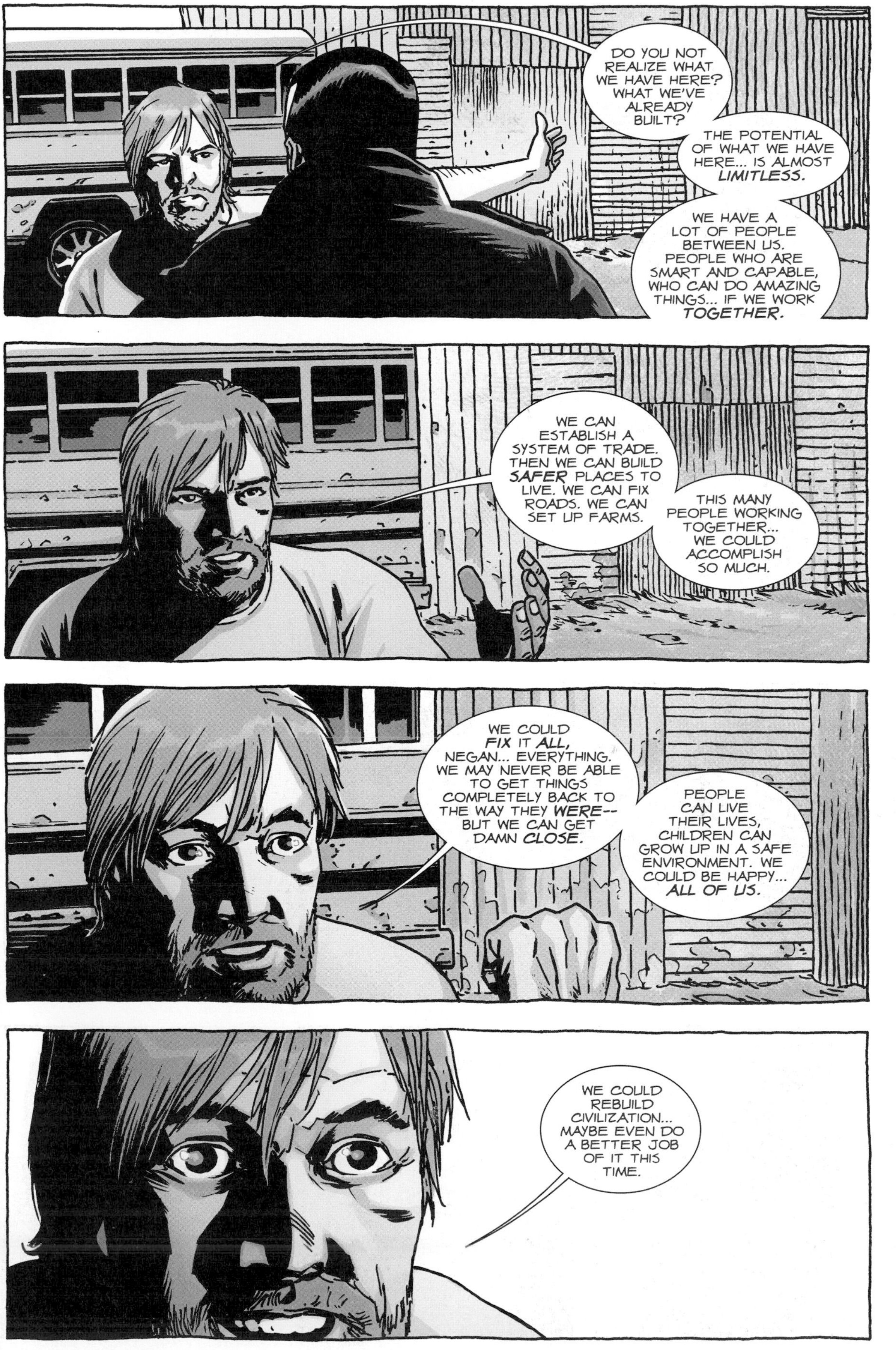
DO YOU NOT REALIZE WHAT WE HAVE HERE? WHAT WE'VE ALREADY BUILT?
THE POTENTIAL OF WHAT WE HAVE HERE... IS ALMOST LIMITLESS.
WE HAVE A LOT OF PEOPLE BETWEEN US. PEOPLE WHO ARE SMART AND CAPABLE, WHO CAN DO AMAZING THINGS... IF WE WORK TOGETHER.
WE CAN ESTABLISH A SYSTEM OF TRADE. THEN WE CAN BUILD SAFER PLACES TO LIVE. WE CAN FIX ROADS. WE CAN SET UP FARMS.
THIS MANY PEOPLE WORKING TOGETHER... WE COULD ACCOMPLISH SO MUCH.
WE COULD FIX IT ALL, NEGAN... EVERYTHING. WE MAY NEVER BE ABLE TO GET THINGS COMPLETELY BACK TO THE WAY THEY WERE-- BUT WE CAN GET DAMN CLOSE.
PEOPLE CAN LIVE THEIR LIVES, CHILDREN CAN GROW UP IN A SAFE ENVIRONMENT. WE COULD BE HAPPY... ALL OF US.
WE COULD REBUILD CIVILIZATION... MAYBE EVEN DO A BETTER JOB OF IT THIS TIME.

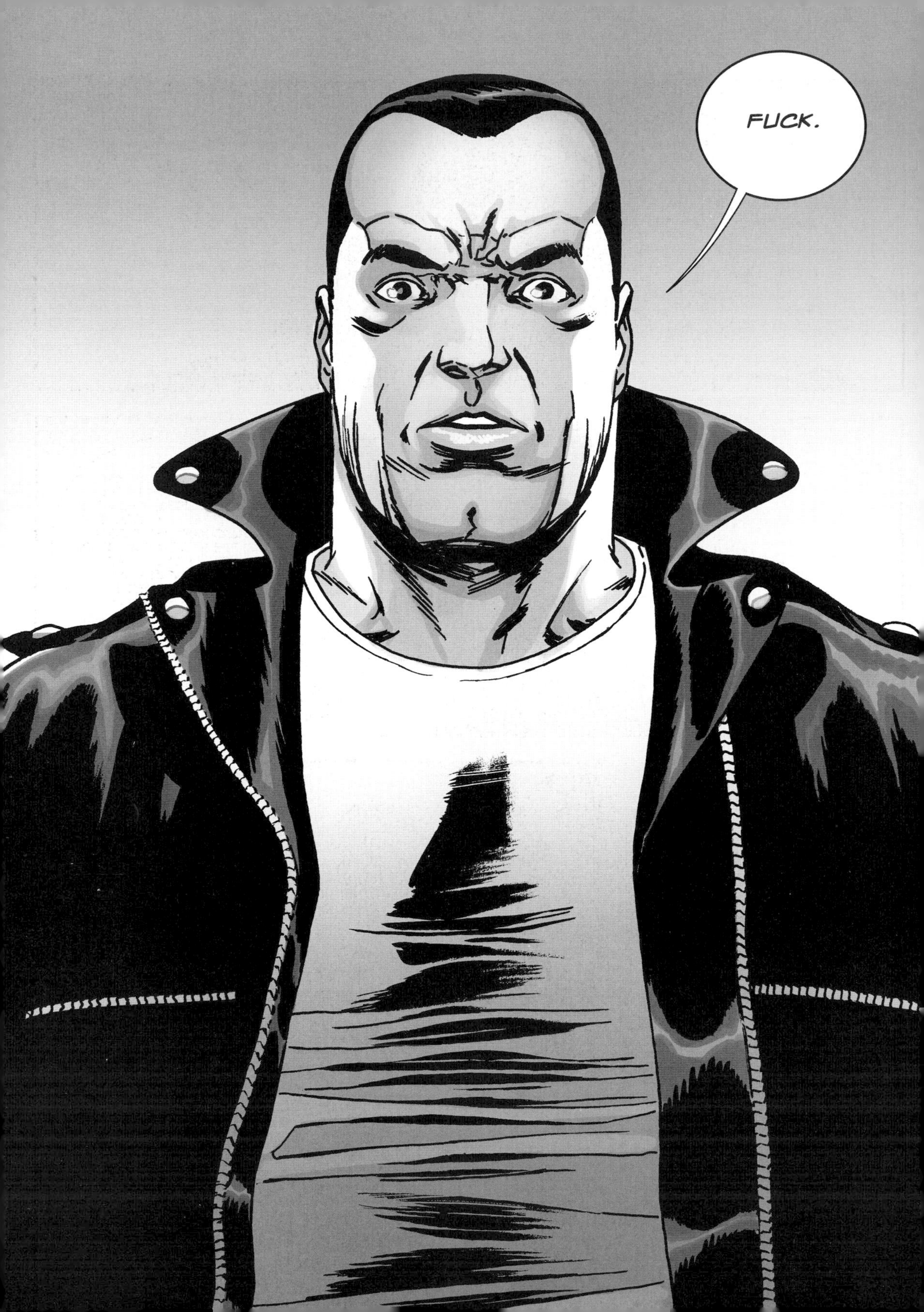
FUCK.

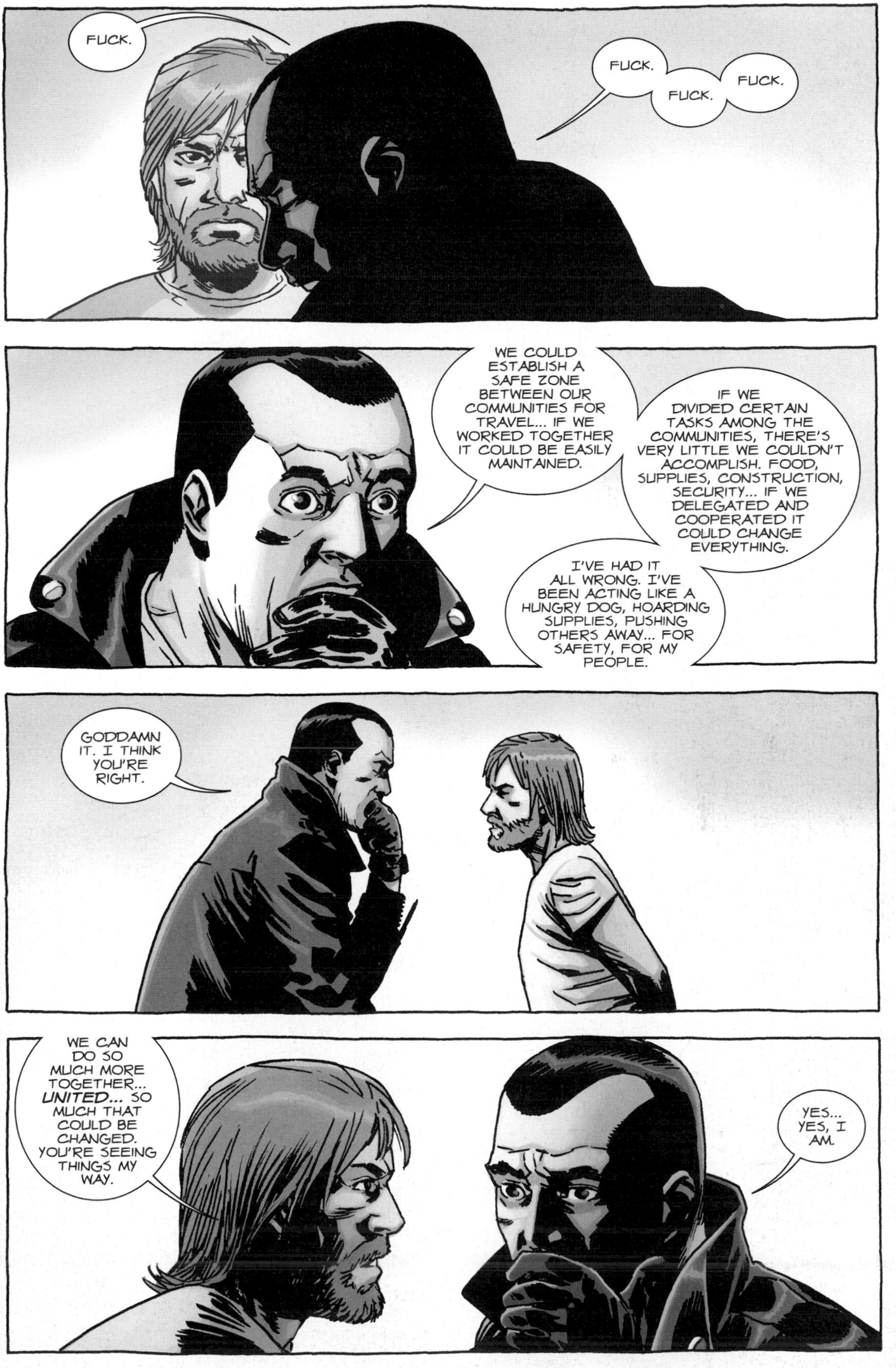
FUCK.
FUCK.
FUCK.
FUCK.
WE COULD ESTABLISH A SAFE ZONE BETWEEN OUR COMMUNITIES FOR TRAVEL... IF WE WORKED TOGETHER IT COULD BE EASILY MAINTAINED.
IF WE DIVIDED CERTAIN TASKS AMONG THE COMMUNITIES, THERE'S VERY LITTLE WE COULDN'T ACCOMPLISH. FOOD, SUPPLIES, CONSTRUCTION, SECURITY... IF WE DELEGATED AND COOPERATED IT COULD CHANGE EVERYTHING.
I'VE HAD IT ALL WRONG. I'VE BEEN ACTING LIKE A HUNGRY DOG, HOARDING SUPPLIES, PUSHING OTHERS AWAY... FOR SAFETY, FOR MY PEOPLE.
GODDAMN IT. I THINK YOU'RE RIGHT.
WE CAN DO SO MUCH MORE TOGETHER... UNITED... SO MUCH THAT COULD BE CHANGED. YOU'RE SEEING THINGS MY WAY.
YES... YES, I AM.

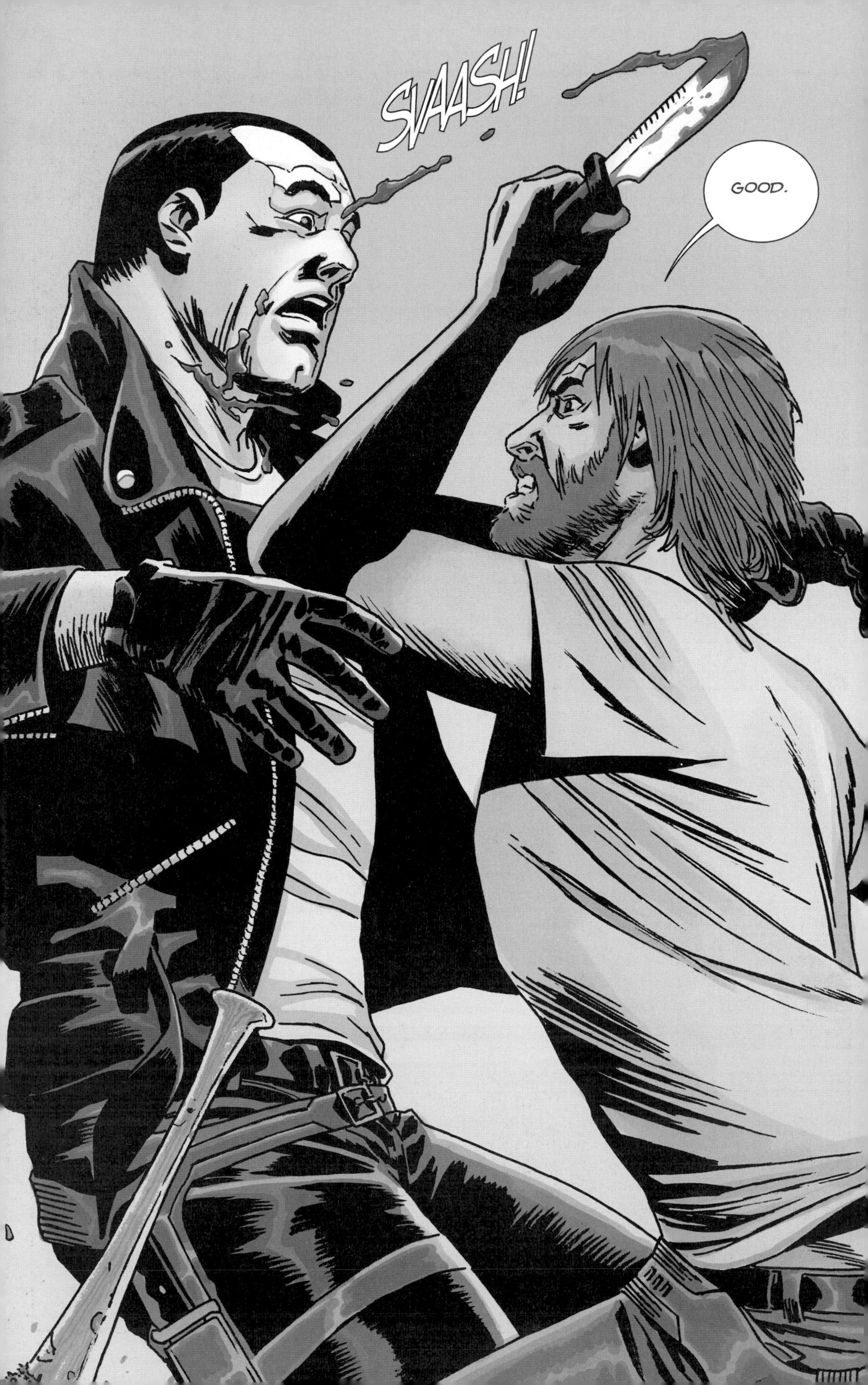
SVAASH!
GOOD.

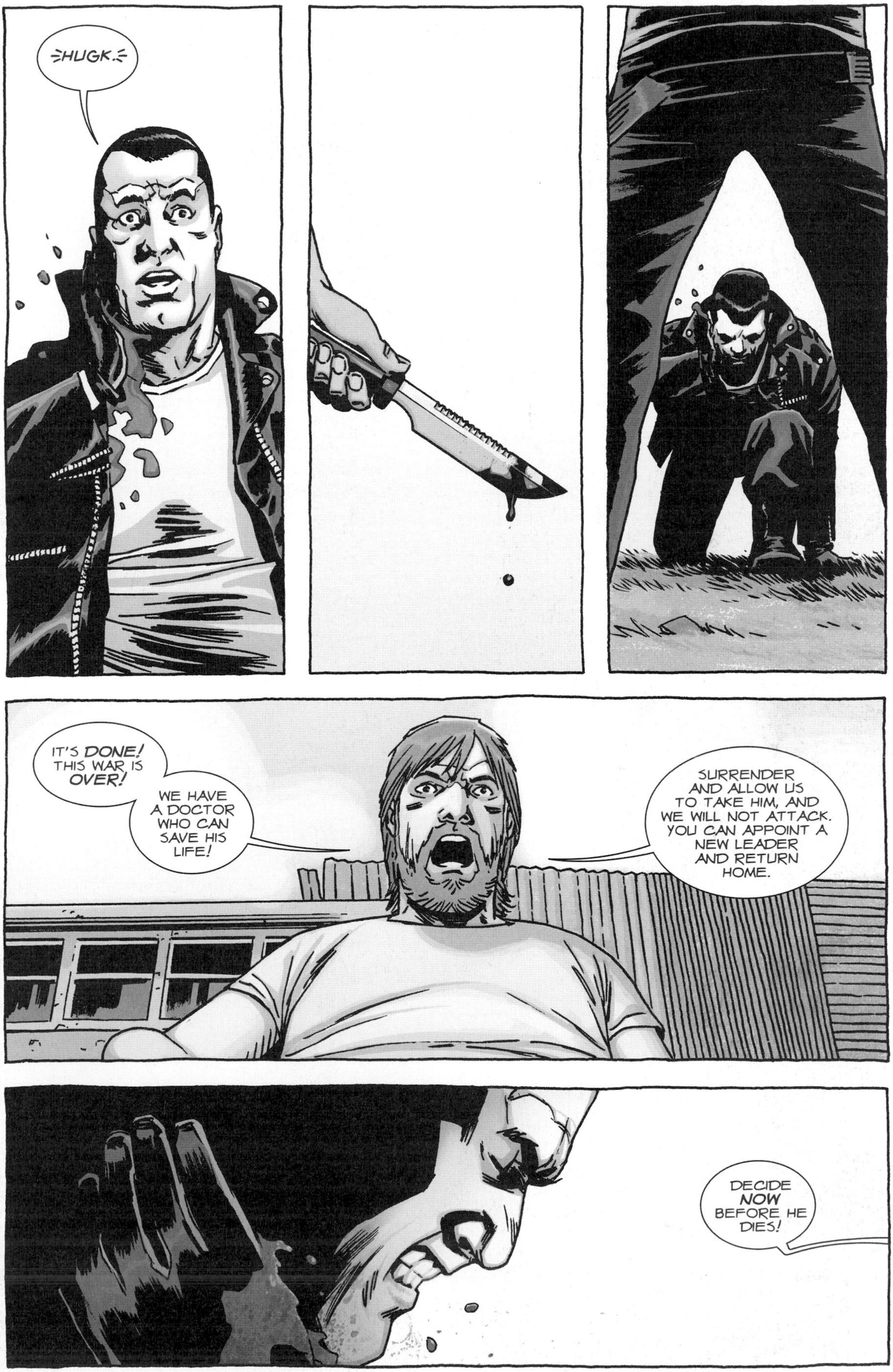
HUGK.
IT'S DONE! THIS WAR IS OVER!
WE HAVE A DOCTOR WHO CAN SAVE HIS LIFE!
SURRENDER AND ALLOW US TO TAKE HIM, AND WE WILL NOT ATTACK. YOU CAN APPOINT A NEW LEADER AND RETURN HOME.
DECIDE NOW BEFORE HE DIES!

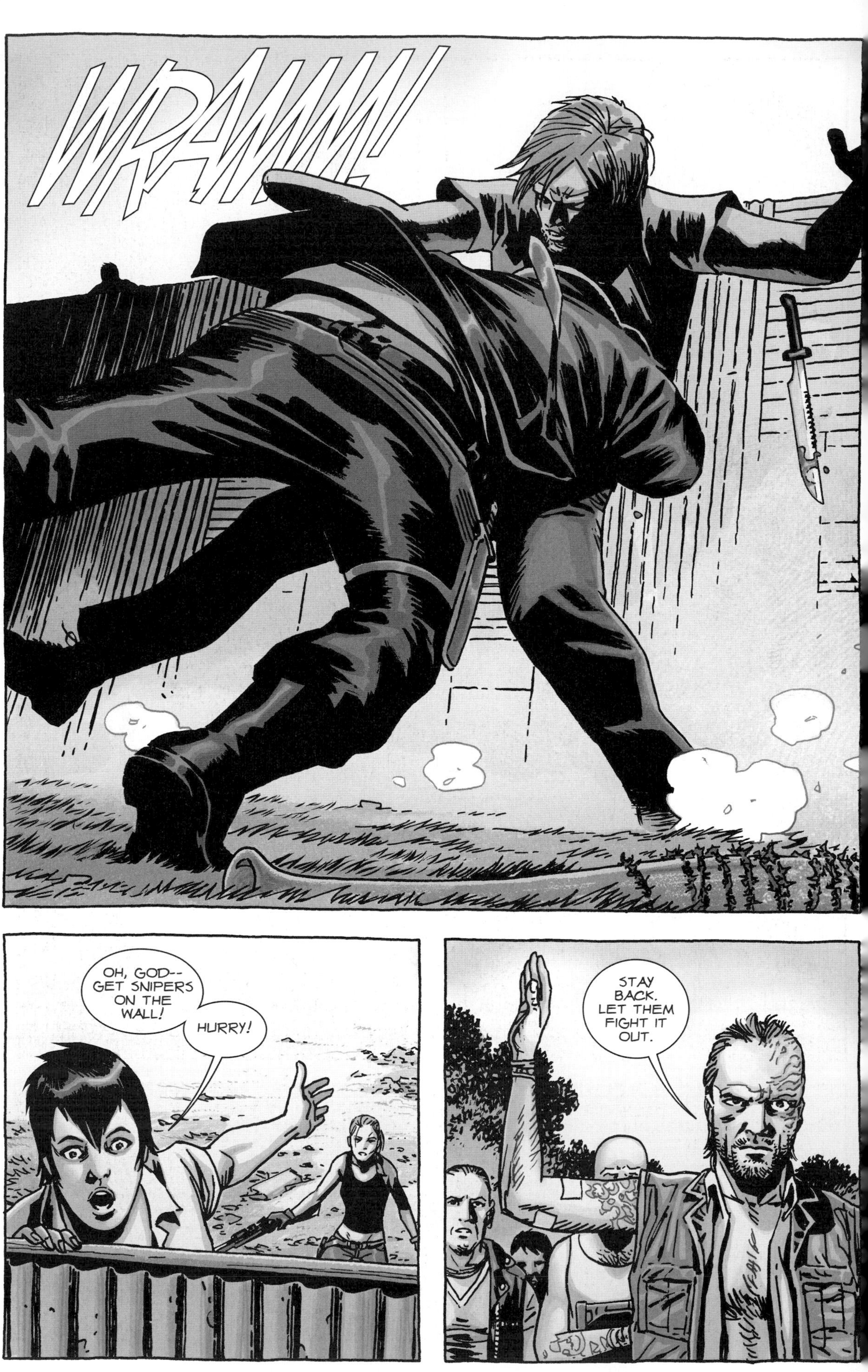
WRAAAAM!
OH, GOD-- GET SNIPERS ON THE WALL!
HURRY!
STAY BACK. LET THEM FIGHT IT OUT.

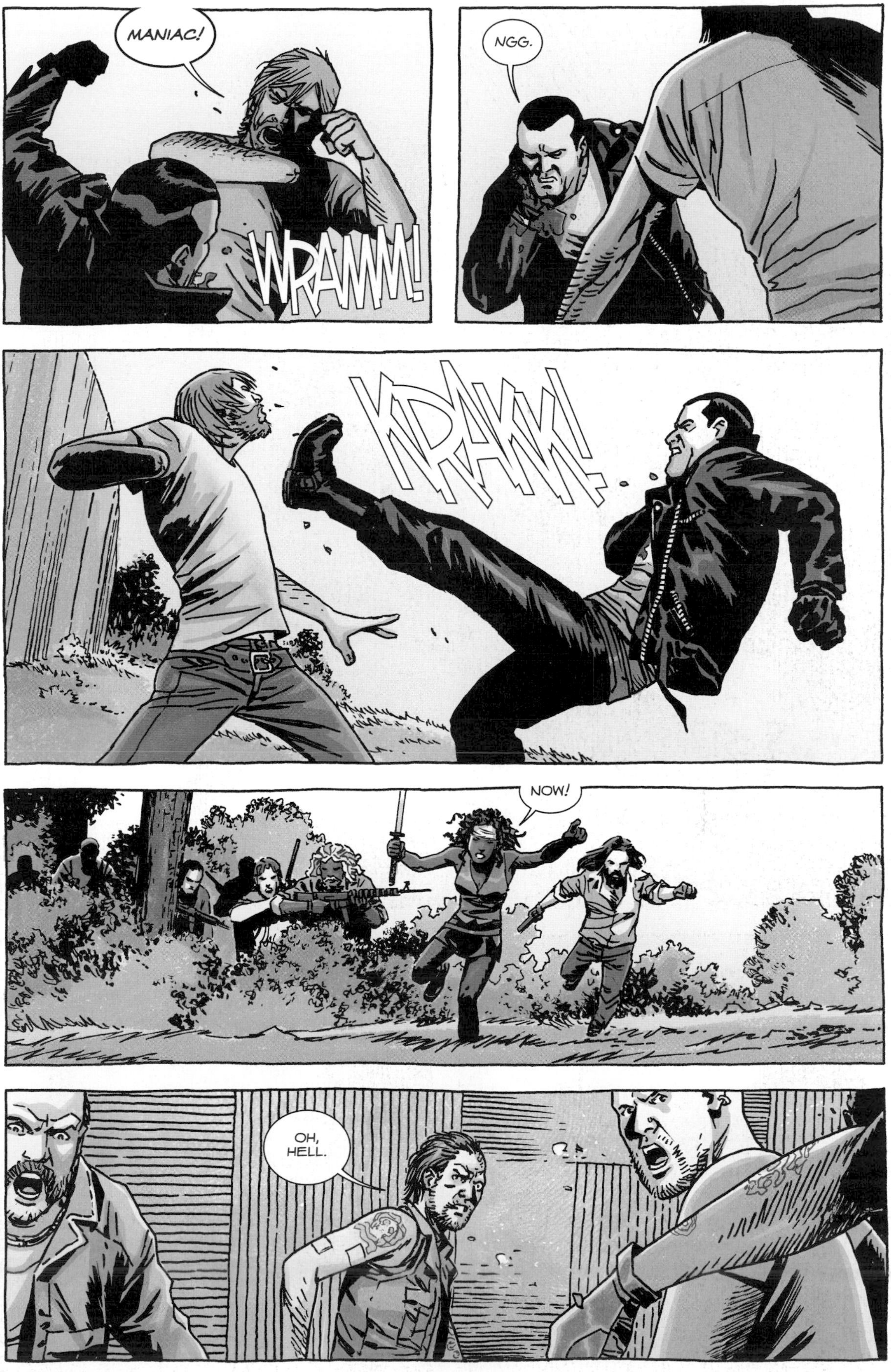
MANIAC!
WRAMM!
NGG.
KRAKK!
NOW!
OH, HELL.

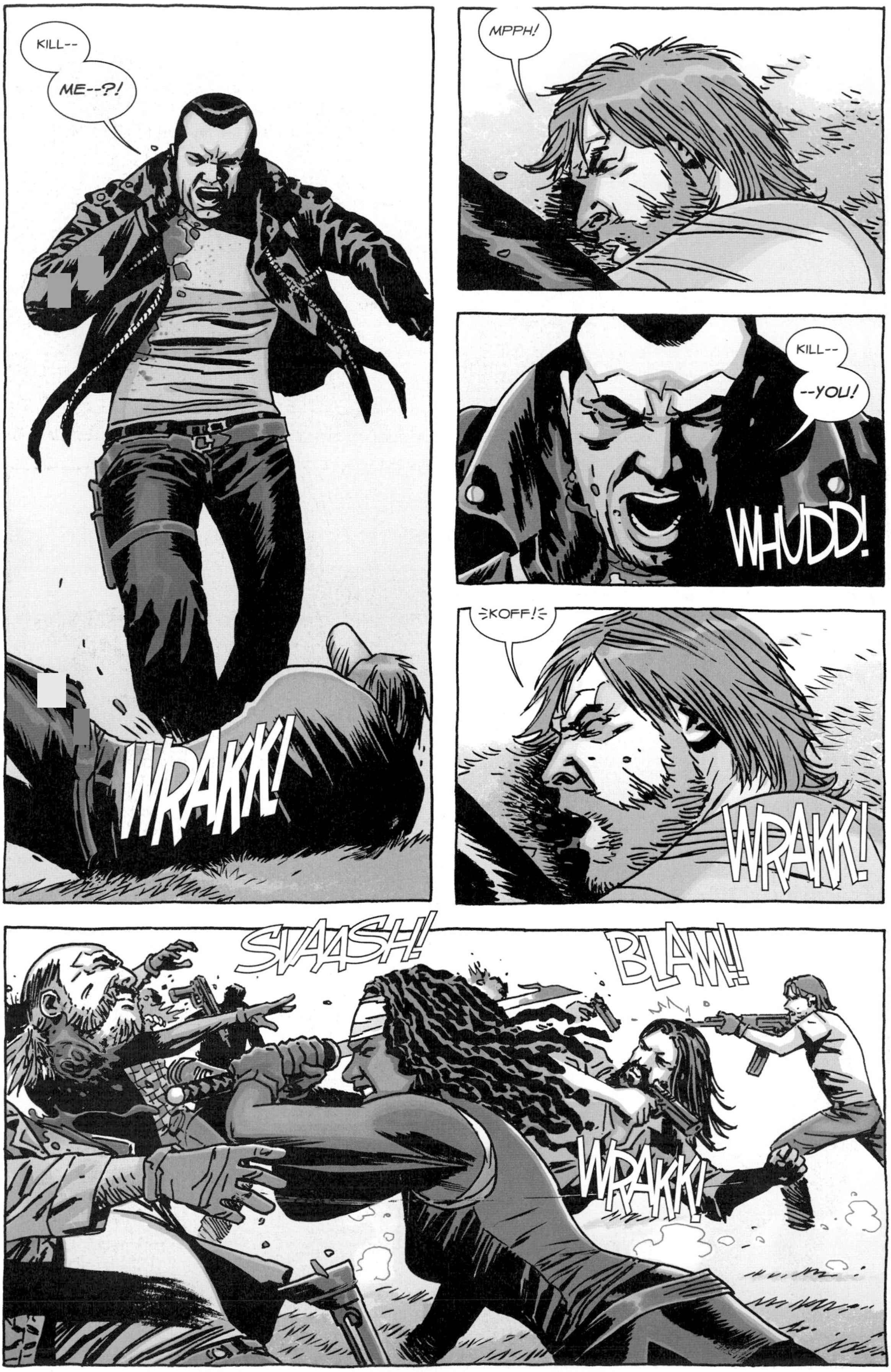
KILL--
ME--?!
WRAKK!
MPPH!
KILL--
--YOU!
WHUDD!
KOFF!
WRAKK!
SVAASH!
BLAM!
WRAKK!

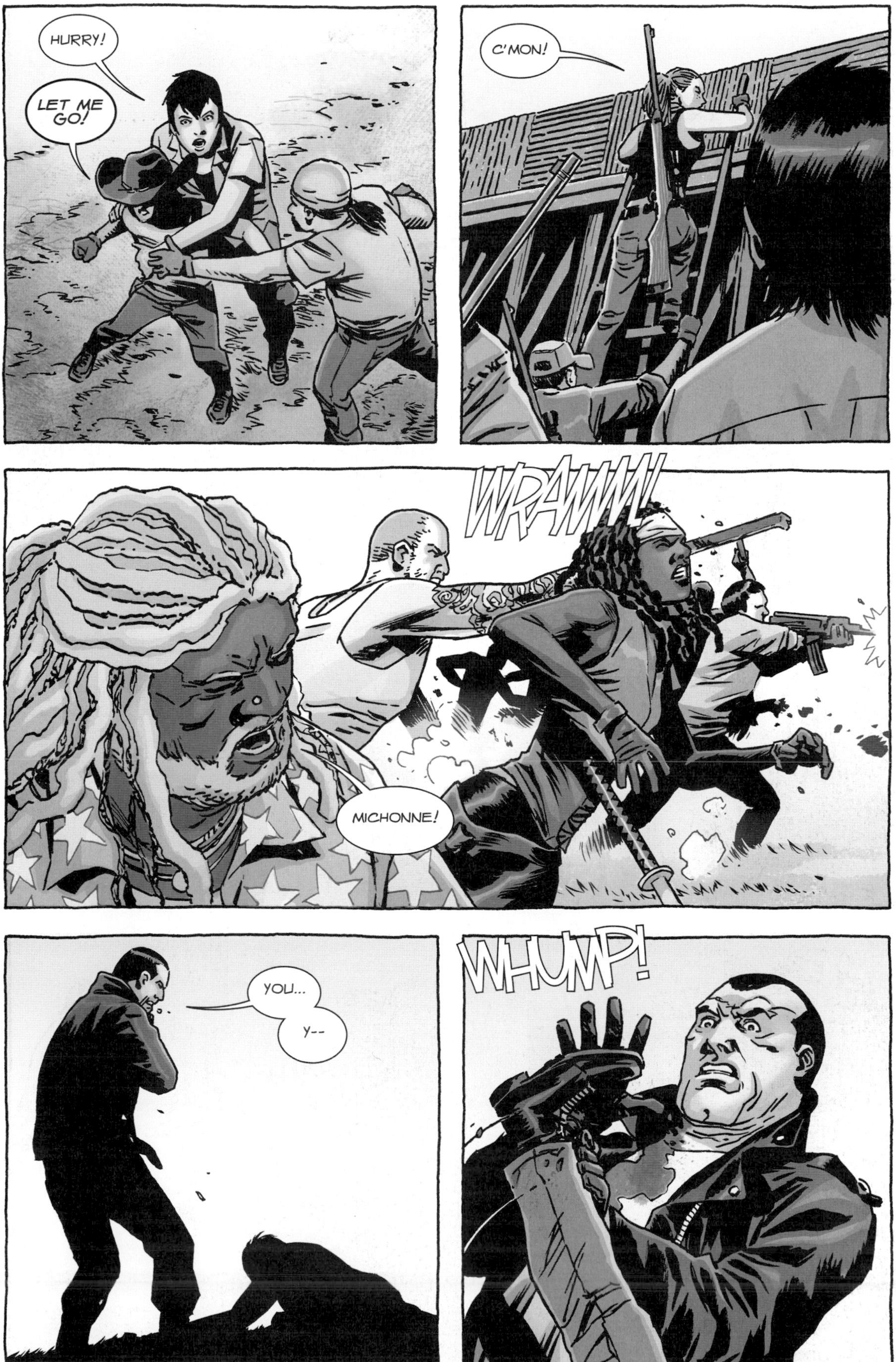
HURRY!
LET ME GO!
C'MON!
WRAMM!
MICHONNE!
YOU...
Y--
WHUMP!

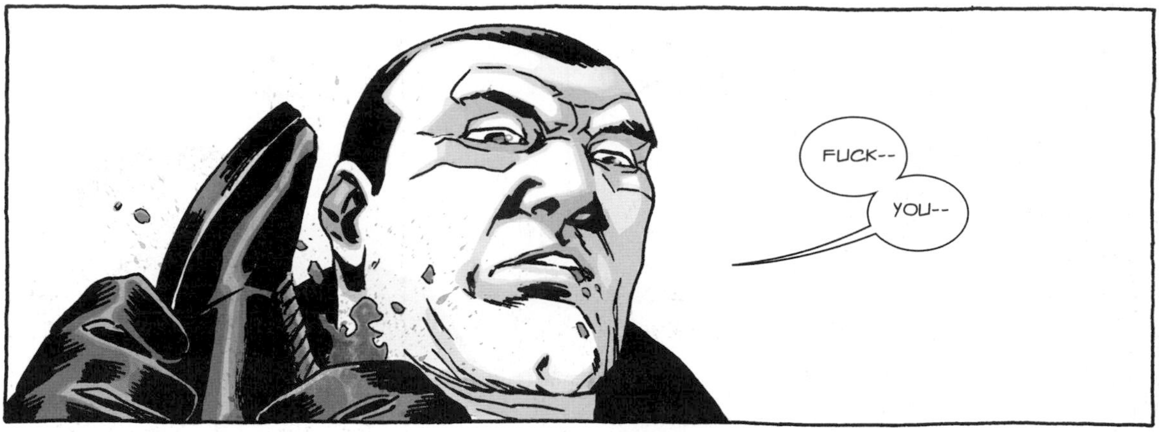
FUCK--
YOU--

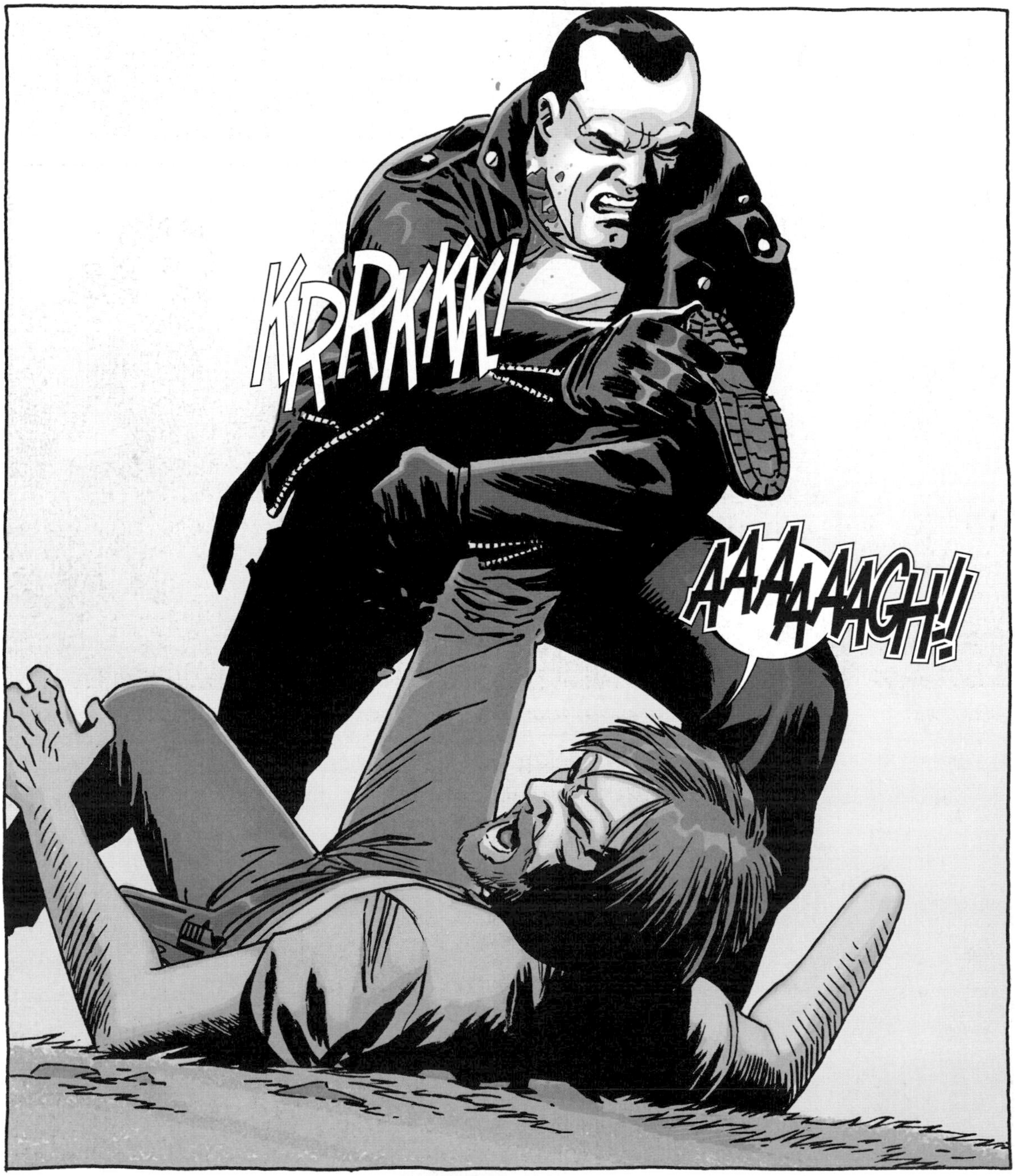
KRRKKK!
AAAAAAGH!!

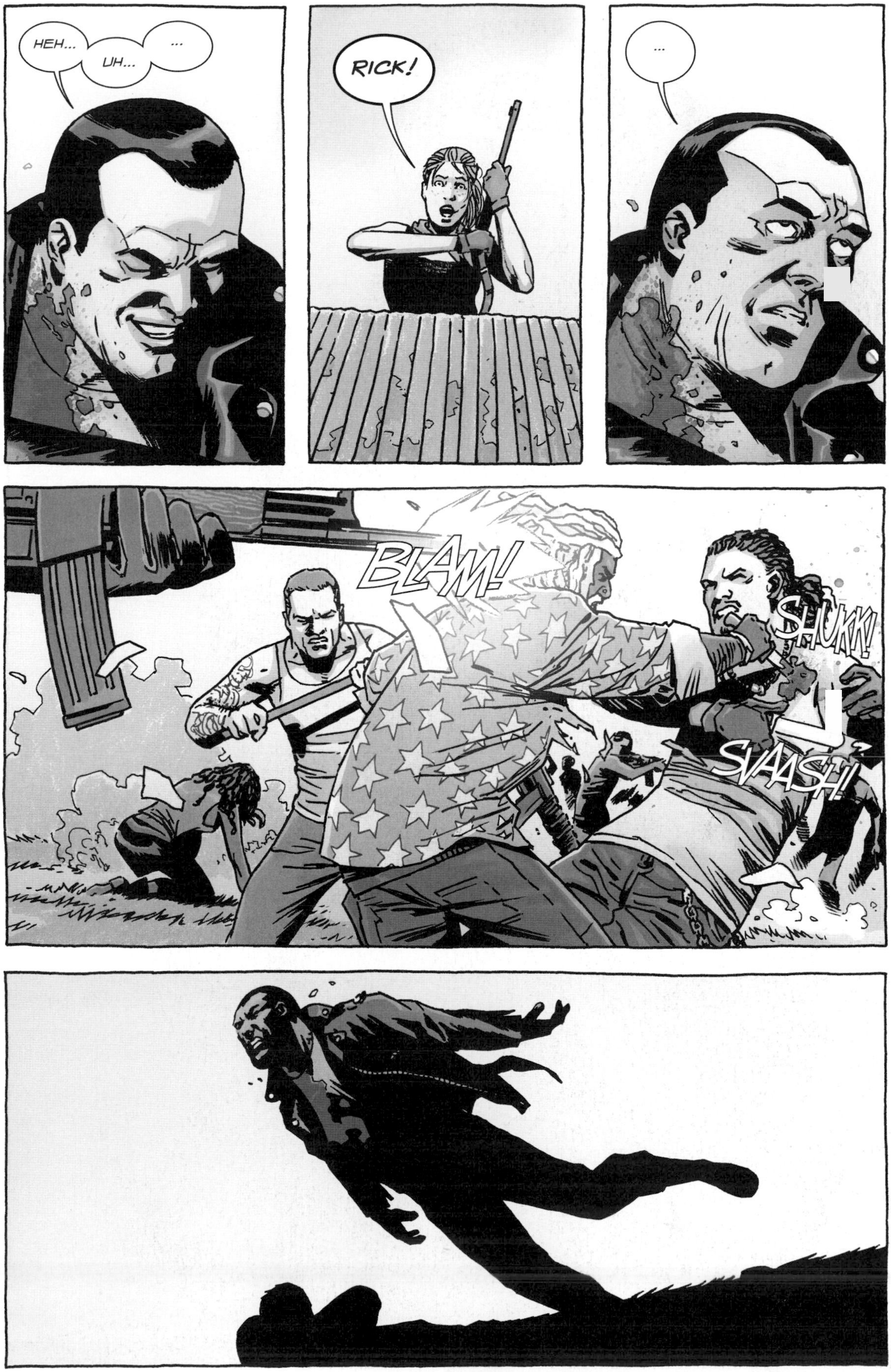
HEH...
UH...
...
RICK!
...
BLAM!
SHUKK!
SVAASH!

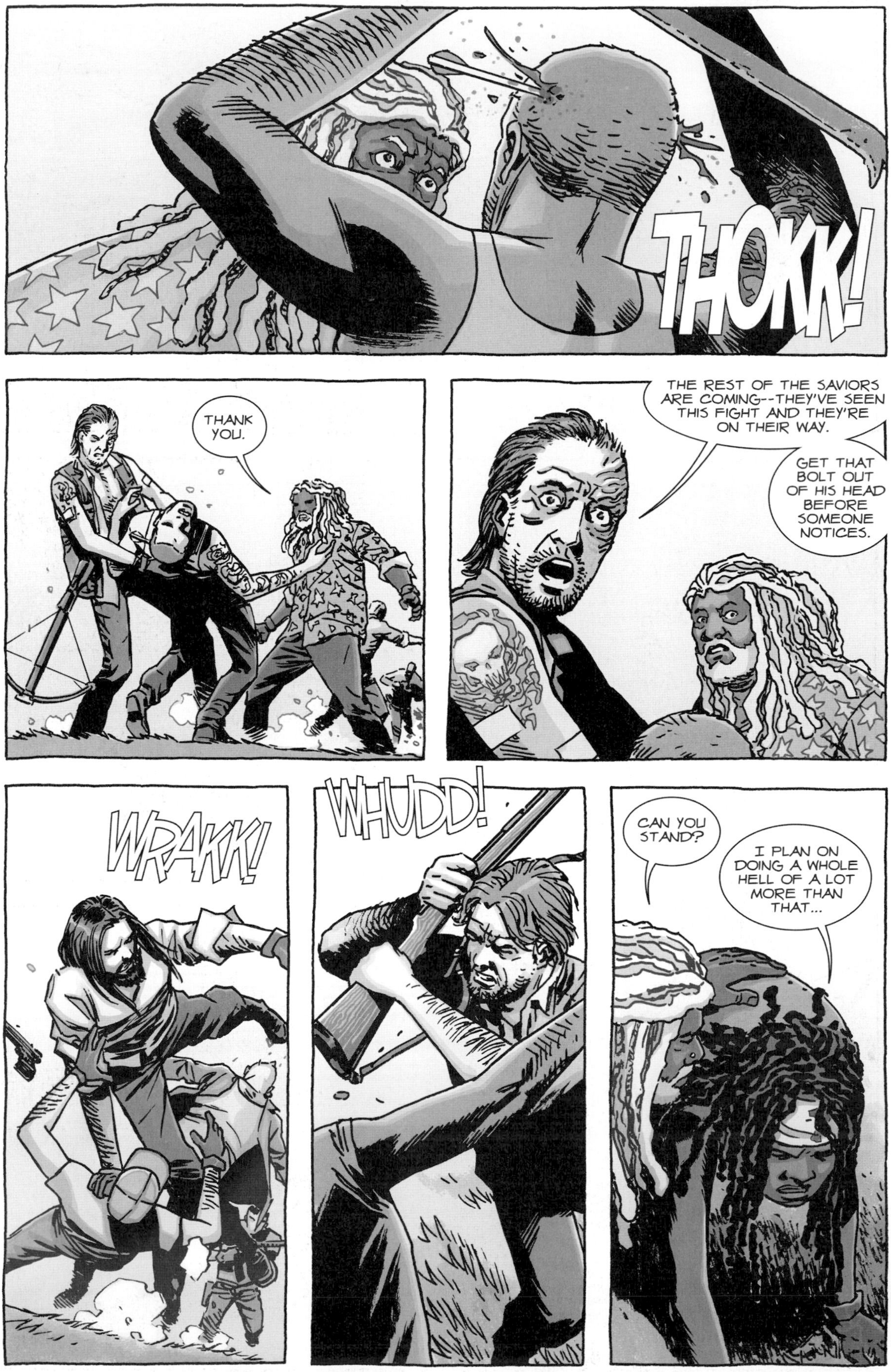
THOKK!
THANK YOU.
THE REST OF THE SAVIORS ARE COMING--THEY'VE SEEN THIS FIGHT AND THEY'RE ON THEIR WAY.
GET THAT BOLT OUT OF HIS HEAD BEFORE SOMEONE NOTICES.
WRAKK!
WHUDD!
CAN YOU STAND?
I PLAN ON DOING A WHOLE HELL OF A LOT MORE THAN THAT...

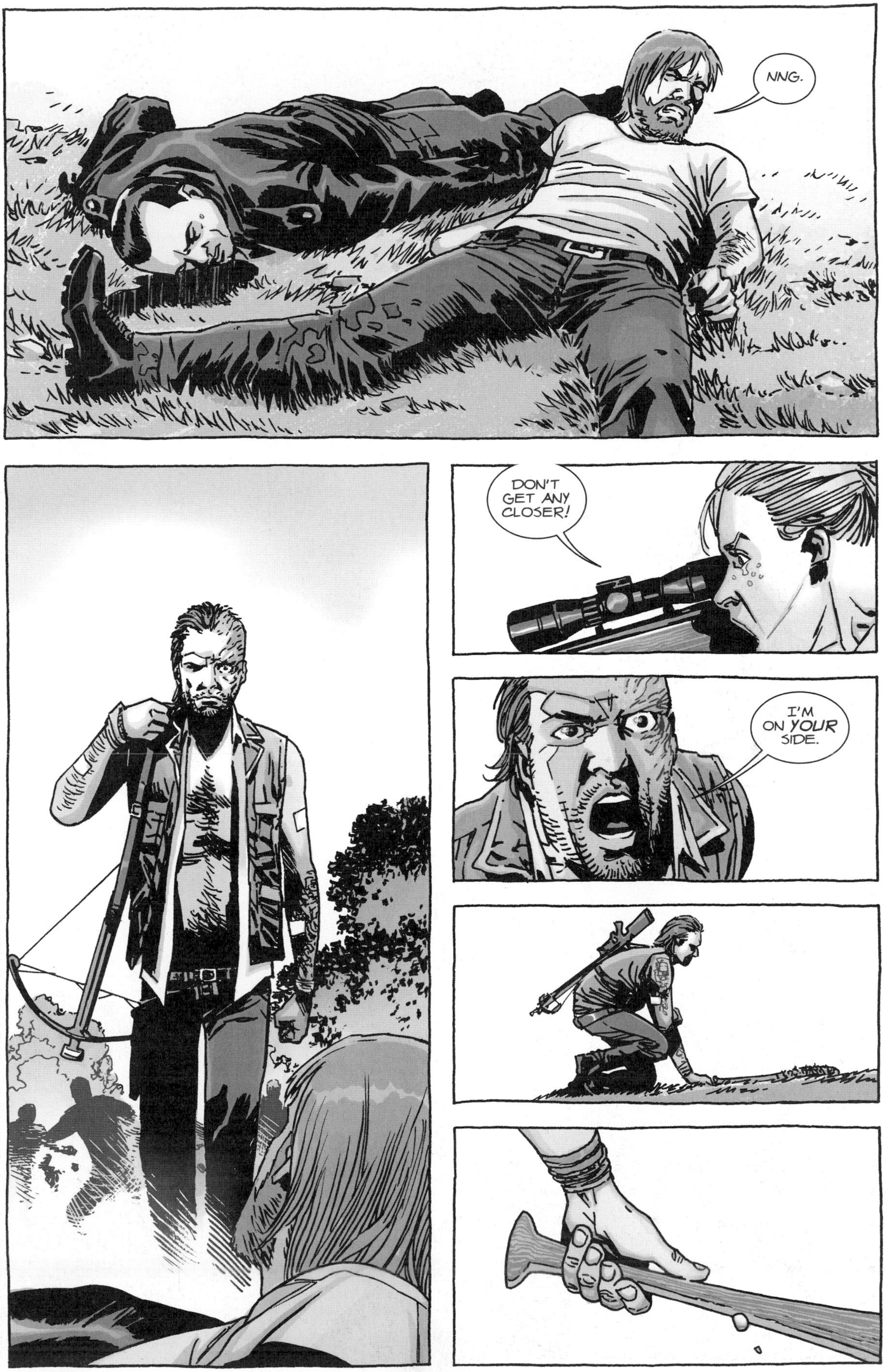
NNG.
DON'T GET ANY CLOSER!
I'M ON YOUR SIDE.

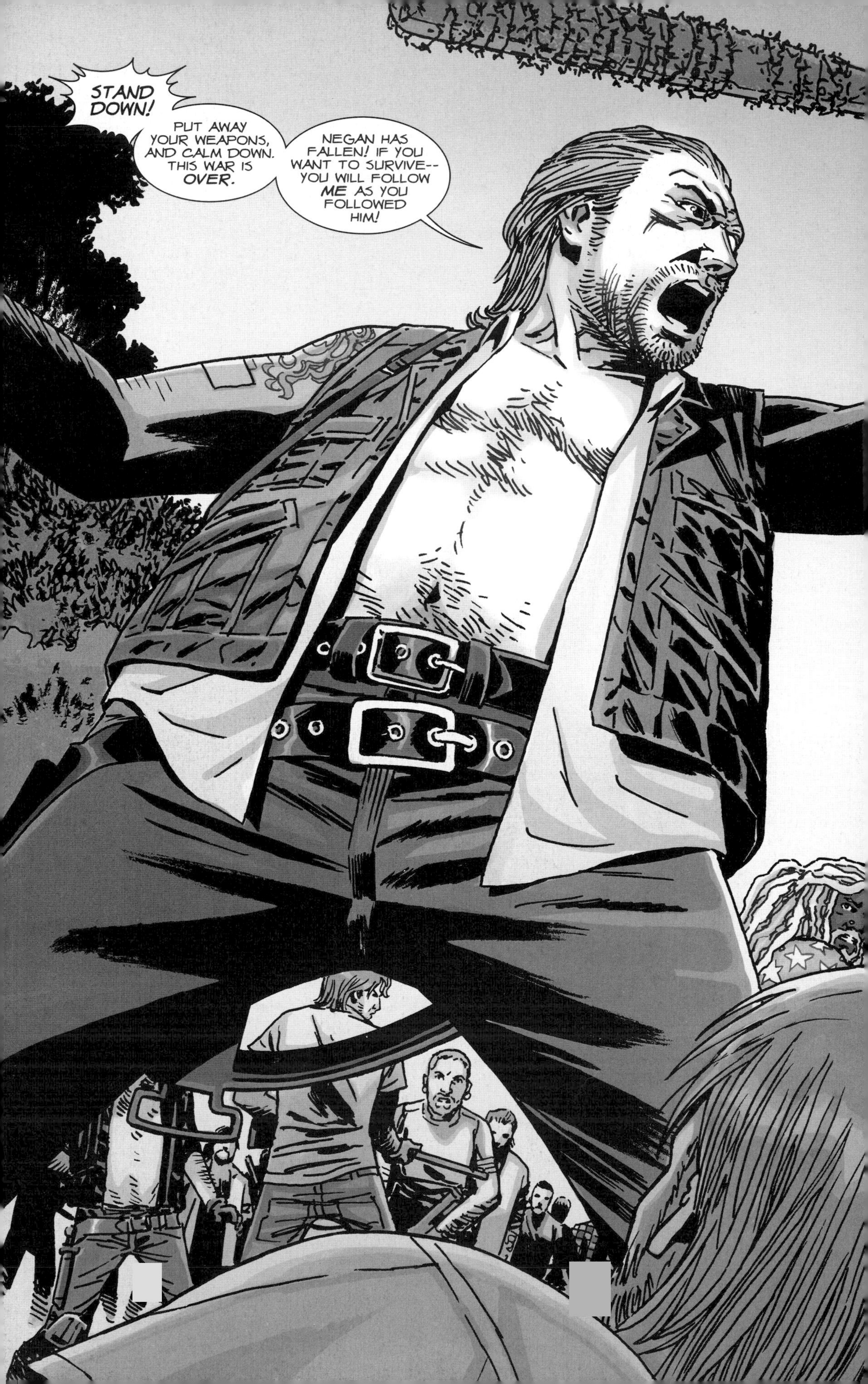
STAND DOWN!
PUT AWAY YOUR WEAPONS, AND CALM DOWN. THIS WAR IS OVER.
NEGAN HAS FALLEN! IF YOU WANT TO SURVIVE-- YOU WILL FOLLOW ME AS YOU FOLLOWED HIM!

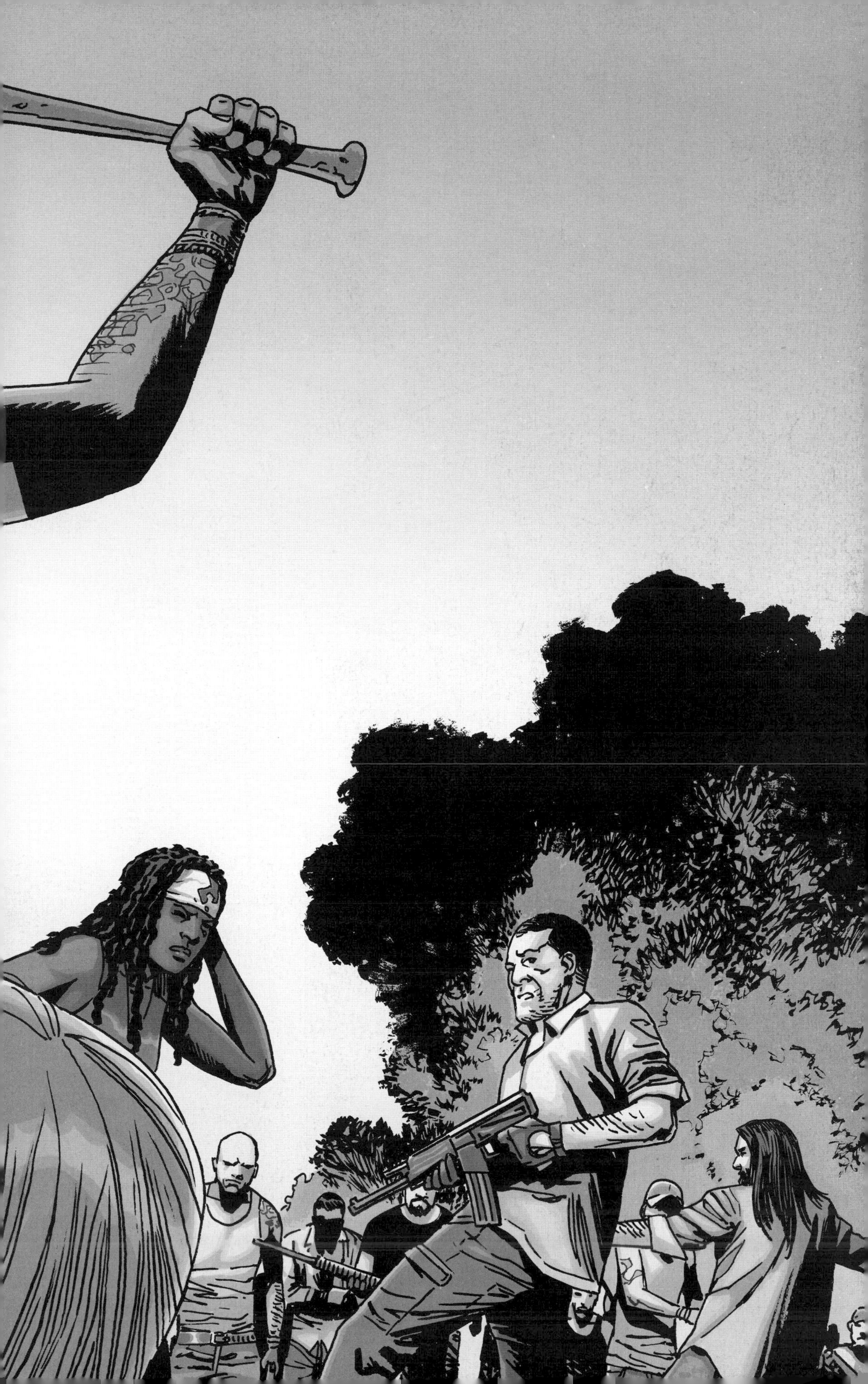

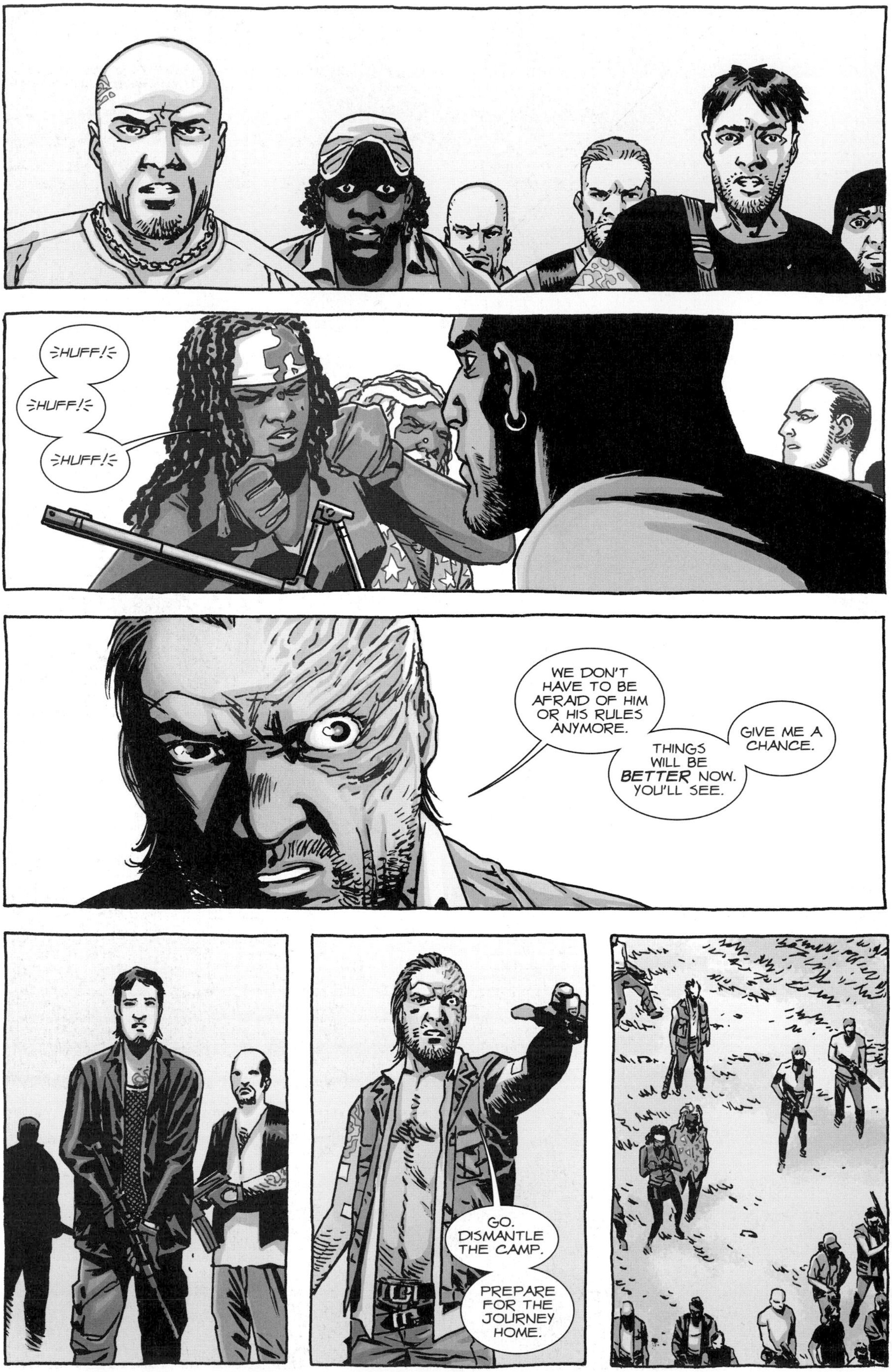

HUFF!
HUFF!
HUFF!
WE DON'T HAVE TO BE AFRAID OF HIM OR HIS RULES ANYMORE.
THINGS WILL BE BETTER NOW. YOU'LL SEE.
GIVE ME A CHANCE.
GO. DISMANTLE THE CAMP.
PREPARE FOR THE JOURNEY HOME.

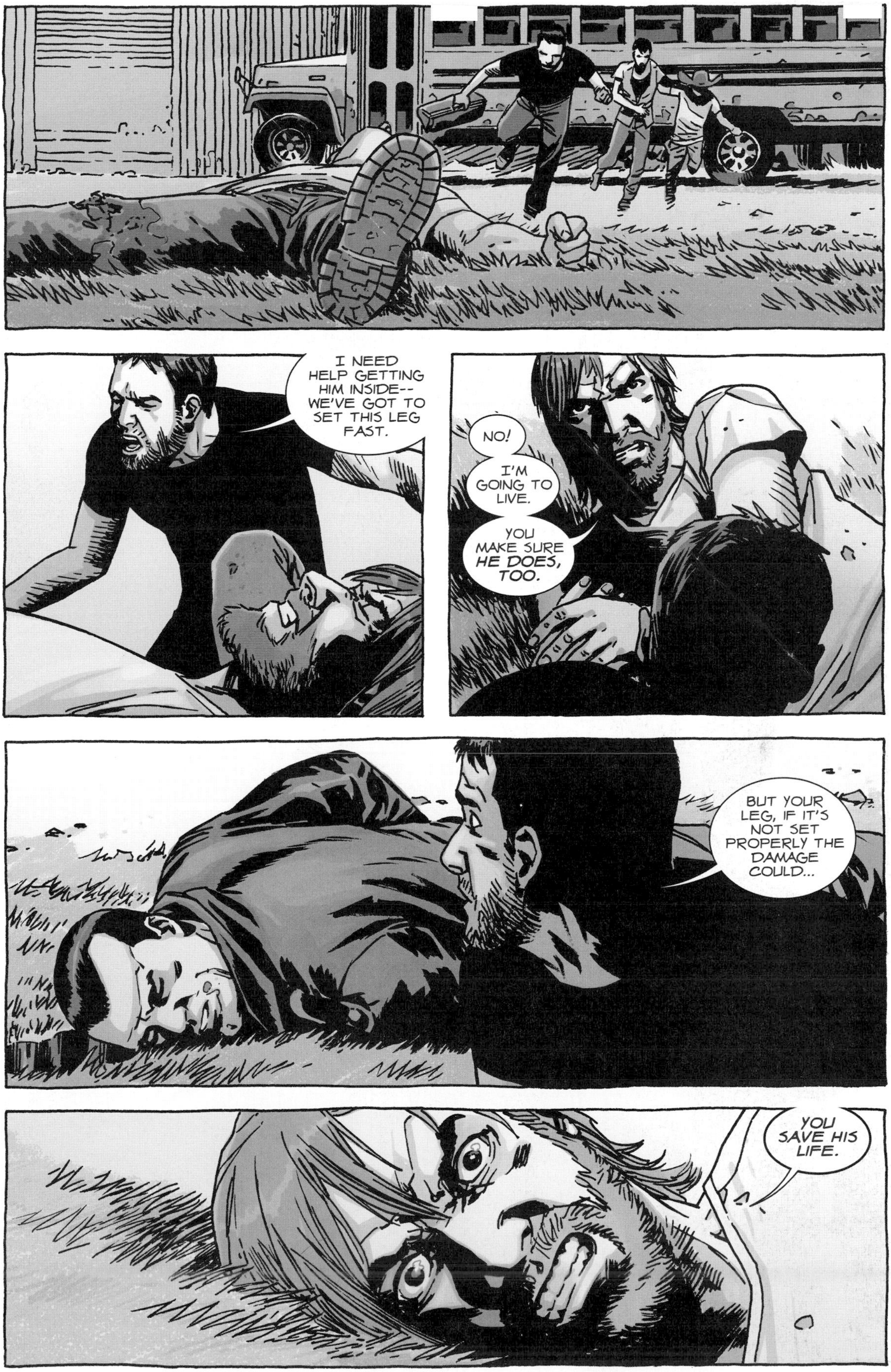
I NEED HELP GETTING HIM INSIDE-- WE'VE GOT TO SET THIS LEG FAST.
NO!
I'M GOING TO LIVE.
YOU MAKE SURE *HE DOES*, TOO.
BUT YOUR LEG, IF IT'S NOT SET PROPERLY THE DAMAGE COULD...
YOU SAVE HIS LIFE.

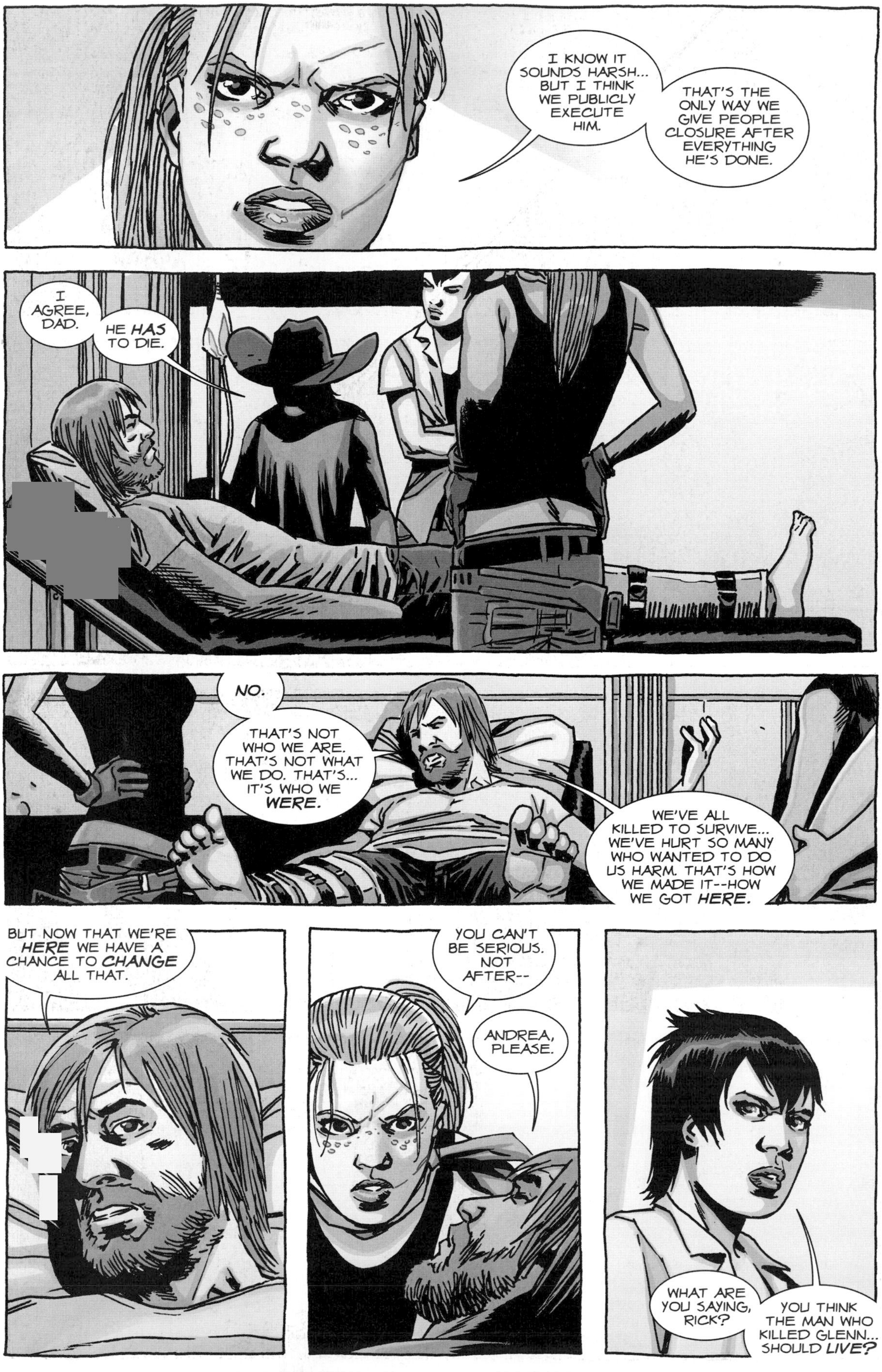

I KNOW IT SOUNDS HARSH... BUT I THINK WE PUBLICLY EXECUTE HIM.
THAT'S THE ONLY WAY WE GIVE PEOPLE CLOSURE AFTER EVERYTHING HE'S DONE.
I AGREE, DAD.
HE HAS TO DIE.
NO.
THAT'S NOT WHO WE ARE. THAT'S NOT WHAT WE DO. THAT'S... IT'S WHO WE WERE.
WE'VE ALL KILLED TO SURVIVE... WE'VE HURT SO MANY WHO WANTED TO DO US HARM. THAT'S HOW WE MADE IT--HOW WE GOT HERE.
BUT NOW THAT WE'RE HERE WE HAVE A CHANCE TO CHANGE ALL THAT.
YOU CAN'T BE SERIOUS. NOT AFTER--
ANDREA, PLEASE.
WHAT ARE YOU SAYING, RICK?
YOU THINK THE MAN WHO KILLED GLENN... SHOULD LIVE?

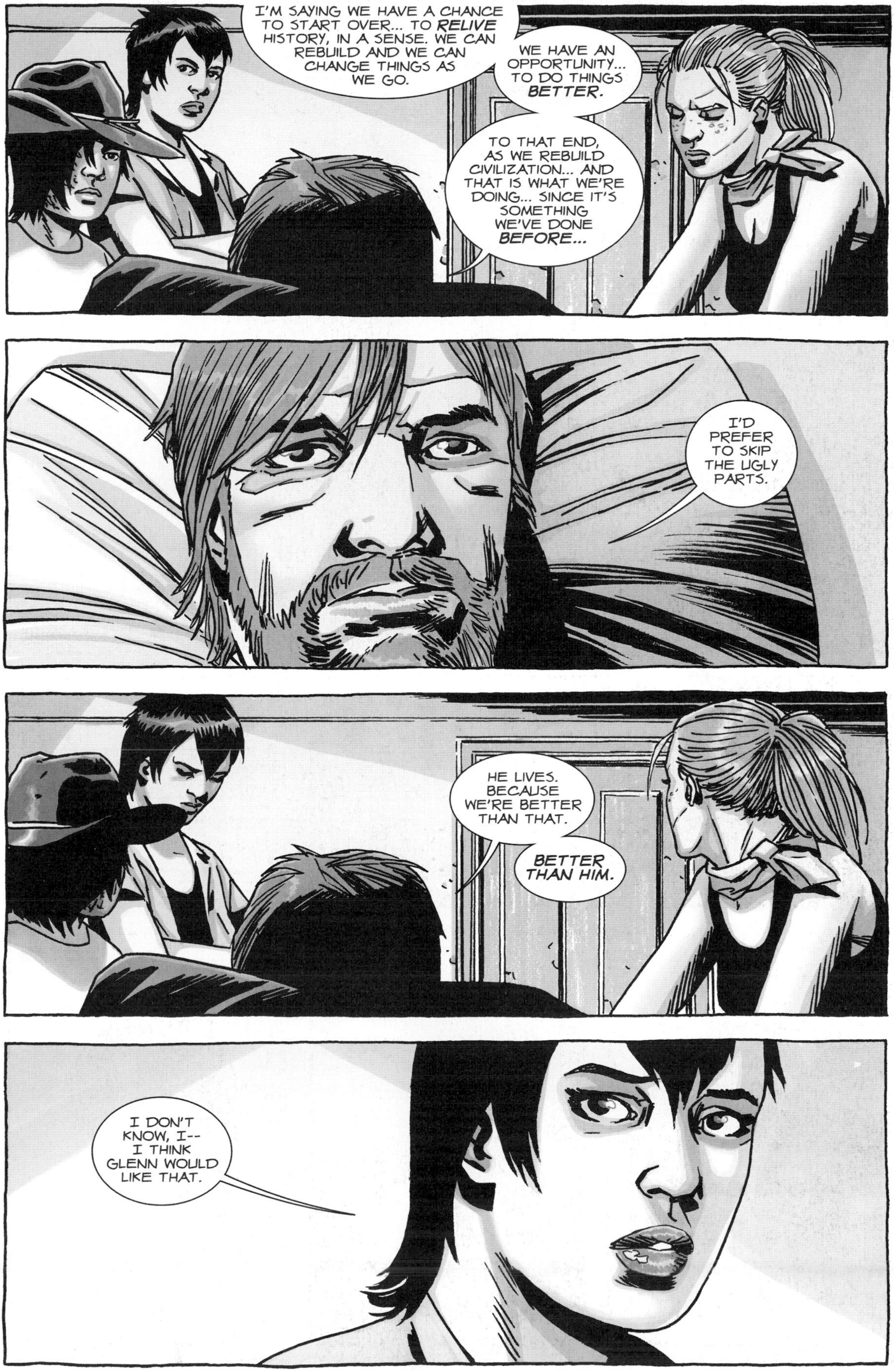
I'M SAYING WE HAVE A CHANCE TO START OVER... TO *RELIVE* HISTORY, IN A SENSE. WE CAN REBUILD AND WE CAN CHANGE THINGS AS WE GO.
WE HAVE AN OPPORTUNITY... TO DO THINGS *BETTER.*
TO THAT END, AS WE REBUILD CIVILIZATION... AND THAT IS WHAT WE'RE DOING... SINCE IT'S SOMETHING WE'VE DONE *BEFORE...*
I'D PREFER TO SKIP THE UGLY PARTS.
HE LIVES. BECAUSE WE'RE BETTER THAN THAT.
BETTER THAN HIM.
I DON'T KNOW, I-- I THINK GLENN WOULD LIKE THAT.

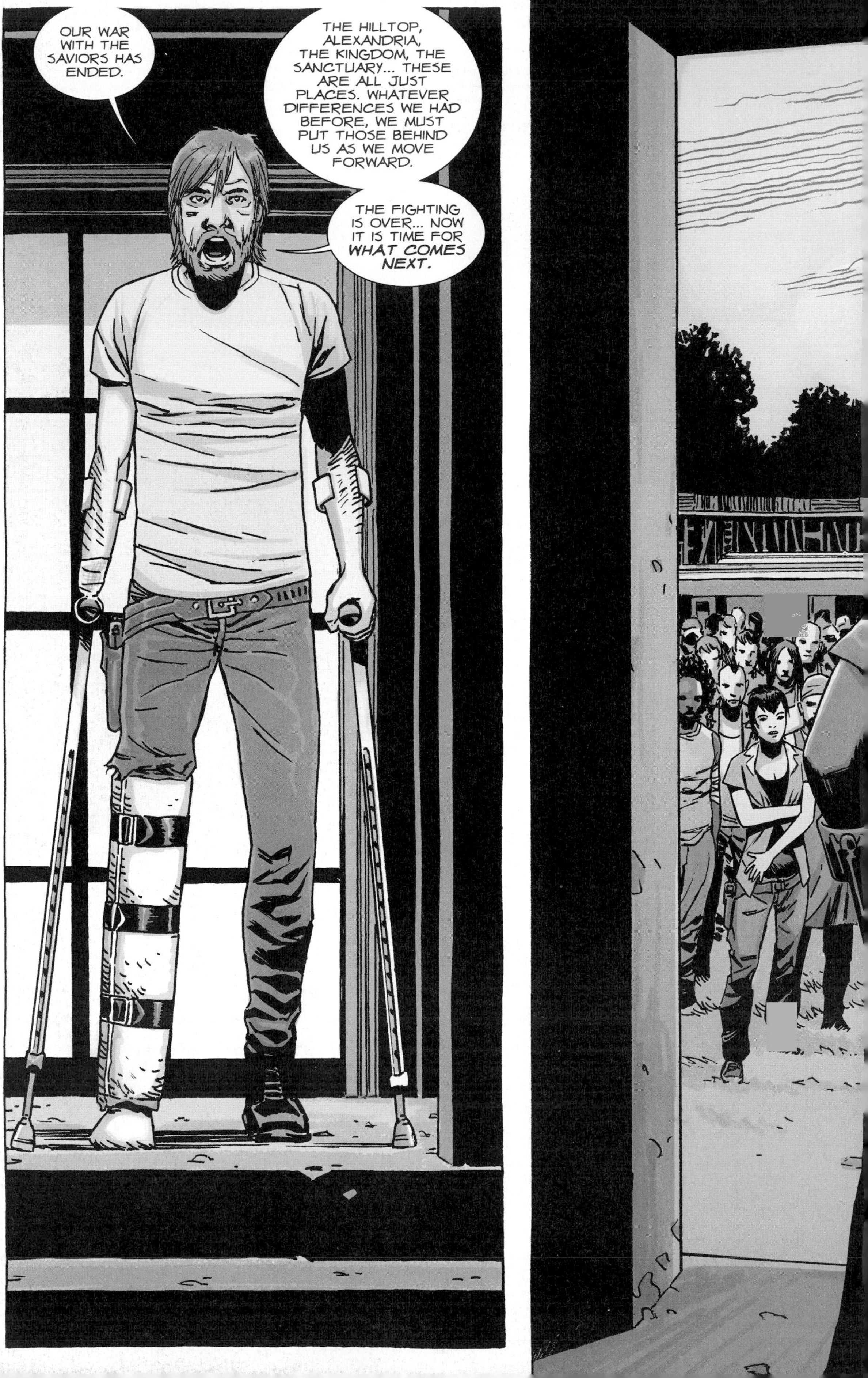
OUR WAR WITH THE SAVIORS HAS ENDED.
THE HILLTOP, ALEXANDRIA, THE KINGDOM, THE SANCTUARY... THESE ARE ALL JUST PLACES. WHATEVER DIFFERENCES WE HAD BEFORE, WE MUST PUT THOSE BEHIND US AS WE MOVE FORWARD.
THE FIGHTING IS OVER... NOW IT IS TIME FOR WHAT COMES NEXT.

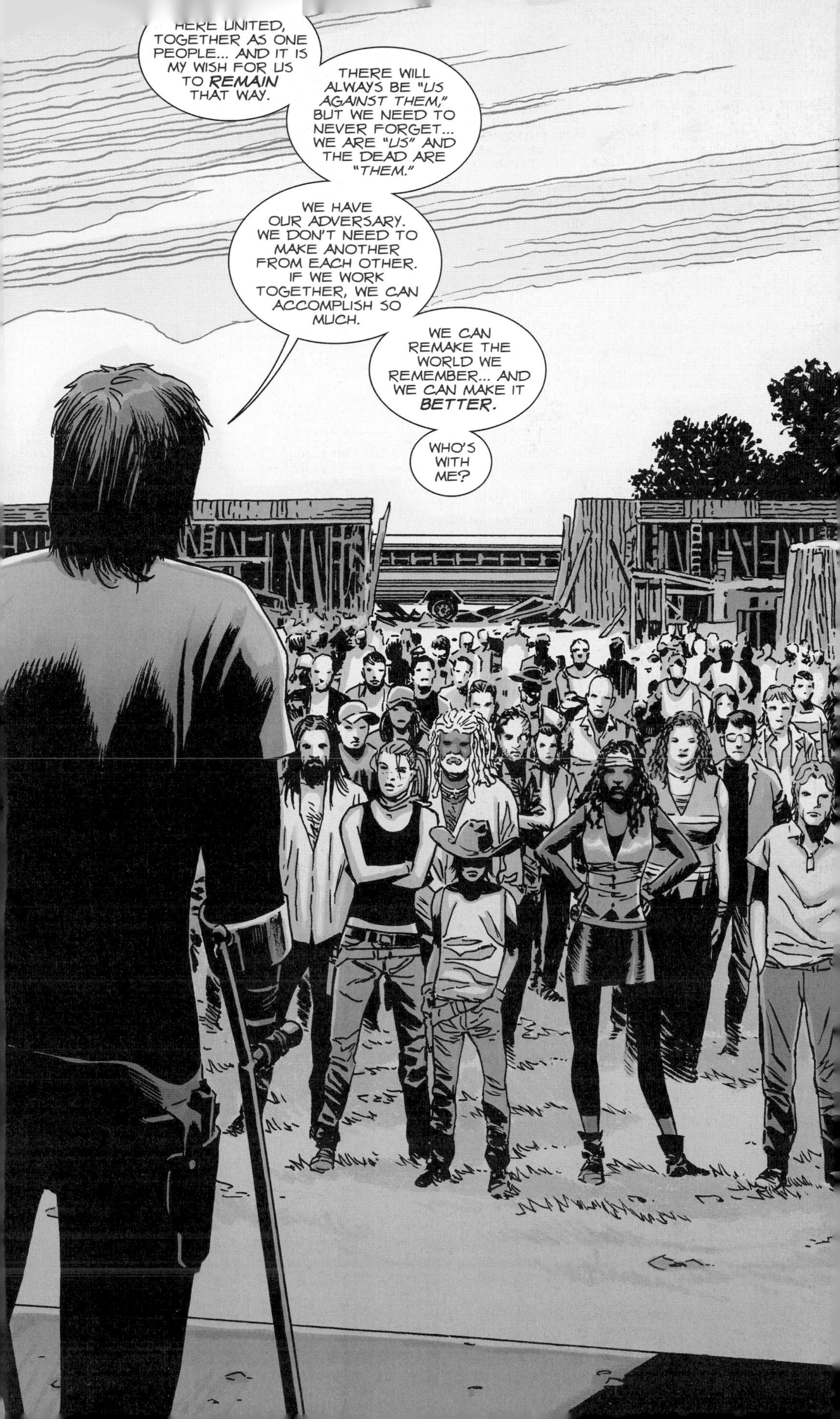
HERE UNITED, TOGETHER AS ONE PEOPLE... AND IT IS MY WISH FOR US TO REMAIN THAT WAY.
THERE WILL ALWAYS BE "US AGAINST THEM," BUT WE NEED TO NEVER FORGET... WE ARE "US" AND THE DEAD ARE "THEM."
WE HAVE OUR ADVERSARY. WE DON'T NEED TO MAKE ANOTHER FROM EACH OTHER. IF WE WORK TOGETHER, WE CAN ACCOMPLISH SO MUCH.
WE CAN REMAKE THE WORLD WE REMEMBER... AND WE CAN MAKE IT BETTER.
WHO'S WITH ME?

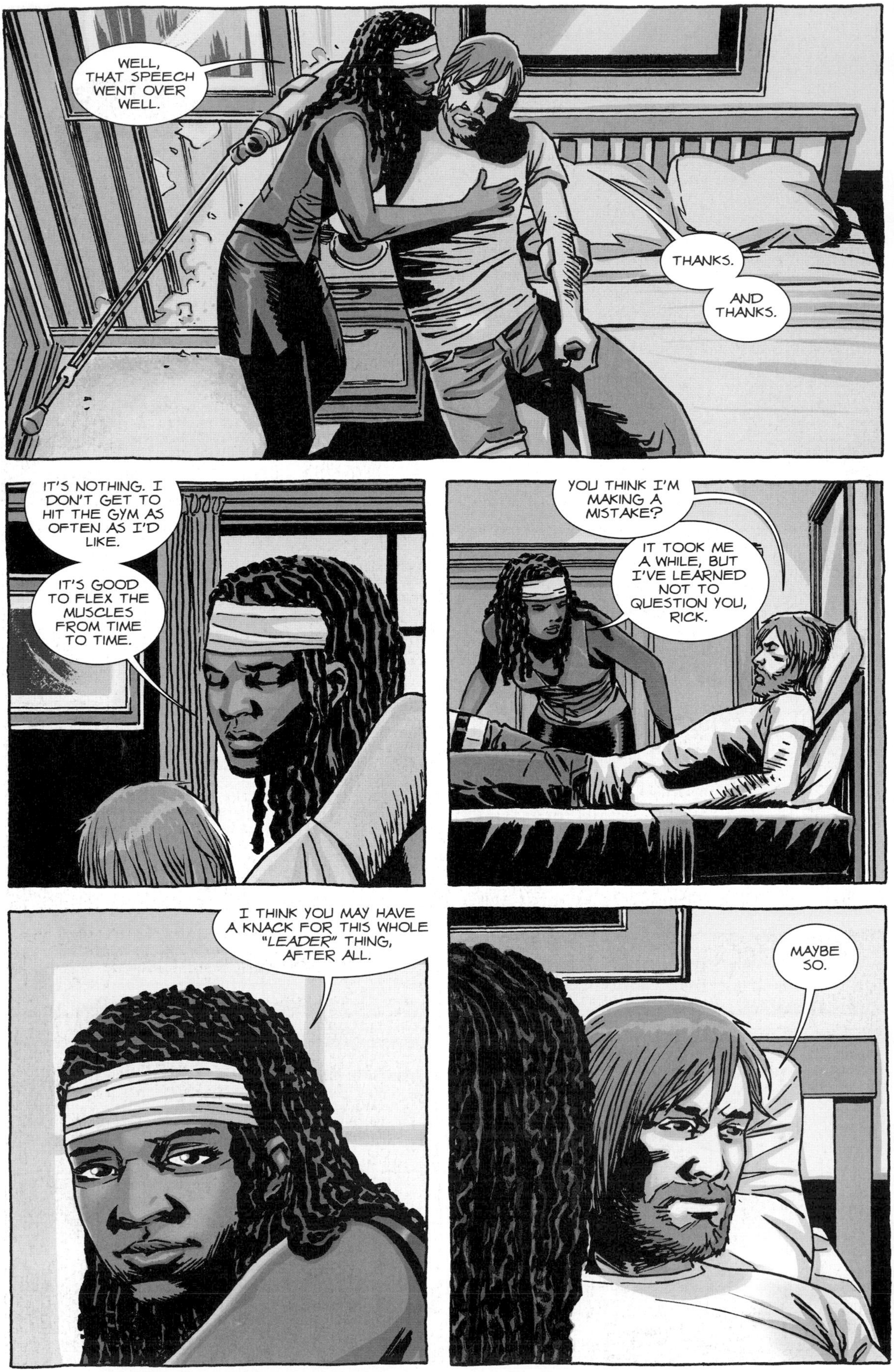
WELL, THAT SPEECH WENT OVER WELL.
THANKS.
AND THANKS.
IT'S NOTHING. I DON'T GET TO HIT THE GYM AS OFTEN AS I'D LIKE.
IT'S GOOD TO FLEX THE MUSCLES FROM TIME TO TIME.
YOU THINK I'M MAKING A MISTAKE?
IT TOOK ME A WHILE, BUT I'VE LEARNED NOT TO QUESTION YOU, RICK.
I THINK YOU MAY HAVE A KNACK FOR THIS WHOLE "LEADER" THING, AFTER ALL.
MAYBE SO.

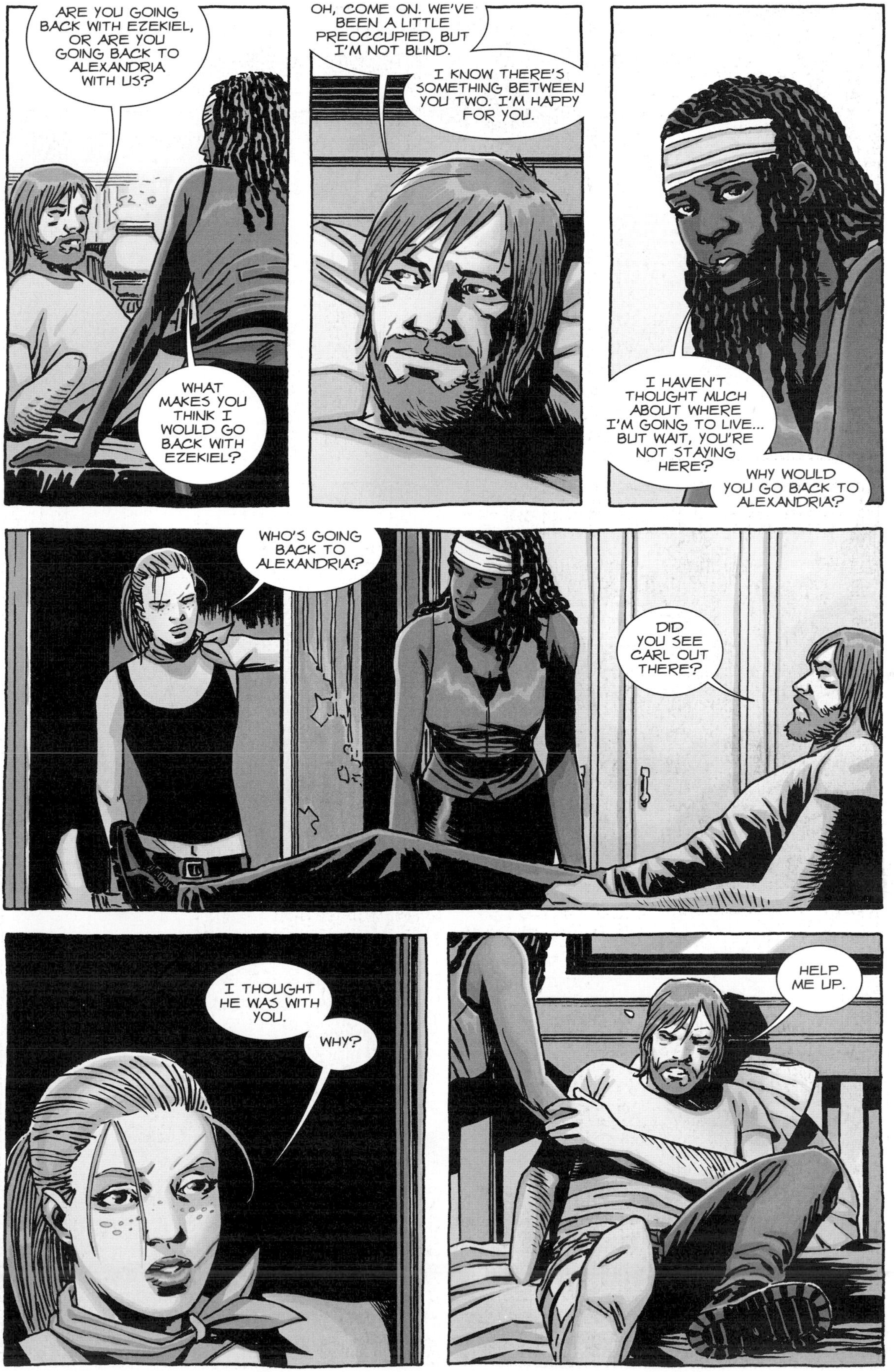
ARE YOU GOING BACK WITH EZEKIEL, OR ARE YOU GOING BACK TO ALEXANDRIA WITH US?
WHAT MAKES YOU THINK I WOULD GO BACK WITH EZEKIEL?
OH, COME ON. WE'VE BEEN A LITTLE PREOCCUPIED, BUT I'M NOT BLIND.
I KNOW THERE'S SOMETHING BETWEEN YOU TWO. I'M HAPPY FOR YOU.
I HAVEN'T THOUGHT MUCH ABOUT WHERE I'M GOING TO LIVE... BUT WAIT, YOU'RE NOT STAYING HERE?
WHY WOULD YOU GO BACK TO ALEXANDRIA?
WHO'S GOING BACK TO ALEXANDRIA?
DID YOU SEE CARL OUT THERE?
I THOUGHT HE WAS WITH YOU.
WHY?
HELP ME UP.

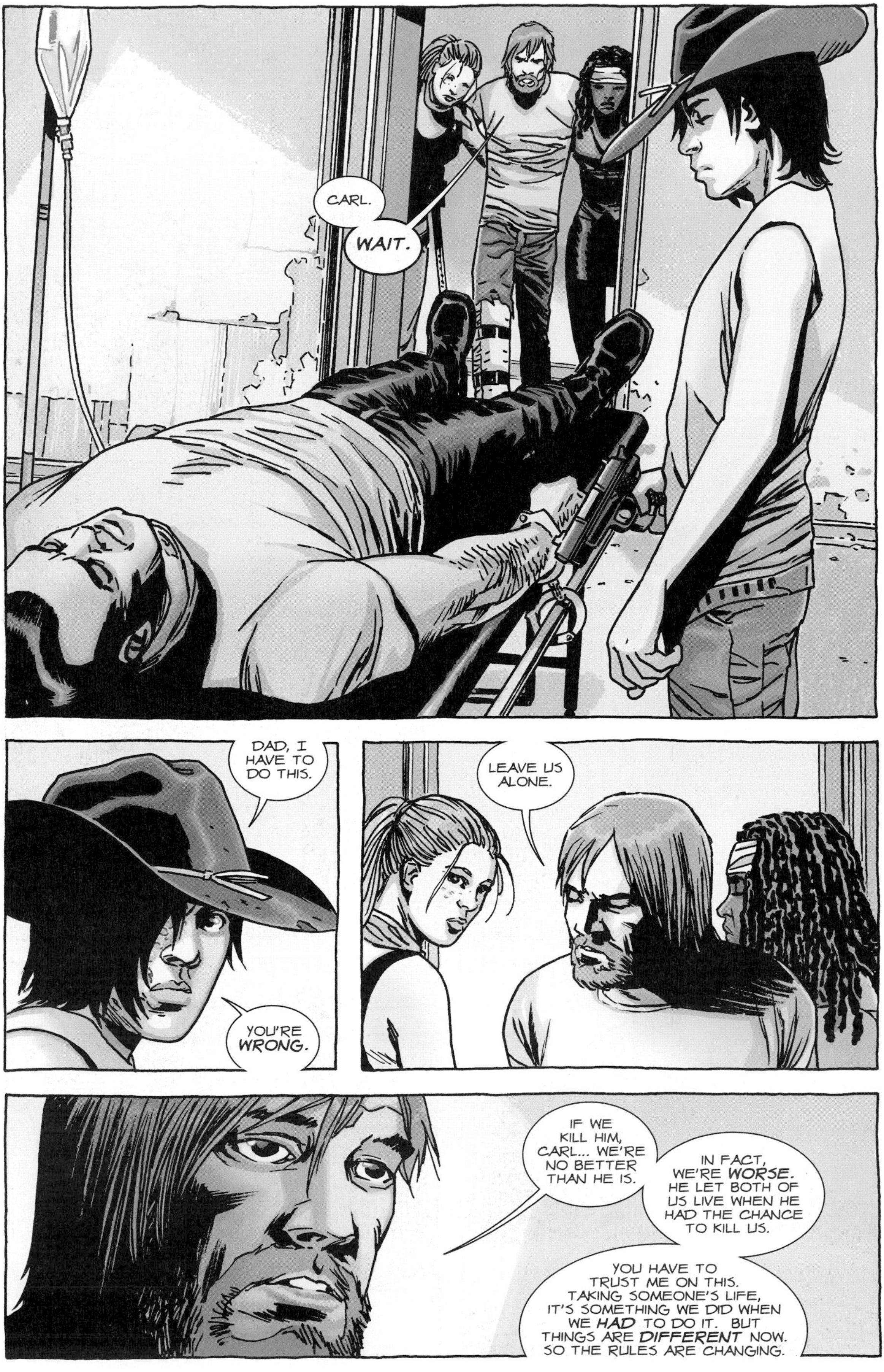
CARL.
WAIT.
DAD, I HAVE TO DO THIS.
YOU'RE WRONG.
LEAVE US ALONE.
IF WE KILL HIM, CARL... WE'RE NO BETTER THAN HE IS.
IN FACT, WE'RE WORSE. HE LET BOTH OF US LIVE WHEN HE HAD THE CHANCE TO KILL US.
YOU HAVE TO TRUST ME ON THIS. TAKING SOMEONE'S LIFE, IT'S SOMETHING WE DID WHEN WE HAD TO DO IT. BUT THINGS ARE DIFFERENT NOW. SO THE RULES ARE CHANGING.

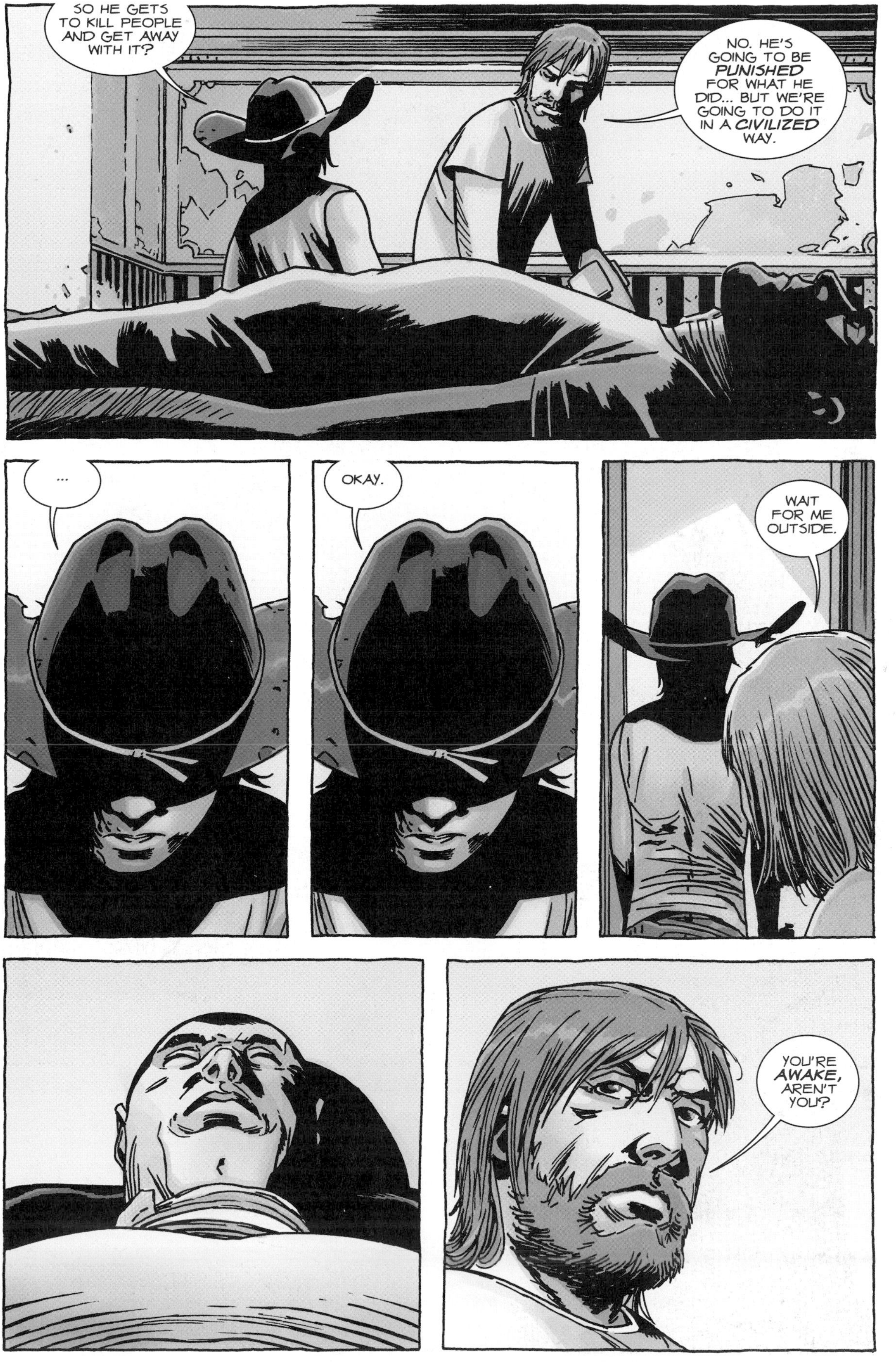
SO HE GETS TO KILL PEOPLE AND GET AWAY WITH IT?
NO. HE'S GOING TO BE PUNISHED FOR WHAT HE DID... BUT WE'RE GOING TO DO IT IN A CIVILIZED WAY.
...
OKAY.
WAIT FOR ME OUTSIDE.
YOU'RE AWAKE, AREN'T YOU?

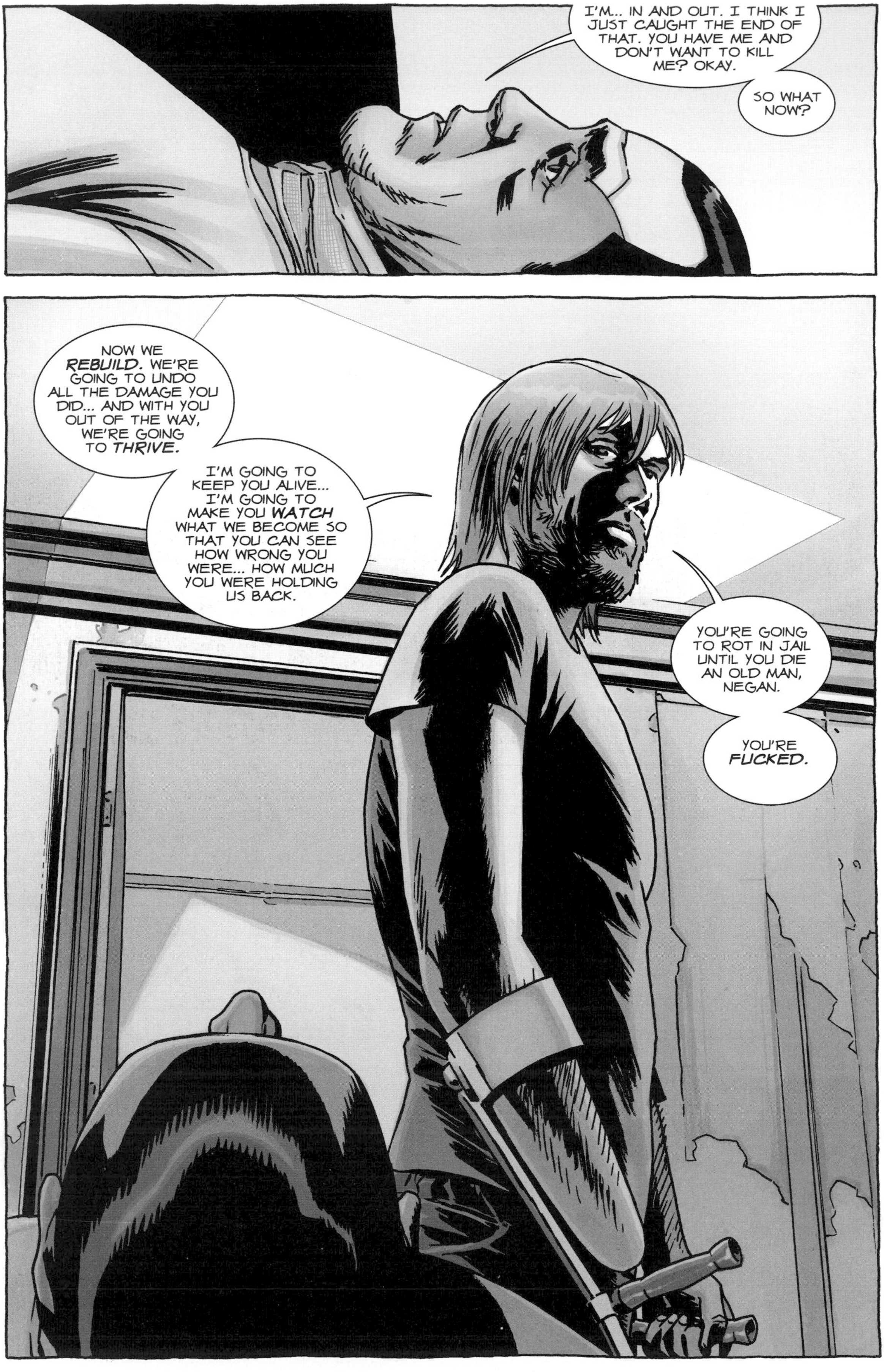
I'M... IN AND OUT. I THINK I JUST CAUGHT THE END OF THAT. YOU HAVE ME AND DON'T WANT TO KILL ME? OKAY.
SO WHAT NOW?
NOW WE REBUILD. WE'RE GOING TO UNDO ALL THE DAMAGE YOU DID... AND WITH YOU OUT OF THE WAY, WE'RE GOING TO THRIVE.
I'M GOING TO KEEP YOU ALIVE... I'M GOING TO MAKE YOU WATCH WHAT WE BECOME SO THAT YOU CAN SEE HOW WRONG YOU WERE... HOW MUCH YOU WERE HOLDING US BACK.
YOU'RE GOING TO ROT IN JAIL UNTIL YOU DIE AN OLD MAN, NEGAN.
YOU'RE FUCKED.

TO BE CONTINUED...

FOR MORE OF THE WALKING DEAD

TRADEPAPERBACKS

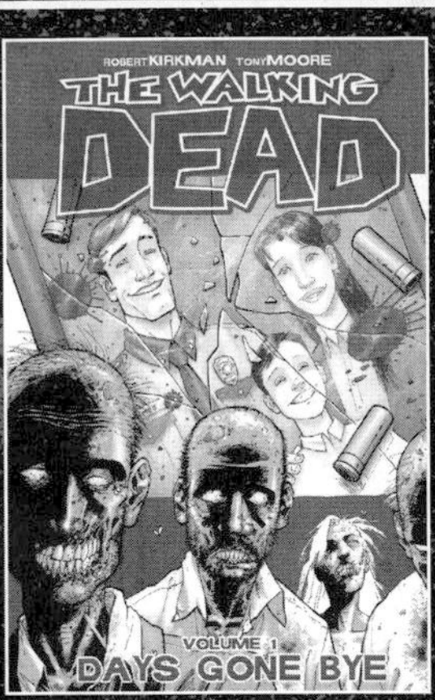
ROBERT KIRKMAN TONY MOORE
THE WALKING DEAD
VOLUME 1
DAYS GONE BYE

VOL. 1: DAYS GONE BYE TP
ISBN: 978-1-58240-672-5
$14.99
VOL. 2: MILES BEHIND US TP
ISBN: 978-1-58240-775-3
$14.99
VOL. 3: SAFETY BEHIND BARS TP
ISBN: 978-1-58240-805-7
$14.99
VOL. 4: THE HEART'S DESIRE TP
ISBN: 978-1-58240-530-8
$14.99
VOL. 5: THE BEST DEFENSE TP
ISBN: 978-1-58240-612-1
$14.99
VOL. 6: THIS SORROWFUL LIFE TP
ISBN: 978-1-58240-684-8
$14.99
VOL. 7: THE CALM BEFORE TP
ISBN: 978-1-58240-828-6
$14.99
VOL. 8: MADE TO SUFFER TP
ISBN: 978-1-58240-883-5
$14.99
VOL. 9: HERE WE REMAIN TP
ISBN: 978-1-60706-022-2
$14.99
VOL. 10: WHAT WE BECOME TP
ISBN: 978-1-60706-075-8
$14.99
VOL. 11: FEAR THE HUNTERS TP
ISBN: 978-1-60706-181-6
$14.99
VOL. 12: LIFE AMONG THEM TP
ISBN: 978-1-60706-254-7
$14.99
VOL. 13: TOO FAR GONE TP
ISBN: 978-1-60706-329-2
$14.99
VOL. 14: NO WAY OUT TP
ISBN: 978-1-60706-392-6
$14.99
VOL. 15: WE FIND OURSELVES TP
ISBN: 978-1-60706-440-4
$14.99
VOL. 16: A LARGER WORLD TP
ISBN: 978-1-60706-559-3
$14.99
VOL. 17: SOMETHING TO FEAR TP
ISBN: 978-1-60706-615-6
$14.99
VOL. 18: WHAT COMES AFTER TP
ISBN: 978-1-60706-687-3
$14.99
VOL. 19: MARCH TO WAR TP
ISBN: 978-1-60706-818-1
$14.99
VOL. 20: ALL OUT WAR PART ONE TP
ISBN: 978-1-60706-882-2
$14.99
VOL. 21: ALL OUT WAR PART TWO TP
ISBN: 978-1-63215-030-1
$14.99
VOL. 1: SPANISH EDITION TP
ISBN: 978-1-60706-797-9
$14.99
VOL. 2: SPANISH EDITION TP
ISBN: 978-1-60706-845-7
$14.99
VOL. 3: SPANISH EDITION TP
ISBN: 978-1-60706-883-9
$14.99
VOL. 4: SPANISH EDITION TP
ISBN: 978-1-63215-035-6
$14.99

HARDCOVERS

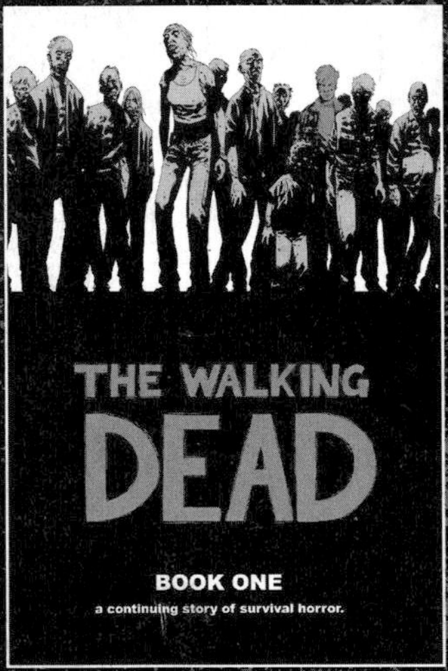
THE WALKING DEAD
BOOK ONE
a continuing story of survival horror.

BOOK ONE HC
ISBN: 978-1-58240-619-0
$34.99
BOOK TWO HC
ISBN: 978-1-58240-698-5
$34.99
BOOK THREE HC
ISBN: 978-1-58240-825-5
$34.99
BOOK FOUR HC
ISBN: 978-1-60706-000-0
$34.99
BOOK FIVE HC
ISBN: 978-1-60706-171-7
$34.99
BOOK SIX HC
ISBN: 978-1-60706-327-8
$34.99
BOOK SEVEN HC
ISBN: 978-1-60706-439-8
$34.99
BOOK EIGHT HC
ISBN: 978-1-60706-593-7
$34.99
BOOK NINE HC
ISBN: 978-1-60706-798-6
$34.99

COMPENDIUMS

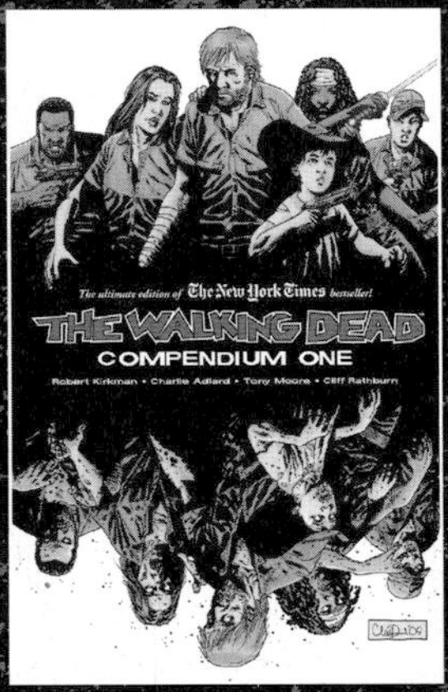
The ultimate edition of The New York Times bestseller!
THE WALKING DEAD
COMPENDIUM ONE
Robert Kirkman • Charlie Adlard • Tony Moore • Cliff Rathburn

COMPENDIUM TP, VOL. 1
ISBN: 978-1-60706-076-5
$59.99
COMPENDIUM TP, VOL. 2
ISBN: 978-1-60706-596-8
$59.99

SPECIALTY BOOKS

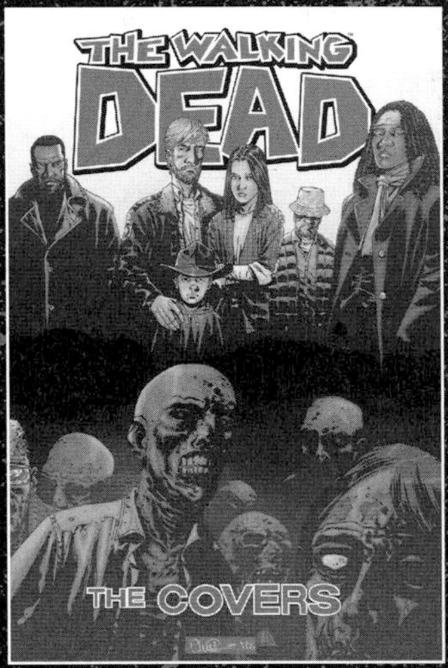
THE WALKING DEAD
THE COVERS

THE WALKING DEAD: THE COVERS, VOL. 1 HC
ISBN: 978-1-60706-002-4
$24.99
THE WALKING DEAD SURVIVORS' GUIDE
ISBN: 978-1-60706-458-9
$12.99

OMNIBUS

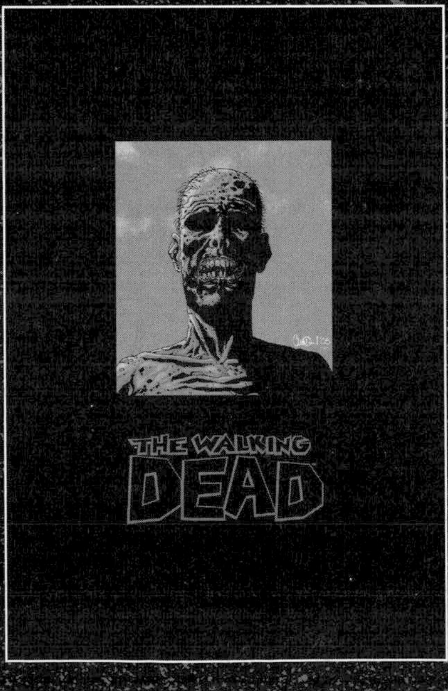
THE WALKING DEAD

OMNIBUS, VOL. 1
ISBN: 978-1-60706-503-6
$100.00
OMNIBUS, VOL. 2
ISBN: 978-1-60706-515-9
$100.00
OMNIBUS, VOL. 3
ISBN: 978-1-60706-330-8
$100.00
OMNIBUS, VOL. 4
ISBN: 978-1-60706-616-3
$100.00